DESTINY'S PATH

Jenna stood before Stefan, shivering, her nerves strained, yet unaware of the storm that raged beyond the windows, aware only of the mounting storm within, as she felt herself lost within the vast blue ocean of Stefan's gaze.

Slowly, Stefan reached out, his fingers brushing gently against the soft curve of Jenna's lips, taking a single droplet of rain on the tip of his finger, then lightly tracing a path along her slender jawline. All thoughts abandoned him, save one, the ecstasy of the satin texture of her skin beneath his hand. Slowly his hands lowered and followed the path of her collarbone, until his fingers closed around her shoulders and her slender body melted into his. Stefan's lips found Jenna's with an intensity that seemed to match the storm, burning, searing, moving with silent desperation as he felt her awakening response.

Jenna did not recognize the yearnings Stefan was stirring deep within her, but she knew that nothing else mattered, except that very moment. . . .

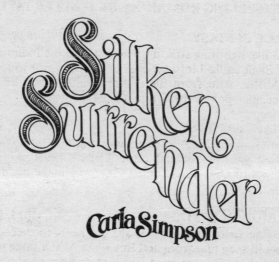

Silken Surrender

Carla Simpson

ZEBRA BOOKS
KENSINGTON PUBLISHING CORP.

For my father, the wise teacher,
and my mother, the romantic.
Thank You!

ZEBRA BOOKS

are published by

Kensington Publishing Corp.
475 Park Avenue South
New York, NY 10016

First printing: January 1986

Printed in the United States of America

Chapter One

London, England
September 4, 1812

The sleek black coach careened wildly. The driver called to the perfectly matched team of bays and fought desperately to control their frenzied pace, as he guided them onto the post road to London. The waning hours of the afternoon refused to yield the day's heat, though the golden sunlight rapidly faded into the gray of early twilight. The calm stillness of the countryside was shattered by the sounds of the laboring horses, as the coach rumbled recklessly down the long road, churning up billowing clouds of dust to mark their flight, as if the devil rode close behind laying the lash upon the glistening dark hides, threatening to consume the team of four if they slackened their frantic pace. The rolling hillsides wore a mantle of thick green velvet that had only just begun to yield to the summer's heat after a long spring of abundant rains that had left thick patches of purple heather waving in the afternoon breeze like brilliant banners. Black-faced sheep with spring lambs by their sides grazed undisturbed as the coach sped across the greensward. The driver wore an expression of grim determination, and had constantly to pay attention to keeping the tricorn atop his head, the uncertain ride threatening to unseat him with each lunging motion. He heartily cursed such a reckless pace, his protests carried on the wind. He knew any further objections would have met with the same obstinate refusal as his earlier warnings. He knew well the young lady in the coach would have listened with patient calmness, and then given the order to continue their journey as before.

Inside the richly appointed coach, the young passenger clung to the handle beside the door with quiet desperation. The heavy shades at the windows had been drawn against the clouds of dust churned up by the hooves of the horses, making the inside of the coach unbearably warm and stifling. Jenna Randolph pressed her lips together in silent vexation, as she was again thrown against the side of the coach and then unseated as the coach seemed to leave the ground, lunging uncertainly over a bump and then settling back to a lurching, rolling motion that set her stomach to churning. Jenna closed her eyes in a silent plea that she might yet survive her impulsive return to London before nightfall. She knew well that better judgment called for a slower pace, but she also knew that time was her enemy.

Jenna fought back her nagging fears about the message that had arrived early that morning at Lord Wingate's country manor where she had spent the last few weeks as a guest of his daughter, Elizabeth Wingate. Her grandfather had suffered several minor heart attacks through the long summer, and she had adamantly refused to consider a vacation to the cooler climes of the country. But she had realized, too, that her constant arguments over the matter with her grandfather perhaps caused greater harm, and she had at last yielded to his wishes. But this last attack, after he had convinced her to leave the oppressive heat of London, had been the worst by far, and Mr. Flint, her grandfather's retainer, had sent a short but urgent note that he would be arriving the following morning to take her back to London. Impulsive and headstrong, Jenna had not waited for Lord Wingate or his son Charles to return from the morning hunt to ask their advice on the matter. Against Elizabeth's better judgment, Jenna had insisted on the use of their coach for her immediate return to

6

London, leaving her dear friend standing in the circular cobbled drive, wringing her small hands in uncertainty at the wisdom of Jenna's decision. In the bright light of day, with Mr. Flint's urgent message clenched in her hand, the decision had seemed the only one she could make. Jenna had stubbornly refused to heed the driver's warnings of the dangers of traveling after dark on the road to London. In her strong-willed determination she refused to accept that they might not reach London before nightfall.

Jenna raised the window shade and peered out the window. A slight frown knitted the creamy softness of her brow. A bright shaft of brilliant sunlight, the last of the day, pierced the mahogany depths of her eyes, setting them aglow until they were almost tawny. The creamy expanse of flawless skin was dusted lightly with soft pink as she gazed into the rose-hued sunset. Her thoughts filled with the memories of her last days at the Wingate estate. Charles had again pressed her for permission to speak to her grandfather of their betrothal. She had stubbornly refused to consider the matter, falling back on the excuse of her grandfather's failing health. The true reason for her uncertainty continued to elude her. Most certainly Charles Wingate, who would one day be the sixth earl of Hampton, was considered one of the most eligible young men about London. Had he not been her best friend's brother, perhaps Jenna could have been more serious about his proposal.

Jenna recognized the crossroads as the coach turned onto the post road, and she realized dismally that they were still quite some distance from London. Anxiously she bit at her lower lip as she noticed the darkening sky. She had given the driver only one order, and she wanted it followed with all haste. She dropped the shade back into place and tried to find a comfortable position among the richly upholstered cushions of the coach. Guilt over her hasty departure swept over her, and she quickly dismissed it. There simply had been no time for questioning her decision. At any rate, it was done, and she would see that the coach was promptly returned to Lord Wingate's

London home, certain that he would understand her reasons in the matter.

Jenna shifted her position as the coach lurched again. She sank back into the far corner of the darkened interior as the driver seemed to find a smoother part of the road, and she thought they must now be very near St. James bridge, which was close to the outskirts of London. The muscles between her shoulders and up her neck ached from fighting to maintain her seating through the long hours of the afternoon, and her hunger nagged at her, as she realized she had not eaten since early that morning. It hardly mattered. Very soon she would be home. Jenna settled back into the soft velvet cushions as the coach swayed gently in a smooth, rocking motion. Her mind was filled with visions of her grandfather. She knew well that the long weeks and months of negotiations for peace with Napoleon had taken a great toll on his health. And now the latest word from London was that Napoleon had deliberately broken his agreements with England by sending his armies into Russia. She could only guess the effect it might have had on Sir Avery, that all his efforts were suddenly cast aside as the "little emperor" boldly continued his quest for complete domination of Europe. For months she had known of Sir Avery's arguments with the prime minister against trusting Napoleon, and now his warnings had proven correct, and at what cost? Impatiently, Jenna wiped at a single tear that threatened to release a torrent if she gave in to the fears that had haunted her through the long afternoon of her return to London.

Securely hidden from view, within the shelter of thickly grown trees that lined the roadway, five riders waited. A signal flashed in the fading light of day as a shaft of light reflected off a small mirror, and the coach swung around the bend and rapidly approached. A sharp command was quickly given, and two of the riders urged their horses across the road before the coach came closer, giving the driver warning of their presence. A third rider rode back, keeping to the shelter of the trees as he sought a vantage point to keep watch for any other travelers who might come along and attempt to give assistance.

The leader of the men silently motioned to his companion, and the burly, mountainous man rode his tall mount into the open road brandishing a pistol and calling loudly for the driver to halt the coach. A single shot was fired over the driver's head, and he concentrated all his efforts on controlling the panic-stricken team as the reins were pulled from his grasp, giving the horses momentary freedom.

Jenna was startled awake by the uncertain lurching of the coach, and she came more fully awake as she was roughly tossed about. She had the impression that their direction seemed to have changed as she was thrown hard against the far side of the coach. She fell to the floor, trying unsuccessfully to grab the handle near the door. The lanterns on the inside of the coach swung wildly in the meager light as she again reached for the handle and was roughly thrown back into the seat. The coach careened wildly, as if out of control, as Jenna pounded frantically on the roof for the driver to halt. If the driver was aware of her frantic message, the motion of the coach gave no indication of it. Jenna concentrated on holding firm to the handle in an effort to prevent being tossed about until every bone was broken.

The coach suddenly swung about with such force that Jenna's grasp on the handle was broken, and she was tumbled over inside the coach, and with sickening reality she knew the coach was rolling side over side into oblivion. The latch on the back-rest of the seat opposite her fell open with the force of the motion of the coach, scattering several pistols and a long sword into the coach from where they had been stored in the compartment. Jenna fell sharply against the edge of the seat and felt a sudden, sharp pain at the back of her head, and then nothing, as darkness closed over her.

The coach rolled over twice after the harness snapped,

9

freeing the frenzied team of horses and coming to a sudden halt on one side, lodged against the sturdy trunk of a massive oak at the base of the hill, below the main road. The burly rider quickly followed the leader, and they descended the hill and reined in their mounts when they reached the coach.

The leader quickly dismounted and with great ease jumped atop the overturned coach. The door to the coach was jammed inside the opening and would not easily yield. The broader, mountainous man nodded gruffly and scrambled onto the coach to give assistance. Drawing a large, curved blade from its sheath, the burly man easily pried the door open. The fading light of day fell across the form of a young woman, crumpled against the far door.

"Christos! A woman!" The burly man exclaimed, raising a startled gaze to his leader.

"Search the baggage compartment. I want those papers found," the man ordered curtly as he slowly lowered his long, muscular frame into the overturned coach.

The darkly clothed leader of the highwaymen carefully leaned over the young woman, his shadow blocking out the fading light as he braced one booted foot against the far side of the coach where she lay. Carefully removing his black leather riding gloves, he rested his fingers along the slender column of her throat feeling for some signs of life. He felt the slow, erratic pulsing beneath the silken smoothness of her skin. She had been fortunate to escape with her life—or perhaps not so fortunate, he thought, as he glanced about the inside of the coach with grim resolve. His attention was drawn back to the young woman as she stirred faintly.

Jenna felt a rush of cool, refreshing air fill her lungs as she breathed deeply, fighting her way back from the dark void that had consumed her. A throbbing pain pounded at the back of her head. She tried to move and felt as if every bone in her body must be broken. A meager shaft of fading light entered the dark interior of the coach. Her eyes fluttered open uncertainly and she tried to move her arm, which was pinned beneath her. A shadow fell across her,

10

blocking the gray light at the opening of the coach. Confused and disoriented, Jenna would have pulled away from those warm fingers that rested momentarily against her throat, but her bruised body refused to obey her commands. Her thoughts cleared, and a sudden fear of the stranger who bent over her welled within her at the memory of Mr. Flint's stern warnings of highwaymen.

Jenna felt herself being lifted, as strong, well-muscled arms reached beneath and closed about her. Too weak to lash out at the stranger who stood over her, Jenna's fingers brushed against cold metal and her hand closed over the handle of a pistol. Gently she was lifted and held firmly against the stranger. He climbed out of the coach as if he carried nothing more than some small package.

The man carried Jenna a small distance and gently laid her against the trunk of the oak tree. He loosened the satin ties of her straw bonnet, which had somehow remained intact, and removed it, freeing a mass of rich, dark hair that tumbled wildly about her shoulders. His breath caught in his throat at the full sight of the unusual beauty who lay before him. A dark sweep of long lashes brushed lightly against her pale cheeks. A faint bruise had appeared across one high cheekbone, but it could not mar the satin perfection of her flawless skin, nor the contour of a perfect profile. He gazed down at the young woman. Her hair, loose in wild abandon from the confines of the bonnet, was long and gently waving, and the color of priceless dark sable—so unusual, when most of the fashionable women of the day chose to wear their hair short and quite curly, in the fashion of the French empress, even though England and France were at war with each other. The silken, luminous softness of the woman's skin seemed to beckon his touch, and he gently traced his finger across her cheek. Under quite different circumstances, he readily admitted he would have enjoyed knowing this young beauty who had crossed his path. He reached for a satin handkerchief and gently wiped at the small trickle of blood at the corner of her mouth. He glanced up as his man approached.

11

"Did you find the papers?" he questioned brusquely.

"There is nothing in the baggage compartment. I have torn the inside apart. There is nothing."

"Search the inside of the carriage, remove panels, everything. I want the papers found."

"You are certain this is the coach?" the broad man questioned.

"The crest on the door is the same. It is the coach," the leader answered tersely. "I had not thought they would use a woman for their purposes."

The burly man grunted disapprovingly. "They must be quite desperate to use women, and one so young, and beautiful."

The leader nodded. "Treachery may take any form, my friend. Always remember that. It is that which you do not suspect that proves the greatest danger."

Jenna heard the soft sounds of voices very near as she slowly opened her eyes. Two men stood a short distance away, discussing some matter of import. The tall, slender man suddenly turned back toward her. Jenna's hand closed shakily around the handle of the pistol hidden in the folds of her dress, where she had hidden it beneath her. The other man, whose size resembled that of a great, lumbering bear, moved in the direction of the overturned coach as the second man approached her. Panic welled inside her as the man approached in long, easy strides. Realizing she would have no defense against the other man, Jenna quickly drew the pistol from beneath her skirts, and without taking careful aim, pulled back the hammer, uncertain that the pistol was even loaded. She closed her eyes tightly as she pulled on the trigger with all her strength.

The air was filled with a deafening blast as the pistol fired, a cloud of smoke filling the air as the spark touched off the powder and discharged the ball.

The darkly garbed stranger reeled backwards as the ball tore into his shoulder. He stared disbelievingly into Jenna's startled dark gaze as the smoke cleared from the air. In the next moment several riders descended the hillside.

The pistol fell from Jenna's grasp as she tried to crawl backwards to escape the fury of the demon who advanced on her. The massive oak at her back and her weakened condition prevented quick escape. In the next moment Jenna was roughly grabbed about the shoulders and hauled to her feet, the mass of her long, dark hair in wild disarray about her shoulders and tumbling to her waist. Her head snapped back as she was crudely drawn against the bold stranger, whose arms closed about her in an unyielding grasp that belied his injury. Jenna's outcry was stilled in her throat as she stared into the dark mask that covered the stranger's face. Dressed completely in black, he was surely the devil incarnate—except for his eyes. Jenna was held transfixed by the brilliant blue of his eyes, which seemed to spark with a fire of their own and yet were as cold as the frozen depths of a lake in the deepest winter. She could feel the warmth of his breath against her cheek. She felt the silent strength that flowed through his arms and his hands as he molded her to him. His lean fingers pressed bruisingly into her skin and seemed to set her aflame. She instinctively sensed the raw power that was barely restrained and could have ended her life in the next moment. Jenna strained away from him, her hands feebly straining to push him away from her. Her eyes widened in surprise as she felt the warm stickiness of his blood spreading across the black silk of his shirt beneath her left hand. His mouth, barely visible beneath the mask, twisted into a cruel smile.

"How fortunate for you, mademoiselle, that pistols have the habit of shooting high of the target, or I might have yielded my life for my carelessness. And you most certainly would then have yielded yours. Now mademoiselle, you will give me the information I seek, or perhaps I shall be forced to instruct you in the art of a finer weapon, such as the rapier. A most effective weapon, requiring great skill and a sure hand to gain victory over one's opponent." His warm voice flowed through her almost soothingly, so that for a moment the cold, menacing

13

threat of his words was lost to her. The blue of his eyes was like a breathtaking spring sky. She felt mesmerized as she stared into their depths.

Desperately, Jenna fought the strange flood of emotions that washed over her. The stranger pulled her to him in a viselike grasp that forced the breath from her lungs. In the next moment his lips crushed down on hers, bruising, searing as they moved over hers, demanding and bold, as if no others stood about them. The darkly shrouded features of the beast who held her fast swam before her as her vision blurred. Against her will, Jenna felt the kindling of her own response as she leaned heavily against him. The heat of his lips against her own suffused her with a glowing heat that seemed to course through her from the far reaches of her being. Her fingers slowly twisted in the silk of his shirt, as if she sought to hold him and prolong the moment that was theirs alone. Instead of the bruising roughness of a moment before, Jenna felt his lips soften against hers as the stranger hesitated for a moment in his assault of her senses. He drew back for a moment, surprised at the response he had felt in her, and then his lips lowered to hers again, now gentle, warm, consuming, as he tenderly explored her gently parted lips with the tip of his tongue, as if first tasting of a rare, priceless wine that must be tasted and tasted again until it is completely consumed—only to leave the soul thirsting for more. Jenna felt as if everything about her had taken flight. A coldness reached up to envelop her as the last traces of her strength slipped beyond her grasp. Jenna collapsed against the stranger.

Gently, the highwayman swung the young girl into his arms, her small head resting gently against his good shoulder as his man approached.

"The wound is bad?" the gruff man questioned as he stared at the younger man.

The leader nodded absently as he carried the slender girl to his horse. Their attention was suddenly drawn to his last man, who now approached from his hidden vantage point further up the road.

14

"Riders approach on the post road."

"You found nothing in the coach?" the leader questioned his bearlike companion.

"Only this. If she carried any message, it is not in the coach." He handed the crumpled message from Mr. Flint to his leader. "I could not make out the English words."

A frown pulled at the corners of those handsome lips as the highwayman stared down at the embossed message. "So, it seems our brave beauty is the granddaughter of Sir Avery Randolph."

The burly man wrestled with his confusion. "What reason would there be for Sir Avery's granddaughter to be the one in the coach?"

"What reason indeed, my friend? Unless she is the link to our traitorous 'friends.'"

"Is she badly injured?"

"I think not. I could find no broken bones." A bold smile flashed in the waning light of day. "But she will have a terrible headache for the next few days from the bruise upon her head."

His gruff companion shook his shaggy head incredulously. "Along a deserted piece of English countryside we seek a coach bearing a traitor with a message of great importance, and you find a girl with beauty to rival that of any royal princess. Always it is so with you. Mark well my words, my friend; one day you will lose your heart or your life at the turn of a pretty face."

The highwayman laughed in spite of the pulsing pain in his wounded shoulder, which increased with each passing moment. "So what is to be, old friend? A princess for the prince?"

"There could be much risk in this. It must be done with great care. We still have not learned of the message that was to be carried," the gruff man warned.

"What of the driver?"

The great giant of a man chuckled heartily. "I would guess he thought us to be the demons of hell descending upon him. He jumped as the coach overturned. When we gave chase, he fled into the trees. I think, not very brave souls, these Englishmen."

"Do not be too hasty in your judgment, my friend. You have seen well the girl's bravery. We must take greater care that we are not discovered. We shall take the girl with us."

"That could be most dangerous. Perhaps others will search for her. It would not do for them to trace her path to our door."

"Easy, my old friend. She will not lead them to us. His Highness Prince Kalinsky shall see her safely returned to her grandfather. And none shall be the wiser for what has passed this afternoon." A wide smile flashed across the face of the leader of the highwaymen, and that bright azure gaze glinted sparks of fire as he contemplated the slender girl who lay against his shoulder, her breathing deep and even, as he gently handed her to his companion. With great effort, he mounted the dark stallion and bent to retrieve the reins, stiffening visibly against the pain in his shoulder. He nodded, and his burly companion gently lifted Jenna into his waiting arms. The command was quickly given, and the riders disappeared into the thick cover of the trees, driving their horses hard, until only the faintest sounds marked their passage through the heavily wooded copse.

Jenna saw neither the bold crimson jacket with the elaborately woven gold frog closures nor the spotlessly polished black Hessian boots, as Prince Stefan Kalinsky carried her easily to her second-floor chamber and delivered her safely to her bed, refusing to allow anyone else to assume the responsibility he had accepted. He lingered for a moment over the slender form of the unconscious girl he had first seen only a short while earlier. He removed his soft leather gloves as he reached to smooth back a stray tendril of hair the color of dark sable that waved enticingly at the side of her face and seemed to beckon his touch. There would be another time, he vowed silently, as the old maid hurried forth to attend her mistress. Indeed, there would be another time. The prince

16

turned on his heel and left the room. The two men who accompanied him quickly followed. A whisper of the evening breeze through the closing door gently billowed the lace curtains in the room, the only sign of their leaving, before the old maid could descend the stairs to show them out.

Chapter Two

Jenna released her breath slowly, concentrating with great effort on the small portrait of her mother, hardly older than her own seventeen years when the miniature had been painted. With each passing moment her impatience grew, and the oppressive heat of the late September morning seemed only to add to her irritation as the seamstress made the final alterations to the filmy, sheer gown, while Jenna stood upon the footstool.

Somehow sensing that Jenna was not in the best of moods, the seamstress quickly called out the changes to be made to her young assistant, in a rapid flow of French. Jenna turned about one more time, for Madame Lessard to make her final inspection, and jumped as she painfully scraped the inside of her arm on a protruding pin. "Enough! I can see no purpose in continuing. I cannot understand why it is necessary that the alterations be done now," Jenna murmured in growing vexation, as she waited impatiently for Madame Lessard to release her from the confines of her cloth prison. The door to Jenna's room was opened, and her maid, Maggie Edwards, entered, carrying a basin of fresh water and a clean linen towel.

"Mademoiselle, your grandfather has given explicit instructions that the gown must he completed in time for the ball this very evening," Madame Lessard responded politely.

Jenna sighed heavily as she turned to her maid and accepted the linen cloth Maggie offered her. Struggling out of the unfinished gown, clad only in the thin silken chemise, Jenna dampened the cloth in the water and pressed the cool cloth against her temples in an effort to ease the pounding that had increased steadily through the long morning. Only a slight discoloration remained at her temple from the blow she had received three weeks earlier, and Maggie had artfully applied a light powder to conceal the purplish mark that had nearly completely disappeared. But her head was still tender from the bad concussion. She looked up at Maggie as she moved to sit before the mirror at the dressing table. The young girl carefully combed through Jenna's luxurious, thick tresses, which streamed down the length of her back like a rich, dark mantle. She then twisted the mass and piled it neatly on top of Jenna's head to offer her some relief from the heat, giving her the appearance of a young Greek goddess.

"Sir Avery insists that you attend the ball," Maggie said gently, knowing well her mistress's stubborn refusal to even consider the matter over the past few days.

"Maggie, I cannot possibly consider attending the ball, when my grandfather is still so weak. I shall merely have to speak with him again." Jenna sighed heavily, as Madame Lessard retreated to the sitting room to complete her final alterations as she had been instructed. There was a faint knocking at the door, and Mrs. Kelly, the housekeeper, entered the room to check on the seamstress's progress. She clucked to herself softly as she crossed the room and closed the large window and drew the heavy drapes to block out the midday sun.

"I cannot remember such heat so late in September. This room is like an oven. Come child, put on a fresh gown so that you may join your grandfather for the midday meal. He has very nearly finished his work for the morning, and will most certainly be waiting for you." Emma puffed as she tried to catch her breath.

Emma Kelly had been housekeeper for Sir Avery Randolph longer than anyone could remember, even

20

before Jenna had come to live with her grandfather, after the death of her parents. Emma Kelly had been both mother and governess to Jenna, and the bond between the soft-spoken Irish woman and the young girl was more than merely that of mistress and servant. The short, stout woman fanned herself gently with her starched apron, her cheeks flushed from climbing the stairs to the second-floor chamber. She deliberately ignored the frown that crossed Jenna's delicate features as she crossed the room to the ornately carved rosewood armoire to select an appropriate gown for Jenna to wear.

Emma could be exasperatingly efficient when she was in a mood to ignore Jenna's occasional displays of stubbornness and, sensing that the issue of the Wingate ball had again come up, she pointedly reverted to the role of housekeeper merely overseeing her responsibilities in Sir Randolph's household. Otherwise she would have had to enter the fray, and she knew well that Jenna would try to enlist her aid in persuading Sir Avery to change his mind in the matter.

Seeing that any further discussion with Emma was pointless, Jenna resigned herself to taking the matter up with her grandfather. She liberally sprinkled the lavender-scented powder down the column of her neck and across the swell of her breasts above the chemise, and then spread it down the length of her arms and absently pushed a stray tendril of curling hair behind her ear, all the while carefully watching the housekeeper in the mirror.

Emma pushed aside first one gown and then another, finally selecting a high-waisted, white muslin one that was liberally sprinkled with tiny, delicately hand-sewn pink blossoms. Short, puffed sleeves were edged with white lace, woven through with pink satin ribbon. The same white lace bordered the low, sweeping neckline, a French fashion introduced a few years earlier by the Empress Josephine. Though the whole of Europe was now engaged in a desperate struggle against the threat of French domination, fashion had not yielded to that primitive desire for survival. Fashionable ladies still insisted on following the style of dress found at the French court, so perfectly re-created by the flood of French emigrées who had fled across the English Channel and established themselves as accomplished seamstresses. Such a one was Madame Lessard, rumored to be of noble birth but forced to leave her homeland under threat of death years earlier when Louis of France had been beheaded and the new order of the Republic of France established.

Emma carefully handed Maggie the muslin gown and smiled down at Jenna complacently. Jenna eyed the woman suspiciously as she lifted her arms and let the filmy gown slip over her shoulders.

"I should like to know your part in this conspiracy to force me to attend the ball. Such affairs are usually quite boring. More often than not, they are merely an over-dressed excuse for matchmaking. I have little patience for such artful ploys," Jenna remarked impatiently, making one last attempt to win Emma over to her side in the argument.

"Dear child, I have little say in the matter. Your grandfather has decided that you are to attend the ball. I cannot deny that a grand ball is an excellent opportunity for young ladies of quality to meet proper young men, and most certainly you would do well to give such matters more consideration. Your own dear mother was well married and already with child when she was your age. And most certainly, many of your young friends have taken a husband or announced their betrothals. Is such a matter so objectionable to you now?" Emma asked as she carefully tied the pink satin sash just below the ample swell of Jenna's bodice.

"It is not that I object to the thought of marriage, but more to the manner in which it is accomplished. I find it deplorable to be paraded before a host of dowagers and their foppish husbands, at endless parties and social gatherings, merely to gain their approval so that their equally foppish sons might be allowed to peer down the front of my gown. It is all quite foolish and unbearable,"

Jenna replied sarcastically, biting off any further comment, for she knew her arguments were better given to her grandfather.

"You know well, lass, that I have little say in the matter. These past few weeks since your return, you have closed yourself inside this house and hardly set foot outside, for your concern and care of your grandfather. But 'tis your future that worries him overmuch, and your lack of interest in it only increases his concern. Your grandfather has a need to see you well cared for; to be assured that after he is gone, you will be happy."

"Emma, I understand what you say, but it is the manner of determining my future that I cannot accept. I will not accept a marriage merely for the fact of being married. I would rather live my life alone than be caught in the lie of a loveless marriage." Jenna's voice was hardly more than a whisper as she admitted for the first time the true reasons for all her objections.

"You are as dear to me as my own child. Indeed, there have been times all these years past, when I have thought of you as my daughter. And if there is one thing I know of a certainty, it is that love takes all shapes and forms between two people. There is the bond you share with your grandfather, and a different bond between you and me. There is the love I once shared with my dear Jamie so many years ago, before he was taken from me. Though all be different, there is a common thing in all forms of love: it grows, day by day. It must grow if it is to survive. If it cannot grow and change, then it dies. The love I shared with my Mr. Kelly is still there. It has changed over the years from what I felt as a girl of fifteen. It is not the same today as it was yesterday; nor is the love you feel for your grandfather. It is different now than when you were a child, because your need of it is different now. What I am trying to say, my dear, is that love may begin only as friendship, and then grow to become much more in time."

"Then you do not believe in love between two people— love that is more than friendship?" Jenna questioned earnestly, her lovely face suddenly quite serious.

Emma sighed heavily, knowing she had been soundly caught in her own trap, for she had loved Jamie Kelly with all her heart and soul, with a passion and intensity that endured to this day, and she had often spoken to the girl of the young husband she had lost, of those few, brief months of her youth, so many years ago, when she had lived and breathed for Jamie Kelly, and then mourned his untimely death with an equal passion.

"You take unfair advantage, mistress."

"Mistress, is it now?" Jenna smiled smugly as she stepped into the white satin slippers and then glanced one last time at her reflection in the long mirror. "You know well, Emma, that you do not believe in a marriage of friendship. You were not willing to settle for such a marriage, and neither shall I."

Jenna's thoughts were suddenly filled with a vision that had haunted her these weeks since her return to London, a vision shrouded in darkness that continued to elude her, a vision of a man whose face was obscure, but whose eyes were the color of aquamarine and seemed to reach into her soul. She had tried to forget that image of the highwayman, and the feel of his lips against hers, bold and certain in his power over her. Her thoughts betrayed her, as her eyes glowed warmly at the memory of his kiss, which had seemed to burn against her lips, so that she was not certain who had received the gravest injury—the highwayman, from the ball that had grazed his shoulder, or herself, branded with the memory of a kiss she could not forget. Jenna could still feel the warmth of his lips against hers, and she reached up uncertainly, her fingers feeling the warmth that still seemed to linger there. She had chosen not to speak of the matter, for fear of its effect on her grandfather in his already weakened condition. Emma's voice drew her back from her thoughts, and she turned towards the door to go and join her grandfather in the dining room below, before Emma could question her about the sudden flush of color that quickly spread across her cheeks at the memory of the mysterious highwayman, whose face was unknown to her, but whose eyes would haunt her for an eternity.

Jenna quickly descended the wide stairway. She halted as she reached the landing, hearing voices coming from the library and realizing that her grandfather had not yet finished working for the morning. A slight frown pulled at the corners of her mouth. Dr. Montgomery had heartily warned him not to overdo after the last attack, allowing him only a few hours's work each day, in the comfort of his library rather than in the offices of the prime minister. Her grandfather had agreed willingly enough, but Jenna was not fooled. Each day he somehow managed to work a little longer than the day before. For the most part, they ignored his complaints and grumblings that he was being treated like a child. But Jenna had found that a constant vigil was necessary in order to prevent him from sneaking in an extra appointment with the other members of the prime minister's staff. On more than one occasion she was forced to intervene, requiring Mr. Flint's presence to end an overlong meeting. In the past she had managed with a polite smile and a simple explanation that it was out of concern for her grandfather's health. But she knew that as his strength increased with each passing day, the time fast approached when her protests and objections would be overruled. Until then, however, Jenna was determined to make the final decisions in such matters. She quietly approached the library door, hoping to determine who the visitor might be from conversation. She knew most of the gentlemen who served the prime minister, for she had seen them all frequently over the past weeks, but the low, even tones of the conversation she heard now gave her no clue to the identity of her grandfather's visitor.

"Mistress, your grandfather has ordered the coach made ready for eight o'clock this evening. Mrs. Kelly said I should inform you of the time." Mr. Flint's imposing hulk dominated the hallway as he stood awaiting her response.

Jenna smiled indulgently at the man, realizing the matter had been taken out of her hands. "Thank you Mr. Flint, but I shall not be needing the coach this evening. I will speak to my grandfather about the matter. Have you eaten, Mr. Flint?" Jenna inquired, as she saw the man's reaction to the aroma from the dining room that filled the air.

"Thank you, mistress. I will be in the kitchen if your grandfather should have need of me," Mr. Flint responded as he bowed his head slightly and moved down the long hallway in the direction of the kitchen, where he knew Mrs. Kelly would have an ample platter waiting for him. Mr. Flint could best most men in a show of strength, but he deferred to Mrs. Kelly in matters that pertained to the household. Jenna smiled at the memory of the mountainous man cowering before the wrath of a broom-wielding Emma, when he had accidentally trod on her freshly waxed wood floors with heavily mudded boots. The scene had reduced Jenna to fits of uncontrolled laughter when she saw the expression of honest fear on the man's face and his hasty retreat when set upon by the stout but diminutive housekeeper. Jenna turned back towards the library, her slippered feet moving noiselessly across that same wood floor, which gleamed now with a rich warmth as a shaft of afternoon sunlight poured through the paned windows of the drawing room.

Jenna knocked gently on the library door, which stood slightly ajar. Her grandfather responded angrily to some comment she could not hear. Without waiting for a response, Jenna pushed the heavy portal open. Her grandfather sat before his large desk in his high-backed, overstuffed chair, listening intently to a tall man who stood beside the desk, his back to the door. At her entrance, Sir Avery glanced up briefly, and he nodded before speaking to the man. The stranger was dressed in a dark green tailcoat that reached to the tops of spotlessly polished black boots, and the collar stood up high and met the brim of his gray felt hat. Even with his back to her, Jenna could sense a strength and energy in the relaxed yet powerful stance. The stranger turned slightly as Jenna stood just inside the open doorway, and she was fascinated by the ornately braided and frogged fastenings of his waistcoat. He leaned toward her grandfather, the spotless ruffles of the shirt at his wrist falling loosely over lean hands concealed by gray doeskin gloves. He murmured something in parting and then turned to leave, but instead of leaving by way of the door, he moved to the glass-paned doors that opened onto the gardens beyond the library. Reaching for the brass handle, the man stopped and cast one last glance over his shoulder. His parting words were for her grandfather, but the look he gave reached over the old man's head. Jenna's breath caught in her throat as her eyes locked with that gaze, which glowed with the brilliance of blue flames upon the hearth.

". . . until our next meeting, Sir Avery; I shall see your message safely delivered." The voice was warm and vital, with a haunting familiarity that was impossible for her to believe, and then the man was gone. Her grandfather turned back to her, absently shuffling through the papers on his desk.

"Grandfather, who was that man? I have never seen him here before," Jenna questioned as she crossed the room to the glass doors and strained for some sight of the man along the garden path that led to the front of the house and the street beyond.

"Oh, merely a messenger from Lord Fallston's office. He brought papers from the prime minister that I must go over tonight." Sir Avery casually dismissed the matter, but Jenna was not satisfied that the man was merely a messenger. Messengers were hardly dressed in the fine garments of a gentleman.

Jenna stretched up on her toes that she might yet see the man as he departed, but to no avail. He had quite effectively disappeared, as if he had never been there at all.

"Come along, my dear. Are you intent that we should both starve while you are given to gazing out of garden windows? I am quite famished, and Mrs. Kelly has promised that cook has prepared a fine meal of roast lamb. And I should like to share your company, for it has been a while since I have had time to sit and talk with you." Sir Avery rose from his chair, still wearing the burgandy brocade robe she had seen him in earlier that morning.

27

"Very well, but I warn you, Grandfather, there is something of import that I would discuss with you. And I am quite determined in the matter." Jenna smiled her most beguiling smile that she knew quite well had a devastating effect on her grandfather. She was not vain, nor was she given to coyness, but she knew well that Sir Avery was most vulnerable where she was concerned, and very likely to let her have her own way in certain instances.

Jenna whirled about as Emma entered the chamber, and the housekeeper wisely kept her eyes averted as she pretended not to notice that her mistress was in quite a high temper.

"Emma, you must please speak with my grandfather. I have been unable to make him understand how I feel about this evening," Jenna moaned with mounting exasperation.

Young Maggie rolled her gray eyes in silent appeal to the older woman, having been unable to convince her mistress to dress for the ball.

"Dear child, Mr. Flint has been waiting for more than half an hour already, and your grandfather is concerned that you may have been taken ill," Emma explained patiently as she retrieved the peach-colored gown that Madame Lessard had finished earlier in the afternoon. Emma braced herself for the storm she saw building in those wide, dark eyes, but she was equally determined to spare her master excessive worry in the matter.

"I simply cannot go to the ball. Emma, can you not see that my place is here with my grandfather?" Jenna pleaded as she saw the firm set to the older woman's jaw. She greatly feared her battle was already lost, for she knew Emma's obstinacy in matters past.

"Listen well, for I have no patience to repeat what I shall say. There is more harm to be done in going against your grandfather's wishes in this, than the slight inconvenience you may be caused in spending the evening at Lord Wingate's ball. I will not see Sir Avery made to suffer for your selfishness in this. Now, Mr. Flint is waiting below. I shall inform him that you will be along presently. And when I have returned, I want to see you dressed in that gown and the prettiest smile upon your face. Do you understand what I am saying?'' Emma asked, her round face suddenly quite red and flustered with her efforts.

Jenna stood in stunned surprise at the woman's outburst, and suddenly felt quite ashamed of the way she had been acting, for she knew the truth of Emma's words. She would indeed be doing more harm by defying her grandfather. She nodded meekly, and then silently turned to Maggie to accept the gown over her head. The door to the chamber closed with a loud thump as Emma Kelly moved with a determined pace across the landing and down the wide stairway.

When Emma returned some time later she was greeted by a vision of loveliness, if not complete willingness, as Jenna stood compliantly while Maggie set the finishing touch to the exquisite gown that draped her lithe form as if it were molded to her. Jenna drew on the long white gloves that reached to the short, capped sleeves of the gown, and accepted an elaborately brocaded satin shawl that matched the creamy peach color of the gown. The rich, dark mane of her hair was freshly washed and drawn smoothly back from the delicate oval of her flawless face, the curling, waving mass of it held back on each side of the crown of her head with matching combs set with double rows of perfectly matched pearls. In contrast to the favored shorter, curly style dictated by the French empress, Jenna preferred her hair long and flowing. Her only jewelry was a necklace of pearls that snugly fit the slender column of her graceful neck, set in the very center with a single large topaz. The fire and brilliance of that stone caught the warm glow of light in her eyes, making them seem almost catlike in the soft glow of candlelight in the chamber.

In the library below, Jenna joined her grandfather before leaving for the ball. Sir Avery turned as he heard the gentle swishing of her gown against the floor.

"How very lovely you are, my dear. Come and let me

look at you more closely." Sir Avery held out his two hands to Jenna and drew her closer to the light of the candles that blazed from the candelabrum upon the desk.

"When I see you like this, I am reminded of how very much you favor your sweet mother, when she was your age. Except for your dark eyes. They were a gift from a Gypsy princess long ago." Her grandfather gazed into the flawless oval of her face, his eyes misting slightly as he looked into those wide, dark eyes fringed with long, sooty lashes that gently brushed against the curve of her high cheekbones. He cleared his throat, bringing his thoughts back to the present moment, when he perhaps would have preferred to remember another time and place.

"My dearest Jenna, you must surely know that you are my greatest treasure, that all I do is for you; to make certain that your future shall be secure."

"I know that, Grandfather. I only wish you would not worry about it so. I see how tired you are, and I fear for your health, if you persist," Jenna responded lovingly as she lifted his wrinkled hand and pressed it tenderly against her cheek.

Sir Avery sighed heavily as he sat wearily in the large upholstered chair before the small fire that had been laid at his request, even in the balmy warmth of the September evening. He drew Jenna down into the chair across from him, and tenderly reached up to caress her cheek.

"I fear, dear child, that there are those who would gladly destroy what we have, with no thought or concern for all the countless generations that must follow. While I may, I must strive to see that that never happens." Sir Avery spoke with a sadness that Jenna had never before heard.

"I have never known you to have fear, Grandfather. I think you are perhaps overtired. Will you promise me to rest this evening? No more work. There will be time tomorrow," Jenna replied softly.

"Time grows short, my dear, and I must see that all is taken care of as soon as possible. Nothing must be left to chance. Do you understand what I say?"

"I am not certain. Grandfather, is there some way I may

help you in your work?" Jenna was suddenly concerned at the ominous tone of her grandfather's voice.

Sir Avery's manner softened as he saw the slight frown that crossed Jenna's face. Above all, he did not want to alarm her, nor jeopardize the plans he had made. He smiled warmly at his granddaughter.

"Have I told you recently, my dear, that you have been the bright sun in my life? My greatest joy has been seeing you grow to the lovely woman you are now, and indeed you are a woman. Why, look at you! There is none to compare to you, with your beauty and fiery spirit. Did I tell you that your grandmother once confessed that there was a dark-eyed Gypsy girl in her family? She only confessed it after we were well married, for fear that I might not approve of it, but I tell you true that I am certain to this day that it was true. And you have the same dark eyes she had; probably a Gypsy princess. My princess, I have a gift for you." Sir Thomas reached to the carved wood table beside his chair and handed Jenna a small wrapped package neatly bound with a satin ribbon.

"Open it, my dear, It is for you. I have kept it for you all these years, and I think it is time that you should have it."

Jenna stared at the package, and then excitedly untied the ribbon and pulled off the paper. She carefully lifted the lid of the box. Inside was a gold box, ornately designed, with small flowers etched into the gold, decorating the entire border of the box. Jenna slowly lifted the lid of the box, and the sweet notes of a melody floated out from inside. Tears filled her eyes as she looked at her grandfather. She had often seen the music box on his desk, and she knew how he valued it. He had given it to her grandmother on their wedding day, and then to her mother when she married. The soft, tinkling notes were familiar to her, for she had often played in the library as a child, and one of her greatest pleasures had been when her grandfather promised her a song from the music box. He had then allowed her to lift the lid, setting the workings of the music box into motion, and Jenna had sat in rapt delight listening to that sweet melody. It was a link to her past, to her childhood, and to her grandfather.

Jenna sprang to her feet and hugged her grandfather fiercely. "It is the grandest gift I have ever received. I will treasure it always. But why are you giving it to me now? Should you not wait until I am well married?" she teased playfully.

Sir Thomas smiled gently. "One never knows who one may meet in the course of a single evening," he answered, winking at his granddaughter. His meaning was not lost on Jenna.

"Is it then your intent that I accept Charles Wingate's proposal?" Jenna smiled sweetly, knowing full well that her grandfather had been showing an increased disapproval of Lord Wingate's son. In the past weeks, though, she was quite at a loss to understand the reason for it.

Sir Avery's gruff manner returned as he rose from the chair and returned to his desk. "It is merely my intent, dear girl, that you enjoy the evening among your young friends. Now be off with you. I have instructed Mr. Flint to return for you at midnight."

Jenna leaned across the desk and lovingly kissed her grandfather's whiskered cheek. "Then you will let me keep the music box, without a husband?" she teased playfully.

"The gift is yours, as I have said. Now go, I have these papers to read tonight."

Jenna frowned slightly. "Only one hour, and I shall instruct Mr. Flint that you will read no more, after his return."

"You are a high-minded bit of a girl. I have a notion to take the box back. 'Tis not a gift for a child."

Jenna darted away from him and made for the door. "I shall hide it upstairs where it will be safe," she teased playfully, casting a loving smile back over her shoulder. "You have given the gift and may not now take it back." Jenna blew her grandfather a kiss as she whirled through the doorway. Down the hallway, Emma stood patiently waiting for her, a delicately woven fan in her hands. Jenna handed Emma the music box.

"Emma, please take this to my room; I have not the time now. And see that my grandfather does not tire himself. I do not like his color this evening. I fear he works overmuch lately." Jenna cast a worried look back toward the library door as she accepted the fan. She bid Emma good-bye and quickly descended the steps to where Mr. Flint stood patiently, holding the door to the coach open for her.

The large, ornate ballroom of Hampton Hall shone as bright as day with the light of many coal oil lamps that cast their brilliant light across the wide expanse of the dance floor. A large crystal chandelier caught the shimmering light of a multitude of candles and reflected that brilliant light on the dancers as they whirled about the room, the vivid colors of the ladies' gowns like brilliantly displayed blossoms in a lush summer garden.

Having given her shawl to the servant at the entrance, Jenna slowly walked through the wide double doors. A uniformed servant stood at each side of the open doorway. Each guest was announced as he or she arrived, and Jenna was aware of her conspicuous arrival, unescorted, even though prior arrangements had been made for her to be the guest of Elizabeth Wingate. She could feel the speculative gazes of the older women as they stared, openly disapproving. Jenna felt the rise of color across her cheeks, but she refused to yield before the line of old dowagers. Indeed, she felt much like the knights of old, forced to accept the challenge of the gauntlet once it is thrown down. She refused to acknowledge the contempt she read in the eyes of one elderly matriarch, who regarded her keenly through a glass eyepiece that dangled from about the woman's wrinkled neck on a gold chain. Across the crowded hall she saw Lord and Lady Wingate and released a sigh of relief as Elizabeth Wingate at last saw her and quickly made her way through the crowd of silk-clad ladies and their escorts.

"Jenna, I feared you might have decided to leave me to

33

face these old harridans alone. I would have been quite upset if you had not come." Elizabeth greeted her warmly, a soft smile lighting up her rather plain features, and Jenna knew her friend was enjoying the evening in spite of all her earlier protests against it.

"I hardly think you have a need of me. It would seem that you are quite well surrounded with admiring young men. And you feared the evening would be boring," Jenna teased her friend, as she gazed across the room to where Elizabeth had stood a moment before and saw the circle of young men who now watched them from across the dance floor.

"You know quite well it is you they are staring at. If you were not my very best friend I would be quite angry with you for the way you have turned every head in this room. Your gown is exquisite; undoubtedly the handiwork of Madame Lessard. You are quite wicked, Jenna. You realize, of course, the woman sews her very finest for you." Elizabeth Wingate pouted playfully as she drew Jenna across the room to join Lord and Lady Wingate.

The lovely lilting strains of music filled the air, and Charles Wingate smiled broadly at Jenna, seizing her gloved hand and drawing her out onto the dance floor before she could even bid her host and hostess good evening. Jenna frowned disapprovingly as she was swept into the swirling movements of a graceful dance, but before she could voice her objections to such poor manners, Charles cut her off.

"My dearest Jenna, how beautiful you are. And quite well recovered from your accident. Surely you shall capture every heart here tonight. And I fear poor Elizabeth will be left the wallflower, so plain is she in comparison. I often wonder that you are friends."

"Elizabeth is your sister, and you know how she adores you. I cannot understand why you insist on being so cruel to her," Jenna replied evenly, hardly in the mood for Charles's biting remarks about her dearest friend.

"Perhaps it is merely that I see the absurdity behind this entire matter. My father hopes to see her wed, and quite honestly, holds great hope that this evening will see a suitable match for her. I do believe that he has plans for Sir Reginald Guilford, although I am certain he would welcome any proposal made for an acceptable match."

"I cannot believe what you are saying. How can you be so cold?" Jenna felt her anger rise.

"I am not cold, merely realistic, my dearest Jenna. Elizabeth is of a suitable age for marriage, and a good marriage could be quite advantageous."

"Is that how you regard your proposal to me—as an advantageous arrangement?" Jenna shot back angrily, her wide, large eyes suddenly dark and stormy. Her slender jaw set defiantly as she glared back at the young man who stood before her. His lean, aquiline features were considered quite handsome by many of the ladies present, yet Jenna had come to consider Charles's aloof bearing quite irritating, as if he played at some game, always regarding her quite coolly behind half-closed lids that hid his true purpose.

They suddenly came to an abrupt halt in the center of the dance floor, while the other couples whirled about them. One by one, the other couples also stopped, and Jenna was aware that she and Charles were the center of attention. Embarrassment was frequently Charles's most effective weapon against people, and she had allowed herself to be drawn into his little game. And how well he enjoyed himself. She realized clearly all her grandfather's unspoken objections to Charles Wingate as a suitor.

As they stood in the center of the large ballroom, Jenna was unaware of a pair of piercing blue eyes that also watched from across the room as she struggled to pull her hand from Charles's grasp. His fingers closed with brutal purpose around hers as he refused to release her. Jenna's gaze was unwavering, as she smiled her most radiant smile and then threatened him from between clenched teeth.

"Release me at once, Charles, or I shall make all your guests aware of the company you keep—all those late evenings when you and your circle of friends frequent the house of a certain lady, unacceptable among those present this evening," Jenna said sweetly, the warm velvet of her eyes, glowing with a sudden intense light.

Charles smiled at her confidently as he sought to play out their little game. "What silly thoughts enter your lovely head, my dearest Jenna; merely gossip that anxious mothers and envious old men spread about when they have nothing better to occupy themselves with."

"Perhaps true, Charles; however, there are sufficient members of Parliament, and titled members of the nobility present, not to mention the Duke of Kent, that I should think you might take care not to jeopardize your stature of respectability for such a trifling matter as releasing my hand," Jenna countered, and she drew no small measure of satisfaction as she saw the conflict that raged within Charles. He wanted to force her into submission, and yet he realized quite well he could not do it in the presence of those about them. With a gallant show of bravado, Charles bent low over her imprisoned hand, gently kissing the back of her gloved fingers before finally relinquishing it.

"There will be another time, my lovely Jenna. It is my intention to speak with your grandfather at the earliest convenience, and then, my love, we shall have a lifetime to play out our little confrontations. I yield the moment, milady, but never the cause." Charles seemed to mock her as he bowed formally and rather stiffly from the waist, and then quite effectively left her standing alone in the middle of the ballroom. If he sought to humiliate her further, he might have considered the matter more thoroughly, for if there was one quality Jenna possessed in great quantity, it was pride, and she stubbornly refused to allow any present to know how his treatment infuriated her.

Jenna felt as if her cheeks were ablaze as she tilted her head proudly. The other couples about her stood awkwardly for a moment and then resumed their fanciful flight about the room in gay abandon to the soft strains of the music that filled the ballroom. Inhaling deeply, Jenna straightened her back, her gaze sweeping along the perimeter of the huge hall. Her eyes locked with that brilliant blue gaze, which sparkled and seemed to pierce

36

her through, so vibrant was its color. She held her breath for a moment as her memory was drawn back to another time and place when for a brief moment she had seen that same gaze, or one so very like it that the memory left her shaken.

Across the wide expanse of the ballroom, the man lifted his champagne glass as if to toast her, and Jenna was aware that he, like the others, had witnessed her entire confrontation with Charles. And now he had raised his glass in mock salute to her.

Jenna quickly made her way to the edge of the ballroom and sought the wide, sweeping stairway, that led to the second floor-sitting rooms. Elizabeth was suddenly at her side as Jenna reached the landing and started up the stairs.

"Jenna, you must try to ignore Charles's mood this evening; he argued with father earlier and seems intent upon making everyone as miserable as he is. You know how he feels about you."

They started up the wide stairs together, and Jenna said, "Elizabeth, you must not defend Charles at every turn. He is quite capable of fighting his own battles." Painfully, Charles's words about Elizabeth cut cruelly through Jenna. How could one sibling be so loving and forgiving and another so deliberately cruel? Jenna hesitated at the next step, her attention drawn back to the ballroom and the vividly gowned ladies and the equally splendid gentlemen, who had chosen to follow the latest fashion dictates set by the gentleman Beau Brummel, who was considered about London to be quite a dandy. Her gaze was again drawn to the handsome stranger, whose gaze had followed her and now lingered over her appraisingly, even at that great distance, from across the hall. Instead of the usual brown or black waistcoats and contrasting doeskin breeches worn strapped over fine leather slippers—worn by all the dandies, as if they had been dressed by the same tailor—the stranger had chosen a military coat of bright crimson, cut away at the waist to reveal flawless white breeches that fit snugly across his lean torso, and down the length of his well-muscled thighs. They disappeared just above the knees into gleaming black leather boots that were tall in front, reaching well above the knee, but cut lower in back to allow ease of movement. His waistcoat was bound across the chest with elaborately braided gold frog closures, and the frothy white cravat of an equally spotless white cotton shirt spilled forth at the neck, the collar of the waistcoat standing up high. It was the same kind of shirt the gentleman she had seen in her grandfather's library earlier that afternoon had worn. The man watched her intently, and Jenna was startled by his lean, handsome features. He had golden-brown skin, deeply tanned, and high cheekbones prominent beneath the gentle slant of those piercing blue eyes, which were of an aquamarine cast and glowed intensely. Light brown hair, streaked golden, waved about his magnificent head, and finely arched brows of that same golden color gave him the look of a hawk watching its prey. He was of equal height with the tallest man in the room, and yet his stature and bearing set him apart from them. Whereas others were dressed to excess in their efforts to exceed the next man's costume, the man who watched her with such intensity seemed to have no need for such affectation. He possessed a confidence that was unnerving without being arrogant, a strong vital energy that was carefully restrained, and somehow Jenna sensed he might feel equally confident leading an army into battle as he would leading a woman across a dance floor. She paused on the second step of the stairway, her gloved hand resting hesitantly on the gleaming wood of the balustrade.

"Elizabeth, who is that man? The one standing near the duke of Kent." Jenna inclined her head slightly toward her friend.

Elizabeth's gaze followed Jenna's across the wide expanse of the dance floor. She leaned forward to whisper discreetly to Jenna as one of the other ladies swept down the stairway past them. "My dear Jenna, that is Prince Kalinsky. He is Russian, although born in France. I have heard that Napoleon seized all of his vast estates in the south of France, when the prince was in St. Petersburg visiting his family. And now that Napoleon has sent his armies into Russia, the prince has sought refuge in England. There are a multitude of rumors about him all over London; not the least of which is his rumored affair with Madame de Stahl. If you had not been such a recluse these past weeks, you would know all of this. Jenna, do you know the prince? It seems as if he has been seen about London with every available lady of title, and several who are not so available. His name is spoken in the highest circles; there is even the rumor that his name appears on the most important guest lists, at the insistence of the duke of Kent. Most certainly he is invited to all the most important social events and seems to have the favor of the prince regent. Jenna, are you all right? You are suddenly quite pale."

Jenna reached up and gently pressed her friend's arm reassuringly. She had known only the name of the man responsible for returning her safely to her grandfather those weeks before, and though she had given the matter some thought, she had not expected they might meet again, certainly not this evening. Jenna only vaguely recalled the rumors about Madame de Stahl and her escapades about London with the elite of English society. Now she wished she had had more interest in Maggie's kitchen gossip about the notorious Austrian blueblooded lady. She smiled wanly.

"I am quite all right. It is nothing, just a silly thought, nothing more."

"Perhaps not, my dearest Jenna, but it seems the prince thinks more of it than you," Elizabeth replied conspiratorially. Jenna turned and her gaze locked with that of Prince Kalinsky as he excused himself from an elegantly dressed lady and made his way around the dance floor with carefully measured steps, until he stood before her. He bowed slowly, the tawny gold of his hair glistening softly, and when he again stood erect before her, Jenna's breath caught in her throat, and she was unable to look away from the intense warmth that glowed in those azure eyes that were as light as a summer sky. She was vaguely aware that Elizabeth made the necessary introductions. Jenna mumbled some simple reply as she tried in vain to excuse herself, but she found herself soundly caught as several ladies descended the wide staircase, preventing her escape. Before she could object, Jenna was drawn out onto the dance floor, the young man who had approached her to claim his dance left standing beside Elizabeth with a somewhat surprised expression on his face. Jenna felt the flood of color rise high in her cheeks as she was swept out into the center of the ballroom. Prince Kalinsky's gaze bore into hers and the warmth of his fingers gently closed over hers as they joined the other couples. Her vision was blurred with the myriad colors of the ornately dressed ladies and their escorts. She was unaware that Charles watched from across the hall, his pale gray eyes suddenly cold and piercing. Indeed, all seemed to watch as the handsome Russian prince, resplendently attired in the crimson waistcoat and flawlessly perfect white breeches, whirled Jenna about the room, in perfect step to the music that filled the night air. Jenna was oblivious to the attention her dark-haired beauty caused in contrast to his well-tanned blond features. Nor was she aware that several of the matronly guests of the evening silently scowled at her, as they drew their eligible daughters aside to instruct them desperately in the finer arts of obtaining a husband.

"I am pleased to see that you are completely recovered from your accident. Indeed, none would ever know of your injury." His words startled Jenna from her reverie, forcing her attention back to that vivid azure gaze. His eyes were like fingers, caressing the entire length of her body, as if he could see beneath the gossamer thinness of her gown.

Jenna tilted her lovely head as she gazed back at him unafraid. "I am grateful for your kindness in seeing me safely returned to London. I fear what might have happened had you not chanced upon the post road when you did."

"Do you fear it indeed, Mademoiselle Randolph? You do not seem capable of fear." Prince Kalinsky smiled with keen pleasure at the lovely girl he once again held in his arms.

Jenna thought she might lose herself in the warmth of that smile that seemed to reach out to her alone, as if they shared some secret that no others could know. She was oblivious of the cold, menacing look that followed them about the ballroom. The music ceased for but a moment, and then the musicians struck up another dance, and Prince Kalinsky firmly refused to relinquish her hand to the next gentleman who tried to claim his dance.

Jenna's gaze traveled the wide expanse of the ballroom, aware that the prince watched her keenly, yet refusing to meet that brilliant gaze as she felt the heat of his bold perusal of her.

Stefan Kalinsky studied the young girl he held in his arms. Her dark eyes, the color of deep amber, gazed steadily past his shoulder as she seemed intent on some point beyond the circle of dancing couples. Her long lashes were thick and framed those dark orbs like a mantle of soft feathers, sweeping across the delicate bloom of her cheeks when she gazed down, as now, as if lost in some deep concentration. Her skin was flawless as satin, a lightly hued blush of soft peach faintly accenting the delicate oval of wide cheekbones. Her nose was delicate and finely boned, sloping gently to the soft curve of full lips, delicately tinged with a soft color that matched her gown. His gaze traveled lingeringly down the slender column of her throat where he could barely detect the faint pulsing just below the surface of her skin. He had not known the full extent of her beauty that late afternoon those weeks before when she had been delivered to his care. An appreciative smile pulled at the corners of his lips as his gaze lingered for a moment over the ample swell of her low-cut bodice, which barely revealed the silken softness of her charms above the sweeping neckline. She was a rare beauty, not like the pale, powdered ladies at court, whose beauty was merely a mirrored image of the latest favored courtesan. Hers was a dark, mysterious beauty, worn unashamedly in the natural dark wave of her long hair, which caught the light of a thousand candles and

41

shimmered with a rich, lustrous life of its own, like a tawny mantle of priceless sable. His gaze bore into her, as he refused to accept her calm nonchalance, willing her dark, wide-eyed gaze back to his, compelling her beyond her own will. He smiled over his small victory as that amber gaze suddenly stared back at him expectantly.

"Do you fear for your reputation after so many dances with the same man, mademoiselle?" His honest question, spoken simply, seemed to beckon the truth from her.

"I have no fear of idle gossip, your highness. It is merely a game others play, out of boredom. I have no use for such games."

"Well spoken. Much what I would expect from the granddaughter of Sir Avery Randolph," the prince answered appreciatively.

"Are you acquainted with my grandfather?" Jenna's curious gaze suddenly lost its guarded aloofness.

"Sir Avery and I have met on occasion. We seem to share the same political opinions. We have enjoyed several conversations as to the future of Europe in these unpredictable times," Stefan Kalinsky responded evenly, divulging nothing that was not common knowledge about London.

"It seems that no one can escape the uncertainty of Napoleon's quest for absolute power. My grandfather has often said that England is the ultimate prize he seeks."

Stefan Kalinsky regarded Jenna Randolph keenly behind the veil of his blue gaze, which was at once cool and appraising. "I find it rare that one possessing such beauty might also possess an interest in such matters."

"I, like my grandfather, value freedom and my heritage. Those who have yielded to Bonaparte's quest for power have lost their heritage and their freedom."

"Ah, the sentiments of the elderly statesman," Prince Kalinsky countered, watching the play of emotions in Jenna's face.

"Not merely my grandfather's sentiments, but also mine, and freely given. These past years I have seen the results of Napoleon's oppression. Indeed, it has robbed my

42

grandfather of his health, though he would give it willingly. I cannot help but think that those who follow Napoleon's cause have merely exchanged one monarchy for another," Jenna replied passionately, her thoughts returning to her grandfather and the past weeks, and how he had constantly disobeyed his physician to spend hours seeking a solution to the endless wars that plagued Europe and threatened them all.

The blue gaze narrowed perceptively as Stefan Kalinsky watched Jenna with unwavering calm. "Do you then disapprove of absolute monarchy, mademoiselle?"

Jenna's startled amber gaze locked with the piercing blue one. What was the answer he sought behind his carefully guarded questions? "I cannot believe that England could long survive without the monarchy, though I know well not everyone would agree with my opinion."

"Who, pray tell, Mademoiselle Randolph, might possibly disagree with you?" Stefan Kalinsky pressed boldly, as he stood before her, the dance suddenly ended.

Before she could reply, Jenna's arm was gently but firmly seized and she was turned about.

"My dearest Jenna, have you forgotten yourself? You have neglected our dear friends, and most certainly myself. The next dance is to be mine, and I will accept no excuses." The pressure of Charles's grasp upon her arm tightened bruisingly, so that Jenna flinched uncertainly at the sudden cruel edge in his voice. Beside her, Prince Kalinsky watched the exchange with keen interest. Jenna hesitated, her temper flaring at Charles's boldness and air of superiority over her as she vainly tried to pull her arm from his hold on her.

Stefan Kalinsky stepped forward boldly, his cold blue gaze fixed with deadly calm upon Charles Wingate. "I believe Mademoiselle Randolph would rather make her own choice for the next dance. You will release her immediately."

Jenna's silent struggling halted as she felt the air suddenly alive with the current of the unspoken challenge the prince had offered before the small circle of people who had gathered about them. None had ever dared question Charles Wingate, certainly not in his own home, before his family and guests. She knew well the boundlessness of Charles's unpredictable temper, for her grandfather had heartily warned her against it. She could hardly believe Stefan Kalinsky would be foolish enough to provoke that wrath. Jenna turned her surprised gaze on the handsome Russian prince and saw no fear behind the cold, unyielding power in that blue gaze, only deadly intent. Charles had finally met his equal.

"Jenna, Elizabeth has been looking for you. I suggest that you leave now to refresh yourself." The command in Charles's voice was carefully hidden behind the simple request, but it was not lost on Prince Kalinsky. The musicians had ceased their playing, and a sudden hush seemed to settle over the ballroom, making the confrontation only more obvious to all. From the open door of the library the chiming of the clock floated softly across the crowded room.

The uneasy mood was suddenly broken as Jenna turned back to Charles. "It is past midnight. Mr. Flint was to have returned for me before now."

The strain seemed to ease from Charles's thin face as he smiled at her indulgently. "There is no cause for alarm, my dearest Jenna. Come, let us enjoy ourselves. I insist on the next dance, and if your Mr. Flint does not appear soon, then Elizabeth can make arrangements for you to remain the night."

Jenna missed the smug look that crossed Charles's face as her concern for the lateness of the hour blocked out all other thoughts. "Grandfather specifically said he would send Mr. Flint with the carriage at midnight. It is not like Mr. Flint to be late."

"Dearest Jenna, you worry overmuch. The first evening you grace us with your appearance, and you choose to leave us early," Charles teased, seizing both Jenna's hands and attempting to draw her out onto the dance floor as the music once again filled the air.

"Charles, please. I cannot stay. I fear something may be wrong. You know well, Grandfather has not been well. Please, I must have the use of your carriage. I will see it returned in the morning," Jenna persisted as she pulled back, gently refusing the dance.

A scowl darkened Charles's face as he refused to yield her gloved hand. "Jenna, you are behaving most badly. I will not allow you to leave yet. Your grandfather is quite all right. It was he who insisted on your coming this evening."

The color rose brilliantly across Jenna's cheeks as she finally gained the freedom of her hand. "Charles, I must leave immediately. I am quite sorry if you fail to understand the reasons. Will you allow me the use of your carriage?"

"I most certainly shall not," Charles stormed at her, his temper suddenly flaring at her boldness before his guests.

"Charles, whether you will allow it or not, I am leaving this very minute." Jenna whirled about, determination worn in every fiber of her slender body, her amber gaze, glinting sparks of gold, meeting the haunting blue gaze of Prince Kalinsky, who stood before her.

"I fear I am without a carriage." Jenna hesitated a moment, suddenly quite breathless with the boldness of her unspoken request.

Stefan Kalinsky smiled softly at his small but significant victory. "Please accept the use of my carriage, mademoiselle. I have no objections to seeing you safely home."

Jenna smiled her relief, not caring who objected to her accepting his bold offer. Without a backwards glance, Jenna accepted Stefan Kalinsky's arm and quickly fled the ballroom, leaving Charles Wingate seething in silent rage at her and the daring nobleman who had openly flaunted his desire for her.

Chapter Three

Jenna was silently grateful for the darkness of the night, which hid all her uncertain feelings at her decision to suddenly return home in the company of a man she had only met hours before, and, undeniably, one of mysterious if not questionable background—even if he was a prince. She was also grateful for the coolness of the night air, which cleared her thoughts of her anger at Charles. They sped through the cobbled streets beyond Grosnevor Square, covering the short distance to her home.

Every window in the stone town house blazed brilliantly as the open carriage drew to a sudden halt. The driver quickly alighted to open the door and drop the step into place, and Jenna quickly alighted, not waiting for either the footman or Prince Kalinsky to give her assistance. She was only vaguely aware of a rider who quickly arrived after them and now stood silently by, as if awaiting some order. In front of their carriage in the small circular drive was Dr. Montgomery's closed coach, and Jenna's heart constricted with sudden fear as she flew up the steps and through the front door.

Maggie's startled, red-eyed gaze held Jenna's as she halted in the hallway. Jenna's voice was hardly more than a whisper as she asked about her grandfather. Her fearful eyes followed the maid's gaze to the library door, which stood slightly ajar. Maggie dissolved into tears as Jenna turned toward that portal. Before she reached the door, it

47

opened suddenly, and Emma Kelly stood silhouetted in the bright glow of light from the room.

"Dear child." Emma's voice broke as she reached out to grasp Jenna's hands in hers.

Jenna brushed past the maid, oblivious to the woman's gentle restraint.

Slumped over his desk, Avery Randolph's head rested on the stack of papers he had been reading earlier that evening. To anyone just entering the library he might have seemed to doze, but somehow Jenna sensed more. Mr. Flint stood across the room, his bulk resting wearily on outstretched arms that braced his weight against the mantel of the hearth. Dr. Montgomery turned abruptly as Jenna entered the room.

"Mr. Flint, she should not see this." The physician's stern warning caused the faithful servant to look up, suddenly surprised to find Jenna standing there. His face was lined with a sudden strain Jenna had never noticed, as if he suddenly felt very old and tired.

Jenna looked questioningly from the physician to her grandfather's retainer. She saw the undeniable truth in their faces. Slowly, she walked toward the large desk. Tears filled her eyes as she slowly reached out to stroke her grandfather's cheek and then leaned over his slumped form, wrapping her arms about him lovingly. The others who watched were unaware of the elegantly dressed man who stood just beyond the open doorway, the light in the hall glowing softly upon the crimson of his waistcoat. Prince Stefan Kalinsky did not miss the disorder in the room, nor the slight trickle of blood at the corner of the dead man's mouth. A dark, deadly expression crossed his handsome face as the sounds of Jenna's softly muffled sobs filled the room. All might now well be lost. He could not know what the others might have found among the papers before striking the old man down. He was convinced Avery Randolph had died defending the secret they shared.

Jenna stood transfixed upon the bleak hillside. A brisk

wind whipped at the black silk of her gown, molding the folds of fabric against her slender body. She was vaguely aware of the priest's words as he gave the traditional service over her grandfather's grave. She stared at the many faces of the mourners who had traveled the distance from London to the small cemetery near Wallingford in the Chiltern Hills, where she had chosen that her grandfather be buried, beside her grandmother, near the small town where they had been married, so many years before. Her grandfather had loved the small, quaint town with its rolling farmlands beside the Thames.

Jenna watched the faces of the mourners, as if she might find some solace in their common grief. She had not known the extent of her grandfather's importance. Members of the prime minister's cabinet had arrived the day before, though the prime minister himself had not arrived until early that morning. Several members of Parliament were present; men whose faces she recognized, but whose names eluded her. The duke of Kent had also arrived that morning, lending his stern countenance to the list of dignitaries who had chosen to attend. Sir Wingate and Lady Wingate had arrived with Elizabeth and Charles the day before, taking rooms in a nearby inn. Indeed, Charles had been most kind in the past days, insisting on helping her with the final arrangements for her grandfather's funeral, even insisting that she stay with the Wingate family in London. Jenna had firmly but gratefully refused. She felt no uneasiness in remaining in her grandfather's house with only the servants to keep her company. Indeed, she had known only love in that house, and it somehow eased her grief to feel that love about her. She had braced herself for one of Charles's frequent tirades when she chose to refuse him, and was pleasantly surprised when he silently, if not happily, yielded to her decision. Prince Kalinsky had been absent the last days since her grandfather's death, somehow sensing Jenna's need for privacy. However, his assistance was not lacking. Mr. Flint had made her aware of a Russian officer, dressed fashionably indiscreetly, who maintained a constant vigil outside the town house, just beyond the front gates, should Jenna need him. It was a touching gesture, one that meant more to Jenna than all the lavishly offered sympathies, which seemed somehow hollow.

The service ended, and Jenna was drawn back to the present as the priest closed the Bible. She moved slowly toward the stone marker and gently placed the yellow and white roses in front of the headstone. She ran her fingers across the elaborately etched inscription, which somehow seemed the final reality of her grandfather's death. A single tear fell upon her cheek. Jenna rose uncertainly, and seemed to stumble. In an instant she felt the strong support of a muscular arm going about her waist.

That brilliant blue gaze, the color of a summer sky, bore into hers. Jenna was far too weary from the last days to know or care about the startled looks that passed among the mourners. She leaned heavily against Stefan Kalinsky as the service was ended.

Charles stepped forward, his left hand firm beneath Jenna's elbow as he tried to pull her toward him. "Jenna, you have guests who will be awaiting you at the inn before returning to London."

Jenna turned to Charles pleadingly. "Charles, I cannot. Not now. Surely everyone will understand."

"Jenna, it is quite unacceptable that you not return. It is expected, especially of the future wife of Charles Wingate." Charles's smug expression could not be masked behind the facade of his sadness for her. Nor could he hide his keen pleasure at the reaction his remark had caused in the Russian prince.

Jenna shook her head wearily. "I am sorry Charles, it is impossible for me to return now. I simply cannot. I must be away from here for a while."

Stefan Kalinsky's voice was gentle beside her, washing over her soothingly. "Perhaps a drive in the countryside would help. My carriage is nearby."

Jenna turned to Stefan, her appreciation spoken in the soft glow of her eyes. With a brisk nod, Stefan swept her away from Charles, away from the sadness of that

50

gray hillside.

Jenna closed her eyes as she felt the rush of the wind against her cheeks. For a time it seemed to whisk away the sadness that had closed about her. Stefan had chosen to drive the carriage himself and settled his lean, hard frame into the cushions beside her, taking her gloved hand gently in his and tucking it into the curve of his arm, a small gesture, but one that somehow forced the cold emptiness from about her heart. Her smile seemed to lose some of its sadness, and she left her hand where he had placed it, not caring who might disapprove. Jenna was aware that with her grandfather's death her own life had somehow changed forever. The safe, secluded shelter of her childhood had fallen away, exposing the bloom of a new flower, one that would grow tall and beautiful even in the midst of a raging storm that would threaten to shatter its lovely petals. Jenna glanced at the leaden sky overhead as the first droplets fell into the open carriage from the storm that had gathered since early morning. A gust of cool wind rustled the silken folds of her skirt, and she reached a gloved hand to secure the veiled hat that covered her neatly coiffed sable tresses. Stefan hastened the perfectly matched team of black geldings over the uneven surface of the road that was soon reduced to a length of muddied puddles. He shouted above the roar of the storm that gathered as a lightning shaft split the darkened sky and expertly guided the team from the main road down an overgrown side road that cut through a heavy stand of alder trees that whipped about wildly in the churning wind.

Jenna's gown was completely soaked, but she felt only the exhilarating rush of the wind as they plunged through the heavily wooded copse at a dangerous speed that threatened to spill them both from the open carriage.

The rain continued in a furious downpour that soaked them both and made it nearly impossible to see the direction they traveled. Deciding that further travel was impossible, Stefan halted the team of blacks under the canopy of a heavily wooded oak tree. Reaching for Jenna, he drew her from the carriage, and they ran together

51

toward the shelter beneath the limbs of that towering tree, whose foliage protected them from the downpour.

Jenna was breathless as they reached the haven underneath the tree. Her gown clung to her like a second skin, the heavy silk, now cold and clammy, set her teeth to chattering as the wind gusted against them. The black silk bonnet had been pushed back by the wind, and the dark, rich thickness of her hair had fallen in wild disarray about her shoulders and down the length of her back, several pins now lost in their frenzied flight from the storm. Her cheeks were tinged with a soft pink that gave her skin a healthy glow in spite of the circles of sleeplessness from the last few nights. The wide, dark depths of her eyes sparkled brilliantly with new tears that formed—whether from her grieving or some uncontrollable joy of the moments past, she could not be certain.

Stefan's dark golden hair was plastered to his head, the black woolen hat having been lost to the wind. His elegantly cut waistcoat and breeches were a sodden mass and clung revealingly to the well-muscled length of his body. Gazing down at Jenna, his gaze devoured her lithe body silhouetted boldly beneath the clinging black silk of her gown.

Jenna's tears threatened to give way to uncontrollable giggling at the sight they made, as Stefan left their woodland shelter for a brief moment, disappearing beyond the curtain the downpour made about them. In a moment he had returned with a carriage blanket he had retrieved from beneath the seat.

Jenna's eyes glistened brilliantly as she watched him lingeringly, fascinated by the raw, animal strength that seemed to guide each movement; something she had never noticed in Charles or any of the young men who had asked for the pleasure of her company. She smiled appreciatively as Stefan wrapped the warm woolen blanket about her shoulders.

"I was not aware you were so experienced with a team of horses."

Stefan smiled down at her, awed by the innocence he

saw behind the amber gaze that stared back at him. Innocent yes, alluring, most definitely, but completely guileless, in a way that touched his heart, when he had thought none ever could.

"They are fine animals. Dmitri acquired them for me, when we first arrived in England. Certainly finer, more delicate animals than in Russia, when I was a child. But they are not as strong or powerful as the fine horses I learned to ride as a small boy. By the time I was eight it was expected that I could handle the troika as well as any grown man." Stefan watched her confused expression with a sudden warmth he found difficult to understand. He had never before cared to speak of his youth or his homeland. In a matter of a few moments he had spoken of both to the drenched beauty who stood shivering before him.

"What is a troika?" Jenna managed from between chattering teeth.

"A troika is an open sleigh, usually drawn by one horse. But the horse must be very strong, with long, muscular legs," Stefan continued, his words not so guarded, the Russian word spoken easily, with only a trace of French accent.

"In Russia, in the winter, the snows are very heavy, making travel by carriage or coach impossible, except in the cities and towns. When one must travel beyond the city, it must be done on horseback, or in the troika. Horseback is perhaps quicker, but the troika is more comfortable when a lady is also traveling. The winters are also very cold. In the troika, there is always heavy sable fur to keep everyone warm." Stefan gathered the edges of the woolen blanket and pulled it more securely about Jenna's shoulders. He could feel the faint shivering in her slender body. He seemed to lose himself in those velvet amber depths, as Jenna stared back at him, unaware of the effect she had on him.

"I have never seen such snow. I should like very much to ride in a troika, but only if you were there to drive it, for I know no one else who would know how," Jenna ventured, at a loss to understand her boldness with this man who was a stranger to her.

"Then I promise you, little princess, one day you shall ride in the troika, through the first snow of a new winter, for it is said in Russia, that the first snow of winter is magic."

Stefan's lean, strong fingers radiated a vibrant warmth as they brushed against the slender column of Jenna's throat, sending a pulsing heat coursing through her veins. His eyes, before cold and unyielding, now glowed that brilliant piercing blue that was so bright it took her breath away, and she somehow sensed that he was capable of seeing deep within her, and was certain he knew the wild tumult of emotions that collided inside her. Jenna was mesmerized by the sudden vulnerability she saw behind that guarded visage, as if for a moment she had glimpsed the boy he had once been. Gently, Stefan's fingers reached behind her neck, through the silken mass of her hair, and cradled her head, pulling her to him. Jenna's breathing seemed to stop as she waited an eternity for his lips against hers, so that she thought she might die of longing for them.

Stefan stared searchingly into the perfect oval of her face, trying to read her thoughts, longing to feel her warmth melting into his, yet realizing well she might refuse him at that final moment. Her head was tilted back no more than a hand's breadth from his, so that he could see the longing in the amber depths of her eyes, which glowed golden with a fire of their own. Her lips were parted in some momentary confusion and trembled visibly, whether from the cold or from some unspoken fear, he could not know. Stefan was aware only of his need to hold her, to caress her, to feel the softness of her lips beneath his, to build within her a passion he was certain she had not yet experienced, until her need of him was as strong as his for her, a need he had known from that first moment he had seen her. Unable to deny the longing hunger he felt within, Stefan's head lowered, his lips taking hers possessively, searing hers with a heat that

54

seemed to burst forth from the center of his being to engulf them both in a flood of white-hot passion that threatened to melt their lips where they touched. His tongue probed the petal softness of her mouth, drinking in the sweetness there, as if his thirst for her could not be satisfied. Boldly his strong hands traveled the length of her back, pulling her into him, molding her lithe young body to his as his hands wandered below the gentle curving of her back, until his hands closed over the tender softness of her derriere, pulling her longingly to him, feeling the exquisite agony of his growing desire for her.

Jenna felt as if her breath had been taken from her, and yet as if she had no need of it; as if Stefan's breath had become hers. Feebly she resisted at first, her mind filled with thoughts of Stefan and the rumors of his indiscreet affairs, and then, unable to resist the fiery heat of his kiss, Jenna yielded to a passion she had never known. Her skin tingled beneath the heat of his caresses, as if it had only come alive at his touch. Her slender body arched against his, hardly aware of the awakening passion within her, responding without knowing of the need that had lain like a sleeping creature just beneath the surface of her awareness, that was now roused under the assault of his passion, coming alive, at first tentatively and then growing stronger, thrusting Jenna forward toward the apex of fulfillment that lay just beyond her grasp.

Stefan's lips left hers and pressed a feverish path down the length of her throat. Her pulse raced uncontrollably beneath the velvet texture of his lips, her eyes closed as she tumbled beyond control, lost to the spell of his warmth against her, as she had never felt with Charles, a warmth that promised and then teased her, a warmth that threatened to consume her and then seemed to be the very essence of life to her.

Above them, the crowning treetops whipped about wildly as the wind whirled its howling fury, adding its own passion to the two who had sought shelter there. Thunder rolled across the hillside, and a brilliant white shaft of lightning split the churning gray sky, illuminating the satin softness of Jenna's face. In her agony of sadness and newfound awareness, Jenna clung to Stefan, burying her face in his lean, muscular shoulder. A second lightning bolt shattered the roar of the wind, and the thunder followed, almost deafening as it rolled away from them.

Jenna clung to Stefan, feeling as if no danger could find her there, safe within his grasp. She could not see the silent wonder upon his lean, hardened features, nor did she feel the gentle brush of his lips upon her hair as he pulled her protectively closer. Behind them, a loud thundering grew in intensity, at first like thunder and then different. From her safe haven within Stefan's arms, Jenna heard shouting, at first distant, and then much closer.

A lone rider reached the crest of the hill and, seeing the carriage, halted under the towering oaks, then quickly urged his mount in the direction the carriage was pointed. A uniformed man of mountainous stature, he reined the horse to a halt a few feet away. His crimson waistcoat was completely soaked, and his dark brown hair, shaggy about the high collar, lay plastered about his great, bearlike head. A long mustache of that same dark brown color dripped rainwater steadily down onto the beard that covered the entire lower part of his face. His black eyes sparkled keenly as he looked at the man and the girl before him.

"So, here I find you, hiding from the storm, or perhaps an enraged suitor? I knew if I searched long enough and found shelter from this ugly storm, I would find you. Sir Charles is most concerned that Mademoiselle Randolph might have come to some harm. And I do not think he was concerned with the weather, my friend." The giant man guffawed loudly and slapped his great, pawlike hand across the soaked expanse of his thigh. The great, gray beast that he rode sidled uncertainly, laying its ears back nervously at the thunder from the storm, and from the man, whose size seemed to dwarf the animal.

"As you can see, Dmitri, we are quite safe." Stefan pulled the blanket protectively about Jenna's shoulders.

The wind had lessened, and only a few droplets of rain fell tentatively before the clouds were rushed across the sky. He turned back to Jenna, an amused grin creasing his face at the sight of the bedraggled beauty beside him. He would have chosen her over any elegantly gowned lady, for she had shown him an honest passion that few possessed.

"I think we should return before you are taken with a chill," Stefan decided. "Most certainly Sir Charles would hardly forgive me for that. I fear he may not soon forgive me for abducting his future bride."

Jenna nodded, her teeth chattering more violently now that Stefan had moved away from her toward the carriage. "Charles presumes too much If ... f ... f ... fear," she retorted brittlely as Stefan lifted her into the carriage. His amusement at what had been an unsettling experience for her twisted within her like a sharp knife.

Stefan looked down at Jenna speculatively. He had known that Sir Avery disapproved of the dandified Charles Wingate as an acceptable suitor for Jenna, but he had not known that Jenna shared those feelings. He masked the slight frown that briefly crossed his face and then called his orders to Dmitri. Stefan easily swung the carriage about and guided the team back toward the main road to London.

Jenna arrived home before Mr. Flint or Emma Kelly, who were delayed at the inn by the storm, greatly surprising Maggie with her disheveled appearance, though she had tried to arrange the waving mass of her hair into some semblance of order. Stefan Kalinsky curtly bid her farewell, but she could not ignore the warm fire that sparkled in that azure gaze as he formally bent low over her hand and pledged his assistance to her before departing. Dmitri's burly hulk disappeared with him, but only as far as the end of the cobbled drive, where the Russian giant took up his post just inside the gate, but well out of sight of those returning later from the funeral.

Jenna sat quietly in the offices of her grandfather's

lawyers for the reading of his will, her hands folded neatly in her lap, as she listened to their droning voices informing her that as her grandfather's sole living heir, she was to inherit the town house, his interest in a shipping company she'd never heard of, and a section of land she had forgotten about in the state of Virginia in the American colonies, now the United States. The land in Virginia she now remembered had once been intended for her mother, though her death, when Jenna was but an infant, had prevented her ever seeing it. The land had been accepted as payment for an old debt to her grandfather, many years ago, and Jenna remembered well that he had received much teasing over the matter. In the years since, the land had been managed by an overseer who planted the annual crops and then sent her grandfather the income from the sale of those crops, retaining a goodly fee for his own labors. More than that she did not know, and the endless details of it all were, for the moment, beyond her grasp.

Jenna gazed pensively out the paned windows of the office, thinking that if this were not all ended quite soon, she would run screaming into the streets of London beyond and let them all think she was quite mad from her grieving. The lawyer's voice continued in that same monotone, and Jenna gritted her teeth as she struggled to maintain an air of control. Behind her, Charles seemed to sense her disquiet and laid a comforting hand across hers and squeezed gently. Jenna's tawny gaze searched his gray eyes, which conveyed a message of concern yet seemed to withhold more than they spoke. His hand upon hers was cool and possessive, as if his claim to her was understood. It was his bold assumption without her grandfather to intercede that perhaps irritated her more than the monotonous details of the last hours. Unable to concentrate on the documents before her, Jenna's thoughts betrayed her, as they wandered to another day, in the midst of the first storm of the season, when she had felt the vibrant heat of a kiss that seemed to rob her of all will to resist, a kiss that beckoned her from the safe sheltering of her innocent youth into the impassioned world of her young womanhood, a kiss that haunted her sleepless nights and reminded her, too, of another kiss, from a bold stranger whose face she had never seen.

At last the lawyer's voice ceased, and Jenna was startled back to the present by Charles's gentle pressure upon her hand. Mr. Flint, Emma Kelly, and each of the servants had been generously provided for, a revelation that reduced the emotional Emma Kelly to recurrent tears. Mr. Flint remained stoical, merely nodding to indicate that he understood he was now a man of comfortable means.

Jenna sat opposite Charles in the closed coach, for the ride home. The entire afternoon she had deliberately avoided his insistent suggestions that she seriously consider announcing their betrothal at the earliest possible date. Stubbornness alone, in the light of her grandfather's wishes in the matter, allowed Jenna to demur politely, with the excuse that it was far too soon for her to consider matters of such import. Charles had retreated to stony silence in the seat opposite her, after Emma Kelly had deliberately taken the vacant space in the cushions beside Jenna. Jenna had coughed abruptly behind her gloved hand, hiding her amusement at the woman's boldness.

Later, in the privacy of her own bedroom, after pleading a headache in order to gain some temporary freedom from Charles's possessive authority, Jenna cast aside the black silk hat with the filmy black veil and then stepped out of the mourning gown of the same color. She would not wear black again; it mattered not to her what others might think. Her grandfather had always hated the color, preferring instead to see her in the bright-colored gowns he had indulged her with. Thoughtfully, Jenna sat before the mirror at the mahogany dressing table. One by one she pulled the pins from the thick mass of her dark hair, until the waving length cascaded softly about her shoulders. She had worn her sadness of the last days dutifully. Now she must see the future. Clad only in a gossamer-thin chemise that revealed more of her slender body than it concealed,

Jenna reached out a slender hand and lifted the lid to the gold music box her grandfather had given her. The haunting notes of the tune of her childhood filled the air, but strangely enough she was not sad. It was a link to her grandfather and the love they had shared. A single, last tear fell upon her cheek, dropping onto the silk that covered the peak of a full, rounded breast. The warmth of the tear seemed to burn into her, and Jenna tentatively wiped away the dampness. Her youthful body betrayed her, as her thoughts were again drawn to the memory of Stefan's touch, the strength of his embrace, the searing heat of his lips against hers, arousing feelings she had not known existed. Her fingers brushed tentatively across the rose-tipped peak, releasing within her a flood of memories of another touch that had seemed to set her afire. Jenna stared back at her reflection in the mirror. Her lips were slightly parted, and her cheeks were flushed with the emotion of those memories, and she suddenly realized she had never before known the girl who stared back at her with wild, stormy eyes and a wild torrent of hair the color of rich, dark sable; as if the woman she might be had been born in that moment in the midst of a raging storm, when Stefan had kissed her, so that she could never again be the girl Charles Wingate had courted with such persistent longing.

Jenna tossed restlessly in her disturbed slumber. Haunting images of the past weeks lurked within the shadows of sleep, just beyond her ability to grasp them. Charles's relentless gray eyes, guarded and emotionless, were calm as he seemed to beckon her at every turn, and always she saw again her grandfather's stern visage, gently warning her against Charles. And, from the darkness of the fog that surrounded her, lean, strong hands reached out to prevent her falling, muscular arms closing about her in an embrace of warmth and protection. A face shrouded in black silk loomed above hers, and when she reached to remove the silken mask Stefan's boldly handsome face, with the lean, well-tanned features of the hunter and bright blue eyes the color of the sky, smiled back at her.

Jenna tossed about so that all the covers were strewn over the edge of the large four-poster bed. A loud crashing sound reached through the fog of her dreams. She tossed from side to side as she tried to see the images that fled before her awakening consciousness. With a start Jenna sat upright in the large bed, her breathing ragged and uncertain as her pulse raced wildly from the truth of her dreams that had fled for a while longer with the darkness of sleep.

Jenna stared about her bedroom, trying to understand what had awakened her. The chamber was bathed in moonlight one moment and then plunged into complete darkness, as clouds passed before the moon. She heard it again. A faint thumping sound downstairs. Jenna reached for the silk wrapper, pulled it on, and crossed the room. The soft glow of a single coal-oil lantern cast long shadows down the hall. Seizing the lantern, Jenna carefully descended the stairway.

Down the hall the door to Emma's room beside the kitchen was closed. No light showed beneath the door. Jenna was certain the maid had been asleep for hours. Across the hall from the parlor, the door to her grandfather's library stood ajar, an odd glowing light flickering beyond it.

Jenna pushed open the door to the library. Her hand flew to her mouth in stunned disbelief. Inside the library, chaos ruled. Every piece of furniture had been turned over. The upholstery was cut and ripped apart, the wool stuffing hanging in shreds from the slashed fabric. Drawers had been emptied and overturned. Her grandfather's desk had been ransacked, papers pulled from the drawers and scattered across the top. The one drawer that was always locked had been pried open, and a slender-bladed knife was embedded in the rich wood of the desktop where the intruder had vented his anger. The soft glow in the room grew brighter, and a crackling sound jarred

Jenna from her shock, as flames spread across a path of spilled coal-oil from a shattered lamp to the full-length velvet drapes at the windows. In the next moment the flames had climbed the full length of the drapes, raced across the top, and fully engulfed the window area that opened onto the gardens beyond. Smoke filled the library as Jenna backed away, calling out for Emma and Mr. Flint in sudden desperation.

The warning cry died on Jenna's lips, as she was roughly shoved from behind against the stones at the hearth. The breath was knocked from her. She saw only a darkly shrouded figure fleeing the library down the long hallway. When next she drew a deep breath, heavy smoke filled her lungs and she was sent into spasms of coughing as the smoke became thicker, stinging her eyes, the intense heat from the flames surrounding her. Unable to see across the room, Jenna blindly felt her way along the wall from the hearth toward the doorway. Tears streamed down her cheeks as she desperately tried to call a warning to the others in the house. If the warning came she did not hear it, as the smoke and heat threatened to overcome her. In that last instant before complete darkness claimed her, Jenna felt herself being lifted and carried away from the heat—or was she dreaming again?

Jenna's coughing came in racking waves, and each time her chest ached when she responded to the rough command to breathe. She felt the coolness of cobbled stones beneath her, and in the next instant, cool, refreshing air. Again that guttural command to breathe deeply. Jenna fought against the hand that firmly held her chin. When she failed to breathe when the voice commanded, Jenna felt herself hauled roughly to her feet and shaken, as if she were no more than a cloth doll. She was shaken until she thought her neck would snap, and when the shaking stopped, she breathed deeply for the first time. Her senses began to clear, and when she opened her eyes she stared back into Emma's worried face, her frilly lace nightcap askew on her graying head. Clad in only her nightgown, the old maid had fled the burning house with little thought of modesty.

"Eh, little princess. You gave us quite a scare. But Dmitri would never allow any harm to come to you. You must stand. It will help you to breathe. The smoke has dulled the senses, but it will pass."

Jenna stared in wide-eyed wonder at the shaggy-headed, bearded Russian who cradled her in his massive embrace as if she were no more than a child. Feebly Jenna grabbed for Emma's hand.

"Maggie and Mr. Flint?" she whispered from between parched lips.

Emma pressed a cool cloth against Jenna's lips. "Maggie has gone to visit her sister this evening, and Mr. Flint was called away." Jenna missed the look that passed between the large man who held her and the old woman. Vainly Jenna tried to stand, her knees giving way beneath her.

"You must go easy, little princess. In a little while you will be all right." Dmitri said gently.

"Emma, the library; all of grandfather's papers, all his work these last months," Jenna croaked with despair, as tears stung at her eyes and streaked the smudges upon her cheeks.

"Dear child, there is nothing to save. I fear all is lost. Even now those dear men are trying their best to save the rest of the house."

Jenna looked in horror past the maid, at a long line of men that had formed across the drive, through the gardens. Each man passed bucketful after bucketful of water from the wagon that stood before the house, filled in back with barrels of water. Inside the front doors of the house, she could see the flames that leaped from the doorway of the library and threatened the rest of the house. Jenna struggled to her feet, slipping from the grasp of the huge Russian. In an instant she gained the front steps and shot through the doorway, past the flames to the stairway that led to the bedrooms on the second floor. Behind her, Jenna was only faintly aware of Dmitri's laboring as he tried to catch up with her.

Inside her own bedroom, Jenna stood in momentary confusion. She whirled about, her gaze sweeping the room, her jumbled senses unable to determine what she should try to take with her.

Dmitri lumbered up the hallway and burst through the doorway, a dark scowl crossing his bearlike face. "Little one, if we are to escape the fire, we must do so now. The men will do their best, but for now I cannot allow you to remain where there is danger. I have been given my orders, and I will see them carried out."

Jenna rubbed her hand across her forehead, momentarily confused by what he had said. What orders? Whose orders to keep her safe? In the next moment, all was forgotten as loud shouting could be heard from the main floor. A warning cry went out for all to leave the house. In the next instant, Jenna seized the miniature portrait of her mother and the gold music box. Anything else of possible value was quickly forgotten as she was grabbed by the arm and quickly propelled through the doorway toward the stairway. The fire had already spread up the stairway, making it impossible for them to leave by the main door. Jenna quickly turned back, pulling Dmitri's towering form behind her.

"What of the servants' quarters? Is there another way out beyond the bedrooms?" A worried frown creased Dmitri's brow, which was all that was visible, except the bright gleam of his black eyes, from beneath all the hair and beard.

Jenna shook her head. "The servants' chambers are all below. I fear there is no other way out; except perhaps for one way." A golden glow sparked in the depths of her large amber eyes, as Jenna led the way back to her room. In quick, easy strides, she reached the tall glass windows and drew back the lacy curtains. In an instant the windows were thrown wide open, and Jenna leaned out. Dmitri joined her, and judged the distance to the ground. A wide smile broke the line of hair and beard. He clapped his huge, pawlike hands together in good humor.

"I think this will be like escaping the prison, except

there are no bars across the windows, and the drop to the ground is not as far. We will need a rope."

Jenna disappeared into the bedroom, and quickly stripped the bed linens from the large bed. In a matter of moments she had tied the ends together tightly to form a long, sturdy rope. Dmitri beamed with pleasure at her sense of adventure.

"I was wrong. You, little princess, are one worthy of any challenge." He seized the bound linens and quickly secured one end about the center post between the two sets of windows. He carefully tested his heavier weight against the knot to make certain it held fast. He stepped back and nodded approvingly.

"You shall go first, my princess. It will hold your slight weight, and I do not care to risk you further."

"No, you shall go first. If it holds your weight, we can be certain it will hold mine."

Dmitri seized Jenna firmly about the wrist and propelled her toward the open window. Quickly lifting her, as if she weighed no more than a feather, he gently set her upon the sill and wrapped the loop of the tied linens about her waist, forming a sling, and, amidst her heated protests, swung her clear of the window and slowly lowered her, taking care not to swing her against the sides of the stone walls.

Jenna clung to the top of the sling with silent desperation. She would much rather have let herself down as she had once done, a very long time ago, when she had sought to escape Emma Kelly's wrath for some broken rule that she had long forgotten. That quick, uncertain drop to the ground below her window had not been forgotten, nor the excitement of freedom only a small distance away. She could still see Emma's face, a mixture of hysterical amusement and barely controlled fury, when she had dropped to the ground at the maid's feet.

She was only a small distance above the ground and the final length of the sling had been let out. Above her, Jenna could see Dmitri's wild waving gestures. She had no idea what he might be suggesting, but she knew well she might easily drop to the ground below. Wiggling out of the sling, with the music box and her mother's portrait secured inside her belted robe, Jenna lowered herself the last remaining distance, until she dangled in midair, her arms outstretched above her. She closed her eyes, inhaling deeply as she let go of the linen.

The jarring landing Jenna expected never came. Instead, she dropped the last small distance into the waiting arms of Prince Stefan Kalinsky.

Jenna's eyes flew open wide in stunned surprise as that piercing blue gaze met hers evenly, the curving of those handsome lips flashing a smile that was exactly as she remembered it from her dreams. Stefan's arms closed about her warmly, his strength bearing her slight weight easily as he held her against him. The full length of her slender body, clad in the silken gown and wrapper, slid easily down the length of his, exposing all her slender curves against the firm, hard line of his body. Jenna's breath caught in her throat as she stared into the vast ocean of that gaze that seemed to wash over her in wild, crashing waves, to leave her breathless.

"I had vowed that we should meet again, and soon. I had not thought it would be quite this soon, mademoiselle." Stefan's voice was rich and vibrant and shot through her like a molten current.

"The fire . . ." Her voice failed her, as she tried vainly to explain, her words coming only in a ragged whisper from her parched throat.

Stefan laid a gentle finger against her lips. "Do not try to speak. Your voice shall return, but for now, I will speak." Behind them there was a loud crashing sound, and Jenna turned about in Stefan's arms. Beneath the window she had just left, Dmitri lay crumpled upon the ground, the linen sling having torn and given way as he descended. For a full, long moment the giant Russian did not move, and then very slowly he moved an arm and then a leg.

"Well, my friend. I see you are taken with leaving through open windows. I would suggest next time that you make certain of the strength of the rope," Stefan chided good-humoredly as he looked upon his bruised friend.

"I will remember your kind words, my prince. And when next time I find myself escaping through the window, I shall let you go first to test the rope. Just reward, I think, for your treatment of me." Dmitri grimaced as he tried to stand, and gently probed his bruised backside.

"Learn your lessons well, when it comes to guarding fair ladies." Stefan turned about and carried Jenna to his waiting carriage. He waited patiently, as Dmitri lumbered across the cobbled driveway and painfully pulled himself atop the carriage. Before Jenna could protest, Stefan gently seized her hand.

"What are you doing? Put me down immediately!" Jenna exclaimed indignantly, struggling to free herself from Stefan's grasp as he set her in the carriage.

"Jenna, look about you. The house is in ruins. It is impossible for you to remain the night, nor would I allow you to wander the streets of London, especially dressed as you are. Although, I warrant, you would quickly find a bed to warm yourself for what remains of the night, I hardly think you would care for the company." A playful smile pulled at the corners of Stefan's mouth as Jenna sat back in the carriage uncertainly, her wide gaze looking past him to the house beyond, where trailing wisps of smoke rose from the structure.

Stefan's smile softened at the distressed look that crossed her lovely face. "For now, you are to be my guest. It can be no other way. My town house is large, with only myself and a few servants, and, of course, my men, although you will not be bothered by them, as they are often kept afar attending certain errands. It is settled, then." Stefan's smile guarded the doubts that nagged at him. Dmitri had told him of the man he had seen in the library, only moments before the house was engulfed in flames. Whoever had been in the house attempted to remove permanently any evidence of his visit. Stefan deliberately chose not to mention any of this to Jenna now. She had suffered enough over the last weeks, without the added burden of knowing that in all probability her grandfather had been murdered, and that the murderer, failing to find what he sought the night Sir Avery died, had returned this night to finish the matter. Stefan could only guess what the murderer had hoped to find—obviously something of such importance that it was worth the risks he had taken. A cold uneasiness spread through Stefan, as he realized that the treachery that had taken Sir Avery's life might now reach out to Jenna.

In the next instant Emma Kelly pulled her ample frame into the carriage, deliberately placing herself between Stefan and Jenna. A practical woman, Emma could easily see the wisdom of the offer of Prince Kalinsky's hospitality.

"We shall accept your kind offer, your highness. Dmitri, be off with you," she instructed firmly, as the large Russian crawled into the carriage seat and seized the reins firmly. "On the morrow we shall return to see what is left of this night."

Jenna sank back into the cushions, her numbed senses only now beginning to realize the full weight of her loss, as the carriage sped away with alarming swiftness from the smoldering house into the darkness of the last hours of night. The chilling night air cut through her thin garments, shocking her into reality. Her slender hand closed over the portrait and gold music box, the only possessions she had saved from the fire.

Chapter Four

Jenna restlessly paced the length and breadth of the elaborately furnished chamber, her bare feet padding softly across the lustrous wood floor, and then muffled silently as she crossed the richly woven woolen rug that occupied the center of the large room. For two days she had remained virtually confined to this chamber, for lack of clothing, after the fire had gutted her grandfather's house. Emma Kelly had borrowed a stiffly starched dress from one of the maids in Stefan Kalinsky's household, and with Mr. Flint had returned to the house the day following the fire. The news of the devastation she brought her young mistress hardly raised Jenna's spirits. All the furnishings, all clothing, everything was lost. They had escaped with only the garments they wore, the portrait of her mother, and the gold music box Sir Avery had given her before his death.

Prince Stefan Kalinsky had most generously offered them his home, but had been strangely absent since the morning following the fire. Dmitri had been seen only once, quickly taking his leave to attend to some matter for Stefan. The remainder of the servants in the large, elegant house seemed to function quite well in their master's absence. Meals were promptly brought to Jenna, and she was afforded every courtesy, except that of a wardrobe, though she hardly expected Stefan Kalinsky to be greatly concerned with such matters.

Emma had left early that morning for the lawyer's with a carefully outlined letter from Jenna, explaining her situation and requesting sufficient funds from her grandfather's estate to remedy the problem. That had been nearly three hours earlier, and Jenna's patience with her dilemma had grown thin with her prolonged wait. She heartily cursed herself for not having paid closer attention to the details of her grandfather's will. She knew that the maintenance of the house and staff were provided for, but all that had now changed.

Jenna stopped before the large paned window that looked out over Grosvenor Square and searched for some sign of Emma, then turned wearily back to her pacing. Reaching the chamber door, she decided to explore the house beyond.

Silence greeted her, as she stood in the carpeted hallway. Downstairs, she heard the faint sound of voices, as the servants chatted idly about some matter and then retreated to another room to attend to their chores. Jenna turned her footsteps to the opposite end of the hallway where several doors stood closed. She knew Emma had been given a smaller chamber at the far end of the hallway. She could only guess that the other doors led to additional bedrooms. The hallway was wide and spacious. Several finely carved lamp tables were set along the long expanse, with coal-oil lamps set to give light at night. At the far end another table stood, gleaming in the sunlight that poured in from an open doorway across the hall. It was set with an elegant crystal vase filled to overflowing with fresh cut flowers, and Jenna could only sadly wonder where the flowers had come from, when her gardens at home had long since yielded the last blooms of the season.

Jenna gently traced the tightly clustered petals of the fall blooms of bright yellow, orange, and amber. Her gaze wandered to the door opposite, which stood ajar. Peering inside, she found the room to be nearly twice the size of her own. The room was richly masculine, with a heavy mahogany bed with crimson velvet coverlet, hung all around with heavy velvet hangings of that same crimson color. A large hearth filled the wall opposite the bed, set with elaborately made andirons formed with the heads of great, fierce-looking wolves on the top of each. The hearth was set in the most exquisite white stone Jenna had ever seen, all flat and smooth as glass. The velvet drapes, also crimson, had been drawn back at either side of the bed to reveal double-glass doors of paned windows, which opened out onto a balcony. A massive armoire stood at the far wall, cut from the finest rosewood, the rich wood gleaming spotlessly, and beside it sat a dressing tale with a wash basin. A brass tub stood in the far corner, discreetly hidden behind a magnificent silk screen with a vivid design of hunting birds stretched in wild flight across the fabric. To her right was an adjoining sitting room, separated by double doors folded back to either side, opening the two rooms to make one large room. At the far end of the sitting room was a large mahogany desk of French design, and a high-backed overstuffed chair. Jenna carefully walked around the large desk. An elegant desk-set adorned the center of the desk, with inkwell, quill, richly embossed paper, and a seal, whose great weight must certainly be solid gold. Jenna carefully studied the embossed parchment. The scrollwork surrounded an elaborately curved letter, and she immediately recognized the first letter of Stefan's name. Jenna looked up and gazed about the handsome room that was so elegant and masculine. The room seemed to emanate the carefully restrained strength and power of the man she hardly knew, but longed to learn more about. She carefully let herself out of the chamber, closing the door softly behind her. Retracing her steps, Jenna stopped before the door opposite her own chamber. She tried the handle and the door opened freely.

The room was smaller than her own, but elegantly furnished, with hangings of satin about the bed. A vast assortment of brushes and combs lay atop the dressing table, with several bottles of fine perfumes, a decidedly feminine touch. Biting her lower lip uncertainly, Jenna swallowed her fears and approached the rosewood armoire. She stepped back in complete amazement, for

71

inside the cabinet were several elegant gowns of varied colors in the latest French fashion. Neatly arranged at the bottom of the cabinet were matching slippers, and on a shelf at the top, an assortment of bonnets to match. Jenna quickly closed the doors of the armoire and fled the room, seeking the privacy of her own chamber, her thoughts in turmoil at her discovery. She had been certain Stefan lived alone.

Jenna's pacing continued until she heard the sounds of a carriage in the driveway below. She was unable to see who had arrived, but ran for the door, certain that Emma had returned with some news from the lawyer's. She stopped in midflight as one of the young servant girls quickly curtsied before her, and then ushered in two other young girls, quickly followed by Madame Lessard.

Jenna stood in stunned surprise as the seamstress gave orders to her assistants in a rapid flow of French. Lengths of brilliant, rich fabrics were carried into the room by a young man, who quickly disappeared. Madame Lessard quickly seized a bright blue satin and set about her work. An assortment of baskets yielded a vast array of trims and elegant decorations. Filmy, diaphanous silk was measured and cut into clingy chemises. Satin ribbon was cut into varying lengths and set about the necklines and sleeves of a dozen gowns, until Jenna could no longer remember them all. Heavier velvets were cut into gowns for colder weather and decorated with lace and satin. Jenna persuaded Madame Lessard to leave the waistline longer in several of the gowns, with the skirts sweeping the tops of her slippered feet. The remainder of the gowns were cut in the current high-waisted fashion. A rich, dark brown velvet was cut into a warm, full-length overcoat, also with a high waist, and set across the front with gold satin braided frogs for closures. Jenna was turned first in one direction and then the other for measurements, and then Madame Lessard clapped her hands together briskly and sent her assistants to work, first marking, then cutting, and then stitching. Jenna could only assume that Emma had indeed been most successful with the lawyers, and she could hardly await the woman's return to give her heartfelt gratitude in the matter.

It was late afternoon when Madame Lessard curtly ordered her assistants from the house. Three gowns lay across the bed in Jenna's chamber, with matching satin slippers. Freshly bathed, with her lustrous dark hair piled high on top of her head, Jenna slipped on a silken chemise of a soft peach color. She had not realized the lateness of the hour, as her stomach suddenly reminded her she had not eaten since early morning. Slipping on the silken wrapper she had worn the last two days, Jenna whirled about as Emma knocked softly on the door and entered the chamber.

"Dearest Emma, you are remarkable. Now I shall not be forced to dine in my room, and tomorrow we shall see about finding a house, until some arrangement can be made for repairing the damage from the fire. However did you persuade Madame Lessard to come on such short notice? You know very well she insists on scheduling appointments weeks in advance. Emma, why are you looking at me that way?" Jenna turned back to the short, round-faced woman, who still stood in the open doorway, her mouth drawn into a slight frown, as she stared at the gowns on the bed.

"I came to tell you that I failed to persuade the lawyers to give you funds from your grandfather's estate. But this . . ." Emma gestured incredulously toward the elegant gowns that draped the bed.

"Emma, if you were not able to persuade them to give me the money, then who provided the money for the gowns? And there are more. Madame Lessard has promised three more for tomorrow and the remainder at the end of the week. If not you, then who ordered the gowns?" Jenna stood in the center of the room, complete bewilderment wrinkling her lovely creamy brow.

"If you will forgive my intrusion, I requested Madame Lessard's presence this afternoon. She was most willing to fill my request for the gowns. She is a very old and dear friend; she was merely returning a favor to me." Stefan

73

stood in the doorway, breathtakingly handsome in fawn-colored breeches, a white linen shirt that flowed with spotless ruffles across his lean, tanned hands, and an elegantly cut, fawn-colored waistcoat, which snugly fit his slim torso, cut away to reveal the flat expanse of his firm, hard belly. Black jockey boots fit his legs snugly, turned back at the cuff revealing leather of the same fawn color. The color of the waistcoat contrasted with the golden streaks in his hair, which waved gently about his head, making him appear somehow leaner, and more handsome, if that was possible.

Jenna had almost forgotten the circumstances of her presence in his house, in her excitement over the improvement of her wardrobe. Nor was she aware at that moment that she stood clad only in the thin chemise and silken wrapper, which outlined her slender body to perfection, leaving no curve unseen. With the rich mass of her hair piled loosely on top of her head and the soft alluring scent fresh from her bath, Jenna was hardly aware of her devastating effect on Stefan's badly strained composure. For a full, long moment she stood lost in the vast blue of his gaze, feeling herself drawn into those depths with their silent message, and then the moment was gone as Emma cleared her throat, aware that Jenna and Stefan were oblivious of her presence.

"We are most grateful, your highness. If you will allow Jenna to dress for dinner, she will be down presently." Not allowing Stefan time to answer, Emma politely but firmly moved to close the door.

Stefan blocked the door with a quickly extended hand that halted Emma's course.

"I shall be dining out this evening. In the morning we shall have time for the discussion I spoke of." Stefan's eyes seemed to devour Jenna, as he hesitated a long moment, and then bowed stiffly from the waist and was gone without further explanation.

Jenna stood in dismayed silence at his announcement of his plans for the evening. She had mistakenly assumed, when he returned, that they might be dining together, for the first time since he had brought her to his house. She was at a complete loss to understand Stefan's sudden cool attitude toward her, or his generosity with the gowns. In sudden exasperation over the frustrations of the last two days, Jenna seized the gold-embossed hairbrush from the dressing table and hurtled it against the far wall of the chamber. How dare he treat her in this way? He had taken it upon himself to have her house watched, of that she was certain. And then, at the moment of the fire, his man had appeared, with no explanation, to take her to safety. What did she know of Stefan Kalinsky? That he was part of the Russian royal family was true, and that he had been exiled from France by Napoleon was also true. About his rumored liaison with several well-known and titled ladies of society she could only speculate, although the armoire full of elegantly designed gowns that she had found that afternoon certainly suggested that he shared more than a casual relationship with at least one of the ladies in question. Perhaps Madame de Stahl? Or some other exiled lady of wealth and title? Most certainly, Madame de Stahl was one of the most highly sought ladies of society, even if she was quite well married.

Emma retreated to her own chamber and later delivered a dinner tray to Jenna's room. When she returned some time later, the meal was untouched. Jenna sat before the dressing table lost in her thoughts, as the maid turned and made to leave the chamber.

"Emma, in the morning, we shall both visit the lawyers, and see what may be done about this matter of finances. They certainly cannot expect us to live in the street, nor can we remain here. Inform Mr. Flint to bring the carriage around early. I intend to spend the entire day, if necessary, to get the answer I want."

Emma nodded, her round mouth pressed into a firm line. She knew well the mood that plagued her young mistress. The lawyers might yet have cause to regret their decision in the matter. Jenna was possessed of a fiery spirit and a stubborn nature and, if pressed, would have her way in the matter, of that Emma was certain.

Propped up on several pillows, Jenna dozed fitfully, suddenly coming awake at the sound of tapping on the glass of the window across her room. The wind had come up sharply through the night, filling the sky beyond with heavy, dark clouds that blocked the light of the moon she had seen earlier and now rattled the tip of a large branch against the panes. Jenna fumbled in the dark for the lamp beside her bed, then realized she had left it on the dressing table across the room. The wind beyond the paned window sent the tree branch chattering loudly, and the skyline of London was momentarily lit by a sudden shaft of lightning that split the night sky. Thunder rolled far away, as the wind came up much stronger now, invading the chamber through the narrow spaces between the framed glass. Jenna shivered from the growing chill in the chamber that sent goose bumps across her bare arms and beneath the thin chemise. She rose and crossed the chamber quickly, her bare feet cold against the floor. The first droplets of rain fell against the panes as she reached high to pull the heavy velvet drapes across the windows to block the draft. She hesitated as a second shaft of lightning splintered the dark sky, much closer this time, quickly followed by rumbling thunder that had hardly ended when another bolt of lightning flashed brilliant white, illuminating the room. A movement in the driveway below caught her attention, and she leaned forward, pressing her nose against the cold pane as she peered below. A coach had stopped in front of the house and now pulled around the corner, in the direction of the carriage-house.

Jenna had no time to contemplate who might be arriving at that late hour. In the next moment, a shaft of lightning seemed to burst into the room, illuminating everything in a ghostly pallor. The wind, much stronger now, gusted full force against the thin panes of glass, rattling the windows in their casements. Instinctively, Jenna reached to make certain the latch was secure, as the wind sent rivulets of rain pounding against the panes, like waves of water suddenly released in the fury of the storm.

Jenna was suddenly thrown back, as another gust of wind rattled the unlatched windows, sending them back hard on their hinges. They flapped wildly against the wood frames, releasing a streaming torrent of rain into the chamber. In a matter of moments, Jenna was soaked to the skin, as she struggled to close the windows against the force of the wind.

The loud roaring of the wind filled the room, sending the heavy drapes billowing wildly to either side of the windows. Jenna pushed with all her strength against the rush of the wind, straining to close the windows enough to set the latch in place. Another shaft of lightning flashed brightly across the sky, lighting the chamber like a midday sun. A loud crack sounded beyond the window, and then a crashing sound, as the large branch tossed wildly in the wind and then yielded to that greater force. It was sent hard against the panes of the window, shattering the glass. In that final moment, Jenna screamed as she felt a strong arm encircling her waist, pulling her backwards, out of harm's way, as the glass showered into the chamber where she had stood a moment before.

Stefan stood before Jenna, his towering height shielding her from the rain that gusted through the shattered portal. His golden hair was wet and hung about his head in dark, damp waves. His piercing blue gaze seemed to engulf her in a flood of uncertainty that sent spasms of shivering through her slender body.

The thin silk of the chemise left nothing to the imagination as it clung to Jenna's sleek body, revealing more than it concealed of every curve and slender limb. Her long, rich, dark hair was wet from the rain and cascaded wildly down the length of her back, and the wild, stormy light that glowed in the amber depths of her eyes made her seem like some wild, untamable creature of the night. The pale, luminous glow of her skin seemed almost unnatural as lightning again flooded the chamber, and Stefan's pulse raced wildly at the sight of the exquisite young beauty who stood before him. The soft color of the chemise blended with the creamy color of her skin, so that it seemed she wore nothing at all. The full, well-rounded curves of her breasts rose and fell rapidly from the strain of her effort to close the windows, the firm peaks taut with the cold of the night, thrusting invitingly against the sheer, filmy fabric, seeming to beckon his touch.

Jenna stood before Stefan shivering, her nerves strained, yet unaware of the storm that raged beyond the windows, aware only of the mounting storm within, as she felt herself lost within the vast blue ocean of Stefan's gaze.

Slowly, Stefan reached out, his fingers brushing gently against the soft curving of her lips, taking a single droplet of rain on the tip of his fingers, then lightly tracing a path along her slender jawline, brushing aside a stray tendril of her hair. All thoughts abandoned him save one, the ecstasy of the satin texture of her skin beneath his hand. Slowly his hands lowered and followed the prominence of her collarbone, until his fingers closed around her shoulders, drawing her to him, until her slender body seemed to melt into his. His lips sought hers with a sudden intensity that seemed to match that of the storm, burning, searing, moving with silent desperation over her, as he felt her awakening response.

Beyond any thought for her actions, Jenna's arms reached up to entwine about Stefan's neck, drawing him to her with an urgency that matched his. He crushed her to him mercilessly, and Jenna reveled in the raw, vital strength she felt within him. She was molded to him, bruisingly, her firm, full breasts crushed against the cold buttons of his waistcoat, her painful outcry muffled beneath his lips, until it was only a soft moan of her aching need of him. Instinctively, Jenna leaned into Stefan, the gentle curving of her hips meeting his. She was powerless to pull away from him, as she felt his hard body full against her, all his desire for her boldly displayed in the firm pressure against her hip. Jenna seemed to have no will of her own as she responded to his kiss. Her lips parted gently, allowing him access to the sweet, softness there, and she reveled in the taste of him, a heady mixture of wind and rain that seemed to fill her senses, as if he had invaded her soul. She felt herself being lifted gently in his strong arms, and she made no move to resist as he carried her from the rain-soaked chamber, down the hallway to his own rooms. Within his embrace there was no sense of time, only his warmth surrounding and protecting her.

Stefan bore Jenna to his bed and gently laid her in the soft covers, which had been drawn back. His gaze seemed to devour her exquisite beauty, the magnificent length of slender legs that were outlined beneath the thin gown, the wild tumble of dark, tawny hair that swirled about her in wild abandon. He gazed into the deep, dark depths of her amber eyes as he leaned over her, trying to know of any uncertainty, any fears that lay beyond that wide gaze. He saw only golden, burning lights that seemed to reflect his passion, but was, in truth, her own awakening desire, beckoning him onward. Mirrors of the soul, he thought, where he could wander forever and never choose to leave. Tenderly he reached to caress the delicate oval of her perfect face, and she gently kissed his fingertips, her lips burning where they touched, as if he had been forever branded by her kiss.

Stefan looked beyond the passion of the moment that he felt for her, and he knew his soul had been bound to hers from their first kiss. He searched beyond the veil of innocence in her gaze, knowing well the treasure he held within his grasp. He kissed her tenderly, his entire being filled with the sight, the scent, the feel of her beneath his hand. Experience cautioned him against taking her quickly, for he knew all her perceptions, all her responses would be guided by the measure of their first time together. His lips pressed a molten path along the curve of her shoulder, gently pushing aside the sheer gown until the swell of a full breast lay exposed before him. His lips returned to hers, and then he rose from the bed, quickly shedding waistcoat and boots, crossing the room to light the fire that had been laid. In those few moments he had given her the opportunity to retreat, and if she had fled his bed he would not have stopped her, but as he turned back toward her, the soft glow of the first tentative flames at the hearth golden across her face, he saw only a beguiling innocence that beckoned him to her side.

Jenna stared in rapt wonder at the magnificent man who stood before her, the firelight playing across the even planes of his handsome face. His golden hair dried before the spreading warmth in the room, and the blue flames that licked at the logs were like the flames that burned in his eyes as his gaze wandered down her full length. All reason cried out that she should flee him, that she forget everything that had passed between them while she still could, but deep within her cried the voice of her awakening passion that had come alive only at his touch and desperately sought a complete fulfillment she had never known. Stefan joined her, the white linen of his shirt in stark contrast to his bronzed hands. Jenna sat up in the middle of the bed, the dark, rich veil of her hair concealing her beauty. Stefan reached out, and gently lifted her face so that he could see her fully. The wide, amber depths of her eyes, darkly fringed with long, thick lashes, spoke of all her innocence, and of her longing for him. Stefan leaned forward, his lips tenderly closing over hers, breathing life into her, giving her his passion, taking away all fear.

Jenna yielded to the warmth that spread through her as she responded to Stefan's kiss with a fire that left them both breathless. His hands gently caressed her shoulders, her back, and in one effortless movement Stefan separated the sheer chemise, drawing it away from her slender body until she lay unadorned before him. A gasp escaped his lips as he drank in the full length of her satin beauty; long, slender legs, well-curved hips, and the small expanse of her waist that rose to the full, rounded contours of her breasts, partially hidden behind the mass of her hair. Her eyes were closed to him, preventing him from knowing her true feeling. She trembled beneath his hand, and Stefan drew her fully against him, giving her his warmth in the cold night air that had only just begun to yield to the flames at the hearth.

Jenna's slender hand reached tentatively to touch the golden skin that lay beneath the open collar of the shirt. Stefan gathered her hand in his and kissed it. His lips sought hers, his passion growing in intensity as he felt her slender body beneath his. Jenna responded openly, exploring the depths of newfound sensations that seemed to come alive from every point of her being. She had no fear of Stefan or of the unknown journey he was about to take her on. She relaxed beneath his touch, reveling in the power he had over her body, but equally amazed that he seemed to anticipate her reactions. She would hardly have believed his wonder of the innocent beauty he held within his embrace. Stefan pulled away from her for a moment, unbuttoning his shirt, looking up in surprise as Jenna rose and knelt before him, brushing his hands aside as she unbuttoned the last buttons and then slowly drew the shirt away, revealing the lean, muscular expanse of his chest, smooth and bronze, like some great handsome creature cast in precious metal. Her hands fanned across that hard expanse, marveling in the feel of him beneath her fingers, experiencing sensations before unknown to her. She stopped and gazed in astonishment at the freshly healed scar on his right shoulder, and then her startled gaze met his, the shadows of the chamber falling across his face, so that she could see only the piercing blue of his eyes.

"You!" Jenna breathed with dawning clarity. "You are the one who stopped my carriage when I returned to London."

The moment Stefan had dreaded was upon him. Gently he tried to avoid the rush of uncertainty he saw in the depths of her eyes.

"My little princess, from the moment I first saw you, our paths have led us to this moment." Stefan pressed Jenna back into the soft bed covers. He traced fevered kisses along the curve of her neck, the creamy softness of her cheek, until his lips claimed hers in a kiss that engulfed them both in a mounting fury of passion. Vainly Jenna struggled against the pressure of his lean, hard body pressing intimately against hers, but all her questions of the moment before, all her doubts, were cast aside as she surrendered to a greater need. Her lips parted in welcoming pleasure to his tongue pressing gently, tasting of her sweetness. Stefan's hand reached to caress the fullness of her breast, his fingers teasing the soft peak to a taut hardness. She shuddered with intense pleasure at the new awareness he created within her.

Jenna arched against his touch of her, drawing back suddenly at the unexpected warmth of his body full against her own, the naked heat of him pressing against her, with but one purpose, their ultimate pleasure of each other. Stefan seemed to sense her trembling spirit as his lips sought that peak, his tongue tracing a molten path where no man had touched. A white-hot fire seared through Jenna as she relaxed beneath Stefan's touch, his hands like soft butterfly wings against her skin, teasing, tantalizing, until he felt her response, as she raked long fingers through the golden mass of his hair, binding him to her where his lips claimed her flesh.

Stefan rose above her, his knee gently riding between hers. His hands boldly caressed and stroked, taking away all uncertainty, all fear as they roamed lower over her young body, impassioned by the silken softness of her skin, drawn smooth over gleaming thighs. His lips reclaimed hers as his hand wandered over the flatness of her stomach and lower still, until he felt of her warmth.

Jenna stared in wide-eyed wonder at the sensations that collided within her, as Stefan took her to the brink of complete fulfillment and then held her back. He wanted to prepare her for that final moment, so that she would have no fear of the pain, so that her pleasure might equal his. Slowly he moved over her, his lips tender against hers, his fingers now tracing along the delicate oval of her face. That piercing blue gaze ignited to a molten flame that glowed brilliantly in the darkness, lighting her soul, until Jenna felt as if she might cry out for him to take her that final part of their journey. As Stefan had taught her by his own actions, her hands wandered over the rounded muscles of his shoulders and down the length of his back. She was awed by the strength she felt there. Her wide amber eyes searched through the dimly lit chamber for some sign of his pleasure of her. Her answer came in the fierce heat of his lips against hers, which left her breathless, his voice oddly muffled in the thick tangle of her rich, dark tresses that swirled about them like a mantle. Jenna felt that molten heat pressed firmly against her hip, and instinctively reached down to touch him as he had touched her.

Stefan's breathing was ragged in his throat as her hand closed over him, her boldness born of innocent passion that he had built within her. Unable to deny that final moment, Stefan guided her, his lean, strong fingers closing over hers as he pressed gently within her. Stefan lingered for a moment longer, desperately wishing he might replace her pain with a passion to equal what he felt for her. He moved slowly within her, feeling the exquisite warmth of her about him as he pressed deeper. Jenna's eyes opened in sudden wonder at the feeling he was arousing within her. She felt pain, intense pain, for a moment, and then it was gone, leaving behind an ache she did not yet fully understand. She had traveled this far; she would not be frightened away. Slowly she moved with him, taking him more fully with each movement. She was keenly aware of the passion that grew within Stefan as he carried her with him, replacing her pain with a flood of warmth that sparked a flame somewhere deep inside and suddenly burst forth to consume them both.

Stefan felt the heat that coursed through Jenna as she moved with him, fearlessly, seeking her own pleasure. He felt the longing within her and knew her pleasure was near. He thrust deeply into her, so that she cried out at that final moment, as pain mixed with passion, and the release she had blindly sought washed over her in waves that carried her with him. She stared up at him in sudden confusion and wonder at the sensations that welled within her. Stefan continued to thrust deep within her, their pleasure met as one. Fiercely he bound her to him, knowing that she, unlike any other, was part of his soul forever.

Stefan gently caressed the silken softness of her cheek, turning her face so that she was forced to meet his gaze.

"I did not wish to hurt you," he murmured, his breath a soft whisper against her forehead as his lips kissed her tenderly.

Jenna reached up, her hand meeting his, their fingers entwining. "There was only a little pain at first, but then . . ." Jenna stopped as Stefan's lips silenced her. He drew back to gaze down at the slender beauty who lay in his arms.

"There are many truths you must know, my princess, but first you must know that you are mine forever. And I will do whatever is necessary to protect what is mine. It is not a threat, but a promise. No man can ever have you as I have you."

Jenna's amber gaze clouded uncertainly. "Who are you? What had you thought to find in my coach that day I returned to London?" She cringed as she gazed into the fierce blue of his eyes, fearing she had perhaps pressed too far.

"I know you have many questions. But you must not seek the answers now. It could be most dangerous. Know only that your grandfather and I sought the same cause." Stefan rose from the bed and bent to place another log upon the hearth that now glowed brightly, chasing away the gloom of the storm that raged beyond the house.

Instinctively, Jenna sensed that he would tell her no more. She marveled at the golden glow of his body, outlined by the firelight as he knelt before the fire. She forced back the demons of doubt, blushing brightly as he rose and walked back to her. His gaze met hers, an amused smile playing across his handsome lips, as he recognized the direction of her concentration. Stefan seized her hand and drew her up against him, the heat of his body melting into hers as his gaze locked with hers. His caresses boldly wandered the length of her body, and Jenna responded with an abandon that surprised them both, as she matched his stroking touch for touch, learning quickly the areas that brought the most excitement in him. Of a sudden, Stefan seized both her wrists in his hands and held her from him, his gaze searching hers, a sly smile creasing his face.

"What is this? Such boldness in one so young and fair that you take my breath away. I fear I may have something to learn of a lady's desires in the matter of making love."

Jenna smiled shyly, realizing for the first time that her actions were hardly those of a demure lady of breeding and title. In the next instant she was lifted from the bed and whirled about the chamber. Stefan seemed to have taken complete leave of his senses.

"I vow, I will take the impassioned young maiden who comes to me so freely over any with much practiced charms." Stefan buried his face into the fragrant softness of her swirling tresses falling with her full length across the large bed, and then, as Jenna joined in the game, he quickly reached out to silence her mock protests, his lips closing passionately over hers. Jenna responded with a fire to equal his. Slowly they turned in the softness of the bed, Stefan's weight pressing into Jenna, until she felt that surging passion welling deep within her and abandoned herself to him, soaring with him, taking him fully, this time without pain, and then giving in return, the searing flames threatening to consume them, until that final moment when they lay in each other's arms, and Stefan's embrace closed about her, protecting her for a while longer.

Chapter Five

Jenna stirred sleepily in the warmth of the large bed, the crackling of the fire at the hearth rousing her slowly. When she opened her eyes, she found Stefan's piercing blue gaze studying her intently. The memory of the night before came back to her vividly, and a pink glow flooded her cheeks as she realized that Stefan's gaze had lowered to where the covers fell away from her breasts. Stefan stopped her hand as she reached to retrieve the covers and gently kissed the tips of her fingers, and then he bent over her, his lips seeking hers possessively, in a kiss that drew her from herself, demanding from her a passion she thought she had only dreamed of. There was a light knocking at the door, and Stefan's lips left hers abruptly, and then, unable to resist her, he returned for a brief impassioned kiss before pulling her beneath the shelter of the covers and acknowledging the knock. Knowing well that she could ill afford to be discovered in Stefan's bed, Jenna snuggled into the curl of his body, delighting in the feel of his strong arms about her.

Dmitri entered the chamber, according to his morning custom, and noticing nothing different from any other morning, went about setting the breakfast tray on the table and then calling for a young servant boy who quickly scurried forth laden down with buckets filled to overflowing with hot, steaming water for Stefan's morning bath. Stefan heartily enjoyed the endless trips required to fill the brass tub that was drawn before the hearth. He took great pleasure in slowly running his hands across the silken softness of Jenna's skin, drawing from her a surprised gasp from beneath the covers as his hand boldly closed over the fullness of her breast, gently kneading her flesh, rolling that rose-hued tip between his fingers, until Jenna thought she might die from the pleasure of it. Bending low into the covers as Dmitri turned to the armoire to lay out fresh garments for the morning, Stefan pressed fevered kisses into the hollow of Jenna's throat, inhaling deeply of the lavender scent she wore, thinking that he had never before so enjoyed the morning ritual of preparing for a bath. Finally unable to resist further temptation, Stefan grew impatient with the slowly measured pace of Dmitri's ministrations.

"Enough of this! The water will be well chilled, at this pace. I will finish myself," Stefan roared at the surprised Dmitri. Dressed in a spotless white tunic, belted over red, loose-fitting Cossack pants stuffed into the tops of spotless black boots, Dmitri cast his master a surprised look. After years of service to Prince Stefan Kalinsky, he knew well the meaning behind the tone of Stefan's voice. He noted without comment the gently curved form beside his master. He smiled to himself before leaving the chamber, thinking there was perhaps some pleasure to be found in this land so far from his beloved Russia.

As the door was closed, Jenna surfaced from the warm covers to draw a deep breath, only to have her lips sealed as Stefan's mouth lowered over hers. She melted into his heated embrace, her slender body pinned beneath his, savoring the taste of him. Gently she nibbled at his lip, drawing a deep-throated groan from him as his passion soared. Her hands spread across the sleek smoothness of his chest, feeling the rippling of the muscles beneath that bronze skin as he closed her in an embrace that drove the breath from her lungs.

Jenna's head was thrown back as she stared at the lean, handsome beast above her, the thick cascade of her sable hair spread across the pillows like a luxuriant fan.

Stefan could resist that silken softness no longer and buried his hands in the thick, waving tendrils that curled possessively about his hand, as if binding him to her. He lowered his golden head, gently nuzzling the soft curve of her throat, where her pulse beat beneath the satin surface of her skin. He pressed Jenna down into the downy softness of the bed, his purpose clear as his brilliant blue gaze turned a shade of soft smoke, and his voice was husky as he whispered in her ear.

"You are mine, Jenna. From this day forth, whatever may come to us, you are mine." His lips closed, agonizingly tender, over the soft peak of her breast, and Jenna thought she might die from it.

Jenna's eyes closed in complete abandon to Stefan's will, as he had his way with her, exploring, teasing, caressing, until he drew a soft moan from her and knew her passion was aroused. In one practiced move, Stefan rolled, taking her with him, so that she now lay over him, her hair tumbling wildly about them. She gazed back at him in sudden surprise, her eyes widening, as his hands rode her hips, lifting her easily and settling her over him.

Jenna leaned over Stefan, her hands resting on his shoulders. She surrendered herself to the exquisite pleasure of his heat searing through her. He guided her, moving with her, as a slow, rhythmic stroking began, building within them both a flame that could not be denied.

Stefan watched Jenna's face intently as she leaned her head back, eyes closed, luxuriating in the warmth of their bond. Never before had he known such pleasure, such need to give pleasure, as he felt now with her. Her eyes opened slowly as the passion built within her, the amber color glowing golden with the fires that burned brightly within her. Shakily she pleaded for him to stop, in her youthful innocence, uncertain that she could endure the final pleasure they were about to share without being consumed by it. Stefan persisted, knowing that beyond her soft whispers were the silent pleas of her need for him. Her breath caught in her throat, her long fingers digging into the bronze skin across his shoulders as he drove her to a final ecstasy that sent pulsing waves through her young body. He thrust deep within her, to join in her pleasure, as a gentle sob escaped her lips, and he felt his own release hot within her, a release that was almost painful in his desire for her.

Tenderly, Stefan turned in the covers, taking Jenna with him, cradling her in his strong embrace, that bond with her as yet unbroken. Gently he brushed aside the veil of dark curls that shielded her face from him. With lean, insistent fingers, he raised her chin, forcing her to look into his eyes. Her lips parted uncertainly, and Stefan's heart was filled with an unexplainable tenderness as he gazed into the wide amber depths of her eyes, filled with her confusion at the passion they had shared. It was a little disconcerting to realize how important it was that he share that first time with her. In the past, he would have scorned the inexperienced virgin for the accomplished courtesan. Indeed, his one experience with a virgin, as a youth, had convinced him they were hardly worth the sleepless nights that followed. But in this beautiful, remarkable creature who lay beside him, he had found a pleasure that far surpassed any courtly lover or mistress. Here was one worthy of any price to keep her beside him. Stefan's lips brushed across the satin texture of her forehead, breathing in her fragrance. He bound her to him fiercely, that he might hold back the demons that threatened them all. How much did she know of her grandfather's work? She had said that Charles Wingate presumed too much in his attentions toward her, and Stefan knew well that Sir Avery had disapproved of the match. How much did Jenna know of the conspiracy they had uncovered?

Stefan watched the slow rise and fall of Jenna's full breasts beneath the linen covers. In sleep, she seemed all the more vulnerable. Gently he eased from her side, pulling the covers high over her gleaming shoulder. He bathed quickly and dressed, leaving the breakfast tray for Jenna when she awoke. He bent low over her sleeping form, gently pressing a kiss against her lips. There was much she would have to know. But for now there was greater safety in her innocence. He dreaded leaving her. He would have cared for nothing more than to remain with her, watching her sleep, as now, but he knew with nagging clarity that events were slipping beyond his grasp to control them. Unless he acted carefully and with all haste, all might yet be lost for them both, for all of England and Western Europe. Stefan seized a single red rose from a crystal vase near the hearth and laid the bloom on the pillow beside her. It was important that it be the first thing she see upon waking, since there had been no time for words.

Stepping into the carpeted hallway, Stefan nodded curtly to the great giant, Dmitri.

"See that Mademoiselle Randolph has all that she needs. I shall return after my meeting." Stefan knew he could trust to his friend's discretion. Through many years together, the bond of friendship and trust between the two men exceeded that of royal prince and loyal servant.

Dmitri nodded his great, bearlike head, already aware that the "little princess" who slept in his master's bed was to be protected against any harm. His black eyes twinkled merrily as Dmitri considered the uncommon spirit of the girl. He could remember none of his master's elegant ladies who could fire a pistol, or escape a burning house down a length of rope. Here indeed was one worthy of the elusive Prince Stefan Kalinsky, who had heartily decried any need of a woman beyond a casual affair. Dmitri quickly dispensed his orders to the young servant boy to prepare more hot water.

Stefan descended the wide stairway, just as Emma Kelly labored up the stairs laden with an elegant filled tray, obviously for Jenna's chamber.

"Mrs. Kelly, there was extensive damage to Lady Randolph's chamber last night from a broken window. It was impossible that she remain in the room. I offered her the use of my chamber." Stefan ignored the stunned look that crossed the woman's face. He would offer no more explanations.

Mrs. Kelly sputtered uncertainly as she stood in the middle of the stairway. "Indeed, the storm was quite fierce, your highness." She fought to regain her composure at his statement.

Stefan's eyes suddenly glowed with a brilliant intensity, a secretive smile pulling at his handsome lips, as he remembered with mounting passion the last hours he had shared with Jenna. "Yes, Mrs. Kelly, the storm was most fierce." Stefan tipped his hat briefly, and then descended the stairway, leaving Emma Kelly in shocked wonder that Jenna had accepted such an arrangement.

Emma Kelly continued up the long stairway, pausing to regain her breath as she reached the top landing. She peered through the open portal to Jenna's chamber. Indeed the protruding tree limb and the shattered panes of glass more than gave evidence to the damage from the storm. Two servants finished rolling the heavy, rain-soaked carpet, brushing past Emma with their sodden burden. The heavy velvet drapes, ruined by the downpour, had already been stripped from their hangings and removed. The delicate lace curtains underneath still remained, badly stained where the crimson dye had run from the heavy velvet. A young servant girl brushed past Emma and set about removing the curtains. Clucking disapprovingly to herself, Emma turned toward the doorway at the far end of the hallway. Before she could reach for the handle, Dmitri's massive paw of a hand closed over hers, seizing the breakfast tray.

"There is no need." The giant Russian spoke gently but firmly in his thick accent. "Dmitri has brought breakfast to the little princess. The boy has brought hot water for the bath. She will have need of you when she has finished."

Emma Kelly sniffed indignantly, not about to be put off by some great lumbering creature who wore the clothes of a peasant, if a well dressed one at that. She firmly stood her meager height, her Irish temper flaring beneath the steady gaze of black eyes that refused to show any emotion.

"I shall attend my mistress as is my custom, and no great growling oaf shall say nay." Emma straightened her back and held her position. She might be a guest in this house, but there were none who would give her orders, except her mistress. With a determined gleam in her eye, Emma nimbly ducked beyond the reach of the giant Russian, quickly darting under his massive arm. In an instant she was through the door, quickly closing it behind her, giving her unspoken challenge that he dare not trespass into a lady's chamber unannounced. Emma whirled around, carefully holding on to the heavily laden tray, her eyes locking with Jenna's startled gaze as she stirred sleepily in the massive bed.

It was a full, long moment before Jenna's senses cleared, as she stared uncertainly at Emma. She gazed about the room, the memory of the night past flooding her with a sudden vibrant warmth as she realized she had not been dreaming, after all. Her wide golden gaze met Emma's evenly before she reached to pull the covers protectively about her naked body, certain the woman must know the truth. But instead of glaring reprimands, Emma quietly crossed the room, placing the heavy silver tray beside the one Dmitri had brought earlier.

"Mr. Flint will have the carriage waiting when you are ready. If you won't be needing my help with your morning bath, I might be of some service in cleaning your own chamber. There is a dreadful mess from the storm last night."

Jenna sighed her silent gratitude. For all the years that Emma had been both confidante and servant to her, she had chosen not to press the obvious question of Jenna's presence in Stefan Kalinsky's bedchamber. Jenna knew for sure that she could not have easily lied to the woman.

"I can manage quite well, Emma. Thank you." Jenna met the woman's gaze unwaveringly, and Emma turned to leave.

"In all the confusion last night, I fear I forgot my wrapper." Jenna spoke softly, refusing to leave the secluded haven of Stefan's bed, with only the covers to shield her naked body.

"I shall bring an appropriate gown for our visit to the

lawyers, and send Maggie to arrange your hair."

"Thank you, Emma," Jenna murmured thoughtfully, her mind already far from the night's events, racing ahead to her confrontation with her grandfather's lawyers.

Emma paused at the door before leaving. "I think it best that other arrangements be made as soon as possible. Most certainly Prince Kalinsky has been most generous, but it is quite impossible that we impose on his hospitality further."

Jenna's eyes locked with Emma's, the woman's message clear in the words she had left unsaid.

"Of course, you are quite right, Emma. More suitable arrangements must be made at once," Jenna added, not at all certain what her success might be with the lawyers, as nagging doubts of her own confidence wavered dangerously. Damn him! Damn Stefan Kalinsky. Jenna was unaware of the door's closing behind Emma's departing figure as she slammed her fist into the mounded softness of the down mattress. How dare he take advantage of her, and then go lightly about his affairs. She could only assume it was his usual practice to rise early, leaving his partner for the night to rouse herself discreetly, leaving before he was caused any undue embarrassment. In sudden vexation, Jenna sprang from the bed, tossing the linen covers away as she felt the rage welling within her. She would be gone when he returned, but hardly to steal away into the shadows of early morning. She would be well rid of that arrogant Russian bastard.

Jenna whirled around as her thoughts returned to the present. Very soon Emma would return with Maggie and clothing. She must bathe quickly. She caught the blurred vision of her own body in the shimmering glass mirror across the room, and she halted in midflight at the sight of her naked body, full-length, unadorned by either chemise or silk wrapper. She approached the mirror, which reflected the image of a young woman, with large, amber eyes that seemed to fill the wide oval of her face, and swirling tendrils of dark hair that tumbled past her waist, curling below the curve of her hips. Jenna stared at her reflection. Nothing was changed. Everything was as it had been before; before Stefan Kalinsky. And yet, as she stood before the mirror, Jenna was aware that she was not the same. She could still feel the warmth of his skin against hers, the feather-softness of his fingers lightly caressing her, making her suddenly aware of the fulfillment to be found in his arms. Surely, it was madness. Surely, she had never bothered to think what lay beyond the casual touch of a hand upon her arm, or a man's arm about her waist. Surely, she had never cared to imagine what might lie beyond Charles Wingate's possessive handling of her. With startling clarity, Jenna realized Charles's touch had never affected her as Stefan's had. Her memory was suffused with the vision of blue eyes as cold as ice with arrogant aloofness, and then fiery hot with the passion he had shown her in their hours together. Tentatively, Jenna reached up, her fingers lightly brushing the tip of her breast where Stefan had touched her. Jenna could almost feel again the exquisite agony of his kisses, his lips possessively taking her to unexplored heights of passion. Her lips parted questioningly as she continued to stare at the vision of the girl, now the woman. The rose-hued peak tautened under her touch, and Jenna closed her eyes, almost able to feel Stefan's heat spreading through her. But it was her own heat, the afterglow of their lovemaking, that spread through her like white-hot liquid that filled her veins, coursing through her, demanding to be fed.

Jenna forced herself back to reality. She willed herself not to think of Stefan Kalinsky, and yet her every thought was of him. From that first moment, on the post road to London, so many weeks before, to her presence in his house, Stefan Kalinsky seemed to wield some power over her. She knew of a certainty that it was Stefan she had seen in her grandfather's library the morning before Sir Avery died. And now, after what had passed between them, she knew it was Stefan who had posed in the disguise of a highwayman. What did it all mean? What had he been hoping to find in the Wingate carriage? Jenna slid into the steamy depths of the bath. She found no answers in her wandering thoughts. The only thing she could know for certain was that when Stefan Kalinsky returned she would be gone.

Jenna lathered the linen cloth with the fragrant liquid soap from the porcelain jar on the table beside the gleaming brass tub. The distinctly feminine scent of roses filled the steaming air, and she wondered vaguely if Stefan had used that same soap. In spite of her strong-willed determination not to think of him, she found it impossible to rid herself of the vision of him, lean and golden, lying beside her in his bed. Jenna ground her teeth in mounting frustration that he might leave her so easily, almost casually, as if such behavior were his custom. Her vision was filled with the memory of the elegant gowns she had found in the chamber across the hall from her own. Did they belong to Stefan's mistress? Somehow Jenna thought not. It seemed unlikely that Stefan would keep a mistress, when all of London's most eligible young ladies had willingly offered their favors. Tears welled in her eyes as she realized she was no different from those overanxious young ladies who presented themselves as the cream of English society, while acting no better than the well-paid whores at the private men's clubs. And yet, in the weeks since their first meeting, she could not recall seeing Stefan in the constant company of any one young lady. She wondered, then, if his attentions were perhaps given to a lady who was not eligible. It was not at all uncommon for a lady of title to take a lover outside of her marriage, when she found her aging husband no longer capable or desirable. Jenna was unable to understand the sudden tightening feeling she felt deep within. She tried to convince herself it hardly mattered where his attentions lay. With a sudden vengeance, she threw the cloth into the cooling water, instantly regretting her show of temper as the splashing water sent stinging soap into her eyes. When she had rinsed her reddened eyes enough that she could see again, Jenna was startled to find that Maggie had arrived to help with her hair. Seizing a linen towel from the table, she rose from her bath, sullenly declaring that she could dry herself. If Maggie thought anything amiss in her mistress's sudden peevish mood, she gave no indication as she carefully hung an elegant gown upon a hook in Stefan's armoire to prevent wrinkling of the watered silk fabric.

Jenna rubbed her skin with a vengeance, as if by that act alone she might remove Stefan's touch from her. Casting aside the towel she accepted the sheer chemise over her head. She drew sheer silk stockings over the length of her slender legs, and a jarring memory suddenly drove all other thought from her mind. Maggie had gone to retrieve the brushes from the dressing table in the other room. Jenna seized her opportunity as she tore through the mass of scattered bed covers for her torn chemise. She groaned her despair as she failed to find the garment, knowing there would be no easy explanation if Emma were to find it first. She vainly tossed aside one down pillow, her assault stopping suddenly as she gazed down at the single crimson bloom Stefan had left for her. Her hand closed over the long stem, and she smelled the strong fragrance that overpowered the faint scent left from her bathing. Perfect petals, as soft as the finest satin, creamy white on the underside, and barely opened to reveal dark crimson on the inside. It seemed as if the petals were so many hands gently sheltering the gift of the beautiful bloom within, now opening ever so slightly to reveal the gift to her, Stefan's gift. A single flower carefully chosen was the greatest gift he could have offered.

Jenna paced the width of the spacious wood-paneled offices of her grandfather's lawyers. She stared beyond the stone planter boxes filled with late-blooming flowers in varied shades of yellow and bronze that adorned the front steps of the building. Beyond the musty, book-filled confines of the office, the streets of London were filled with a jumble of activity this early October morning. Sir Lawrence Renfield had been called away on a matter of grave importance, leaving Jenna to wait, idly contemplating her plan of attack. All of Emma's urgent pleadings about their dire predicament following the fire had failed to stir the renowned barrister from his decision that he could not possibly release extensive funds from her grandfather's estate into her inexperienced hands. Inexperienced she might be, Jenna thought ruefully, at least in matters of finance and business, but she would not be put off in this matter. Surely Sir Lawrence could be made to see the matter clearly. Jenna smoothed the emerald-green watered silk of her high-waisted gown to still the trembling in her hands. At the sound of voices beyond the door, Jenna turned to meet her challenge, all her confidence borne in the regal tilt of her chin.

Sir Lawrence Renfield, senior member of the prestigious London firm, greeted Jenna warmly, extending his rounded hand to gently seize hers, patting her gloved hand reassuringly.

"My dearest Jenna, how very lovely you look, hardly the destitute, homeless figure Mrs. Kelly would have me believe."

"You are very kind Sir Lawrence. But all is not as it seems. You are aware of the fire that burned my grandfather's house. It is quite impossible for me to return until the necessary repairs have been made."

"Jenna, please, must we be so formal? Have I not watched you grow from a young child to the exquisite young woman you are now? You have been well provided for, and your grandfather entrusted me to see that you would continue to be well cared for. I will not neglect my responsibility as your grandfather's lawyer, and now yours." Sir Lawrence smiled placatingly.

Jenna braced herself mentally. She could see that he was well prepared to evade her requests. "Sir Lawrence, you have made it quite clear that you are not prepared to release funds for the necessary repairs until the cause of the fire has been determined. You have also refused to release funds so that I may find another residence until the repairs can be made. It seems, sir, that you are quite unwilling to cooperate with me on any level in this matter. I easily recognize that I may be ill prepared for the events surrounding my grandfather's death, but I also recognize that I may make my own choice of lawyers in this matter, and I am prepared to do so.'' Jenna quickly withdrew her hand, hardly in the mood for idle pleasantries. She thought she noted a slight twinge of annoyance behind his carefully guarded gaze. And then the professional smile returned.

"My dearest Jenna, there is most certainly no need for this. I am quite prepared to release from your grandfather's estate whatever funds might be necessary for either the repair of the house or the cost of an alternative residence, or both." Sir Lawrence smiled vaguely as he noted the surprised look on Jenna's face.

Jenna was hardly prepared for such cooperation. After Emma's report of her meeting with Sir Lawrence the day before, Jenna had been prepared for a struggle, even for further legal action, if it were necessary. If she had failed, she was hardly prepared to face Stefan Kalinsky. Her only alternative would have been Elizabeth Wingate. Messages had begun arriving at her grandfather's house the morning after the fire, inquiring after her whereabouts and her health. Jenna had responded, saying only that she was unharmed and that all would be taken care of. She had graciously refused Lord Wingate's insistence that she stay with them until the repairs could be made to the house. Though it had been Lord Wingate's invitation, Jenna had sensed Charles's possessive assumption that she would stay with them. The decision had been an easy matter. The solution might not be as easy. Now Sir Lawrence stood across from her, smiling that benign smile that revealed absolutely nothing more than what he had said.

"I'm afraid I do not understand, Sir Lawrence. Yesterday Mrs. Kelly returned to inform me that you could not consider the matter," Jenna responded quizzically.

"Dear child, I am quite prepared to consider any course of action you might suggest. But I must make you understand that although I am aware of your plight, and heartily agree we must find a solution, I am bound by the strict law concerning your grandfather's will and the provisions of his estate.''

Jenna fought back the confusion that crowded her. It seemed they were speaking of the same matter, although it hardly seemed they were arriving at the same solution. She inhaled deeply as she continued.

"Sir Lawrence, are you then prepared to release the necessary funds for the repairs and a place of residence until the repairs are completed?'' There, she had forced him to answer the issue directly, cutting away all his legal nuances, of which she had little understanding or concern about at the moment.

"Jenna, I am afraid you do not understand my position. As executor of your grandfather's will, I am bound by his requests as set forth in that will. Most certainly the repairs of his residence shall commence immediately. Under the provisions of your grandfather's will, you are to be supplied the funds necessary for the maintenance of the house and staff, as well as additional funds for your own purposes. However, I am afraid that until your twentieth birthday, almost two years from now, all other properties and funds must remain in trust. That is of course, unless you should choose to marry, in which case, all properties and funds will immediately be released to your husband.''

Jenna stared in stunned disbelief at Sir Lawrence. A barely perceptible gleam crept into his beady eyes, the first sign of any emotion since he had entered the office. She could hardly believe what she was hearing. True, she had been amply, if not lavishly provided for upon her grandfather's death. If Sir Lawrence was to be believed, it was also true that nothing but the most essential funds was available to her until she turned twenty years old. Jenna braced herself for the answer to her next question.

"According to my grandfather's will, Sir Lawrence, how much additional funds am I to be allowed for 'my own purposes'?'' Jenna fought back the wave of anger that threatened to overrule all caution.

"The sum is one thousand pounds, quite adequate I am sure.'' His arrogant smirk was more than Jenna could bear.

"Hardly adequate, Sir Lawrence, for payment of an additional residence. It would seem that your legal restrictions have me quite soundly caught."

"Not at all my dear. Your grandfather was a man of great importance, and well liked among his friends. I am certain you will receive a great many offers of assistance. It has been brought to my attention that Lord Wingate has already offered his home and whatever assistance may be at his disposal. In view of your friendship with Lady Elizabeth Wingate, and your pending betrothal to Sir Charles, I think it would be quite acceptable to accept their kind offer, with certain proprieties of course." His attitude was completely detestable.

Jenna straightened to her full height, as she fought to refrain from clawing his eyes from his pale, powdered face. She would not allow him the satisfaction of seeing the tears that threatened. Jenna swallowed hard as she regained her composure.

"You are quite right, of course, Sir Lawrence. You must adhere to the strict instructions of my grandfather's will. I will take a draft for the one thousand pounds now."

Sir Lawrence's pale complexion seemed to drain of any remaining color, if that was possible. "You wish the entire amount, now?"

"Yes, immediately. There are important matters I must take care of. The remainder of the funds for the maintenance of the house and staff is to continue as before. Mr. Flint, my grandfather's retainer, will advise you of our location. I want to thank you most kindly, Sir Lawrence, for your time and concern." Jenna bit off her last words sarcastically, the brittle edge unmistakable as she extended her hand, playing out his game to the bitter end.

Jenna picked up her woven shawl and matching silk reticule. Having nothing further to discuss, she whirled on her heel and disappeared through the wide portal, in a rustling of silk, loudly slamming the heavy door behind her so that a full score of heads in the outer offices, snapped up in startled surprise. She swept through the law

101

offices, wishing sorely that she might have been born a man, so that she might enjoy the immense pleasure to be found in laying a sound blow to one Sir Lawrence Renfield.

Beyond the stagnating confines of the offices, Jenna stepped into the crisp coolness of early fall. A gentle wind gusted about the skirts of her gown and seemed to cleanse the spirit as she breathed deeply. She nodded briskly to Emma as she stepped into the open carriage. Jenna settled into the soft leather of the cushions, tilting her head back to feel the brush of the breeze against her skin. Her gaze was suddenly filled with the brilliant blue of the autumn sky, achingly vibrant, hauntingly familiar, as her memory flooded with the vision of eyes as blue as that sky. His eyes—Stefan's—that seemed to find her wherever she looked, and she wondered with a sudden wistfulness what his memory would be of their night together. Undeniably like any other nights he had spent with some lady favored for an hour or two, or perhaps a day. In his leaving, without a word for her, he had made his purpose abundantly clear.

Jenna tilted her trembling chin a little higher. She would forget Prince Stefan Kalinsky. He was the same as other men, such as Sir Lawrence Renfield, who cared only for their own purposes. She would forget the feel of his hands across her skin, the gentle touch of his fingers in her hair, the exquisite tenderness of his lips seeking hers. Indeed, she would forget, as easily as he had forgotten.

"Mistress?" Mr. Flint startled her from her reverie, and she realized he waited for her instructions—but what should she tell him?

Jenna clutched the draft for the funds tightly in her fist, unable to determine what their destination should be. She turned as Mr. Flint shouted a greeting, and pointed to the burly, mountainous figure of a man approaching on a horse. Dmitri's size alone set him apart from other men. And now he seemed to dwarf the fine mount that carried him with no small effort toward their carriage.

"Ah, little princess, I have found you at last. His

highness was most concerned to find you gone upon his return. The girl, Maggie, said you would be here. Prince Kalinsky has asked that I escort you." Dmitri's face was almost indistinguishable behind the scraggly thick furring of his unkempt hair and beard.

Jenna fought her growing desire to yield to Dmitri's wishes. At that moment she would have cared for nothing more than the safe haven Stefan might offer her, though she knew it quite impossible. "Dmitri, I am grateful to his highness for his hospitality, but surely you must realize that I cannot return."

"*Da, da.* Yes, of course," Dmitri responded absently in his thickly accented English. Without giving her the opportunity for further excuses, the giant Russian Cossack leaned across his horse, giving Mr. Flint some instruction.

With a curt nod of his head, Mr. Flint expertly guided the matched team of bays through the milling throng of carriages and people crowding the cobbled street in front of the offices and shops. Jenna's persistent questions about their destination were met with stony silence, and she realized Dmitri would say nothing until he had delivered her, according to Stefan's instructions.

Chapter Six

Hallston House stood imposingly silent among the other Georgian homes that lined the cobbled street across from Highleigh Gardens. A tall wrought-iron fence surrounded the grounds, offering a measure of privacy to those within, although Jenna knew quite well that no one had occupied Hallston House for more than a year, since the death of Lady Eugenia Van Dyne, the last remaining heir to Van Dyne shipping. The stately home had been the object of much speculation as several families of title had sought to purchase the London residence. All had been summarily refused. Jenna knew that Lord Wingate had also sought to purchase the manor for himself, to then offer his own smaller, though equally elegant town house to Charles as a wedding gift. Jenna had never chosen to question who the intended bride might be. Charles's constant companionship over the last year and his unrelenting determination to announce their betrothal earlier in the summer had been answer enough. Only Jenna's stubborn refusal to accept, because of her grandfather's illness, had temporarily curbed Charles's intentions.

Jenna accepted Mr. Flint's hand as she stepped down from the carriage, at a loss to understand why Dmitri had brought them here. Behind her, Emma alighted from the carriage just as the front door of the manor was thrown open. Both women stared in surprise at the man who stood ready to greet them.

Dmitri greeted the man and called him Alexei. He bowed stiffly before Jenna. A spotless white tunic was belted over crimson Cossack pants, the same as Dmitri wore, the pants tucked into the tops of gleaming black Hessian boots. Jenna nodded to him briefly as Dmitri escorted them through the foyer into the main drawing room.

Jenna stared about the large, elegant room in disbelief. The walls were covered with cream-colored satin fabric, accented with royal blue velvet stripping from floor to ceiling. The mahogany floor gleamed with the rich, lustrous glow of recent waxing. A large woolen carpet dominated the room, set with clusters of flowers in the design. Single blooms, set like a magnificent woven chain, bordered the carpet, in a vivid deep red the color of rich, claret wine, interspersed with tiny blue violets. Heavy velvet portieres of that same deep wine color, richly edged with a gold satin fringe, draped the large floor-to-ceiling paned windows that opened out onto a rose garden beyond, while sheer, diaphanous curtains were hung underneath. Two large overstuffed wing-back chairs, covered with royal blue velvet, were set before the ornate fireplace. Beside one chair was a small, rosewood table, set with a crystal decanter filled with wine, and several crystal goblets. At the far side of the room, set near the large windows to catch the light, was a round rosewood gaming table set around with four chairs. Over the ornately carved mantel was hung a round gilt-framed mirror that reflected the image of the magnificent room. Jenna stood in stunned silence. She had thought the manorhouse empty. She had hardly been prepared for the elegant furnishings of a home that seemed to wait only for its master and mistress. At the sound of heavy booted footsteps from the hallway, Jenna whirled around, already certain of that brilliant blue gaze, which watched her intently.

"Welcome, Jenna. I hope everything meets with your approval. There was little time for more, although I think Maggie and Mrs. Kelly will find the kitchen and staff will meet their needs." Stefan's voice was vibrant and warm as his gaze lingered over the beautiful young woman before him. He would not have believed it possible that she could be more beautiful than when he had last seen her, curled naked in his bed. Now he realized it was possible. The shimmering emerald silk gown clung to her lithe form enticingly, the plunging sweep of the neckline revealing the ample swell of her breasts above the perfect cut of the bodice, the filmy, sheer lace about the edge discreetly shielding her charms. The emerald-green color had been an excellent choice, as he knew it would be. The color caught the glow of her amber eyes, mesmerizing him with a warmth that seemed to move instantly between them, like some invisible bond. Her dark hair had been pulled back and piled high upon her head, left unadorned, except for the matching set of combs set with several rows of small pearls. If she felt uncertainty at that moment, it was not to be seen. She was at once strong yet vulnerable, proud yet demure, defiant yet yielding, as she had been the night before, when she had come to him uncertainly yet passionately.

"Why have you brought me here?" Jenna answered shakily, feeling herself drawn by the warmth of his gaze.

"This will be your home. At least for the time, until the repairs can be completed. I thought it hardly acceptable for you to remain my guest, although I would never deny the pleasure such an arrangement might offer." Stefan smiled at Jenna warmly, a playful smile pulling at his mouth, as he watched the noticeable rise of color across her high-boned cheeks. A wicked glare leaped into those amber eyes, and Stefan was pleased to see her spirit return so quickly. She was one worthy of keeping, of that he was certain.

"This is quite impossible," Jenna bit off sharply, when she would have added that his treatment of her the night before hardly gave him the right to intervene in her life.

"You will find that Maggie has brought your wardrobe. The remainder of the gowns will be delivered tomorrow. I purchased additional furnishings for your comfort.

Dmitri will see that you have whatever additional furnishings you require. You have but to ask."

Jenna stared at Stefan incredulously. This was madness, and quite impossible. In spite of his words the night before that his cause and her grandfather's were one and the same, she could not help but wonder at the motives of such a man. She advanced toward him a few steps, and then stopped as she remembered Mr. Flint and Emma were in the room. A curtly given nod from Stefan and all were ushered from the room by the overpowering Dmitri. Only Emma dared to flash the huge man a warning glance as he guided her to the kitchen and the servants' chambers beyond. Jenna turned toward the bright light streaming in through the windows in an effort to sort her tangled thoughts. She whirled about as she heard the double doors of the drawing room being drawn shut. All her quickly assembled protests died on her lips as she stared into the vast brilliance of Stefan's blue gaze, which seemed to devour her.

"It is quite impossible for me to remain here. Surely you must know that," she whispered shakily. "What is the true purpose of a royal prince who must hide behind the disguise of a highwayman? What dangerous game are you playing?"

"If only this were all just a game, my lovely Jenna, then we might all go home safely when the game was ended. You must trust in me, as your grandfather trusted me. I can say no more. As for this house, it is a suitable arrangement that no one could object to. And it will be much easier to make certain there are no more 'accidental' fires. You might not escape again so easily."

All the questions that demanded to be answered fled as Stefan approached. Jenna's breath stilled in her throat as he stood before her. He reached for her hand. Though she tried to pull away from the warmth of his fingers about hers, she found it impossible to break his grasp. Jenna willed herself not to look into his eyes, for fear she might lose herself in the depths of his gaze. Try as she would, she could not deny how handsome he was. The perfectly cut brown waistcoat was molded to him like a second skin, contrasting elegantly with the fawn-colored breeches. She dared not trust herself to further inspection for fear her gaze would betray her. With growing vexation, she noted the faint smile that turned his lips.

"You see, my dearest Jenna, I am quite aware of the answer you received from the lawyers this morning. Sir Lawrence Renfield is to be commended for his singular loyalty. He has offered you a solution as to your residence, and remained favorable in the eyes of his most esteemed client, Lord Wingate."

"But you are mistaken. He only mentioned the possibility that I accept Elizabeth's hospitality."

"Not Elizabeth Wingate's hospitality, but that of Charles Wingate. And what better way to press his cause."

Jenna shook her head uncertainly, but knew she could hardly deny Charles's persistence during the last weeks and, more recently, since her grandfather's death.

"True that may be. However, Elizabeth is my friend and offers her home out of friendship. I dare not say what favor I might be obligated to give in accepting your offer. I fear I could not meet the price."

Stefan bowed low over her hand, his lips lingering again at her fingertips, sending a river of molten heat flooding through her.

"I think perhaps an agreement can be reached. You have need of a home. This house has been empty for quite some time. I think a contract might be drawn, allowing you the house for one year, for the sum of one hundred pounds sterling. Would such an agreement be acceptable to you, my little princess?" His twinkling blue eyes glinted with his good humor of the moment.

Jenna found him completely maddening. "That is impossible. You cannot make such an offer; the owners would think you quite mad."

"But my dearest Jenna, I am the owner. And it is my decision to offer you Hallston House for the sum of one hundred pounds sterling, as you see it now. Is that acceptable to you?"

Jenna bit at her lower lip, her thoughts racing, as she tried to understand his reasons for such a ridiculous proposal, and yet she knew she had little choice in the matter. He was offering her an honorable arrangement, or so it seemed.

"I find I have little choice in the matter. I accept your offer, your highness."

"A rule in my house, Jenna. There must be no formality between us. It is quite impossible after last night."

Her startled amber eyes met his piercing blue ones, as she fought against a sudden stifling heat in the room. She felt the firm pressure of Stefan's arm beneath hers, his fingers closing possessively about her elbow. For a long moment, Jenna was certain he would pull her into his arms and kiss her. Had she acknowledged the truth of her own feelings, she would have known how she longed for the feel of his lips against hers. Instead he pressed another kiss against her fingertips, before gently releasing her.

"I believe you will find everything you need. Alexei will remain as part of your staff. Dmitri will call upon you frequently to see to your requests. I have one request of you now. A new play is opening at the theater, Saturday next. I insist upon your company for the evening. Shall we call it a small down payment on the contract for the house? Good day, Jenna." Stefan bowed his head to her with great formality, the gesture broken only by the twitch of the smile on his lips. Turning abruptly, he left the drawing room, the sound of the heavy front door announcing his departure before Jenna could recover from their meeting.

Immediately the following morning, Jenna pressed a draft for one hundred pounds into Dmitri's large hand, with firm instructions that it was to be delivered to Prince Stefan Kalinsky. She felt some measure of satisfaction in the payment, though she knew quite well it was a paltry amount. Inexperienced as she was in matters of finance, she did know that her grandfather had once paid such a sum for a fine coach horse. For the remainder of the morning, Jenna occupied her time with settling into the chamber she had taken for her own. There again, Stefan seemed to have made the choice for her. A finely carved rosewood armoire filled with gowns he had purchased for her stood across from a huge postered bed. It was far more effort than it was worth to move the heavy furnishings merely to satisfy a foolish whim. And she could hardly find fault with Stefan's choice for her. The bedchamber was magnificent. A large white woolen rug, with a floral pattern woven in the yarn covered the wood floor. The walls had been covered with pale blue moire silk. Velvet drapes of a darker shade were hung across the double set of french doors that opened out onto a stone terrace overlooking the grounds beyond the manor. An elegant dressing table stood across from the bed, covered with jars containing varied scents and powders, far more than her own dressing table at home. A delicately carved wood-handled brush and comb set that Stefan had given her had been neatly set there also, as if but waiting for her hand. Indeed Stefan had provided for her every necessity or want, save perhaps one—which Jenna was hardly aware of. Jenna's thoughts were suddenly interrupted as Maggie knocked anxiously on the door and then burst into the room not waiting for Jenna's response. Jenna stared at her maid in surprise.

"Maggie, whatever is the matter?"

"You must come quickly. It is a surprise, and most grand." Maggie fairly bubbled over with her excitement.

Jenna stared at the girl as if she had taken complete leave of her senses, then followed Maggie down the long hallway and the sweeping staircase. Jenna followed Maggie across the foyer toward the drawing room, where Emma stood in the doorway shaking her graying head from side to side in disbelief. Jenna halted in midstride as she entered the drawing room and stared at the surprise that awaited her. Everywhere about the room were clusters of elegant crimson roses. In vases set upon the mantel, and the gaming table. In an embossed, silver bowl. Everywhere she looked, the fragrant blooms dominated the room. Jenna stared about her, until her gaze rested on the silent, mountainous Dmitri who had vainly tried to make

111

himself less conspicuous.

"What is the meaning of this?" Jenna asked, astounded at the great quantity of roses, when most gardens had yielded their last for the season.

Dmitri coughed uncomfortably, searching for the correct words, that she might understand.

"His highness ordered the flowers delivered. He also asked that I inquire as to your needs, and deliver this message." He handed her a sealed envelope.

"I should also like to know the meaning of this?"

All eyes turned in startled surprise, as Charles Wingate, unannounced, strode into the room.

"I rang several times, but there was no answer. I thought perhaps Elizabeth might have misunderstood the message she received from Mr. Flint. Regrettably, I see there was no misunderstanding." Charles sniffed disapprovingly as his gaze swept the elegant room and the brilliant floral display.

"It would seem, my dearest Jenna, that you have an admirer, or perhaps several."

Jenna was not unaware of the caustic edge to Charles's comment, beneath the carefully disguised pleasantries.

"Charles, how nice of you to call. I was not expecting you. You are my first caller. Has Elizabeth come with you?"

"No, Elizabeth was greatly occupied this afternoon at the dressmaker's, having the final alterations made to her wardrobe for the theater. It was in the matter of the theater that I wanted to speak with you, and of course to see for myself if Mr. Flint had spoken correctly. It would seem he has."

Jenna could see that warning glint in Charles's pale gray eyes that she had come to know so well. He was extremely upset and quite intent on letting her know of it.

"Actually Charles, the matter of my living arrangements was settled by Sir Lawrence Renfield, my grandfather's lawyer." Jenna was immediately aware that she had struck a sensitive place with Charles. The surprise in his face was quickly masked by that condescending smile of his that she found so infuriating. He knew quite well of her meeting with Sir Lawrence. Jenna completed her role as the perfect hostess as she asked Maggie to bring them tea and cakes. With much rolling of her dark eyes, Emma followed Maggie, pointedly leaving the double doors to the drawing room wide open for easy inspection.

As soon as the servants were beyond immediate proximity, Charles whirled on Jenna.

"Will you please explain the meaning of all this to me? I find it quite deplorable that you should choose to refuse my and Elizabeth's offer of hospitality, in favor of taking residence in this house. Jenna, it is quite unacceptable that you should behave in this manner," Charles stormed at her, the color suddenly rising across his pale cheeks.

Jenna was hardly prepared for this outburst. Charles looked as if he were about to suffer apoplexy. Jenna poured a goblet of the dark wine from the crystal decanter and thrust it into his hand. Charles quickly downed the liquid, slamming the goblet down with such force that Jenna flinched, fearing the delicate crystal would shatter.

"Aren't you going to read the note?" Charles spoke from between clenched teeth as he fought for some measure of control.

Jenna pushed the sealed envelope aside on the table, thinking it perhaps wiser that she wait. She brushed past Charles as Maggie entered with a silver serving tray laden with tea and cakes. Jenna took the tray from Maggie, quickly dismissing the girl, not wishing to subject her to Charles's tirade. She also quickly dismissed the girl's whispered concern for her safety. She knew Charles's temper well, and would not tolerate his boorish behavior in her house. Smiling sweetly, Jenna filled a delicate cup and offered it to Charles. He absently accepted the cup, his troubled gray gaze watching her every move.

"My purpose in coming was also to ask if you would accompany me to the theater. Naturally, Elizabeth and Father would be there to share the evening with us. It is the first performance of the season. The prince regent has planned to attend, as well as other members of the royal family. It promises to be quite a grand affair. I know it is quite soon after the loss of your grandfather, but I had thought since we will soon be announcing our betrothal, an exception in propriety might be made."

Jenna's face suddenly paled noticeably as she turned to pour herself a cup of tea, the cup rattling badly in the saucer. She quickly set the cup upon the table. She had forgotten about the theater, and that Stefan Kalinsky had informed her of his intentions to escort her. She clenched her slender hands together to still their trembling as she whirled to face Charles, offering a charming smile that carefully concealed her rising panic. It was completely impossible for her even to consider his invitation. To do so would be disastrous. She had been more than aware of the instant conflict between the two men on the night of Lord Wingate's ball. And though she knew as well that Stefan would hardly accept any excuse, her most pressing problem was Charles Wingate.

"Charles, you are quite right, of course. I had not considered attending the theater. It is still too soon." There, it was said, and that would be the end of it. She simply would not attend the theater, and her excuses were quite acceptable. She noted the pinched look about Charles's eyes and knew he was not pleased.

"Very well, Jenna. Of course, I would not presume to press you in this regard." Seizing her hand, Charles raised her fingers to his lips. How odd that Jenna felt only a sudden desire to retrieve her hand when all will failed her with Stefan.

"But I warn you, my dearest Jenna. Your mourning will come to an end, and I shall be present to escort you about London, so that all may congratulate us on our betrothal." Charles smiled confidently as he held her hand imprisoned for a moment longer.

"Before the new year is upon us I vow I shall make the announcement."

Jenna smiled silently, not wishing to hear herself repeat the well-worn excuses she had previously offered. Indeed, what excuse could there now be, after her grandfather's death. She was quite alone, and as Emma frequently reminded her, of an appropriate age for marriage and family. Why then did the prospect of marriage seem so dismal and unappealing?

Charles bid her good-bye, lingering for a moment, and then seizing the opportunity to plant an impassioned kiss on her cheek. Jenna was immediately aware that her startled reaction was hardly what Charles had expected.

"Charles, please." Jenna pulled away from his grasp, and noticing Emma beyond the open door, effectively completed her escape.

"Thank you, Charles, for calling, and thank you for your invitation." It was simply spoken, but had the effect Jenna desired. He could not remain without causing himself embarrassment before Emma Kelly.

Charles nodded stiffly, and then seizing his last opportunity to gain the upper hand, bent forward, planting a kiss upon her lips that spoke of familiarity. He barely acknowledged Emma's surprise in her stiffly arched brow as he swept from the room.

Jenna sighed heavily. Charles was determined in his cause, and had made it quite clear that he would have his way in the matter. Jenna forced all thoughts of Charles Wingate from her mind as she turned back to the drawing room, marveling at the exquisite, if lavish beauty of the roses. It was absurd. Where could anyone find so many perfect roses this time of year? Jenna seized the small parchment envelope from the table. The note was penned with firm, strong strokes of the quill to the letters of Stefan Kalinsky's name. And above it, a short, simple message: "To seal our contract." That was all.

Jenna's hands trembled, though hardly from faintness. She could hardly explain the rush of warmth she felt surging through her veins. And yet, even as she read the message, she felt nagging disappointment that she would not be able to accept his invitation to the theater.

Her decision was made. It would hardly seem appropriate for her to accept Stefan's invitation, when she had only moments before refused Charles's. Jenna seized a single bloom from the vase; a small bud of the rose that was yet to be.

She rose early the following morn and busied herself helping Emma make the necessary list for market. The list compiled, she quickly dispensed Maggie and Mr. Flint to purchase the necessary items, and then retreated to the quiet solitude of the rose gardens, which had grown to neglect. The October morning stretched into late afternoon. Jenna looked up from her labors to find Emma scowling at her.

"Here I find you still cutting and digging like a common servant, when there are others to do this. And you have not even touched the meal I prepared for you. Dear child, this is enough for one day. Already the afternoon light is fading, and I have prepared a fine dinner for you."

"Emma, please. I could not bear to look upon the beautiful roses inside, and think of these poor bushes in such a sad state. If they are not attended, there will be no blooms for the next year."

"But 'tis not work for your hands." Emma clucked disapprovingly as she seized Jenna's stained hands.

"Go now, upstairs. Maggie has drawn you a fine, hot bath. And mind you, scrub well. I want no dirt upon those hands when next I see you."

Jenna smiled her resignation as she relinquished the soiled apron she had donned over her gown. When Emma was determined, as she was now, there was simply no point in arguing. She might win her point by authority, but it was hardly worth the woman's sour disposition later.

Jenna mounted the stairway, finding that she was quite stiff from bending over through the long afternoon. Stepping out of the muslin gown, she slipped slowly beneath the steamy surface of the hot bath, losing herself to her thoughts of the elegant roses still fresh in the drawing room. She had earlier dispensed Alexei to Stefan's house to inform him that it was impossible for her to attend the theater that night. Alexei had returned a short time later and said nothing of Stefan's response. So the matter was settled.

Jenna quickly dried and slipped on a silk wrapper, preferring to take her dinner in her room, rather than in the large emptiness of the dining room below. She was ravenous. An abundance of fresh air had done wonders for her appetite. Jenna had just finished a last bite of roast lamb, when she heard the commotion from downstairs. Setting aside the wine glass, Jenna left her chamber to see what was causing such excitement. She halted in stunned surprise at the top of the landing, staring down the wide sweep of the stairway into the most handsome face she had ever seen.

Prince Stefan Kalinsky, resplendent in crimson uniform elaborately decorated with gold braid and worn tightly over equally tight white breeches, slimly tapered into black boots, bowed from the waist as he met Jenna's gaze from the top of the stairs.

"Good evening, Jenna." His blue eyes twinkled warmly, and the curve of his smile had the most devastating effect on her.

Jenna stared in disbelief.

"I asked Alexei to inform you that I could not attend the theater this evening," Jenna managed weakly.

"Alexei is most efficient in his duties. I would not have him with me if he were not. Your message was delivered. But it was quite unacceptable," Stefan responded evenly.

"It would not seem appropriate," Jenna added unconvincingly, when she felt herself drawn into the depths of that azure gaze.

"Jenna, I am well aware of the depth of your loss," Stefan said gently. "You know as well as I, your grandfather would not see you in black to mourn his death. Nor would he deny you your happiness." The last was almost whispered, as if holding his hidden message for her alone.

Jenna's cheeks flushed crimson at his unmistakable

meaning. He could be so very arrogant; arrogant and handsome. She found it impossible to look away from him. Thick waves of golden brown hair framed his head perfectly, accenting the golden-bronze color of his skin. And that thought stirred more memories than she would have dared to admit. Jenna stared uncomfortably into Emma's questioning face. She had made her decision, but Stefan Kalinsky had also made his.

Stefan quickly stepped forward, his booted foot firm on the first step of the stairway, his intent clear in the set of his jaw.

Jenna rushed forward to halt his ascent.

"No. Please, if you will give me a few moments, I will be ready." Jenna deliberately refused to meet Emma's startled glance.

Stefan smiled his small victory.

"Of course, you shall have a few moments. But be certain if you are not ready by the end of the time, then I shall be forced to come up these stairs, and I think that is hardly a fate you would tempt." Stefan smiled confidently as he watched Jenna disappear in a whirl of satin from the top of the stairs. He could think of no better way to enjoy the evening than in the company of the most beautiful young woman in all of London, even if that young woman had chosen to remain distant and aloof. Nor could he deny himself the opportunity to mingle with the titled nobility and elite of London society. It was now his only hope of learning the information Sir Avery Randolph had given his life for.

Chapter Seven

The Theatre Royal, Drury Lane, in the heart of London, glistened like a brilliant star in the center of the universe of mankind. The cobbled streets were crowded with a multitude of richly appointed carriages, as royalty and titled nobility arrived for the first performance of the season and the occasion of the reopening of the theater, after its destruction by fire three years earlier. Gas lamps glowed brightly along the street to light the way, as elegant ladies and their equally elegant escorts alighted from their carriages in the long procession that lined the street.

Jenna and Stefan had ridden the short distance in silence. She was grateful for the darkness that surrounded them, broken only by the soft glow of the gas lamps along the street that briefly outlined his handsome face, making her acutely aware that he studied her intently, his piercing blue gaze reaching across the small expanse of the carriage, then disappearing into darkness as they passed beyond the last lampost. Jenna knew she should have refused his insistent demands that she accompany him. Her refusal had come so easily for Charles. But she was already keenly aware that in the matter of Prince Stefan Kalinsky, her strong-willed determination often deserted her. Only now, as the glow of myriad lights upon the theater facade cast its brilliant invitation into the darkening night, did she have cause to doubt her sanity at such foolishness. She knew of a certainty that Charles and Elizabeth Wingate would be in attendance, for the reopening of the theater had been a much-heralded event for all London Society. Tickets had been sold out for weeks, and the only still available seats belonged to those possessing a theater box. Jenna swallowed uneasily as the driver, elegantly liveried in crimson and gold, reined the perfectly matched team of black horses to a stop a short distance from the theater entrance. Her courage failing her, Jenna lingered momentarily in the safe confines of the carriage. In the next moment all doubts fled before the assault of warmth coursing through Stefan's fingers as he gently reached for her hand, his power and strength invading her, driving away all doubts and fears. Propriety be damned. At that moment, there was no other place she cared to be.

The milling throngs of the cream of society seemed to part momentarily and then close about them in a multicolored wave of silk and velvet, as Stefan led Jenna from the carriage. She felt reassuring strength as Stefan tucked her gloved arm through his. Their gazes met for a brief moment, his lightened mood infecting her with a sense of abandon, the corners of his lips curving slightly into his mysterious smile, as if he guarded some special thought. Jenna felt a sudden warming spread across her cheeks, as she thought of another time when he had flashed her that secretive smile, when they had lain in each other's arms and Stefan had drawn from her a passion she had not known existed. May the devil take the curious stares and slyly whispered comments, of the gossipmongers. Jenna was suddenly aware that it mattered little what others might think. For the first time in days, she felt vibrantly alive, as she had felt that one night when Stefan had taken her sadness and fears and replaced them with fire and passion. Jenna tilted her head a little bit higher as they climbed the last steps to the theater entrance.

Stefan was not unaware of her inner turmoil. His golden head inclined slightly toward hers, as he bent to whisper close beside her.

"It is very much like facing a duel on the field of honor, don't you think?"

Stefan's voice was vibrant and carried an unmistakable warmth that rippled pleasurably through her, sending delightful shivers across her skin. Jenna smiled up at him in answer, thinking that he was quite right.

"There is much danger to be found in both."

"Do you fear such danger, my lovely Jenna?"

Jenna gazed into the depths of his blue gaze, feeling as if everything about them had ceased to exist, as if her only reality was Stefan Kalinsky.

"Only if I should have to face it alone," Jenna answered, suddenly quite wistful as she thought of her grandfather, realizing how much she missed him.

"Then there is nothing for you to fear, little princess, for I vow you shall never be alone." That mysterious smile appeared again briefly and then spread into a wider grin, a devilish light springing into the blue gaze.

"Shall we then rush onto the field and meet our opponent?" He was smiling at her, but his full meaning was not lost to her.

Jenna returned a dazzling smile that set the golden lights blazing in her own amber gaze. At that moment, she might have braved the most formidable enemy for just the next few hours beside him.

Elaborately uniformed attendants accepted the gold-embossed tickets from each patron, escorting those with gallery seating. Those with theater boxes were escorted through the main foyer, up the wide sweeping stairway. The rebuilt theater greatly resembled its predecessor, although a wider gallery had been planned, and the number of individual boxes increased and now connected, separated only by a small half wall to allow privacy. The increased number of boxes greatly added to the theater's capacity for each performance.

Jenna's attention was drawn to Stefan's ticket as the attendant accepted it. The embossed gold seal of the prince regent was brightly displayed. They were quickly escorted up the stairway to the arched opening that led to the span

121

of boxes reserved for royal patrons. She hesitated momentarily as the attendant stood aside for them to pass through to their seats within the royal enclosure, immediately to the left of the duke of Kent and his mistress.

Stefan's golden brows lifted slightly as he noted her hesitation.

"If you object to the seating, other arrangements might be made." Stefan eyed her oddly, as if sensing some reservation.

Jenna was aware that the duke of Kent had turned in his seat to greet them. She leaned forward discreetly, fixing Stefan with a dazzling smile.

"Certainly, I have no objections. It is only that I had not thought it possible for you to acquire such fine seating when you have been in England such a short time," Jenna whispered, the fresh scent of her hair filling his senses as she leaned against his arm, the swell of her breast pressing into him.

"My dear Jenna, I have been in England for quite some time. The invitation was extended by the duke of Kent."

Jenna turned a thoughtful gaze on Stefan Kalinsky as they took their chairs. She had not been aware that he was personally acquainted with the duke of Kent. A memory stirred. Her grandfather had worked closely with the duke of Kent. There had been many private meetings between the two men at her home, instead of at the less private royal residence. She gazed thoughtfully at the Duke of Kent, a man very near fifty years old, and Madame St. Laurent, his mistress of long standing. Jenna wondered what her grandfather's acquaintance with Stefan Kalinsky had been. Stefan had spoken of matters of great importance regarding her grandfather on the night of the fire. Her suddenly pensive mood was interrupted by the fanfare from the orchestra as the esteemed Mr. Elliston, favored actor in the theater, came forward to give the opening address for the evening. Moments later, the curtain rose on the first act of *Hamlet*, the Shakespearean tragedy, and Jenna lost herself to the performance.

* * *

The audience applauded the fine actors appreciatively as the curtain was lowered for intermission after the third act. Jenna's smile was radiant with her enjoyment of the evening. Her wide amber gaze swept from the stage as she felt the pressure of Stefan's hand upon hers. He drew her against him momentarily, as they stood aside to allow the duke of Kent to pass through the arched, velvet-draped entrance.

"You are enjoying the play?" Stefan whispered warmly against the curve of her cheek.

Jenna's hands were flattened against his chest, but she hardly resisted against the pressure of his embrace as his arms closed about her. She breathlessly smiled her answer, as they stood a moment longer secluded in the shadows of the heavily draped partition. The box was completely empty now, and only a handful of people milled about on the floor of the theater.

"I think, my little princess, that if we do not join the other guests, we may provide tonight's guests with a greater subject for scandal. Be warned my love, I am not above finding our pleasure in a darkened corner."

Jenna's cheeks flamed crimson at his obvious meaning, and she vainly tried to pull away from his unrelenting hold on her. He could be maddeningly arrogant, maddeningly handsome when he looked at her as he was looking at her now, as if he might easily have made love to her there in the balcony of the theater. But more than his arrogance, Jenna was unnerved by her own lack of resistance. She knew well if he had chosen to take her there, in the corner where they stood, she would have offered him no resistance, such was the uncontrollable passion he had released within her.

Stefan chuckled low against her ear, the sound rumbling from low in his chest.

"Are you so distressed, little one, to realize that you desire me, as I desire you?"

"Stefan, please. . . ." Jenna's protests were silenced under the pressure of his lips against hers. She felt herself drawn tighter into the strength of his embrace, as if she might melt into him. She felt no will to resist. A flame

123

ignited within her brain and seemed to flood through her entire being. The full, firm roundness of her breasts, exposed above the scooping neckline of her gown, pressed into the heavy gold satin cording of his tunic. Her slender arms wrapped possessively about his strong neck, molding him to her, and she responded with a fire of her own that made him breathless, as none before her ever had.

Stefan fought to regain his shaken composure. Gently he seized her slender wrists and held her away from him. He was aware that she was more than a litle shaken by her own response. Suddenly uneasy, she refused to meet his slightly amused gaze. Stefan raised her gloved hand to his lips, tenderly kissing her fingers. His humor increased as he saw her inner struggle to master her shaken composure.

"Perhaps we should join the others. I think a strong port wine will restore your spirit."

"There is nothing wrong with my spirit," Jenna retorted defensively, as she quickly brushed past Stefan, his low chuckling of humor rankling her temper. Why should he enjoy a joke at her expense?

Beyond the confines of the theater box, Jenna and Stefan joined the other guests for wine to celebrate the reopening of the theatre. Familiar faces passed among the crowd as they joined the duke of Kent. Jenna watched carefully for sight of Charles, and wondered what her excuses might be if he approached. her. She was silently grateful for the press of the crowd, which hardly allowed for milling about and socializing with anyone other than those beyond their small circle. Stefan was involved in some lengthy discussion with the duke of Kent, and Jenna relaxed somewhat as she sipped her wine.

"Jenna, what a surprise to find you here!"

Unable to escape in the crowd that surrounded her, Jenna turned around to smile weakly at Elizabeth Wingate.

"Jenna, I am so glad to see that you decided to attend this evening. I believe a bit of entertainment to be the best cure for sadness. Although Charles seemed certain you would not attend." Elizabeth looked past Jenna, in an obvious attempt to learn the identity of Jenna's escort for the evening. Her eyes widened in stunned surprise as Prince Stefan Kalinsky bowed formally in acknowledgment.

"Your highness, how thoughtful of you to escort Jenna this evening," Elizabeth stammered excitedly.

Jenna suddenly felt as if her knees would not support her. She inhaled deeply as she met her friend's inquisitive gaze. She hardly knew what explanation she might offer.

"You are most kind, Mademoiselle Wingate. I, too, could not bear the thought of Jenna's continued mourning. As it is, I had promised her grandfather some time ago that I would be honored to escort Jenna to the opening of the theater season. I felt bound to honor my promise to so fine a gentleman."

Jenna's stunned gaze met Stefan's, twinkling with high humor at the lie he had told. He had managed to make their relationship seem most innocent and acceptable. He was indeed not only a skilled highwayman, but a most accomplished liar. With those mesmerizing blue eyes and that irresistible smile, she had no doubt he could charm a miser out of his last coin.

"Is Sir Charles with you this evening? We have a most interesting conversation to finish," Stefan continued.

Jenna silently grated her teeth in misery. He was deliberately trying to provoke a confrontation with Charles. She silently vowed to take better aim, when next she held a gun on him.

"Charles decided not to attend. He mentioned something about meeting his friends at the club. He was quite disappointed that you refused his invitation, Jenna," Elizabeth added as she turned a coquettish smile on Stefan Kalinsky.

Stefan's gaze narrowed perceptively.

"Does Sir Charles frequent Watier's often?" It was an artfully disguised question to gain more information.

Jenna stared at Stefan thoughtfully, unable to understand his sudden interest in Charles's choice of clubs.

"Charles does not attend Watier's. He belongs to White's, as does Father," Elizabeth offered innocently. She then proceeded to engage Jenna in some inane chatter about young ladies they were both acquainted with, and their escorts.

Jenna only responded vaguely to Elizabeth's idle chatter, nodding absently, or mumbling some reply. She was more interested in Stefan's sudden change of mood. She watched him thoughtfully as he excused himself for a moment and disappeared through the crowd.

"Jenna, you simply must tell me everything about him," Elizabeth whispered excitedly, an attractive pink flush spreading across her plain features.

Jenna turned back to her friend, unaware that Elizabeth had watched as her gaze followed Stefan's tall, commanding form through the throng of people.

"What were you saying?" Jenna murmured absently.

"My dear Jenna, the most spectacular moment of the evening was not the curtain raising on the first performance in three years, but learning who would attend with Prince Stefan Kalinsky. Carolyn Lamb is quite beside herself. It is said that she held off accepting Lord Byron's invitation, in vain hopes that Prince Kalinsky might favor her for the evening. Who would ever have guessed he was to be your escort? Although, as I remember from the ball, he was absolutely taken with you."

"Elizabeth, please. I was not aware you were given to spreading senseless rumors."

"Ah, but these are hardly senseless. I have it on good faith that Carolyn Lamb has already moved from the London residence she has shared with Lord Byron these last two years, to make herself available to his highness. And you can hardly deny the well-known fact of his acquaintance with Madame de Stahl."

Jenna turned to stare at her friend. She could not deny that everyone about London knew quite well that Prince Stefan Kalinsky had been seen in the company of Madame de Stahl on several occasions, even returning from her residence at very indiscreet times of the night. She could hardly deny it, since she had been witness to at least one of his late-night excursions when she had accepted his hospitality before moving into Hallston House. Jenna's high spirits suddenly faded before the truth she could not deny. Before she could find some excuse for Elizabeth, she noticed that flirtatious smile returning. There was only one who seemed capable of drawing such a response from her shy friend. Jenna turned about as Stefan Kalinsky moved easily through the crowd of people. He returned Elizabeth's smile, but his gaze was locked with Jenna's. Quite masterfully, he reached for Jenna's slender hand, taking it possessively in his own.

"You must forgive me, Jenna. I have been called away. But it is my wish that you remain for the rest of the performance. Dmitri will accompany you, and escort you home after the play."

Jenna stared past Stefan at Dmitri's imposing height and width as the large man met with little resistance passing through the foyer of the theater. She turned back to Stefan, at a loss to understand what might be of such importance to call him away. He had left shortly after Elizabeth joined them. Jenna's thoughts raced back over their conversation, wondering what might have prompted such urgency. She could think of nothing other than idle pleasantries; except Charles's unexpected absence. She searched the depths of Stefan's gaze, suddenly aware that she had struck at the heart of the matter. Elizabeth had volunteered that Charles had decided to meet friends at White's. She was not unaware of the undercurrent of intense dislike between the two men.

"Stefan?" Jenna's fingers closed around his, holding him beside her for a moment longer.

Stefan's blue gaze softened to a gentle glow at the sound of his name upon her lips. "Do not frown so, little princess; there is nothing wrong. Only a matter that I must attend to; matters of political importance that I fear you would find quite boring."

Jenna was not fooled. Behind the handsome mask that

had fallen into place, she sensed a certain urgency. She might be wrong. It might have nothing to do with Charles Wingate and his friends at White's. She hesitated for a moment longer, as Stefan made his farewell to Elizabeth and then turned to leave the theater. She reached uncertainly for his arm, her gloved hand brushing the sleeve of his uniform. Stefan turned back for a brief moment, and she felt again that silent message that seemed to be theirs alone. She could not deny a sudden coldness that seemed to grip her heart, as if something were very wrong.

"You will be careful?"

That mysterious smile pulled at the corners of his mouth. "I am quite flattered by your concern, little princess. There is nothing to fear. My only regret is that I must shorten our evening together."

Jenna tried once more. "Charles has a most violent temper. He carries a small pistol inside his waistcoat."

Stefan stared at Jenna in stunned surprise. He had said nothing of his intentions, yet she had somehow guessed his destination. Her warning to him meant far more than any spoken concern for his safety. She had innocently given him proof of her innocence in the conspiracy. At that moment he wanted nothing more than to take her into his arms, and again feel the soft, beguiling warmth of her slender body molded against his. He faintly acknowledged the warning she had given him with a slight bow of his head. His gaze seemed to devour her as he raised her hand to his lips, and Jenna's breath caught in her throat at the boldness of his silent message.

Stefan Kalinsky turned quickly on his heel. Making his polite excuses to others in the crowd, he disappeared through the large double doors of the theater.

Jenna felt the discomforting stares of others in the foyer, as she turned back toward Elizabeth. She chose to ignore the questioning stares as one matron whispered slyly to another. Her gaze was filled with the imposing sight of Dmitri as he stood before her like some great giant, uncomfortable in the confines of the elaborate uniform he had been forced to wear. She could not suppress a smile of humor at the sight of the tall man.

"It is good to see you smile, little one. There is too much sadness about with the war the French emperor brings. One so beautiful is not meant to be sad."

"Dmitri, are you quite certain you are not part Irish?" Jenna fixed her large companion with a radiant smile.

Dmitri looked back at her uncertainly, not at all sure how he might be mistaken for being Irish.

Jenna laughed good-naturedly as she accepted his arm to follow the other guests back to their seats for the next act of the play. She cast one last glance over her shoulder at the large doors to the theater.

"Do not fear, little one. He will not come to harm." Dmitri spoke gruffly as he watched the direction of her gaze.

Jenna's cheeks suddenly flamed with her embarrassment that her feelings were so obvious to the burly Russian.

"There is no harm in truth, little one," Dmitri added as he gazed ahead over the heads of those ahead of them, seemingly unaware of the curious stare she fixed on him.

"But there is perhaps great harm in idle speculation," Jenna countered, hoping to end the conversation.

Dmitri seemed to find great humor in her discomfort. He roared with laughter as he firmly held her hand upon his arm. Jenna withdrew her hand, suddenly uncomfortable that her feelings should be so obvious to the towering Cossack. Russians, she decided, were all arrogant and insufferable, and far too honest for discretion.

"I think, perhaps, my young prince has met his match. It will be a great pleasure to see who offers the next challenge."

Jenna's cheeks flamed brilliantly, and the air in the theater seemed to have become quite stifling as she passed through the arched entrance to their box, Dmitri following close behind. The gaslights were suddenly dimmed about the theater, and Jenna was able to retreat into the temporary safety of darkness as the curtain raised on the fourth act of the play. Behind her Dmitri, took up his solitary post as escort and protector.

The great Shakespearean tragedy ended to a thunderous round of applause. The gaslights flickered momentarily and then glowed brilliantly in the theater as the performance was ended and the guests rose to find their carriages outside.

Jenna rode in the open carriage, lost to her own thoughts as she contemplated the evening, and wondered what course Stefan had taken after leaving the theater. Across from her, Dmitri too rode in silence, his great bulk having trouble remaining upon the seat. She was certain he would have preferred to ride a horse. He was so quiet that had it not been for the sparkle of his dark eyes, glistening like two live coals, she might have thought him to be dozing. She knew, though, that he would follow Stefan's instructions completely, and that included seeing her safely home for the evening. Stefan's carriage rounded the park across from Hallston House. The driver sent the team clattering up the wide sweep of the cobbled drive, reining them to a stop before the steps to the main entrance. Dmitri quickly scrambled out of the carriage and assisted Jenna down the two narrow steps. Alexei stood waiting for her with an oil lantern to light the steps. The two men exchanged brief greetings in Russian, and then Dmitri called to the driver and settled his huge frame into the carriage for the short drive to Stefan's town house.

In her own second-floor chamber, Jenna quickly undressed, laying her gown over the chair beside the dressing table. She loosened the pins in her hair, letting the heavy, thick mass cascade down the length of her back. Deciding against the silken chemise, she slipped beneath the heavy coverlet, luxuriating in the feel of the linen sheets against her naked skin, as she had that night with Stefan.

The room took on the chill of early autumn, and Jenna snuggled further into the depths of the down bed, for a while content with her own solitary warmth, until her dreams returned again to haunt her with the vision of a lean, golden body entwined with her own, so real that she could feel the heat of his fingers boldly exploring her, eliciting from her a soft moan that escaped her parted lips. Suddenly coming fully awake, Jenna stared wide-eyed into the darkness of the chamber, her skin fevered with silent longing to feel his touch upon her again. She trembled as she tentatively touched the firm, taut peak of her breast, a deep, longing ache suddenly filling her with a consuming need, a need she had discovered with Stefan. She turned away from the truth of the longing that welled within her, but it was some hours before sleep again released Jenna from her silent torment.

Through the next days, with no word from Stefan, Jenna could only fear the worst after his hasty departure from the opening night at the theater. Her fears were heightened by the memory of Charles Wingate's unreasonable anger in matters past; to be eased only when Dmitri finally appeared at Hallston House to hastily inform her that Stefan had been called away from London the last days. Dmitri's sudden appearance at the servants' entrance threw Emma Kelly into fits of turmoil. He was a man accustomed to strict military code, with little thought to the more refined elements of city life. His imposing presence in an elegantly furnished dining room or in Emma's spotless kitchen unnerved the woman. She disliked finding a muddied boot heel on her gleaming, polished floors. His gruff manners, acquired in the company of men rather than in a formal household, reduced Emma to much muttering and head-shaking. For herself, Jenna welcomed his visit, for it gave her the reassurance she needed of Stefan's safety.

Charles Wingate, however, was another matter. Sunday afternoon, the day after the theater, Charles had appeared unannounced and sought to reduce her to tears for her lack of manners, or affection. Whatever reaction Charles had sought, he failed miserably, and he had left as quickly as he had arrived, his lean, angular face quite flushed, either with the effort of his speech, or with restrained fury, Jenna was not certain. Two days later, Charles sent his man,

Langley, with a formal invitation for her to dine at the Wingate estate. Jenna accepted only out of courtesy to Elizabeth. She hardly felt inclined toward more of Charles's lectures on her behavior. But the evening had been a pleasant surprise. Warm and charming, Charles's manner had reminded Jenna of how he could be when not ruled by anger. It had been an enjoyable evening, followed by Charles's insistence that they plan a day for riding through nearby Kensington Gardens. Jenna had hesitated at first, reluctant to encourage Charles's attentions, but the last weeks of sadness and confinement after her grandfather's illness had finally convinced her to accept his invitation.

Afterwards, she had cause to regret her decision.

As the day arrived, she hardly felt in the mood for a ride. Indeed, the last days she had been short-tempered and uneasy, and completely at a loss to understand the cause. More than once, upon hearing a heavy-booted foot on the wood floor in the foyer, she had anxiously flown down the wide stairway, only to find Dmitri or Mr. Flint conversing with Alexei or one of the maids. It disconcerted her no small amount to find that she constantly listened for Stefan's footfalls in the entry or his voice in conversation at the front door. His thoughts or concern for her seemed quite obvious. Hers for him she understood less easily.

Jenna idly stared out the paned window of the drawing room. Crisp morning and evening temperatures, leaving a mantle of frost upon the ground, had taken the last of the roses from the gardens at Hallston House. She was a vision of elegantly restrained energy, dressed in a riding gown of rich dark brown velvet, the color glowing with golden light next to the peach-hued softness of her skin. A collar of satin-edged brown velvet stood high at the back of her neck, sweeping low in front to meet across the front of the bodice, held together with brown satin closures. The white lace-edged collar of her underblouse snugly fit the slender column of her throat. A single satin ribbon of the same rich brown color had been tied over the lace collar, much like a man's cravat. The puff of slightly flounced sleeves was inset with rich brown satin inside the folds, then tapered snugly over her slender arms, flaring into cuffs turned back at the wrist, revealing a border of the same satin ribbon and the elegant white sleeves of the underblouse, also edged with delicate lace. The bodice of the gown tapered to a form-fitting waistline beneath her well-curved breasts, the skirt falling away just above her slender booted feet. A small brown velvet hat with a narrow brim was set upon the mass of carefully coiled hair, a long, dark veil trailing down her back. Soft leather riding gloves on the sofa table waited only for her hands.

Chapter Eight

Kensington Gardens was an elegant pastoral panorama of country manors, enhanced by the presence of Kensington House at the end of the well-groomed green connecting a varied display of gardens and pathways. Kensington House had served as primary residence first to Queen Mary, nearly one hundred and fifty years earlier. The accomplishment of the noted architect, William Wren, the rambling red brick mansion now served as residence for members of the royal family other than the sovereign, most notably the duke of Kent.

Jenna held a firm hand on the reins of the gray stallion Mr. Flint had saddled for her. While other fashionable young ladies preferred the relative comforts of riding in open carriages, Jenna preferred the singular freedom to be found on horseback.

The morning air was brisk, and the gray snorted with high spirit as he strained against the bit, trying without success to gain firm control of the bridle. Charles had been right about one thing—the ride had been good for her. Jenna's spirits matched those of the gray, as if she had too long strained against some invisible bonds and now anxiously sought to break free of them. She knew Charles would have much preferred the confines of the carriage, for his own purposes. Riding atop a horse hardly afforded the opportunity for the private, lingering conversations that Jenna was determined to avoid. She knew well the direction such conversations would lead. Charles's horse sidled nervously at the screeching of nearby children at play, and Jenna stifled a mischievous smile as she overheard Charles's muttered curse beneath his breath. Without waiting for Charles to reach her side, Jenna eased her hold on the reins and urged the gray forward, herself eager to feel the rush of wind against her face.

With great skill, Jenna guided the gray away from the slower-moving procession of carriages on the cobbled pathway that wound leisurely along the green from Kensington House to the royal gardens. She expertly negotiated a set of quick turns along the well-traveled pathway as she sent the gray toward the open field ahead, which was golden brown with the dry, pungent grass, dampened by recent rain. Somewhere behind her she heard Charles calling after her, but she paid little heed. Much like the stallion, she could no longer contain the energy within that demanded release. She knew the gray was a skilled jumper, and with little regard for propriety, she sent him thundering toward the expanse of split-rail fencing that bordered the field. The wind rushed against her face with such force that she could not draw a breath of air. Her eyes watered, and the vision of the fence before her blurred momentarily. Feeling the magnificent ripple of muscles of the fine animal beneath her, Jenna crouched low, touching her riding crop against the column of his finely arched neck, demanding an extra burst of speed as they catapulted toward the fence. For one breathless moment Jenna felt that singular exhilaration of flight, as the gray gathered himself, and launched across the fence, landing easily on the other side, continuing their abandoned flight without missing a pace.

Following the course of a narrow stream, Jenna felt the gray tiring beneath her. She eased their pace and met no resistance as she held a firm rein, until the stallion had slowed to a walk.

"There, my fine friend. A good run was all that was needed. I fear you, like myself, grow weary of our confinement of late. We shall take a run more often."

Jenna firmly patted the animal's warm neck as she reined in to let him drink briefly from the stream. On a grassy knoll on the far side of the stream, Jenna's wandering gaze watched a carriage beneath the spread of a giant oak tree. An elegantly gowned lady, whose face was hidden behind the curve of her hat, seemed to be alone, except for her driver. In the next moment, Jenna saw the form of a lone rider emerge from the far side of the carriage. The rider circled around toward the lady. Jenna hesitated as she started to turn the gray about. There was an odd familiarity about the rider. She watched for a moment longer, her answer coming as the man turned to the side in conversation with the lady. Jenna stared in stunned surprise as she recognized that lean, well-tanned profile. Without seeing them, she was certain of the brilliant blue color of his eyes. And the elegantly gowned lady with wide-brimmed hat was none other than Madame de Stahl, the sun illuminating her round face as she gazed up at Stefan.

Jenna stared for a moment longer at the two who conversed with such rapt attention for one another, a frown wrinkling the smooth perfection of her brow. Deep inside she felt a sudden wrenching that left her unable to draw a deep breath. She was unaware that Charles had finally reached her side, and was easing his own mount to the stream's edge.

Charles Wingate followed Jenna's gaze to the far side of the stream. He immediately recognized the elegant lady and the horseman beside her carriage. His gray eyes narrowed keenly as he noted Jenna's troubled expression. A slight smile twitched perceptively on his thin lips. He had hoped for just such a moment as this.

"It would seem his highness, Prince Kalinsky, has already found the advantages of this secluded location, although his relationship with Madame de Stahl is well known about London. Those of royal blood always consider themselves above other men, as if they possess some singular power. One day they will all be made to realize their blood flows as easily as any man's," Charles added with a sudden coldness in his voice that Jenna failed to understand, for certainly his own family was distantly connected with that of the regent.

Across the stream, Stefan's fine black stallion responded to the gray, momentarily drawing his attention to the far side of the stream. Through Alexei, he had been aware of Jenna's plans to ride with Charles Wingate from the moment the invitation had been given. He tipped his head slightly in acknowledgment, well aware of her cool, stilted response. His eyes narrowed as he studied Charles Wingate, and the look of smug satisfaction that spread across his lean, sallow features. Stefan had known quite well what Jenna's reaction would be. He leaned forward, seizing Lillian de Stahl's gloved hand and bringing it to his lips, feeling no satisfaction in the game he played. The sound of departing horses was the reaction he had hoped for.

Well rested, the gray stallion once more grew restless under Jenna's hand and snorted his displeasure at their delay. Jenna's hands tightened on the riding crop, as if it were some weapon she contemplated using as she glanced once more at the couple across the stream, now engaged in what seemed a most intimate conversation.

"I have had quite enough of riding for one day. It has suddenly become quite cold. I should like to return home," Jenna said solemnly, feeling as if she had suddenly been drained of all energy. She turned the gray about and urged him into a gentle canter, until they were some distance from the stream and Stefan Kalinsky.

They rode for a short while in silence, Charles quite content to allow Jenna to contemplate her encounter with Stefan. Emerging from the woods very near Kensington House, Charles sought to press his advantage.

"Jenna, it has been some time since your grandfather's death. I was hoping you might now consider announcing our betrothal." His careful suggestion not meeting with Jenna's usual excuses, Charles pressed his cause.

"You must now think to your future. Certainly you must be aware of my feelings for you. Your happiness is most important now. I am certain Sir Avery would agree with me if he were alive. Father and Elizabeth are making plans for the Christmas holidays in the country, after the usual round of parties and celebrations. I would like very much if you would consider our announcing our betrothal then. It would be most appropriate with everyone together."

Jenna stared moodily ahead, concentrating on the path underfoot, when she had hardly given it a moment's thought in her wild run through the woods earlier. She could offer Charles no valid argument against his plans. None, except that she knew she did not return his feelings. Try as she might, she could not rid herself of the vision of Stefan Kalinsky, his golden hair and sun-bronzed skin. She willed herself to be angry for the hurt he had brought her. How foolish she had been to think that he cared for her in some small measure. That night when he had protected her from the storm and taken her to his chamber, she had thought he cared. She realized how impossible it had been. His reputation was well known. It had been there from the very beginning, only she had refused to see it. She had seen the proof in the gowns she had found in the room at his home. He had promised her nothing. And yet, at that very moment, in her deepest despair, Jenna could not deny that she would gladly have gone to him again, if only for a short time, to feel the exquisite passion he had given her. She nodded her lovely head absently, hardly hearing Charles's words.

"If you wish, I will say nothing until the announcement at the Christmas celebration. It will be a delightful surprise. I know how pleased Father will be, and of course Elizabeth. She has long thought of you as her sister."

Jenna looked up as they passed the royal residence. "Please, Charles, must we discuss this now?"

"Of course, my darling, how inconsiderate of me. Until Christmas then, this will be our little secret."

Jenna sighed wearily, feeling only a nagging annoyance at his persistence. Charles immediately took her silence for agreement, leaning forward to press her hand affectionately. Jenna pulled away abruptly, feeling increased aggravation at his attentions. Why was it that she could not feel some measure of caring for Charles? Was it merely her grandfather's vague, unspoken objections, or was it the lingering memory of another man's caresses that made it impossible for her to consider another? She urged the gray stallion to a greater pace, unable fully to understand her anger with Charles, when Stefan had brought her such pain.

Lillian de Stahl leaned back into the carriage, staring speculatively at the handsome Russian, knowing quite well his thoughts were not on her.

"My dearest Stefan, you play a most desperate game. I fear for you." Madame de Stahl smiled softly as she gazed into that crystal-blue gaze, wishing circumstances might have been different. At thirty-eight years of age, Lillian de Stahl no longer resorted to coquettish charms to entice men to her side. Her affairs were numerous and well known. But the one man she continually sought to lure to her bed chose to remain merely her friend.

"Dear Lillian, there is nothing to fear, when the jackal remains in its lair." Stefan smiled devilishly as he kissed her hand.

"Quite true, my brave prince. But the jackal now seeks fairer prey, and may yet draw you out. I know well your feelings for Sir Randolph's granddaughter. Guard well that your feelings do not endanger you both. The jackal can be a deadly enemy."

Stefan's smile faded as he met the beautiful woman's gaze evenly, that azure gaze suddenly as cold as ice.

"Then the jackal must be struck down," he whispered harshly as his gaze returned to the far side of the stream where Jenna had been a moment before.

Jenna stormed through the front door of Hallston House, the loud slamming of the massive doors behind her evidence of the fine temper that raged within her. Her amber gaze, alive with inner fire, met Emma's startled expression as the housekeeper came quickly from the drawing room, a feather duster raised in her hand uncertainly.

"Saints preserve us all. Have the French invaded England?" Emma asked uncertainly, as she noted the feverish light in Jenna's golden gaze.

Jenna fumed silently as she removed her riding gloves and threw them, together with the leather riding crop, upon the long table in the hallway. She struggled for some inner control. Damn Stefan Kalinsky! Damn him! Damn her own foolishness! Hadn't she been warned of his reputation? Even dear, sweet Elizabeth had been completely taken in by his charming manner. Jenna fought back the haunting memory of ice-blue eyes, and the lean handsome strength of his tanned face. Damn his arrogance, and his eyes, and the touch of his fingers against her skin. The memory betrayed her even in her moment of anger. Gazing about her in sudden desire for vengeance, Jenna seized a porcelain figurine and sent it hurtling against the hearth across the room. The figurine shattered against the finely cut stone of the hearth. Maggie rushed from the kitchen. The young maid stared in stunned surprise at the shattered figurine on the carpet before the hearth. Emma warned the young girl to silence and waved her from the room.

"Of all the arrogant, insufferable boorish behavior," Jenna spat out as she at last found some release for the anger within.

"I fear your grandfather was quite right about Sir Charles. You seem ever at odds with each other," Emma ventured cautiously.

"This has nothing to do with Charles," Jenna fumed as she whirled about and started for the stairway.

"I will have Maggie bring hot water for your bath." Emma called after her, not wishing to pursue the matter of her mistress's anger when she was in such a high temper. Emma Kelly had learned well when it was best to leave matters until a later time.

Jenna charged through the door to her own chamber, slamming it with great force behind her.

"The house is well built. But I am not certain it is strong enough, if you insist on slamming each door."

Startled, Jenna whirled about in stunned surprise at the sight of Stefan Kalinsky.

"Dear Jenna, I know how angry you must be. . . ." he began.

Jenna stared at him incredulously.

"You are bold. How dare you come here! What gives you the right to walk into my home? Get out of here now," Jenna ordered, her voice rising with her mounting anger as she turned back to the door, intent on being rid of the man who had caused her such torment.

"Jenna, I must speak with you," Stefan began, staring at the exquisite young woman before him. She was extraordinarily beautiful, especially now, with stray wisps of her dark hair trailing about her face, the color high in her cheeks. A warning sparked in the depths of her amber eyes, which narrowed almost catlike as she faced him.

"There is nothing you can say that I wish to hear. Leave this house at once or I shall be forced to call for Alexei."

An amused smile played across Stefan's lips, having a maddening effect on Jenna's badly shaken composure.

"I hardly think Alexei will interfere in such matters. He has his orders."

Jenna stared at him as a slowly dawning realization took hold.

"And I suppose that was your reason in offering me this house, so that you might come and go as you please. Let me assure you, you are quite wrong." Jenna whirled about, intent on finding some assistance in removing him from her bedroom. Her path was blocked as Stefan moved between her and the door.

"Jenna, there is so much you do not understand. I had hoped it would not be necessary to involve you, but now I find there is no other way." Stefan's hands closed around Jenna's arms as he drew her toward him.

Jenna twisted within his grasp, intent on gaining her freedom. "Let me go," she spat from between clenched teeth, her flaring temper blinding her to all reason except being rid of Stefan Kalinsky.

"I will let you go after you have listened to what must be said." Roughly Stefan pulled Jenna across the room and pushed her into the high-backed chair that sat before the hearth.

Jenna immediately started up out of the chair, but found her way soundly blocked by the lean hardness of Stefan's body. His arms closed about her, as he saw no other way to gain her attention.

"Jenna, I do not want to hurt you. You must listen to me." With gentle but forceful strength, Stefan grabbed both Jenna's wrists, pinning them behind her back as she tried to strike at him. He pulled her slender body against him in a viselike embrace that forced the air from her lungs, quelling further objections as she struggled just to draw a single breath.

Jenna stamped her booted foot in frustration, failing to make any contact that might have caused him pain. She ground her teeth in silent agony, realizing she was soundly caught. She might scream until she was hoarse, but she knew that none would come to her rescue. Indeed, she was certain Alexei would carry out Stefan's instructions completely. Her head thrown back, she stared at Stefan warily. If he thought the matter so easily settled, he was in for quite a surprise. Gathering her strength, Jenna stood motionless within his embrace. Her thoughts were in complete turmoil. She was angry. She wanted desperately to hate him, and yet standing there molded against his body, feeling the strength of his arms about her, she felt only a desire never to leave his embrace. Jenna closed her eyes as she felt the tears well within her. The last thing she wanted was for him to see her weakness.

Stefan felt the trembling in her slender body and knew the conflict that raged within her. His voice was low and oddly muffled against her ear as he pressed her against him.

"I never meant to cause you pain, my little princess. How I wish that I might protect you forever."

Jenna might more easily have dealt with his aloofness or his arrogance. She found it impossible to deal with his tenderness. She tried to pull away from him, fearing the emotions that flamed within her, feeling her resistance wavering dangerously under the assault of his nearness.

"Jenna, you must listen. Listen to what I have to say. Then if you wish me to leave, I shall go without another word. But you must first listen," Stefan continued. Jenna ceased struggling, though she remained wary and unyielding within his embrace.

"My dearest Jenna, how can I say this and not cause you pain?" Stefan struggled to find the words that might ease the shock of what he was about to say. He could find none. His arms about Jenna tightened, as if he might protect her in some small measure. "Jenna, the night of the Wingate Ball, when you returned to find your grandfather dead, there was much more that you did not see. I had thought it possible that you would never need to know of it."

"What are you saying?" Jenna whispered hoarsely.

Stefan held her gently in his arms, cushioning her small head against his shoulder. It tore at him to cause her pain, and yet he knew no other way.

"To all who entered the room that night and knew of your grandfather's recent illness, it appeared that his heart had failed. Before Mr. Flint was to return for you, he checked one last time on your grandfather, and found him slumped upon his desk. Mr. Flint also found signs of struggle, papers scattered about the library, although your grandfather was hardly in any condition to protect himself against attack. His heart failed in the struggle. Whoever attacked Sir Avery knew well of his condition. Under orders of the regent, your grandfather's physician was convinced to say nothing of the matter." Stefan pressed a kiss against Jenna's hair as he held her tightly. He could feel a faint trembling in her slender shoulders.

"I don't understand. Why would anyone want to harm my grandfather?" A sob escaped as Jenna tried to find some understanding of what he was saying.

"Because of what he knew."

"What are you talking about? Stefan, please, I don't understand anything you are saying."

Stefan gently lowered Jenna into the wing-backed chair before the hearth, his lean, strong hands holding hers.

"I was not certain of your innocence in all of this, not until the evening of the play, when you warned me against Charles Wingate. I knew then that you knew nothing of the conspiracy."

Jenna stared at him in confusion.

"What conspiracy? Stefan, what are you talking about?"

"You must never say anything of what I am about to tell you. Not to anyone. Your life and many others' may well depend upon it." Stefan stared at her solemnly.

Jenna nodded her agreement.

"I knew your grandfather quite well. We met many years ago, when I was a young student at Oxford. We were introduced by the duchess of York, who is also my first cousin. I greatly admired your grandfather as a man of integrity and honor. I returned to France, and did not meet with Sir Avery again until I was forced to leave my country, when my lands were confiscated by Napoleon. Through Sir Avery, I found acceptance in England. Through your grandfather, it was possible for me to bring my family out of France to safety. My debt to your grandfather was enormous, one I felt I could never repay."

"I don't understand what this has to do with my grandfather's death," Jenna interrupted with mounting confusion.

"In his work over the last two years, your grandfather discovered a conspiracy against the English Crown. At first he was reluctant to believe what he had learned. But after the assassination of the prime minister last spring, he could no longer deny the possibility of a conspiracy. Because of his position in the prime minister's cabinet, because of his outspoken loyalty to the Crown, he found it impossible to learn more of the conspiracy. He had only been able to learn that it was part of a plan to seize control of England for Napoleon. If England fell, Napoleon's domination of the entire world would be assured, with only the American colonies to stand in his way. Because I was privileged to certain social circles and private clubs, Sir Avery enlisted my aid to learn what I could of the conspiracy. In the last months before his death, we had learned that the conspiracy possibly involved those of the nobility, with certain access to the regent. However, we failed to learn the identities of the conspirators. I cannot help but think we must have been very close to learning their names. Someone knew what Sir Avery was about and feared what he might have learned. The success of the conspiracy depended on your grandfather's silence."

Jenna stared at Stefan in stunned disbelief, her mind not willing to accept what he had told her, yet unable to deny the secrecy and desperation that had surrounded her grandfather's work over the last months. It easily explained the conferences behind closed doors with members of the prime minister's staff, and the evasive answers Sir Avery had offered her when she pressed him as to the importance of work that robbed him of his health. Her last conversation with her grandfather in the library, on the night of his death, had told her more than she'd realized. He had spoken of some great threat that endangered them all. Jenna only now understood what he had spoken of. Indeed, there had been great danger, and her grandfather had given his life to stop that threat. Jenna rose on shaky knees as the dreadful truth filled her thoughts.

"My grandfather was murdered?" she whispered as she stared up at Stefan, the wide depths of her amber gaze filled with the tears of her pain and confusion. All resistance, all anger of the moments before had flown.

Stefan seized Jenna by the arms, once more folding her within his embrace, meeting with no resistance now, as he felt the trembling of her sobbing.

"My little princess, I never wished to cause you such pain." His voice was hoarse with his own emotion as he fought back his own anger and frustration that he had not

146

been able to protect her from this harsh truth. His lips warmly brushed her forehead. Gently he stroked the silken softness of her hair.

Jenna turned her gaze to search his. She saw her own torment mirrored in the depths of his blue eyes. Her lips parted in silent question, a sob escaping. Her mind had only just begun to accept the horrible truth he had given her, and deep within she felt an aching that demanded ease.

The anguish he saw in the amber depths of her wide eyes tore at Stefan's heart. He pulled her to him, feeling the satin softness of her cheek against his as she buried her face in his shoulder.

Jenna's slender arms reached up around Stefan's neck, seeking comfort in the strength of his embrace. Her eyes closed tightly as she let her sorrow flow in the sobs muffled in the soft wool of his coat, her head tucked beneath his chin. She found comfort in the silence of his understanding. This man knew more of her than she herself understood. Long moments later, Jenna raised her head, her wide gaze searching his. She reached up tentatively to gently touch the firm line of his jaw. Her lips sought his, uncertain at first, and then with silent longing and desperation. She cared not what his thoughts might have been for her boldness. She cared only to feel the warmth of his touch that she might hold back the cold dread of truth.

Stefan's senses were filled with her as he responded to the tentative warmth of her lips against his. He was aware of the scent of her, the feel, the heat of her slender body pressed hungrily against his own. His arms closed about her possessively, as she strained against him with a desperate passion that drove all caution from his thoughts. His lips left hers, to press a molten path of kisses along the slender column of her throat above the lace of the high collar.

Beneath the warmth of his lips against her skin, Jenna moaned with her aching need of him, a need that had come from their first time together, a need she had denied and now could deny no longer. His name was a whisper of pain and longing upon her lips. With trembling hands, Jenna unbuttoned his waistcoat, gently pushing the coat from his shoulders until she could feel, the lean hardened muscles across his chest, beneath the shirt. She felt the warmth of his skin, her fingertips lightly grazing his neck as she untied the cravat. In the next moments, the white silk shirt lay discarded beside the waistcoat. Jenna's hands moved tentatively across the rippling planes of his chest, as if she suddenly feared the heat of that contact. In the next moment she was crushed against him, the fullness of her breasts beneath the sheer silk of her blouse melding with the heat of his bare skin. Her breathing seemed to stop as she felt the pressure of Stefan's fingers against her bodice, loosening the closures, her gown sliding easily over her hips, until it lay on the floor, forgotten.

Stefan's fingers pushed aside the straps of the chemise with exquisite tenderness, luxuriating in the feel of her skin beneath his hands. The pale satin of her skin seemed to glow golden in the fading light that penetrated the chamber, and Stefan lingered with agonizing slowness before letting the chemise drop to the floor. His hands returned to gently caress her neck, spreading into the thickness of her hair until it hung loosely about her shoulders, tumbling free to her waist. Her eyes were closed in silent expectation, as Stefan bent to sweep her into his arms, slowly lowering her to the carpeted floor before the hearth.

Jenna opened her eyes. In the fading light within the chamber she watched the lean, muscular outline of Stefan's body as he joined her, his sleek nakedness molding against her own. There were no words, only the silent communication of his touching her, stroking her, as she entwined her lithe body with his.

Stefan's lips closed over Jenna's, tasting her sweetness. Her scent was a mixture of lavender and sunshine and leather from her ride. It was a devastating combination as he felt her respond to his own growing urgency. Stefan groaned as he felt her hands boldly caressing the length of his back and then moving across his thighs. Her slender

148

legs opened to him, demanding that he release the passion within her.

Jenna responded to Stefan's caresses with a fire of her own. Desperately she sought his warmth within her, arching against him, feeling the heated pressure as he entered her, his hands firm upon her bottom as he drove deep within. There was no pain, only her passion joining his as she met him fully in that most exquisite union.

Stefan had never before experienced abandoned passion to match his own. With others, he had known only physical release, quickly forgotten beyond the moment's necessity. With Jenna, from the first moment he had held her in his arms, it was as if his soul had crossed some invisible barrier and joined hers, to become one soul, each incapable of life without the other. His eyes closed as he abandoned himself to the warmth of her body surrounding him, feeling the exquisite heat as she took possession of him, demanding and then giving in the fevered stroking of her body against his.

Jenna arched against Stefan, molding him to her as her mouth grew hungry under his. All thoughts were abandoned to the aching need within, as she reveled in the penetration of his body within hers. Her hands glided across the smoothness of his shoulders as he drove her beyond the limits of her own passion. Jenna's eyes opened wide as he thrust deep within her, pushing her beyond control, until she felt the first spasms of release engulfing her. Her fingers were buried in the thick, golden waves of his hair as she cried out against his shoulder, her eyes now closed in complete abandonment to the pleasure he had given her.

A molten heat surged through him, almost painfully, as Stefan moved against Jenna, finding his own release in the depths of her strong, young body wrapped about him, his face buried in the silken mass of her dark hair that swirled about them in their frenzied need of one another. For long moments they lay entwined, as the waves of passion receded, leaving them spent with their mutual pleasure in each other's arms.

Jenna remained still within Stefan's embrace, not wanting the moment to end. She luxuriated in the contact of his warm skin against her own. She tried without success to ignore the faint tickling against her breast. She resisted a moment longer, her eyes flying open in pleasurable surprise at the touch of Stefan's mouth teasing a full peak to tautness.

"I think, my little princess, I shall find great enjoyment in learning what pleases you. I have often thought there are pleasures to be found beyond the confines of a bed. Now I realize a hard floor can be quite soft when one has the appropriate cushion," Stefan teased playfully, trying to draw her from her sadness of the moments before.

Jenna flushed beneath his casual gaze, yet could find no fault with his discovery. The soft glow in her amber eyes washed over him wantonly.

Jenna and Stefan both jumped at a sudden light knocking at the door. Jenna's startled gaze met Stefan's as she realized the scandal that might follow if they were discovered in their present position. Her silent struggling to regain her clothing met with firm resistance, as Stefan refused to release her. From beyond the closed portal Alexei's voice, not Maggie's, discreetly inquired if Stefan required anything.

A wry smile danced across Stefan's lips as he dismissed the faithful servant. And then with measured slowness he began to explore all the soft beguiling, hidden places of Jenna's body that concealed a bounty of pleasure awaiting only the release of his touch.

Chapter Nine

Jenna crossed the room quickly, the cold of the chamber sending goose bumps across her naked skin, as she laid new wood upon the glowing embers of the fire Stefan had laid the night before. The deep amber lights in her eyes sparked golden with sudden heat at the memory of the night now past. Deep within she felt a ravening hunger that had nothing to do with lack of food. As the flames flickered tentatively and then caught at the fresh wood she had laid there, Jenna stole quietly back to the warmth of the postered bed and snuggled deep into the covers, seeking Stefan's warmth to drive away the chill that had taken hold of her. His cursing was muffled against the sweet silken mass of her hair as he pulled her against him.

"I would swear it impossible for such a cold maiden to hide such fire within. It defies all reason." His lips were warm against the curve of her neck as he sought some tender fare to satisfy his own appetites.

Jenna giggled underneath his wandering lips and hands, thoroughly enjoying the invasion of his heat. Her cold feet elicited only the slightest groan of displeasure, as she felt a greater warmth pressed against her thigh. Her amber eyes suddenly darkened as she opened to him, feeling that exquisite pressure of him moving deep within her. Jenna responded with abandon, luxuriating in the warmth that Stefan built within her, that quickly drove the early morning chill from her.

Later, as the first gray shafts of light stole through the closed drapes, Jenna snuggled into Stefan's embrace, her cheek pressed against his shoulder, her lips lightly grazing against his neck. Sleep would not return. Instead, Stefan's words of the night before crowded her thoughts. It had seemed impossible to believe the truth of her grandfather's death, and yet it had been there all along. Only she had been too grief-stricken to see it. Perhaps if Mr. Flint had been there through the evening, and not taken away to drive her to the Wingate ball, perhaps if she had not attended, but had remained home that evening his death might have been prevented. Jenna squeezed her eyes tightly shut, her tears rolling silently down her cheeks, until they mingled with the saltiness of Stefan's skin. As if he had felt the tears she cried, Stefan reached to take her tears upon his fingertips. She had not known he was awake.

"You must not be sad, Jenna, not now. Your grand-father knew the risks well, and he took them willingly. His only regret was the danger it might bring to you. He was a very brave man. It is one thing to face the enemy on the field of battle. It is quite another to bravely seek the enemy in the shadows of deceit and treachery. Your grandfather's one wish was to provide a better, safer world for you. It was a wish we both shared. But not the only thing we shared," Stefan whispered gently, the strong, lean lines of his face softened in the soft glow of first light that crept into the silent room.

Jenna reached up, her small, slender hand seeking his, her fingers entwining with his lean, bronzed fingers, feeling his strength flowing into her.

"What other secret are you about to confess? What else did you share with my grandfather?" Jenna smiled sadly as she tilted her head back on the down pillow that she might gaze fully into the calming depths of his eyes.

Stefan turned her hand toward him, the gentle pressure of his lips on her fingers sending a tingling heat coursing through Jenna, driving away the last traces of her sadness before a greater passion that could not be willed away.

"We were each bound by our love for you, my dearest Jenna."

The breathless smile upon Jenna's lips faded as she gazed with wide-eyed uncertainty at Stefan. Never before had he spoken of his feelings for her, and she suddenly thought she knew little of this Russian prince who seemed to rule her heart, her very life, since their first meeting. A faint smile returned to her lips, as she thought perhaps he was trying to play some joke on her. Stefan's gaze remained serious, the blue of his eyes hauntingly brilliant, and she realized that he had spoken with complete honesty. Jenna could not return that unwavering gaze, and she looked away as she pursued the answer to a question that had haunted her the last weeks.

"What of your love for Lillian de Stahl?" As soon as she had said it, Jenna hated herself for her words, knowing well she was prying into matters that might well bring only heartache. Her answer came in the sudden painful pressure of Stefan's fingers closing with brutal strength around her slender wrist. Her startled gaze shot up to meet his.

"Know well Jenna, that I do not pledge my love easily. Whatever I may share with Lillian de Stahl has nothing to do with what passes between you and me. I have vowed my love for you. It cannot be taken back. It is a live thing, which has become a part of me since the first day we met on the post road outside of London. It is like a creature that haunts my every moment, finding ease only when you are with me, as you are now." The last words were spoken almost painfully as Stefan flung her from him and immediately rolled away from her side, the lean contours of his body outlined in the meager light of the chamber as he rose from the bed.

Jenna choked back a silent sob. He had given her the words she had longed to hear, and yet she had flung them back at him by questioning him about another woman. Charles or any other young man would have fallen at her feet with well-rehearsed excuses. She found she had much to learn of Stefan Kalinsky.

"I don't believe I much care for angry Russians. You are far too easily angered, and too unpredictable. I don't like anger or half-truths, and I don't want you coming here anymore," Jenna stormed, her bruised emotions retaliating against his evasive answer about Lillian de Stahl. May the devil take him and his conspiracy, and see what she cared. Jenna was unaware of the warning light that sparkled in the depths of that blue gaze as she bent to wrap the sheet about her slender body.

Stefan descended on Jenna, his strong fingers closing with bruising purpose around one slender wrist as she reached with the other hand to tear away the sheet. Jenna's head snapped back in stunned surprise at his assault, her heated objections silenced beneath the heat of his lips against hers, drawing her breath away. She was defenseless against his towering strength as he drew her slender body full against his, molding her to him so that no part of them did not touch.

Somewhere in the far reaches of consciousness a flame sparked, and it burst forth in consuming anger against this man who boldly thought to dominate her with passion where force might fail. Jenna struggled against his hold, and finding no release, bit down on his lip against hers.

A loud oath filled the chamber, and Stefan jerked away from her in stunned surprise, a look of disbelief on his handsome face. The eyes that met Jenna's seemed shot through with intense heat as he reached up to feel the small wound she had left. In one catlike movement, Stefan descended on Jenna again, seizing her arm and twisting it cruelly behind her as he drew her against him.

"Ah, my lovely Jenna. Perhaps it is truth you speak of my anger, but only where there is danger to something I value highly. Unpredictable; I think not. It was quite predictable that I fall in love with you. How could I possibly resist such strength, such courage, and a passion to match my own? No Jenna, you cannot deny it, for I have known those qualities in you."

Jenna tried to twist away from Stefan's unyielding

154

grasp, refusing to meet that piercing gaze that seemed capable of knowing her thoughts.

"The only strength I possess is one born of necessity, and the courage you saw was only my will to survive," Jenna spat back at him, finding words were now the only weapons left to her with her arms soundly pinned behind her back.

"And what of passion, Jenna? Would you deny the pleasure you have found with me?"

Jenna's struggling continued as she realized that there was no reasoning with him.

"Jenna?" His breath was the softest whisper against the column of her throat, as he drew her tightly against his body to still her struggling.

Jenna groaned inwardly, feeling her resolve weaken. Her skin tingled beneath the warmth of his lips as Stefan sought to prove his point.

"Jenna?" His voice was oddly accented as he spoke her name and gently whispered of his longing in words she could not understand. His grasp about her arms loosened, and he pulled her more fully against him, his lips lingering achingly over the tip of her breast as he bent her back over his arm.

Jenna shuddered with undeniable pleasure as she stroked her long fingers through the tousled mane of his golden hair, at first desperately seeking to hold him from her, and then yielding to feverishly bind him to her.

"Say it, Jenna. The words wait only to be spoken." All anger had fled before Stefan's desperate need to hear the words from her lips.

He had released her from the boundaries of innocence. He had given her the ultimate pleasure to be shared between a man and a woman. Jenna knew that no matter what words she might have spoken in denial, they would have been lies. Like other truths she had chosen to ignore, it had been there all along.

"No!" Jenna's answer was barely more than a whisper, which was silenced beneath Stefan's lips. And then Stefan pulled away from her, an amused smile pulling at his lips as he gazed down at his slender captive.

"I want more from you Jenna. But it is enough that you have admitted what you feel." He playfully waved a warning finger at her, like some instructor at his lessons.

"One day, the words will come easily. I shall wait for that day. Until then I shall say them for you, whenever and wherever the moment suits me. Be warned Jenna, I care little for the English affinity for discretion. Above all else, I speak freely and honestly of what I feel."

"It would seem I have a great deal to learn of Russian manners and Russian princes," Jenna countered tartly.

"Only of one Russian prince, my lovely Jenna. For no other would dare trespass in this matter," Stefan warned playfully, as he left her side to retrieve his breeches and shirt.

"What of an English gentleman?" Jenna pursued artfully.

"Charles Wingate is no gentleman. I cannot give the reasons for what I say, only that they go beyond any petty jealousies. You are mine Jenna, but in that there is great danger. Do not anger Charles Wingate, for I fear him to be unpredictable in certain matters, and I would not want you caught between us in this."

Jenna looked up, her gaze fastened on Stefan Kalinsky. What was he trying to tell her?

"You think Charles is somehow involved with the conspiracy, don't you?" Jenna tied the silken wrapper about her, and when Stefan seemed to ignore her question, she followed him across the room, where he sat pulling on his black leather boots. She knelt before him, her hands gently stopping him as he tried to pull on the second boot.

"My grandfather suspected Charles to have some part in the conspiracy, didn't he? Stefan, I have to know. Did my grandfather learn something that involved Charles in all of this?"

Stefan gazed into the delicate oval of her exquisite face, a faint, peach color still on the delicate arch of her cheeks, beneath the wide, mahogany depths of her eyes.

"Three days before you returned to London, when your

grandfather became ill, we received a message that connected Charles Wingate and several others to the conspiracy. All we were given were names, and places of meetings, nothing to prove what we had learned. The proof was to be found in a packet of secret documents, supposedly being sent to London by Charles Wingate."

"You were looking for those documents, when you stopped the coach."

"Yes, but it would seem, your grandfather's illness, which hastened your return to London, thwarted Charles Wingate's plans to deliver the message on the family's return to London. It would also seem that Charles discovered someone knew of his plans. The man who gave us the information about the documents was found dead two days later. I can only believe that the man died without telling the conspirators the extent of what we had learned. Your grandfather's involvement was well known in certain circles. I am certain the conspirators thought to end the investigation with Sir Avery's death."

Jenna looked at Stefan with a sudden dawning fear. "It is possible they know of your involvement."

"Quite possible. And that would explain Charles's wariness toward me—that, and jealousy." Stefan arched a golden brow as he turned toward Jenna.

"Jealousy?" Jenna stared incredulously at Stefan, and then her amazement faded. It was possible that Charles suspected something of her relationship with Stefan, although certainly neither of them had given any public indication of what passed in the privacy of the bedchamber. Jenna looked up to find Stefan staring at her. She reached out tenderly to caress his cheek.

"Then Charles must have nothing to be jealous of, not if we are to be successful."

"Successful? Jenna, what are you talking about?"

"I am talking about the conspiracy. If it is true that Charles suspects your involvement with my grandfather, then you can hope to learn nothing. Charles is quite clever. He will never allow himself or any of his friends to be found as part of some plot against the Crown. Don't

157

you see, the only hope you possibly have of learning the information you need is through me?"

"No! I will not allow it!" Stefan fairly roared, his voice seeming to echo in the chamber, in the early morning silence of the great house.

"Stefan, please, you must reconsider this. You must surely know that Charles has long spoken of plans for our marriage. Who would better have access to their plans than someone he trusted? I know well from listening to my grandfather that Napoleon presses his cause against England with each passing day. Already he has pressed deep into Russia. If he is not stopped now, everyone who stands in his way will be crushed. I do not understand this conspiracy of Charles's. But I know my grandfather opposed Charles Wingate. Now I know the reasons. My grandfather could not complete his work to save England. Somehow I must try to continue where he left off. I owe him that much, for the love he gave me. My darling, can you not understand?" Jenna pleaded with Stefan, her voice trembling with a sudden coldness that seemed to have invaded the chamber.

Stefan's fingers closed about hers. He could not deny the truth in her words, and yet his heart too suddenly felt the coldness all about, at the danger she was risking.

"I could not bear it, for any harm to come to you." Stefan's voice was a harsh whisper.

Jenna smiled bravely at the sudden emotion in his voice. "I have nothing to fear. I have a Russian prince to protect me."

Stefan stood suddenly, drawing Jenna to her feet.

"I must not be seen here."

Jenna smiled ruefully. "How shall I explain your presence last night?"

"Only Alexei will know of my presence here last night. But if I do not leave now, I shall be tempted to return you to that bed once more. There are still words I wish to hear from you."

Jenna quickly pushed Stefan aside as she moved to the door. He moved past her into the dimly lit hall. They met with only silence from the still sleeping household.

Stefan turned back to Jenna one last time before turning down the hallway, his arm encircling her slender waist as he drew her to him.

"Be careful, my little princess. We play a very deadly game."

Jenna's eyes softened and then closed as his mouth closed over hers, her senses consumed by a sudden aching deep inside.

"Send Mr. Flint to me with your messages. Alexei will remain close by at all times, but will not always be known to you. It is safer that way. Always remember, the moment Charles Wingate suspects anything, you will be in great danger."

"I will remember." Jenna kissed Stefan's cheek, and then he was gone, disappearing down the far end of the carpeted hallway through a door that led to the servants' chambers on the ground floor. Jenna fervently prayed he would not meet with Maggie or one of the other staff. When no sounds reached her from below, Jenna turned back to her own chamber. Her breath caught in her throat at the sight of Emma Kelly standing reprovingly across the hallway. It was impossible that Emma had not seen Stefan leaving Jenna's chamber. But instead of lecturing, she merely shook her graying head as she preceded Jenna into the chamber.

Jenna thoughtfully combed through the dark, sable-colored lengths of her hair, studying Emma's stout frame reflected in the mirror of the dressing table. She had stubbornly refused any mention of Stefan Kalinsky, although Jenna knew quite well nothing had escaped the woman's attention. Through the course of Jenna's morning bath, Emma Kelly had remained stoically silent, going about her usual chores, straightening the chamber, putting away garments, sending out Jenna's riding habit to be cleaned, and then ordering up a hearty breakfast, all as if nothing were amiss. Jenna somehow felt as if this were merely the lull before the storm that was certain to come.

"Well?"

Jenna's brush clattered loudly on the top of the dressing table, as the storm suddenly broke within the chamber.

"What can you possibly be thinking, dear child? Carrying on with that Prince Kalinsky? I should have seen it coming from the very beginning. I blame myself in the matter. You were innocent in such matters, and quite grief-stricken over the loss of your dear grandfather. I should have made certain that you were protected against such things. You must not see him again. I will make certain of it. But I must have your solemn promise that you are done with the matter."

Jenna let Emma's tirade continue until she could stand no more. Rising from the stool before the dressing table, Jenna whirled on the older woman, having had enough of the woman's wild ravings.

"Silence. I will have silence. You know little of the matter. It has nothing to do with any failing on your part. You could have done little to prevent what has happened. I met Stefan Kalinsky long before the night of the Wingate ball. And I will give you no such promises."

Emma's face blanched ashen as she stared in stunned disbelief at her young mistress.

"Dear child, you cannot mean what you say."

"I mean exactly what I say." Jenna caught herself before she might have spoken more of what had passed that night between herself and Stefan Kalinsky. As much as it might hurt, she dare not trust even Emma, though the woman's loyalty was unwavering. The fewer who knew what she was about to do, the greater the possibility for success.

"The matter is quite done with. Prince Kalinsky will not return to this house."

Emma had not thought to win her argument quite so easily. Indeed, she suspected something more that had not been said.

"And what if in the months to come you should find yourself carrying his babe? What then will your answer to

160

me be?" Emma spoke bluntly. "What fine young, gentleman of title would accept another man's bastard child? Can you answer me that?"

Silence filled the large chamber. Jenna could offer no assurances against what Emma had suggested. Indeed, only time would tell. If she failed to gain the information Stefan needed to stop the conspiracy, there would be little future for any of them. Jenna tilted her chin slightly, hoping the trembling that she felt was not obvious to Emma.

In the next moment, Emma crossed the wide span that separated them, wrapping her short arm about Jenna's waist protectively.

"If it is love, it will endure. We shall not speak of it again." Emma patted Jenna lovingly on the arm, and then moved across the chamber, dabbing at her tear-filled eyes as she tried to select a gown for Jenna.

Jenna recognized their silent truce in the old woman's gesture of love. She dabbed at her own eyes briefly, before inhaling deeply. There was much to be done.

"I will be working in the rose gardens this morning, Emma. I have much thinking to do. I shall be attending Almack's this evening for dinner. Madame Lessard has promised the yellow velvet gown will be delivered this afternoon, in plenty of time."

"Will you be seeing Prince Kalinsky this evening?" Emma ventured quietly.

"I believe Prince Kalinsky has other plans for the evening," Jenna responded thoughtfully as she slipped into the muslin gown, pulling back the long, cuffed sleeves.

Jenna worked her way slowly through the maze of thorny bushes, working carefully to trim back the branches as her grandfather had showed her long ago. It was part of him, she thought, this love of land and growing things. She could remember walking along beside him as a child, holding onto his coattails, watching

161

him prune the rosebushes of his own gardens, until she was old enough to handle the shears without cutting herself. With his failing health in later years, the complete care of the gardens had fallen to her. It was a responsibility she accepted lovingly, for she realized all her efforts would be greatly rewarded when the roses once again burst forth in abundance. She trimmed back one last bloom, once brilliant red, now dried and withered, and her thoughts returned to that first rose Stefan had given her. Never again would she be able to look at a red rose without thinking of Stefan.

Jenna willed herself to think of Charles Wingate. How was it possible that Charles had become involved in a conspiracy against the Crown? What madness could have led him to such desperation? Or was it desperation? She remembered hearing, more than once, Charles's outspoken dislike of the regent, but she had thought it hardly more than the common grumblings against a prince not greatly liked. But conspiracy? She had known Charles and Elizabeth Wingate most of her life. Sentiment cried out that she not believe what Stefan had told her, and yet logic could find no other explanation. Her grandfather's continual warnings against Charles, his obstinate refusal to accept Charles's pleadings for their betrothal, spoke a truth she could not deny. Her grandfather had given his life for that truth.

Jenna cast aside the shears in favor of the rake and vigorously cleaned all her cuttings into a neat pile at the edge of the garden. When she had finished, she could feel the strain in the muscles of her back. The midday sun was well overhead as she straightened from her labors, her thoughts clear as she turned toward the sound of a small plain carriage turning up the cobbled drive.

Madame Lessard alighted from the carriage, her arm looped through the handle of a large basket.

Jenna wiped her hands on the coarse cotton of the heavy apron and entered the house through a side entrance off the gardens. Her plan was firmly made. She would be patient through Madame's fitting, and the hours that remained of the afternoon. And then she would set her plan in motion. She would try, this evening, to learn what Elizabeth might know of Charles's activities with his friends. There was every possibility that Elizabeth knew nothing. In that event, Jenna would be forced to strengthen her relationship with Charles, in hopes of learning something from him.

It was later than Jenna had thought, and she was forced to rush through a quick bath and dressing, pausing only long enough to down a few bites of the meal Emma had brought to her room. Jenna chose to ignore Emma's look of disapproval as she picked up her dinner, quickly setting the tray aside as Maggie entered the chamber to announce the arrival of the Wingate coach. With only a hasty glance to her appearance in the large mirror, Jenna seized her wrap and departed the chamber before Emma could scold her for her meager appetite. Had she delayed a few moments longer, she would have known that Emma Kelly was only slightly displeased with Jenna's preoccupation that evening. The maid was silently grateful that Jenna had shown some enthusiasm for her evening with Elizabeth Wingate, and their invitation to Almack's.

Emma Kelly held no illusions about what she had learned that morning upon finding Prince Stefan Kalinsky leaving Jenna's chamber before the sun was well risen in the sky. Nor was she easily fooled that the affair was nothing more than a passing dalliance. Long before Jenna had been aware of Prince Kalinsky's attentions, Emma had been aware of the look that came into his eyes whenever her mistress entered the room. She could only fear that such a relationship was ill fated. There were far too many rumors about his other affairs. Emma had her sources among the staff and servants. She had heard much of Prince Kalinsky's discreetly active reputation about London. She was not eager to see Jenna become part of that reputation. Emma Kelly sighed heavily as she folded Jenna's silk wrapper and straightened the chamber. Placing the carved brush and comb where Jenna might easily find them, the old woman's hands brushed against the gold music box. She knew it well, for she had seen it often in Sir Avery's possession. She knew how he valued it for the memories it held. She had also known of Sir Avery's intentions that last evening to make a gift of the music box to Jenna. Absently, Emma lifted the lid of the small box, immediately setting the mechanism to movement. Tinkling sounds filled the chamber as the tune played. A piece of clear glass lay across the top of the box, protecting the delicate mechanism from dust. On top of the glass lay a perfect pressed rosebud. Emma closed the lid of the music box, feeling as if she had somehow interfered in something very private. She could only guess where the rose might have come from. Indeed, over the last few weeks, it seemed the house never lacked for roses.

Jenna had accepted the engraved invitation from Countess Lieven to attend Almack's that evening, originally to please Elizabeth. Only earlier that morning, after Stefan had left, had she realized the evening might provide an excellent opportunity for her to learn some valued piece of information about the conspiracy. The countess, together with Lady Jersey and Lady Castlereagh, Princess Esterhazy and Lady Cowper, controlled the greatest social events to be found at the height of the season in London. It was even rumored that the prince regent consulted this elite circle of titled ladies as to the functions and social events planned by the Crown. Almack's was a very elite, very private club for ladies, where a mixture of dining, dancing and exchanges of gossip were the fare of the evening. As dictated by the titled hostesses, gentlemen guests, invited by certain young ladies, had to be greatly accomplished on the ballroom floor. It was required that they wear knee breeches and white cravats. No exceptions were ever allowed. It was a well-known fact that the duke of Wellington had been refused entry to Almack's earlier in the season because of the trousers he had chosen to wear. Not even royalty were allowed exceptions to the strict mandates of the patronesses who established the rules of the house. It was a young lady's greatest disgrace if she did not receive at least one invitation to Almack's through the course of the official social season. Jenna had declined all previous invitations in deference to her mourning after the death of her grandfather. Now she realized that such an evening might easily be advantageous.

The ballroom at Almack's was a glittering display of white and gold in every detail. Walls painted white were inset with panels depicting scrolled designs of gilt-edged flowers. At the far end of the ballroom a full orchestra struck up a waltz, each member resplendent in white coats trimmed with gold satin braid. The gleaming mahogany wood floor reflected the brilliance of crystal chandeliers, suspended at even intervals from the vast ceiling and set with small gaslamps that resembled a multitude of candles. Across the crowded dance floor Jenna recognized Beau Brummell and his circle of equally dandified young gentlemen, surrounded by openly admiring young ladies. Jenna found herself searching the crowded ballroom for someone of taller height, with golden hair and azure gaze. She mentally chided herself for thinking that Stefan Kalinsky would have any interest in attending Almack's. It was well known that many enduring relationships were formed at Almack's, as well as betrothals sealed between titled young ladies and gentlemen. Stefan Kalinsky was not one to seek such devices for affairs of the heart.

Jenna absently handed the attendant her wrap, turning about to acknowledge a greeting from Countess Lieven.

"My dearest Jenna, at last you grace us with your presence. How very wonderful that you could attend this evening, although I quite understand your reluctance. Now it is time to put aside your sadness. Tonight there must be no sadness, only gaiety and lively spirits."

"You are most kind, countess. I was not aware that you knew my grandfather."

"Sir Avery was a man of vast accomplishments and purposes. And a most astute businessman. He advised my husband on several matters, and he always found your grandfather's advice to be most accurate. In later years, he valued your grandfather's intense devotion to the cause against Napoleon. Your grandfather was also the consummate diplomat. One day I shall tell you a fine story of the supreme test in diplomacy that resulted in my marriage to Count Lieven. Ah, I can see I have revealed something of your grandfather that you did not know. Be assured, Sir Avery was not always the overworked advisor to the prime minister. But come now, dear child, I have someone who wishes to meet you."

Jenna was drawn across the ballroom, her arm firmly entwined with Countess Lieven's. She cast a resigned glance over her shoulder at Elizabeth, only to find her friend already engaged in rapt conversation with a young man Jenna recognized as John Whitmore. Their conversation seemed anything but casual, and Jenna could only guess that Elizabeth had insisted on her attendance to provide the opportunity for meeting with John. She knew that Charles heartily disapproved of Elizabeth's choice in the young man, thinking the match not of adequate advantage for Elizabeth. Jenna sympathized with her friend, for she knew how forceful Charles could be when he became determined in other matters.

"Jenna Randolph, I would like to introduce Madame Lillian de Stahl. I do not think you have been previously introduced."

The remainder of Countess Lieven's introduction was lost to Jenna as she stared at the elegantly dressed woman who stood before her. It was a long moment before she recovered her composure sufficiently to acknowledge the woman's greeting.

"Mademoiselle Randolph, I specifically requested that Countess Lieven make the appropriate introductions, as I thought it highly unlikely that Stefan would extend that courtesy."

Lillian de Stahl watched the exquisite young woman before her for some sign of shaken composure. She found none in the calm, wide amber gaze that regarded her evenly. If Jenna Randolph was at all shaken by their meeting, she was to be congratulated as the consummate actress. Nothing in her manner or response indicated that Stefan Kalinsky's name held any meaning for her, although Lillian de Stahl was well aware of Jenna's acquaintance with Stefan.

"I have known Stefan for a long time, long before he arrived in London. We have shared an extremely close relationship, which I value highly. Because of that relationship, I have come to know Stefan well, and I speak of it now only to offer you some advice."

Jenna coolly returned Lillian de Stahl's speculative gaze, refusing to allow the woman to know that their meeting had shaken her badly. The last thing she had expected was a confrontation with the woman who was rumored to be Stefan's mistress. Indeed, Jenna had forced herself not to think of Stefan's relationship with the notorious Lillian de Stahl, as if by ignoring the obvious she might allow herself to believe Stefan's words of love for her. If she had indeed been a fool, she was not about to allow Lillian de Stahl any satisfaction with that truth.

"I have received ample advice over the last weeks, Madame de Stahl, regarding a number of matters. I hardly think there could be any further advice that you might offer me."

"What I would offer you, my dear, hardly pertains to matters of finance or estate, but rather matters of the heart. And in that, my dear Jenna, I think experience weighs rather heavily. You my dear, have none, at least none of value to you, in the matter of Stefan Kalinsky. What you might hope to call love is nothing more than a momentary passion for Stefan, and indeed he has many passions. It would be sad to see an innocent, such as yourself, caused pain and sadness because of that momentary passion."

Jenna regarded Lillian de Stahl coolly.

"I am indebted to Prince Kalinsky only for his generous offer of assistance after the sudden death of my grandfather. Your concern is well noted, Madame de Stahl, but hardly warranted. I shall speak to Prince Kalinsky of your concerns when next we meet. Please, do enjoy your evening."

Lillian de Stahl regarded Jenna evenly. She now realized this was no ordinary affair for Stefan Kalinsky.

Not only was the young woman before her an exceptional beauty, but she was also possessed of great spirit. Where any other young lady might have cowered before her obvious warning, Jenna Randolph remained cool and polite, as if her relationship with Stefan Kalinsky had never gone beyond the bounds of casual friendship. Here indeed was no dimwitted young woman whose only thought might be to an advantageous affair. Jenna Randolph was a woman of intelligence, poise, and most of all, discretion. Lillian de Stahl fluttered her lace-edged fan with an air of sudden annoyance, as she realized she was in danger of losing Stefan Kalinsky forever. His plan to use Jenna Randolph to gain information about the conspiracy had already become more than a casual affair, of that she was certain. The pinched lines that had formed about Lillian de Stahl's mouth relaxed, as she realized there was still an advantage to be gained. If her sources were correct, the man approaching them at that very moment might give her that advantage.

With a slight tilt of her head, Jenna brushed past Lillian de Stahl, desperately hoping the shaking of her knees could not be heard over the music of the orchestra. She vainly sought Elizabeth across the ballroom, feeling as if the evening were already doomed to dismal failure. Jenna turned about suddenly at a gentle, but insistent hand on her arm.

"Charles!" Jenna's gloved hand flew to her mouth in stunned surprise.

"My dearest Jenna, are you so surprised to find me here? Indeed, when Elizabeth finally revealed her plans for this evening, I found the invitation to share your company irresistible. You had but to ask, and I would have accompanied you."

Jenna fought to regain her composure as Charles drew her out into the middle of the ballroom.

"I only accepted for Elizabeth. She thought it necessary that I be seen at Almack's, although I am not certain about her reasoning."

"Nor am I. Surely Almack's is reserved for fashionable

168

young ladies seeking fashionable arrangements, possibly betrothal. Jenna, you wound me deeply, that you would have others think you seek such an arrangement when you already have my pledge for marriage."

"Charles, please. I have already explained that I attended out of friendship for Elizabeth."

"Then I shall have to speak to Elizabeth and tell her that I heartily disapprove of her plans to lead you astray."

"It was hardly her thought to lead me astray," Jenna retorted evenly, at a loss to understand how Charles always managed to put her on the defensive.

"As I can well see. It seems Elizabeth seeks relationships of her own. I shall be certain to advise father of her conduct."

They suddenly came to a stop in the center of the floor, and Jenna laid a restraining hand on Charles's sleeve.

"Please, Charles. Elizabeth is quite fond of John Whitmore. And I am certain he returns those same feelings for her. What possible objection could you have to him?"

"Dear, sweet Jenna, you must surely know that father intends a more suitable arrangement for Elizabeth. After all, one must think of title and position, mustn't one?"

Jenna studied Charles thoughtfully. She could not be certain, but she sensed more beneath his carefully spoken words than merely his concern for the acceptability of Elizabeth's marriage. She forced herself to look beyond the cool facade of Charles's manner.

"Then *you* also must have great concern for an arrangement of suitable title and position. Therefore, I find it difficult to accept your affections for me," Jenna countered.

Charles's gray eyes narrowed as he took up the challenge that forever seemed to loom between them. He stepped back, and seizing her hand, pressed her gloved fingers to his thin lips.

"There are none who will decide for me. My choice has already been made. My greatest concern now is for your protection."

"Protection?" Jenna stared at him incredulously, her

amused surprise quickly turning to uncertainty as she noticed the unnatural gleam in his eyes.

"What is it you think you must protect me from?" Jenna ventured cautiously, knowing Charles might choose to evade her questions with some casual response. She accepted his arm as he led her to the far side of the ballroom, where they accepted filled wineglasses from one of the servants.

"It is 'whom' I must protect you from, Jenna. He is known to you. It is Prince Stefan Kalinsky, a most dangerous man, dangerous to you, dangerous to England."

Chapter Ten

Through the last days of October and the early weeks of November, Jenna's days and nights were filled with a constant round of balls, dinner engagements, and social events. She attended the circus, delighting in the colorful costumes of the performers, enthralled by the animals, but especially drawn to the black Russian bears that performed perfectly to the commands they were given, in exchange for some tasty morsel as their reward. She took frequent walks through Vauxhall Gardens with Elizabeth, and was more often left to her own wanderings, as Elizabeth stole a private moment with John Whitmore. Most often, Charles declined to accompany them, begging a previous engagement with a friend or acquaintance. Jenna readily admitted she would have liked to know exactly where his mornings and afternoons took him. She had chosen to ignore Charles's concerned warnings against Stefan, hoping he would not press her further in the matter. Though his reasons had remained vague, Jenna had become uneasy at the sudden passion that seemed to possess Charles, as if he considered Stefan Kalinsky a demon that he must extricate from her life.

The weather remained unseasonably mild through November, the days cool but sunny, the nights tinged with the crispness of frost. The earlier rains in October seemed to have abated for a time, and Jenna was not surprised to learn that the prince regent had planned a week of royal parties and fox-hunting at his country estate outside of London. She was surprised, however, to receive a gold-embossed invitation that read more like a royal summons to join in the round of festivities. She soon learned that all London was astir over the names of those who had received the honored invitations. Even though Edward was not overly popular with his subjects, there were none who could deny their enthusiasm at receiving an invitation to be seen among the royal set. For Jenna it would be an excellent opportunity to move among the titled nobility, for she had failed to learn anything during the last weeks about the conspiracy, so that she had begun to wonder about the truth of what Stefan had told her.

While Emma busily took charge of her wardrobe for the journey to the country, Jenna quickly dispensed Mr. Flint to Stefan's town house with a hastily penned message about the invitation she had received. Though she had sent several messages to him over the last weeks, she had received none from him, only Mr. Flint's assurances that the messages had been delivered to Dmitri. Indeed, her only contact with Stefan were the brief exchanges dictated by social etiquette when they chanced to meet at the opera or the theater. Stefan's manner remained aloof, even disinterested. He was seen all about London with Lillian de Stahl, so that Jenna found it necessary to remind herself continuously of their common cause.

Charles had become increasingly confident of their imminent betrothal, and his manner of late had relaxed with that confidence. Jenna could even admit that his manner was almost pleasant. His rude, temperamental outbursts seemed to have disappeared, so that Jenna found herself enjoying his company, although she readily admitted it was no greater than her caring for Elizabeth, after a lifetime of friendship.

Jenna struggled with the inner turmoil of her feelings for Stefan Kalinsky. Her apprehensions through the days of that first month quickly disappeared, and she tried without success to forget the stolen moments they had shared with each other. Unable to deny the truth of Lillian de Stahl's words about Stefan, she easily recognized the foolishness of a continued affair with him. In her hectic social schedule she found it easier to accept that. In the solitary loneliness of her bed, at night, her conviction was completely stripped away, as she tossed and turned restlessly, continuously haunted by the touch of his fingers across her skin, the heat of his lips against hers, the memory of his body taking possession of hers. Instead of fading with the passage of days into weeks, the memory of their time together became a haunting passion. Only a passion of equal strength provided Jenna with the conviction to continue her dangerous pursuit of the truth. She would not casually accept her grandfather's death, as Charles and so many others had argued that she must.

On the Thursday morning before the Monday on which Jenna was to depart for the country, Elizabeth Wingate arrived unannounced before Jenna had dressed for the morning. She was a vision of absolute misery, bewailing the fact that while the entire Wingate family had been invited to the royal estates, John Whitmore had not received an invitation. Jenna spent the better part of the morning trying to ease Elizabeth's anxieties about being separated from John for more than ten days. By the time Emma announced luncheon in the dining room, Jenna had managed to convince Elizabeth that she would indeed survive the ordeal of time. After luncheon she convinced the red-eyed Elizabeth that a separation of a few days might serve her well in her crusade to convince both her father and brother of the merits of John Whitmore. Elizabeth seemed to consider the validity of such arguments, and reluctantly agreed to make the best of the royal invitation.

The next days passed rapidly, with a flurry of activity. Jenna had earlier refused any participation in packing for the journey to the country, her own enthusiasm greatly lacking. However, as Monday fast approached, she received a brief message from Stefan that he had been called to Dover on a matter of grave importance. It could only mean that he had received some information about the conspiracy. Now, she was most eager for the next days to pass quickly, until she could return to London to find out what Stefan had learned.

Foxmoor House was hardly a house, but more an elegantly furnished hunting lodge comprised of a series of wings housing an endless number of rooms that had been added in a continuing effort to accommodate the prince regent's penchant for elaborate hunting parties. Only a day's ride from London, Foxmoor House was nestled in the forested beauty of Huntington Wood. Here, the rapid approach of winter was more readily felt in temperatures that demanded woolen coats and fur mufflers. Traces of the winter's first snow weeks earlier could be found only in shaded seclusion beneath the massive pine trees. The bright midday sun amply warmed the long caravan of coaches, wagons, and riders, which almost took on the atmosphere of a traveling fair.

Lord Wingate had refused to accept any excuses Jenna might have offered against riding in the Wingate coach. He silently hoped that Jenna's lovely presence would lift Elizabeth's morose spirits. His plan was not altogether unsuccessful. By midmorning Elizabeth's dour expression of the last days had disappeared, as Jenna drew her out of her melancholia with idle chatter about the coming few days and about who might be attending. Charles had chosen to ride his own mount at the last minute, insisting that it would allow them more comfort in the coach. But Jenna was not fooled. Being on horseback afforded Charles easy access to others in the caravan of coaches. She could only speculate on the conversations that passed between Charles and his friends, and she somberly wondered if they were connected with Stefan Kalinsky's hasty departure to Dover.

The royal party arrived at Foxmoor House just as the last light of day was dipping low behind the towering pinnacle of pine and oak trees. As each coach arrived in turn at the entrance to Foxmoor House, it was met by a member of the royal staff, which had been in attendance for days prior, in anticipation of the royal arrival. Jenna and Elizabeth were given adjoining rooms that opened out onto a large balcony overlooking the green that stretched from the north wing and spanned the full distance to the stables beyond.

Instead of fatigue from the day's journey, Jenna felt only a nagging restlessness from being confined in the coach. The evening meal in the banquet hall below would not be for another hour, and Jenna seized the opportunity for a walk, while a young maid unpacked her clothes. Elizabeth had chosen to rest before dinner, affording Jenna the opportunity to explore the entire north wing of Foxmoor House at her leisure. It might well be the most unstructured time she would be allowed for several days to come. She knew that a full schedule of hunting, riding, and other activities was always planned at these events, and Charles had spoken of his intentions that she ride to the hunt with him, though he knew well she cared little for the sport. Jenna quickly discovered that Charles and Lord Wingate had also been given separate chambers across from each other at the far end of the hall.

Returning from her walk to freshen herself before dinner, Jenna nearly collided with a man who had just emerged from Charles's chamber. He was an odd-looking man; short and dark complexioned, and he moved quickly past her, with only a brief, nervous look in her direction before disappearing down the opposite end of the hall. He somehow seemed strangely out of place among the royal guests, and Jenna could not remember having seen him earlier that day as they journeyed from London. Her hand resting on the doorknob to her own chamber, Jenna could not help wondering what Charles might have discussed with such a man, and in the privacy of his chamber, when they were just arrived from London. Of course, Charles would hardly have expected her to be out walking just before dinner, when Elizabeth had suggested they would both be resting.

Jenna carefully let herself into her own chamber. She

stood quietly in the shadows of the room cast by the single oil lamp on the dressing table. Over the last weeks she had been able to learn nothing that might have any significant connecton with her grandfather's death or the conspiracy Stefan had warned her of, so that she had begun to doubt it was anything more than a lie. Indeed, Stefan's continual absences over the last weeks might have borne out her suspicions. And now the first communication she had received from him in weeks informed her he had gone to Dover. All her questions of Mr. Flint had gained nothing more. Either the man knew nothing or had been instructed to say nothing. Jenna whirled about at the sound of light knocking on the door.

Quickly casting aside her woolen coat and pelisse, Jenna hesitated before the mirror at the dressing table, which caught her reflection in the soft glow of the lamp. She smoothed back a few stray tendrils of her dark hair. Charles had said that he would escort her to dinner promptly at eight. The ornately carved clock that sat on the mantel over the fireplace had struck the hour as she returned from her walk. Jenna lightly powdered her cheeks to subdue the brilliant pink that flushed across her high cheekbones from the cool night air. It would not do for Charles to know she had been walking about unescorted. He would merely take it upon himself to occupy her every spare moment in the next days, and Jenna had already begun to feel smothered by his lavish attentions of late.

The next days passed quickly. Jenna rose before the first light, and with the help of her maid, donned riding habit and soft leather boots to accompany those intent on riding to the hounds. The weather remained mild for November, the sun rising high to warm the greensward, sending swirling vapors of mist about the riders as they sent their mounts chasing after the hounds, all in pursuit of the hapless red fox. Shivering in the first light of day, as the riders assembled, Jenna had cause to envy the slight cold

Elizabeth had come down with. She heartily wished that she too might linger beneath the soft, downy warmth of a heavy coverlet in her bed. But those thoughts brought a flood of other pleasant memories that soon warmed her beyond the early morning chill.

By Saturday, Jenna found she could stand the morning ritual of the hunt no longer. She restrained the eager black mare with a firm hand on the reins, lagging behind most of the riders as they charged across the small clearing beyond the lodge. Very soon the sounds of the dogs baying in the cold morning air was nothing more than an echo that reached Jenna as she slowed the mare again, and then drew her to a halt. In the rider's frenzied pace to outride their regent and keep pace with the reckless hounds, they had failed to notice one rider who dropped far behind and then stopped altogether.

The black pawed nervously, chomping on the bit, as Jenna watched the last of the riders disappear from sight.

"Good morning, Jenna."

Jenna whirled about in the small saddle. She had not heard another rider approaching.

Only a short distance away, hidden in the shadows of a large pine tree, a lone rider sat astride a tall black stallion. The black stallion pawed excitedly at the scent of Jenna's mare, the rider finally urging him forward a few paces. The sun glistened on waving golden-brown hair framing a handsome face. Jenna felt a sudden weakness as her wide amber gaze met brilliant blue. And she realized, almost with sadness, that all her thoughts of the last weeks had been of the next time they would meet.

Stefan Kalinsky halted the stallion with an almost unnoticeable pressure on the reins.

"I must speak with you. But not here; there is too much risk in our being seen."

"Have you been to Dover?" Jenna could not restrain her nervous excitement as she leaned toward Stefan, resting her gloved hand on the sleeve of his jacket. In her eagerness to find out what he had learned in Dover, Jenna was unaware of the devastating effect she was having on his tightly controlled emotions. Jenna had refused the small hat she usually wore, instead wearing her rich, dark hair loose and flowing to her waist, restrained only by a length of dark green satin ribbon that entwined with the vibrant flowing mass that seemed to drape to her waist like a rich mantle. The sunlight caught the golden lights in the sable-colored tresses, as if releasing threads of priceless gold hidden there. The soft oval of her face was as flawless as satin, a bright rosy hue spreading across her cheeks, accenting the slight tilt of her large, dark eyes, which met his and seemed to convey a silent message of uncertainty and longing that she would have denied had he asked her. Jenna quickly looked away, idly twisting her gloved hands in the reins, as she realized that no matter what she might have told herself over the last weeks, no matter the logic of such an affair, she had longed to see him again. And now that she had, she realized the foolishness of it all. Lillian de Stahl's words returned to tear at her.

"Are you also a guest of the prince regent?" Jenna was not aware of the sudden cold edge to her words as she urged the mare forward. The mare sidled nervously as Stefan's hand shot out, grabbing the reins, and jerking the mare's head about none too gently.

"Jenna, it is of grave importance that I speak with you." Stefan noted the sudden defiant gleam that had sprung into those wide amber eyes.

"Your message said you had to leave immediately for Dover. That was five days ago. And now you are here. With the fastest horse, it would still be impossible to ride to Dover and then ride here, in five days." Jenna bit off the last words, not at all certain why she felt such anger toward Stefan.

Stefan realized the danger of their being seen together if they remained in the middle of the open field, where the riders and Charles Wingate might easily return at any moment. In one quick movement he leaned forward, jerking the reins from Jenna's grasp.

Almost unseated as the mare was pulled around behind Stefan's stallion, Jenna needed all her efforts to remain in

178

the saddle. By the time she was able to think of retrieving the reins, Stefan had already led them deep into the woods, far from the path of the riding hunters. They rode on silently, Jenna realizing that any efforts to gain her freedom would have been hopeless, unless she chose to walk back to the lodge. Her temper overwhelming her caution, Jenna kicked her booted foot free of the stirrups and slipped from the saddle, tumbling to the ground. She quickly scrambled to her feet and started in the opposite direction, which led back to the riding trail.

Stefan swore, in a mixture of French and Russian, as he whirled the stallion about, releasing the reins to Jenna's mare. In a matter of moments he had caught up to her, easily sliding from the saddle to stand imposingly blocking her path.

"Jenna!" Stefan warned as he reached out to entrap a slender wrist in lean, strong fingers.

"It has all been a lie, hasn't it? There never was a conspiracy. This has all been some elaborate trick, and I believed it all quite easily."

Instead of listening to more of her tirade as she struggled to free herself, Stefan whirled about, dragging Jenna behind up an uncertain path that took them deeper into the woods, through brush that tore at Jenna's clothes and tree branches that snagged at her hair. It took all her efforts to protect herself along the path. When she stumbled and would have gone down on her knees, Stefan hauled her to her feet and continued their journey into the shaded darkness deep within the forest. When they at last came to a halt on the edge of a small clearing, it required all Jenna's drained strength to draw a ragged breath that hurt her aching lungs. Unable to protest, she beat feebly at his unyielding grasp of her wrist.

Halting only a moment, Stefan pushed Jenna ahead of him into the small clearing. At the opposite side of the clearing stood a small gamekeeper's cottage. Made of stone to stand the test of time, the cottage had fallen into neglect, wooden shutters missing from the windows, several panes of glass broken.

Jenna strained away from Stefan on shaky knees that suddenly would not support her. In the next moment, Jenna felt herself being lifted in Stefan's strong arms and carried to the cottage. Kicking open the loosely hinged door, Stefan carried her inside, depositing her in the middle of the dusty floor, none too gently. Only just beginning to draw an even breath, Jenna struggled to her feet, as if she thought to leave the cottage. She wanted none of Stefan Kalinsky's artful excuses or carefully contrived lies. She was immediately halted by Stefan's arms closing about her gently, but firmly.

"Jenna, you must listen to what I have to say. It is of grave importance."

"There is nothing you can say that I want to hear. Now please stand aside and let me pass," Jenna countered boldly, realizing there was little she could do if he chose to prevent her.

Stefan's blue eyes flashed with mounting frustration and anger, as he realized there was more to Jenna's sudden coldness than the meeting at Dover.

"Jenna! You must listen to me; you *will* listen to me!"

"I am not Dmitri, or even Mr. Flint, who seems to have given you his complete loyalty. I will choose what I will hear and whom I will hear it from." Jenna twisted within his embrace, trying without success to gain her freedom. Tears welled in her eyes, blurring her vision, so that she struck out at Stefan blindly.

"Jenna." Stefan's voice was no longer commanding and harsh, but a softly whispered warmth against her ear that filled her senses with sudden confusion and then undeniable longing.

"No. I don't want to hear your excuses."

"Jenna, I shall never give you excuses; only truth. Whatever you may believe, I have not wronged you. You must at least listen to what I came here to tell you. Then you may go, if you choose. Once you have heard it, I will not attempt to hold you against your will."

Slowly Jenna relaxed within Stefan's embrace. He held her for a long time, feeling the wild beating of her heart against his own. Reluctantly he released her, setting her gently into a chair that looked as if it might hold her slight weight. When she remained in the chair, Stefan knew she at least considered his words.

The damp shadows of the abandoned cottage sent a shiver through Jenna's slender body.

Stefan quickly removed his coat, wrapping it about her before disappearing out the front door of the cottage. He returned a short time later, his arms laden with sticks and twigs for a fire. Within moments, a small fire kindled tentatively, and then grew, the flames stealing through the dampened twigs and brush to flare smokily. When the fire had grown sufficiently, Stefan placed bigger pieces of wood on it, which quickly caught. A growing warmth began to pervade the cottage. The room soon became warm and cheery, the darkened corners yielding a collection of spider webs and dust that had accumulated over many years of neglect.

Jenna felt life returning to her chilled limbs as she huddled before the fire. Her gaze met Stefan's as he drew a small bench across the room and sat beside her.

"I left for Dover the same day I received your message. You are right, it would be quite impossible to reach Dover and ride here in five days. When I reached Dover and found what awaited me, I knew it was gravely important that I reach you as soon as possible. My yacht brought me as far as Harwich. I rode the remaining distance, arriving this morning in time to see you ride out for the morning hunt."

Jenna stared at Stefan uncertainly. She wanted desperately to believe him.

"What did you learn in Dover?"

Stefan moved to place another log on the fire. He straightened, leaning on outstretched arms against the stone mantel above the hearth.

"Two days earlier I had received an urgent message from a man who insisted on meeting me in Dover. His message said he could provide me with the name of a man who was part of the conspiracy, but whose loyalties were

181

questionable. He thought the man might possibly be persuaded against the conspiracy. The message demanded that I meet with this man in Dover immediately. I could not risk telling you more of it before I left. When I arrived for the meeting at the appointed place and time, I found the man murdered. I can only assume that someone knew what he was about and was determined to prevent the meeting. That also means that whoever murdered the man knew of his contact with me."

Jenna's startled gaze met his.

"Who was this man?" Her voice was hardly more than a whisper.

"His name is hardly important now. He was a Frenchman. I knew him many years ago. His family lived at Villandry, when I went there as a small child. I was without my family. His family became my family. The bonds of friendship formed as children were strong, and continued long after the Revolution. My friend was very outspoken against Napoleon. My cause to regain Villandry became his cause. It was through my friend that we first learned of the conspiracy. Now, they have silenced him."

"You are in great danger," she whispered, a sudden fear taking hold of her, causing the cold shivering of earlier to return.

"Jenna, it is not for myself that I fear. It is for you. If the conspirators know of my involvement they may also suspect you. I fear for the danger I have brought you." Stefan's voice was suddenly hoarse with his own emotion as he gazed down at her, wanting more than anything at that moment to take her into his arms, that his love for her might prove strong enough to keep her from harm.

"That is why I want you to do nothing more in this. Nothing! No one must suspect that you know anything of this."

Jenna stared at Stefan with dawning realization. He was asking her to forget their plan.

"Stefan, I can't. My grandfather . . ."

Stefan cut her off abruptly. "I will see that those

responsible for your grandfather's death are made to pay for their crimes. Jenna, can you not see?" Stefan stood before her so close that she could still feel warmth in spite of the fact that his towering height blocked the heat from the hearth. It was his heat burning through her, melting the coldness she had built against him.

"My friend was cruelly murdered, but he suffered long before the murderers ended his pain. He was a true friend, and brave. I pray he told them nothing, but I cannot be certain. Jenna, if any harm were to come to you, I could not bear it." Tenderly, Stefan reached to cradle her face in his hands, his strong, warm fingers caressing her skin, reaching to disappear into the loose tendrils of her thick hair, the ribbon lost on their wild journey through the forest.

"I would give my life to keep you safe."

Stefan's last words were a soft whisper against her lips as his mouth lowered to hers, tearing down the last of her resolve with a kiss that removed all doubts, all fears that had grown within her the last weeks.

Jenna wanted desperately to believe him, needed desperately to believe him. She pushed aside the doubts that crowded her mind, and yielded to the physical desire that burned deep within her brighter than any flame. Her hands were flattened against the soft silk of Stefan's shirt as his arms closed about her slowly.

There was within them both an urgency to feel again the exquisite joining of their bodies. And yet Stefan delayed almost painfully as he slowly undressed Jenna, reveling in the soft, silken contours of her lovely young body until she stood before him unadorned.

Stefan's shirt fell to the floor beside Jenna's garments. She reached up, her slender arms entwining about his neck, molding her hungering body full against his. Her full breasts pressed into the flattened planes of his chest wantonly, seeming to burn where their skins touched.

Stefan breathed in the woodsy fragrance of Jenna's hair, which wrapped about them like a warm cloak as his hands slid down the satin softness of her back and closed over the gently rounded fullness of her derriere, pulling her into him, feeling the lingering agony of her young body thrusting against him. With a sudden feverish longing, Stefan lowered Jenna onto his jacket spread before the hearth. Within moments his breeches lay with their other clothes, and he joined her, his kisses setting her skin aflame where they touched. Jenna moved beneath him with an urgency to match his, her long fingers raking across his skin, reaching to bind him to her as she arched against him, feeling as if she might not endure another moment without fulfillment. Stefan's hands reached beneath her, closing over her bottom with brutal strength as he pulled her against him, thrusting deep within the searing heat of her young body, like a live creature beckoned by the warmth of the flame only to be consumed by it.

Jenna cried out against Stefan's shoulder as she felt him deep within her, replacing the aching need of the last weeks with a burgeoning passion that could not be sated with one moment or one night, but only with a lifetime of love.

Stefan moved with Jenna, his strong body forcing her beyond the realm of pleasure they had known before. He felt a sudden tension in her sleek young body, heard her sudden gasp, and then the pulsing spasms that drew his own shattering release within her warmth. Stefan wrapped Jenna in a strong embrace, refusing to release her, wanting to hold her against him always.

Jenna slept peacefully for the first time in weeks, safe in the shelter of Stefan's embrace. Only when the fire had died on the hearth did she rouse with a slight shivering as the damp coldness of the cottage stole over their naked bodies with icy fingers. She remained motionless in Stefan's embrace, not wanting to relinquish their moments together. Another spasm of shivering spread through her. She felt the warmth of Stefan's lips against her forehead.

"You would not last long in the bitter cold of the Russian winter. You do not have enough fat on your bones to keep you warm," Stefan mumbled playfully against her ear before rolling from her side to place more wood upon the fire.

Jenna sat up, drawing her knees against her chest for more warmth, while she watched Stefan at this most simple of tasks. She thought she might want nothing more in life than a small, meager cottage such as this, as long as she might have Stefan to share it with her.

"You did not seem to object to these meager bones a little while ago," Jenna retorted saucily, an impish smile pulling at her lips.

Stefan turned back to gaze at her passionately as he recalled the time they had shared. The fire caught, and he turned to place more wood upon it, daring to hope they might share a few more hours.

Jenna could not resist the temptation of his lean, bronze body, naked before the spreading glow of the fire. She crawled forward until she knelt very near, and then leaned forward, pressing a trail of feather-light kisses against the skin across his muscular back. Her kisses soon became gentle nibblings as she persisted in her play. Stefan turned before her abruptly, so that her last kiss landed on the lean, taut smoothness across his belly. Before she could pull back to some remote safety, Stefan had closed her within his embrace, crushing her fiercely against the wide expanse of his chest. Momentarily breathless from the strength of his grasp, a soft sigh escaped her lips, as she realized he might easily crush the life from her and she would offer no struggle, as long as she might remain in his arms forever.

Stefan pressed Jenna back upon their crude bed, now slowly exploring all the tantalizing pleasures to be found in her lithe, young body, as he kissed her softly rounded shoulder, his lips lowering across the ample swell of her breast. He felt her breathing still in anticipation as he continued his slow meandering across the satiny softness of her skin, his strong hands moving with agonizing slowness across the softness of her body, exploring with her all the pleasures to be found in a single touch, a caress—as he had learned them many years before, but

185

never fully believed until he gazed into the fiery depths of her amber gaze to see the passion he built within her.

Jenna responded with abandon as she returned his exploring, touch for touch, stroke for stroke, each caress seeming to release a multitude of sensations that built to fevered pitch.

Stefan's kisses trailed along her finely boned hip, down the length of her gleaming thigh, where he lingered, pressing brief impassioned kisses into the soft, vulnerable skin behind her knee. Jenna thought she might die from the pleasure he gave her. Very slowly, Stefan turned Jenna, his tongue moving with deliberate slowness across her knee and then up across the softness of her thigh, her hip, the flatness of her stomach. Tenderly he kissed the softness of her skin suddenly taut with expectation. She did not halt his explorations. Slowly Stefan's head lowered, the brilliant gold of his tawny hair soft against her skin. Jenna's breath caught in her throat at that first contact, her eyes flying open in confusion at these new feelings Stefan was releasing within her. She had thought he had taken her to the farthest reaches of her awareness, but now he was taking her beyond. Jenna's hands reached out to push him away at the contact, the deepest, most exquisite pleasure. Stefan's strong hands restrained her, as he continued in the pleasure he gave her, until Jenna could deny him no longer, her long fingers reaching to hold him to her as the first waves of passion built within her. At that final moment Stefan joined her, stroking deeply within her, finding his greatest passion in the pleasure he had given her.

Stefan woke Jenna slowly, wanting desperately to prolong the hours, the minutes that seemed to flee so quickly. He dressed, leaving the cottage to see to their horses, returning a short time later to find Jenna dressed, trying to bring some order to her wild mane of hair.

"Your mare is gone. She'll return to the stables before nightfall. It is late."

Jenna nodded sadly. The sun was well overhead. If she did not return soon, others might be sent to search. They could not risk being seen together. In spite of Stefan's words to her, she was more determined than ever to learn anything that might lead to the men who murdered her grandfather.

"We will ride together to the lodge."

"It's far too dangerous. I can walk. It can't be far," Jenna responded evenly.

"It is quite far, and I will not risk your coming to some harm in the forest. We shall ride together. After all, I am an invited guest. My presence will not be unexpected."

Jenna followed Stefan out the door of the cottage and waited while he mounted the black stallion. She reached up as he took her hand, lifting her into the saddle before him. Jenna leaned back into the firm strength of Stefan's chest, and they rode for a while in silence.

Stefan guided the stallion with unerring accuracy over fallen timbers, around thickets, and across a stream that bordered the hunting lodge. He halted the animal as they emerged at the edge of the forest, across the green from Foxmoor House.

"Jenna, I must leave you here. It will be easily accepted that you fell from your horse." Stefan leaned forward, pressing a passionate kiss against Jenna's lips.

"What will you do now that the man at Dover cannot give you the name of the one man?" Jenna pressed, unwilling to allow the matter to be forgotten. She could feel the tension in Stefan's strong hands as he quieted the stallion.

"I must continue as before," he answered solemnly.

"It will be difficult without someone to help you."

"I have my sources. They may prove a bit more time consuming, but they are highly efficient."

"Dmitri and Alexei are too easily recognized. It would be impossible for them to move among these men without suspicion. And I think Madame de Stahl has other interests beyond the importance of uncovering the conspiracy," Jenna boldly replied, aware of the effect of

187

her words in the sudden flexing of muscles she felt in his arm about her waist.

"Stefan, already Napoleon has suffered great losses in Russia. The winter snows have driven him from St. Petersburg. It is logical to assume he will turn his concentration to England with more determination than ever."

Stefan sighed heavily. He was not unaware of the latest movements of Napoleon's Grand Armée. His sources in Vienna, even in Paris, had kept him informed of certain military policies that had been adopted in the last few weeks. His uncle, Czar Alexander, from the remote safety of Varykein had sent a courier with dire warnings that time was growing short. After the winter, it was safe to assume that Napoleon would send the major thrust of his army against England. If England fell, Russia remained the final prize for complete world domination.

"You should know there is a man I have seen meeting with Charles. I have never seen him before, but since we arrived I have seen him with Charles twice and once with Lord Wingate. His name does not appear on any official invitation, nor does he stay in the main lodge. He always stays among the handlers or groomsmen, but I have yet to see him handle the dogs or groom the horses." Jenna gave a detailed description of the man to Stefan as they lingered for a few moments longer.

"Does it mean that they may plan an attack against the regent here?" Jenna pressed. Stefan fell silent for a moment as he considered her words.

"Jenna, it is more important than ever that you not continue in this. The man you have described to me may possibly be the same one seen leaving Dover shortly before my arrival. He may be responsible for the death of my friend."

"You do believe they may attempt a move against the prince here."

"Jenna, in order for their plan to succeed, they must eliminate the prince regent and the succeeding members of the royal family. Yes, it is possible, but I rather believe it

188

will be a highly coordinated plan to eliminate all members of the royal family at the same time, thereby eliminating the possibility of raising an army against the French."

"You know as well as I that there is no one else who might be able to give you the information you need in time. Stefan, my grandfather's death cannot have been a waste. I must try." Jenna spoke softly, but passionately. Before Stefan could object, she slipped to the ground, refusing to meet his eyes, afraid of the anger she would see there.

Stefan remained firm in his determination. "Jenna, I will not allow you to endanger yourself further."

His words cut through her. How dare he not *allow* her? Jenna's small chin tilted defiantly, and she met his gaze without wavering.

"Whether you will allow it or no, Prince Kalinsky, I will do what is needed." Jenna squared her slender shoulders and whirled about, her firm strides carrying her quickly across the greensward to the front steps of the hunting lodge. Behind her she heard the sounds of a single horse as the rider headed for the stables.

Reaching the steps, Jenna was startled as the heavy oak door was suddenly thrown back on its hinges. Charles emerged, his face a mask of concern and anger.

"Jenna, where the devil have you been?" Charles rushed to her side as she mounted the steps.

"Charles, the devil has nothing to do with where I have been, but rather an unruly mare. My horse and I parted company shortly after the rest of you gave chase after the hounds. I spent the last hours walking back."

"You are certain you are not harmed?"

Charles Wingate was the essence of caring concern. Had she not known otherwise, she would have found it difficult to doubt his love for her.

"If you are quite all right, you must dress quickly for dinner. Madame de Stahl has arrived this morning from London, and the regent is proclaiming tonight's dinner in her honor."

Charles was not unaware of the startled expression that

crossed Jenna's lovely face at the mention of the notorious courtesan.

"It seems she arrived with Prince Kalinsky. He chose to go for a ride this morning. It is a pity that you did not see Prince Kalinsky. It might have made your return much quicker."

Jenna forced the innocent smile onto her lips. Charles was playing out a vicious game and loving every moment of it. She could only guess what he might have seen from the lodge just now, when she and Stefan returned. Did he know she lied? As they passed through the hallway toward the stairway that led to the north wing and Jenna's chamber, she cast a furtive glance out the wide sweep of windows that looked out onto the greensward beyond the lodge. At this time of day, the entire perimeter of the forest was a mass of long shadows as the sun sank low in the sky. She could see nothing but the vague outline of the treetops in the pale blue sky. Jenna fervently prayed Charles had seen nothing more.

Chapter Eleven

Jenna suffered through the dinner party that was given in honor of Lillian de Stahl. Among so many others, the notorious courtesan had managed to attract the devout attentions of the prince regent. For all Madame de Stahl's dire warnings to Jenna, Stefan Kalinsky seemed only barely attentive to the French courtesan. The evening's lavish celebrations hardly provided for any exchange with Stefan, and Jenna excused herself early, begging a headache after the morning ride. Elizabeth insisted on accompanying her, with the excuse that the celebrations of the last days had grown tiresome. Charles was most considerate of her excuses, offering to escort her and Elizabeth to their chambers. Jenna bit off a sharp reply that she had no desire to share his company. Charles had been most congenial the entire evening, except for insisting on taking possession of her hand whenever Stefan was around. At first annoyed by his persistence, Jenna later began to feel seething anger, as she realized he was merely toying with her.

Bidding Charles goodnight at her door, Jenna quickly set the lock in place. Unable to sleep, she paced the chamber restlessly. A fire crackled invitingly in the ornate fireplace, but could not drive away the haunting chill that seemed to have crept into the room. The clock on the mantel struck ten, and Jenna still wandered the length of the chamber. Finding herself before the door, Jenna was suddenly seized with an idea. Letting herself out into the hallway, she could hear the distant sounds of the dinner party, the prince and his guests obviously still enjoying their fine meal with stories of the day's hunt.

Jenna paused outside Elizabeth's door. Silence and the darkness beneath the door told her Elizabeth had retired for the evening. Jenna quickly turned her footsteps in the opposite direction, toward Charles's chamber.

Jenna listened carefully for any sound from the chamber. Not one to miss an evening's celebrations, Charles had surely returned to the elegant dining hall below. With a hand that trembled visibly, Jenna tried the knob. It turned freely, and in the next moment she stood submerged in darkness inside Charles's room. Silvery streams of moonlight invaded the chamber, casting a pale glow on the furnishings in the room. Once her eyes adjusted to the darkness, Jenna moved about easily. She was not certain what she sought; something out of the ordinary that might give evidence to Charles's involvement with the conspiracy.

Jenna went first to the large cabinet across the room from the bed. She carefully pulled out first one drawer and then another, finding only finely tailored silk shirts and other garments. The armoire yielded an ample supply of waistcoats, hunting jackets, and breeches. The bottom of the armoire was lined with spotlessly polished boots, but nothing that looked out of the ordinary.

Jenna turned next to the dressing table with wash basin. It held a brush and comb, powder, and a light cologne some of the more dandified gentlemen insisted on wearing. Jenna turned about in disappointment, her gaze resting on the small writing desk beside the bed. She found only a few plain pieces of parchment and envelopes, a quill pen, nothing more.

Jenna carefully let herself out of the room. She was not certain what she had hoped to find.

"Good evening, Mademoiselle Randolph."

Jenna had only just stepped away from the door to Charles's room and whirled around in stunned surprise.

She forced her most radiant smile as she faced the man she had seen speaking with Charles on several occasions since their arrival at Foxmoor House.

"Good evening. We have not been introduced, although you seem to know quite well who I am." Jenna sought to divert the obvious questions she saw in those sharp, dark eyes, which seemed to miss nothing as they roamed over her entire length appraisingly.

"It is my responsibility to know each of the guests, Mademoiselle Randolph," the man said benignly, his gaze unwavering, as he seemed to wait for her excuses for being in the hallway outside Charles's door.

"You are part of the royal staff?" Jenna ventured, as she refused to reveal how his sudden appearance had shaken her.

"It is my responsibility to see to the needs of each of the guests."

He had quite effectively avoided answering her directly, and Jenna felt a growing coldness in that gaze that never wavered as he continued to regard her impassively. Jenna's thoughts raced for something she might say to explain her presence in the hallway.

"I thought Sir Charles might have chosen to retire also. I wished to discuss a matter of importance with him."

"Sir Charles has returned to the evening's celebrations. I shall inform him of your desire to speak with him."

Jenna fumed silently. This miserable wretch of a man was taking great delight in seeing her discomfort at being caught in the hallway outside Charles's chamber. She was not about to give this sallow weasel the satisfaction of seeing her fear.

"I do not wish to disturb Sir Charles. It will keep until the morning."

"You said it was a matter of great importance. Perhaps I could carry a message to Sir Charles?" the weasel pressed, studying her closely for some sign of nervousness.

"In matters of love, monsieur, many things are of paramount importance. What I wish to discuss with Sir Charles will wait until the morning. I could not possibly say the words to another." Jenna smiled demurely, watching the man from beneath the sweep of her eyelashes as she gave the pretense of sudden shyness. She fairly choked on her words, but managed the most convincing of smiles as she brushed past the man and turned to go into her own chamber.

"Good evening," Jenna ended sweetly, disappearing through the door, and closing it, leaning back against it with strained relief. Of one thing she was certain. That shrewd creature would carry to Charles a detailed description of their encounter that evening.

Jenna spent a restless night behind the remote safety of her locked door, rising late to find that everyone had already left the large hall for a ride to a nearby meadow to participate in a round of sporting events that the regent hailed as a contest between the finest of his friends and subjects. Jenna was informed by her maid that Elizabeth had joined the others, venturing beyond the lodge for the first time since their arrival. After eating a light meal of spiced hot chocolate and croissant, Jenna donned her woolen shawl against the morning chill that had lingered over the landscape.

Jenna was more than a little irritated that the maid had failed to waken her in time to join the others. She wanted desperately to speak with Stefan of her meeting with the stranger outside Charles's chamber, although she knew well such a conversation was highly unlikely. Stefan had made his intentions abundantly clear: She was to have nothing to do with the matter of the conspiracy.

Her late morning walk took her past the vegetable gardens, which in warmer weather would have offered an abundant crop for the royal pallet. Beyond the greensward she heard voices in the direction of the kennels.

The kennels were a long row of small outdoor pens standing behind an equal number of enclosures to protect the royal hunting dogs from colder weather. Several litters of half-grown pups joined in wild excitement as they heard Jenna's approach. Within minutes the call had gone out the full length of the kennels, and eager muzzles thrust through the fencing in excited greeting. Jenna could not resist the temptation to pet the young pups, and soon received any number of eager licks on the hand. A young lad emerged from the far end of the stables at the excited sound of the dogs. A shrill whistle ended their wild outburst as the lad approached Jenna.

"The master of the kennels doesn't care to have anyone walking about when he's not here, mum," the lad offered politely. As Jenna looked up from where she knelt beside one enclosure and fastened him with that dazzling smile, the lad swallowed hard. He had seen her before, countless times, about the stables before the morning hunt, and had admired her firm hand with a horse. Seeing her for the first time this close, he knew he had been right. There was none who could compare with her, of that he was certain.

"I didn't mean to cause any harm. They are quite magnificent. My grandfather used to say there was no finer hunting hound than those kept at Foxmoor House. 'Tis rumored that the Americans import some of these fine hounds each year to improve their own stock," Jenna replied knowledgeably. The young lad smiled appreciatively. It was rare to find one such as her, with such beauty and appreciation of animals.

"Aye, Master Cody has a gentleman's agreement for a full score new hounds each spring with a gentleman in Virginia. He gets his pick of three top litters each June, and pays handsome for it too, what with giving Master Cody first pick of the finest colts born each year on the farm in Virginia."

"A gentleman's agreement?" Jenna mused, wondering how it might be possible for such an exchange when England and America were again at war with each other.

"Aye, 'tis true. The gentleman sails to England once each year and makes his selections. That be in early spring. In late summer Master Cody sails to Virginia with the young hounds, to make his selection of the three finest colts born at Petersborough."

Jenna smiled up at the young boy, unaware of the

devastating effect she was having on him. She was oblivious to the dazzling gold lights that played across the dark satin of her hair, or the peach-hued softness of her skin, blushed by the coolness of the morning air.

The young lad coughed nervously, a startled expression suddenly on his face, as his gaze moved past Jenna. The moment of friendship was broken as the lad bowed stiffly before her and started to return to the stables. Jenna whirled around to see what had caused such a sudden change of spirit in the boy. Charles Wingate stood at the far end of the kennels, a look of bemusement on his thin face. He was dressed for the part of the country gentlemen, in fawn-colored breeches and flowing white silk shirt. A cravat of white lace was tucked inside a dark brown velvet vest. Jenna noted the heavy leather gloves that covered his hands and extended far up his arms.

"Bewitching young boys, my lovely Jenna? How I enjoy the beauty of your smile. Ah, but now it seems to have faded. Come, join me. I was merely exercising some of the royal falcons." Charles's smile carefully masked the irritation he felt at her little display with the boy.

Jenna was soundly trapped. There was no excuse she might offer that would not seem like one. She smiled faintly as she joined Charles. They walked a small distance to the greens that bordered the north wing of the lodge. Dismally, Jenna wished she could flee to the lodge.

"I thought you had joined the others for the sporting tournaments," Jenna ventured casually.

"I grow weary of royal company, always chatting inanely about the latest fashion, or invention, or the latest fad that has sprung up about London," Charles answered absently as they reached the middle of the green where a young gameskeeper stood waiting patiently. On his arm, the young man held a magnificent Peregrine falcon, hooded, and tethered to his arm with a leather strap.

"I much prefer the hunt. There is far more excitement to be found in chasing one's quarry." Charles extended his arm, taking the Peregrine from the gameskeeper. She fluttered wildly at the unexpected movement and then quieted as Charles stroked the silken smoothness of her breast. Disoriented by the thick leather hood that covered her head, the falcon shook her fine head and grappled for a better position on Charles's arm, sending the small bell above one taloned foot, tinkling in the morning air.

Jenna stood aside, watching Charles with keen interest, wondering if there was more that had kept him from attending the sporting events. Certainly, there would be several others to join in a contest of falconry. She found it disconcerting that Charles had chosen to remain at the lodge. Jenna wondered if he had made that decision before or after learning of her meeting with his "friend" the evening before. Jenna forced an expression of mild curiosity onto her face. She had never cared for the senseless killing of birds or animals, merely for the sake of sport. For the moment, though, she must endure Charles's little exhibition.

Charles reached up and carefully unfastened the leather hood. The Peregrine twisted her fine head about in all directions to gain her bearings. Her fine senses picked up the sounds of the game birds securely penned in baskets at the feet of the gameskeeper. At a nodded command, the boy selected a dove from the basket. At a second command, he released the dove. Jenna watched her frenzied flight of momentary freedom, already aware of the bird's fate. The dove circled once, and then gained altitude in a desperate bid for freedom. In the next moment, Charles sent the Peregrine aloft.

A skilled huntress, the Peregrine flew higher and higher, her keen vision at last making her mark. With breathtaking swiftness the falcon plummeted toward her target. Jenna watched, spellbound as the falcon dropped from the sky with amazing swiftness. Unaware of its fate, the dove soared, beating its wings one last time. In less than a heartbeat the Peregrine reached the dove, those lethal talons slashing at the helpless prey. In the next moment, the dove hung lifeless in the Peregrine's talons, her neck quite effectively severed by that gleaming yellow beak.

Charles whistled a sharp command, and the Peregrine soared back over the green, dropping her lifeless kill as she returned to her perch. The obedient hound beside Charles awaited his own command and then raced to retrieve the fallen bird. The Peregrine obediently returned to her perch on Charles's arm. She cocked her sleek head to catch some faint noise on the wind, the fresh blood of the dove on her beak. Charles rewarded her with a small morsel of raw meat.

Somberly, Jenna wondered if Charles's performance were for her benefit. She glanced across the green at the sound of a carriage approaching as Charles again sent the falcon aloft, the gameskeeper releasing a second dove.

Jenna would have known the rider who approached anywhere. Beside Stefan Kalinsky, Lillian de Stahl rode in the comfort of her carriage. Jenna glanced away as they approached, unable to hide a sudden frown at the sight of the bold courtesan. Her memory was filled with thoughts of the afternoon before with Stefan at the cottage in the forest, and she lamely wondered if he had taken Lillian de Stahl there also. She refused to meet Stefan's piercing blue gaze as they approached, concentrating instead on the efforts of the falcon.

Charles turned to greet Stefan and Lillian de Stahl coolly.

"I had thought you much preferred contests of brutal strength to ones of more refined skills, Prince Kalinsky." Charles regarded Stefan with cold indifference, which quickly melted before the heat of restrained anger.

"I am afraid it was I who became quite tired of the games. Stefan was most considerate to accompany me," Lillian de Stahl replied, with hidden meaning.

Jenna was aware that the comment had been meant entirely for her benefit. If she had dared to look at Stefan, she would have seen the momentary flicker of anger that glinted across his eyes. As it was, she was left only to her silent doubts as Lillian de Stahl pursued her lost cause.

"I was showing Lady Randolph the finer skills of the

falcon, an exquisite creature, sure and swift," Charles continued.

"I, too, prefer a sport of finer skill. I think it requires little skill to thrust the falcon skyward. It is her skill that reaps the reward of satisfaction, not the handler's," Stefan countered, without the slightest trace of the anger that was barely controlled. His keen blue eyes watched the elusive prey he now stalked.

Charles whistled again for the falcon, retrieving her easily. He left the leather strap untied, and all but Stefan seemed unaware that he failed to reward the bird for her efforts. The Peregrine fluttered nervously from her human perch on Charles's arm.

"There is skill to be found in falconry, as in any sport. Ages ago these fine birds were used as weapons against opponents. Instead of the dove as prey, the falcons were used against other men." In one swift movement, Charles jerked his arm toward Jenna, the sudden movement causing the falcon to leap away from his arm, flapping her wings wildly, those lethal talons not more than a hair's breadth from Jenna's face. A piercing whistle split the air as Stefan extended an unprotected arm and beckoned the falcon. The Peregrine settled uncertainly on her new perch, and Stefan slowly handed her over to the game-keeper.

In that one instant, Jenna had raised her arms to protect herself, aware that it would have been little use against those slashing talons. She stared wide-eyed at Charles, the sudden fear causing her to tremble. To all who had witnessed the incident, it surely seemed the bird had become momentarily upset. If not for Stefan's quick actions to halt the bird, Jenna might have suffered irreparable damage. She was not fooled. In that one moment of fear, she had seen an expression on Charles's face she never wanted to see again. It gave reality to all her grandfather's dire warnings against Charles Wingate.

And in that one moment of anger, Stefan realized how futile his efforts might be to keep Jenna safe. He brought his nervous horse under control. He knew well the game Charles played. Charles had deliberately taunted him, trying to force some response he only suspected. He remained cool, realizing the wrong response could well place Jenna in even more danger.

"As I have said, Sir Charles. It is the falcon's skill, hardly the man's. I much prefer more refined skills."

Jenna turned startled eyes on Stefan. She fought to regain her composure. She dared not let Charles know how badly he had frightened her. Fear was the one thing Charles loathed in anyone. Her hand shook visibly as she reached to smooth a stray tendril of hair. She could not know how that one gesture tore at Stefan's heart.

"I believe I have had enough of sporting for one day." Jenna spoke with a calmness that belied the frantic beating of her heart. As Charles handed over the gloves and turned to accompany her, Jenna turned on him coldly.

"Please, do stay, Charles. I wouldn't think of depriving you of your sport. Perhaps you can provide Madame de Stahl with some valued advice on the skills of the hunter." Jenna whirled about and fled in the direction of the main entrance to the hunting lodge.

During the entire evening Jenna was afforded little opportunity to speak with Stefan about the man she had seen outside Charles's chamber the night before. Always when she looked for him across the crowded dining hall, Lillian de Stahl seemed to have captured his complete attention. When she looked for him much later, she felt a small amount of satisfaction that Madame de Stahl had been left to her own entertainments. Stefan was nowhere to be found. When Jenna thought she could tolerate Charles's smothering attentions no longer, she made her excuses and left the large dining hall. At the far end of the vast room a set of double glass-paned doors had been left open to allow some fresh air into the stifling room. Jenna stepped outside onto the flagstone landing and inhaled deeply of the crisp night air, which somehow steadied her nerves and cleared her thoughts of the day's events. She pulled the woolen shawl more closely about her shoulders as a faint evening breeze rustled dried leaves at her feet and sent icy fingers through the silk of her gown. Clouds had gathered before sunset and now stole silently across the path of the moon, casting shadows of silent stalking figures across the greensward, where a moment before the entire grounds about Foxmoor House had seemed almost as brilliant as day. Jenna shivered, the thin shawl hardly providing ample warmth against the building storm that gathered. She felt a sudden light pressure upon her arm. She whirled about, a sudden fear rising within her that she had ventured away from the safety of the crowded dining hall. The unuttered cry died on her lips as she was drawn into the shadows beyond the doors by strong arms that closed about her with unyielding strength, a warm hand pressed firmly across her mouth preventing her from crying out.

"Jenna, do not be frightened." Stefan's voice was warm and vibrant against her ear as he held her against him. He felt the tension immediately ease from her young body. Slowly he drew his hand away, gently stroking her cheek as he gazed down at the soft oval of her face.

"It was important that I speak with you. I fear for you in the company of Charles Wingate. He is an evil man, Jenna. You must take greater caution. Never, for an instant, trust in him."

Jenna turned her face, gently kissing Stefan's fingers.

"It is you who must take great care. Charles has a violent temper. If he were to suspect anything between us . . ."

Stefan laid a silencing finger against Jenna's lips.

"I would defend you against all danger; you must believe that. For any harm Charles Wingate might bring to you, his life would be forfeit."

"Stefan, no! You must do nothing. Charles will not harm me, not as long as he thinks to make me his wife. But you must take greater care." Jenna quickly told Stefan of her meeting with the man in the hallway outside Charles's chamber.

"Jenna, it is more important than ever that we have no

contact until the conspiracy is broken. Charles may suspect my involvement through my friendship with your grandfather. I cannot risk his thinking you to be a part of it." Stefan stare down into the wide amber depths of Jenna's gaze, where the myriad lights from the dining hall beyond sparkled like so many fires. His mouth lowered, taking possession of hers in a tender and silent promise.

Jenna surrendered completely to the warmth of Stefan's embrace, wishing desperately for the solitary silence of their woodland cottage.

Slowly Stefan released her, his hands warm and strong, holding hers for a moment longer.

"So, here it is that I find you." The heavily accented, lustily feminine voice from the doorway was unmistakable.

Lillian de Stahl ventured into the chilling night air, casually eyeing Stefan and the young woman who had quickly snatched her hands beyond his grasp.

"You should not venture so far away, my darling, when we have so much of the night yet to share. It is quite cold this evening. I believe we are in for a change in the weather. Perhaps winter will come at last. I shall have a need of your warmth this evening, Stefan. Please, do excuse us, Lady Randolph." Lillian de Stahl's meaning was unmistakable.

Stefan politely refused her ample arm through his, instead opening the french glass doors to allow Jenna to pass before them. He then seized Lillian de Stahl by her well-rounded wrist and efficiently guided her back to the festivities of the evening through another entrance at the far end of the dining hall. Anyone who watched would have seen Jenna returning from a stroll about the grounds. Stefan and Lillian de Stahl entered by a less obvious entrance near the servants' quarters.

The following morning Jenna was awakened early by her maid, who informed her that Lord Wingate had decided they should return to London that day. Elizabeth Wingate had taken an unexpected turn for the worse, and he insisted they not delay further. Jenna left the maid to do the necessary packing and hastened to Elizabeth's chamber, unable to understand her friend's sudden relapse when she had seemed in such fine spirits the evening before.

Jenna knocked lightly and let herself into Elizabeth's chamber. She found her way soundly blocked by Charles.

"Charles, I came to see Elizabeth." Jenna tried to brush past him in her concern.

"Elizabeth will be quite fine when we are returned to London. Father thought it best. It would seem we are in for a bit of nasty weather. She will be more comfortable at home," Charles informed her, seizing her hand and guiding her from the chamber.

"Would it not be wiser to wait out the storm? If Elizabeth is worse, a long, exhausting ride in a cold coach will hardly do her good," Jenna suggested with mounting concern.

Charles laughed amiably, seizing her hand and lifting it to kiss her fingers.

"My dearest Jenna, how I should treasure causing you such concern for myself. Elizabeth will be quite right when we are in London again and our physician has given her a visit. She is resting for now, and I should not wish to disturb her. I have arranged for us to return in a separate coach; less likely the danger of catching this malady of hers."

Jenna was not about to be put off by Charles's excessive thoughtfulness.

"That is complete nonsense. I shall return with Elizabeth. I have no fear of such illness. She may well have need of me." Jenna turned back to her own chamber.

"I can see you are quite determined in the matter," Charles said, suddenly quite irritable.

Jenna knew well that Charles often responded to a smile and a softly spoken word, rather than an argument.

"Charles, it is only out of concern for Elizabeth that I make such a decision; concern for her, and for you." Jenna found the last words unusually difficult. She could see that they had the necessary effect on Charles, however, or was he merely playing another game with her? She found that mysterious smile quite maddening, as if he was considering some other matter behind the mask of that mild expression she knew so well.

"Very well, I shall inform Father that we shall be leaving together."

Jenna was suddenly taken aback by Charles's yielding manner. She was certain he was up to something in insisting that they return in separate coaches. She was hardly prepared for his sudden cooperation. Jenna smiled at him faintly, thinking that there was indeed much to be careful of with Charles Wingate.

Within the hour, the coach stood ready before the massive entrance to Foxmoor House. The baggage was secured and all made ready. There had been no time to get word to Stefan of their unexpected departure. Jenna had been informed that Prince Stefan Kalinsky had departed with the duke of Kent before dawn and was not expected to return until late in the day. She thought to leave a hastily scribbled message, and then decided against it. There was too much danger of the message's falling into the wrong hands. She dared not risk it. Stefan would learn quickly enough of their return to London. Jenna had every confidence that Lillian de Stahl would inform him of it personally.

Jenna settled back into the soft upholstered seat of the coach. Charles climbed in behind her and took the seat next to her. She would much have preferred to sit with Elizabeth, but that place was already taken by Lord Wingate, who stared impassively out the window of the coach while Charles gave the final instructions to the driver. The coachman called to the team, and the coach lunged forward with a sudden lurching motion. Jenna stared across the darkened enclosure of the coach at her friend. Elizabeth was dressed warmly against the coldness of the winter day, a heavy fur muffler drawn high about her neck, partially hiding her features from view. A dark fur hat had been pulled low for warmth, so that the only part of her that remained visible was the somber light that shone in the depths of her eyes, before she closed them and sank back into the seat of the coach. Not a word was exchanged, and Jenna had cause for concern at her friend's sudden silent manner. Certainly, they had weathered childhood maladies before, but never with such dismal silence.

The rolled shades at the windows were soon dropped into place to afford more protection from the gusting wind, leaving the coach momentarily in darkness as Charles reached to turn up the small flame in the lamp. He took advantage of the darkened interior of the coach to seize Jenna's hand in his own, holding her soundly imprisoned by his heavy shoulder against hers. There was no escape. Jenna could hardly cause a scene before Elizabeth and Lord Wingate. Grinding her teeth in silent vexation, Jenna settled back into the seat, resigning herself to her temporary situation and praying fervently for fair weather to speed their journey to London.

Through the long hours of the morning and afternoon, as they sped across the gloomy countryside, darkened by the storm that descended, Jenna cast concerned glances at her dear friend with increasing frequence. Elizabeth remained stoically silent in the far corner of the coach, and neither her father nor Charles attempted conversation with her. Jenna's nerves wore thin by early afternoon, when they stopped to exchange the team of horses for fresh ones for the remainder of their journey. Lord Wingate assisted Elizabeth from the coach, and Jenna followed. They sought warmth inside the roadside inn, where a crackling fire had been built against the increasing cold of the day. Dark clouds overhead predicted they would have snow before nightfall.

Inside the inn, Elizabeth took a place at a table very near the hearth, smiling her gratitude as a young servant girl brought her a cup of hot tea. Jenna watched her friend with interest. Elizabeth was hardly the sight of some poor, stricken invalid. Though her eyes were reddened, there was little evidence of the malady that had sent them all returning to London with such haste. They took a light meal quietly before the fire, Charles excusing himself to see to the delay in readying the team. When Lord Wingate excused himself to attend other matters of privacy beyond the inn, Jenna took the seat opposite Elizabeth.

"I hardly believed Charles's words of your illness. Now I see it is not so. Elizabeth, what has happened?"

"Jenna, please. I really have not been well this entire trip. You know quite well, I hardly ventured beyond the lodge. This sudden change of weather gave me a dreadful chill last night."

"Is that what Charles instructed you to say?" Jenna looked at her friend unfalteringly. She knew well that Elizabeth had not the spirit for lying.

"Jenna, please. Do not press this matter," Elizabeth whispered as she looked pleadingly at Jenna for understanding.

"Then you are not ill!" Jenna whispered back fervently, from between clenched teeth. She had suspected as much. First Charles's determination that they ride in separate coaches and, failing that, his intervention to keep them from having any conversations. Indeed, Charles had gone to great lengths to insure that she not learn the truth of his little ruse.

"I would be willing to wager that you have not a trace of the cold left. You're hiding something. For heaven's sake, Elizabeth, what is it? You must tell me. I am your friend, I would never betray your confidence," Jenna implored desperately, somehow sensing that her friend was hiding something of grave importance.

"Jenna, I . . ." Elizabeth suddenly halted as the door to the inn gusted back wildly, the first flurries of new snow swirling into the inn with intense abandon. Charles dusted the snow off his heavy woolen overcoat.

"I can say nothing now. When we are returned to London, I must see you. Say nothing to Charles, or father," Elizabeth whispered passionately, resuming her role of the invalid, retreating into the far corner of the table, seeming to concentrate on the cup of hot tea she clutched with silent desperation between her hands.

Jenna knew it would be foolish to pursue the matter further. She rose abruptly, as if she sought to warm her hands before the blazing fire at the hearth.

"The horses are quite ready. Elizabeth, Jenna, we should be on our way. The storm has worsened considerably," Charles offered, stepping forward to guide Elizabeth to the waiting coach.

Jenna followed, stepping easily up the two short steps into the coach. She felt the possessive pressure of Charles's hands about her waist, supposedly to give her assistance. Once again, Jenna settled into the seat opposite Elizabeth. She hardly noticed that Charles sat very close to her, when ample room in the wide seat hardly called for crowding. The remaining hours of their journey, Jenna silently contemplated her friend's silent warning and wondered what secret Elizabeth protected.

Once they were in London, Jenna would make certain she learned what had prompted their quick return under the pretense of Elizabeth's illness. She could not rid herself of the feeling that it was somehow connected with the events of the past days, and she wondered if Lillian de Stahl had made it a point to mention the chance meeting with Stefan the night before to Charles. She had no fear of Charles's anger; indeed, she had much experience in handling his raging tantrums. It was his silences that frightened her more than she dared admit. His silence gave no warning of the fury he concealed.

Chapter Twelve

Jenna sat alone in the small tearoom that was located at the far end of the long arcade of shops near St. James Square. From her vantage point she could easily see everyone who strolled along the cobbled walkway, busily shopping in the many clothiers' shops or fashionable bootmakers shops that lined the square. She glanced impatiently at the clock tower that stood at the far end of the square, realizing that she might easily have missed Elizabeth in the press of holiday shoppers eager to find the perfect gift for the Christmas celebration.

The duchess of York, a Prussian princess, might well be held accountable for helping to make the Christmas holiday an exceedingly profitable one for the varied merchants along the square. With her marriage to the duke of York several years earlier, the custom of gift-giving at Christmas had become a fashionable exchange among friends, as well as family. The German custom had grown in popularity over the last years, so that the annual Christmas shopping had become a major social event often requiring several days of venturing into the market-place, interrupted for fashionable luncheons or teas, which afforded the greatest opportunity for gossiping and exchanges of the latest news of the war with France.

Earlier that morning, Jenna had made the last of her own purchases, which included a porcelain figurine of a ballerina on an ornately decorated pedestal for Elizabeth.

When the pedestal was turned, the ballerina began to whirl about in fanciful dancing movements to the sounds of tinkling music from the music box contained within it. She remembered Elizabeth's enjoyment of the ballet and thought the porcelain dancer with delicate hand-painted features a perfect gift. She had much earlier purchased a finely woven woolen shawl for Emma Kelly, delicately carved combs for Maggie, and a rosewood carved walking stick for Mr. Flint. Her most expensive purchase had been a silver and crystal brandy decanter for Lord Wingate. The selection of a gift for Charles remained her biggest problem. Anything she might have chosen seemed far too impersonal and she feared he might take some offense. More personal items somehow seemed inappropriate.

Jenna's purchase of the porcelain figurine for Elizabeth had taken her into the shop of the watchmaker her grandfather had often frequented. The shop contained not only clocks, but a vast array of music boxes. Jenna had stood in rapt delight as the shop owner had taken great pleasure in playing each melody of his collection. Each was lovely and unique in its own way. Jenna learned that Sir Avery had purchased her own music box for her grandmother from the same shopkeeper many years before. He took great delight that his creation had been passed from mother to daughter over three generations. The next hours had passed all to quickly as the shopkeeper told her of his first meeting with her grandfather as a young man, and of Sir Avery's instructions that the gold music box must be the shopkeeper's finest creation, for it was to be a wedding gift for the young man's bride. Jenna's eyes had filled with tears at the story, imagining her grandfather as a young man, desperately in love with her grandmother. Their time together had been so very brief, and yet she knew they had known great happiness. Their love had endured beyond death, beyond time. Jenna had sighed wistfully, realizing with sudden clarity the loneliness her grandfather had endured for so many years.

Jenna had accepted the shopkeeper's kind offer of tea and cakes, while he attended to some matter in the back room. He emerged sometime later with yet another sample of his fine workmanship. Jenna had stared in silent wonder at the carefully designed ring he presented on a cushion of blue velvet. It was by far the most magnificent creation she had ever seen. It was at once ornate yet simple in design. It was oval in shape and set into a fine gold setting with small, delicate filigree loops instead of prongs to hold the setting in place. A perfect, luminous pearl oval provided the background for a single fragile rose set in the very center. The brilliant crimson bloom was created by the arrangement of perfectly matched teardrop-shaped rubies, set atop a stem with leaves crafted from the finest gold. It was an exquisite creation, even more so because of the single red rose, which held a special meaning for Jenna. Noting her fascination for the ring, the shopkeeper insisted she try it on her hand. The fit was perfect, as if it had been made for her. After a moment longer, Jenna reluctantly surrendered the beautiful ring. She could hardly justify the purchase of such a ring for mere sentimentality, especially when her funds were so meager for the next months. She graciously thanked the shopkeeper for his kindness and stepped into the chilled morning air with her few purchases, burying her hands deep inside the fur pelisse for warmth. Jenna was unaware of a lean, dark-caped man across the square who watched her intently and then followed her measured pace down the length of shops. Nor was she aware of his presence sometime later when she entered the tearoom for warmth against the biting chill of the morning while she waited for Elizabeth.

Jenna watched out the paned window, which fogged over from her warmth. A moment later, the Wingate coach stopped beside the cobbled walkway in front of the tearoom.

"Jenna, please do forgive me for being so late. I had not thought so many people would be about with the weather so dreadful," Elizabeth offered apologetically.

Jenna smiled reassuringly, thinking how her friend had recovered quite nicely from her mysterious malady over the last weeks since their stay at Foxmoor House.

"I think it adds to the holiday spirit. I have ordered tea for you to warm yourself—and then we can shop," Jenna added, innocently enough. She had tried several times without success to lure Elizabeth beyond the confines of Wingate House, so that they might speak of their return journey from Foxmoor. In the nearly three weeks since their return, Elizabeth had remained at home under the pretense of recovering from her illness. Jenna was not fooled. She knew well that Elizabeth had recovered long before. She found it quite odd that Elizabeth should refuse all social commitments at the height of the season in London.

Elizabeth's cheeks flamed brightly in the warm room, and Jenna tried to pass the time with idle chatter, while Elizabeth warmed her hands.

"Have you a gift yet for John Whitmore?" Jenna asked lightly as she accepted a second cup of tea.

Elizabeth's cup rattled in the saucer with her sudden discomfort, causing Jenna to wonder what might have alarmed her friend in such an innocent question.

"I . . . I hadn't a chance to find anything," Elizabeth answered quietly.

"Well, perhaps we shall find the right gift today. There is a fine shop down the street. I made a purchase there myself."

"Jenna . . . I won't be purchasing a gift for John," Elizabeth said solemnly.

Jenna could not mistake the sudden strained silence that had come between them.

"Have you seen John since our return from Foxmoor?"

"No, I haven't. That is, I mean . . . I thought it best that we not see so much of each other for a while." Elizabeth eluded Jenna's question uncertainly.

"Elizabeth, I thought you cared a great deal for John Whitmore. I had thought it to be quite serious."

"It is, it was. I mean . . . oh Jenna, I'm not certain what I mean. I sent word to John that we couldn't see each other for a while."

"What are you talking about?"

Elizabeth twisted her small hands uncertainly and then attempted to hide her uneasiness with a casual smile. Jenna was not fooled by her friend's brave attempts to find an explanation.

"I wasn't certain that John felt the same way I did. It seemed quite foolish to pursue something that held no meaning for him."

"How could you not be certain of his feelings? It is quite obvious in the way he looks at you. Whenever you walk into a room, it is as if everyone else ceased to exist. His every conversation is filled with words of praise for you." Jenna leaned across the elegantly draped table, her deep amber eyes suddenly glinting a passionate fire. She had little patience for foolishness, least of all in one she cared for as a dear friend. And she was suddenly quite certain Elizabeth was hiding the truth from her for some reason that was impossible to understand.

Elizabeth was suddenly a vision of absolute misery, as she reached into her reticule for a lacy handkerchief, her eyes suddenly filling with tears. Unable to find the elusive handkerchief, Elizabeth's tears flowed unrestrained with mounting sadness and frustration.

"You cannot possibly understand," Elizabeth sobbed under her breath, her nose now quite red as she found the handkerchief and dabbed at her eyes and then her nose.

Jenna stared at her dear friend in sudden vexation.

"How can I possibly understand anything when you have told me nothing? Elizabeth, you will tell me everything, now!" Jenna scolded as quietly as she possibly could in the tearoom, which was now quite empty as other holiday shoppers dispersed to continue their purchases.

Elizabeth stared back at Jenna, suddenly beset with a fit of hiccoughing.

"How could everything be so wrong, when I love him so much?" Elizabeth wailed into her handkerchief, as a fresh wave of tears threatened to drown them both.

"Stop this, now! Elizabeth! Stop this immediately!" Jenna commanded.

The crying persisted, and Jenna could see that Elizabeth was quite overwrought. Leaning across the small table, Jenna smacked Elizabeth sharply across the cheek, her hand smarting from the blow as she sat back in her own chair. She looked across the table at her startled friend.

"Oh Jenna, I am dreadfully sorry. This is all such a mess."

"Start at the beginning and tell me everything. How can I help you, if I know nothing of what's happened?" Jenna reasoned.

Jenna waited patiently for Elizabeth's hiccoughing to subside, and then offered her friend another cup of tea.

"Now!" Jenna commanded, feeling very much like a mother trying to console an upset child.

Elizabeth inhaled shakily as she blew her nose as quietly as possible in the empty tearoom.

"John had planned to join us at Foxmoor. He received an invitation, and we thought it an excellent opportunity to tell Father of our betrothal."

Jenna was not greatly surprised. She had known of Elizabeth's deep affection for John Whitmore.

"John owns several warehouses near the waterfront. Two ships were delayed because of heavy storms, and he stayed to meet with the owners to make certain the cargoes arrived safely. He accompanied Prince Kalinsky and Madame de Stahl from London." Elizabeth hesitated a moment as she saw a flickering of emotion in Jenna's amber eyes.

"There was a dreadful confrontation with Charles. He wouldn't allow John to explain, much less speak with Father. Oh, Jenna, he lied to John. He told him Father had agreed to my betrothal to Sir Reginald Guilford. John didn't want to believe Charles, but you know how convincing Charles can be. I might have been able to convince John of the truth if Lillian de Stahl hadn't interfered."

"Madame de Stahl?" Jenna's deep, dark eyes widened with startled surprise.

"She came forward to offer her congratulations on my

214

betrothal to Sir Guilford. Oh, Jenna, it was so dreadful. Afterwards, there was nothing I could say that would convince John of my love for him. He left that very morning without seeing Father. I haven't heard from him since we returned from Foxmoor. What am I going to do?"

"You must speak with your father. He is a reasonable man. Surely he will see John, and all of this can be straightened out."

"Jenna, you don't understand. Father has gone this very morning to meet with Sir Guilford to make the necessary arrangements." Elizabeth seemed on the verge of another wave of uncontrollable tears.

Jenna reached out a comforting hand.

"Why would your father and Charles be so determined in this? Surely John is a very fine man, and not of meager means. You would be quite comfortable. And I have heard it said that he is a fine businessman, with an excellent eye for trading. The Whitmore family is well established. I cannot understand Charles's objections."

Elizabeth brightened visibly at Jenna's praise of John Whitmore. His attributes were quite well known about London, indeed in every port along the coast where the trading business flourished. She smiled bravely as she dabbed at her tears.

"John is a fine businessman. He understands so much of the shipping business, and he loves it so. He has been very successful over the last few years. It was not always so. When John was young, his father fell into difficult times. He lost everything the family had. He died in debtors' prison. John's mother took a position as governess and raised John by herself. There was an inheritance from John's grandfather. Most of it went to cover the remaining debts. The remainder provided for his mother, while he apprenticed as a clerk in a shipping office. He saved enough money to attend the university. After completing the university, he took a position with a shipping firm in Liverpool. In three years he purchased a partial ownership in the firm. Five years ago his partner died, leaving John the entire company. John purchased the warehouses in

London and has done quite well, although the war with the colonies and the French has hurt his business. But even so, we could live comfortably, and John says the wars will soon be ended, and then shipping will be a very lucrative business." Elizabeth's enthusiasm suddenly faded and she bit at her lower lip uncertainly as she continued. "Father has substantial commitments involving Whitmore Shipping. He threatened to cancel all shipping agreements with John's company unless I agreed never to see John again."

Jenna stared aghast at Elizabeth, who had suddenly grown quite pale with the truth she had hidden over the last weeks. Jenna found it impossible to believe that Lord Wingate could be so unreasonable. Indeed, Jenna had thought Lord Wingate greatly admired John Whitmore's drive and ambition. Jenna shook her head in disbelief. Furthermore, she found it impossible to understand Lord Wingate's sudden preference for Sir Reginald Guilford, who, despite an impeccable lineage, had a reputation about London of a gambler who had managed quite effectively to lose most of his family's great fortune over the last years.

"I had not known your father was a close acquaintance of Sir Guilford."

"He is not a close friend of father's. He is well known to Charles. Charles has convinced father that my marriage to Sir Guilford would be a far more advantageous alliance than marriage with John Whitmore. One must think of suitable arrangements." A bitter edge sharpened Elizabeth's last words.

"Why would Charles be so concerned with such matters? Surely you should be free to marry any suitable young man. I should think it far more important that Charles marry well," Jenna said thoughtfully, adding, "I was not aware that Charles and Sir Reginald Guilford shared any interests."

"Obviously, they have some interest in common. They belong to the same club, and Sir Reginald attends all the same meetings with Charles," Elizabeth said as an afterthought.

Jenna's attention was suddenly drawn back to her friend.

"What meetings?"

"Some sort of private meetings. They hold them at Watier's, or other private places. They met at Wingate Hall once," Elizabeth replied absently, hardly aware of Jenna's keen interest.

"When was this meeting?"

"It was the opening evening of the theater. You attended with Prince Kalinsky. When I returned home early, I overheard Charles and his friends in the library. He seemed quite upset that I had returned earlier than expected, and wouldn't consider introducing his friends."

"Did you hear any of their conversation?" It was difficult for Jenna to remain calm, realizing she might have chanced upon important information, but she realized the danger of involving Elizabeth, and forced herself not to show any excitement.

"I overheard two of the men talking. One had a very thick accent. I didn't realize who he was until we were at Foxmoor."

"You saw him again at Foxmoor?"

"It was the Frenchman. Surely you must have seen him. His name is Edmund Duvalier. Charles knows him quite well."

Jenna tried to remain calm. She reached a reassuring hand across the small table as she noticed Elizabeth had grown suddenly quite pale. Jenna's eyes followed Elizabeth's glance to the door of the tearoom.

Charles Wingate stood conversing briefly with the proprietor. He looked up, his gaze locking with Jenna's. His expression was at first cold and unyielding, and then the mask of a perfect smile fell into place.

Elizabeth stiffened visibly, her hands twisting nervously in her lap as she shot Jenna a pleading glance.

"Elizabeth, you gave us quite a scare. Do you really think it wise to venture out on such a cold morning when you are so recently recovered?"

To all who watched his performance, it seemed Charles had only deep concern for his sister. But the anger that lay just beneath the surface of his calm exterior was obvious to Jenna. In the polite words he spoke she heard his silent message to Elizabeth. Jenna fixed her most radiant smile on her lovely face as she came around the end of the small table, slipping her slender arm through Charles's, to divert his attention.

"I am afraid I am to blame in the matter. I needed Elizabeth's company and good advice in the choice of a gift. She agreed to meet me here. I was not aware that the weather would be so forbidding. Elizabeth seems quite well recovered. Do not blame her. If you must blame someone, it must be me. I simply would not accept her excuses," Jenna said sweetly, practically choking on her honeyed words, when she would much rather have confronted him about his meeting with the French stranger. Jenna had not wanted to believe Charles's involvement in the conspiracy. Somehow it all seemed so impossible, and yet there was so much of Charles Wingate she did not know.

"Very well. You have convinced me not to be angry with Elizabeth. But out of concern, I must insist that she return home immediately. Perhaps I may be of service in your purchase of a gift," Charles offered.

Jenna could play the game, as well. She seized Elizabeth by the hands and drew her from her chair.

"It was quite foolish of me to risk your health. We shall plan an outing when you are fully recovered. And, of course, there will be a full round of holiday parties to attend. Take very good care of yourself. We shall talk again soon about the gowns we shall wear for the Christmas ball." Jenna leaned forward to plant an affectionate kiss on Elizabeth's pale cheek, whispering a quick message for Elizabeth to have faith that all was not lost. Her friend smiled wanly as she turned to leave, Charles escorting her to the waiting coach.

When Charles returned, Jenna fixed him with a sweet smile that gave no indication of the anger she felt at his intervention, except perhaps for a fevered glow that kindled in the depths of her dark eyes. She was determined that Elizabeth would not be forced into this arranged marriage.

Three days later Lord Wingate made the official announcement of the coming marriage of his daughter, Elizabeth Wingate, to Sir Reginald Guilford.

"What am I going to do? I would rather die than be married to Reginald Guilford. His youngest daughter is older than I am," Elizabeth wailed with mounting misery as she sank into a large chair before the hearth in her sitting room.

Jenna had come to spend the afternoon with Elizabeth with the pretense of discussing their choice of gowns for the Christmas ball. She instead furnished an unending supply of fresh linen handkerchiefs to her dear friend, who was practically distraught with unhappiness.

"Don't marry Sir Reginald," Jenna stated flatly. It was a full, long moment before Elizabeth's sobbing subsided sufficiently for her to be certain she had heard correctly.

Elizabeth wiped at her reddened nose and puffy eyes as she looked at Jenna across the room. She sniffled pathetically and then blew her nose once more.

"What are you saying?" Elizabeth mumbled from behind her handkerchief.

Jenna turned back from the window, rimmed with a pattern of frost still upon the paned glass from the hard freeze the night before. The look upon her lovely face was one of complete determination.

"I have never understood the purposes of arranged marriages, where both the man and woman are forced into an alliance they care nothing for. The man takes a mistress, who bears his bastard children, who then in turn demand recognition. I fail to see what has been accomplished, except that many people are made very miserable.

If you do not want to marry Sir Reginald, then do not marry him."

"How can I not marry him, when father has given his approval? Arrangements are already being made."

"Do you love John Whitmore?" Jenna persisted insistently.

Elizabeth stared at her in complete bewilderment.

"Of course, I love him, and he loves me. At least once he loved me. I cannot be certain of his feelings now. He thinks I have betrayed him." Elizabeth sobbed into her handkerchief with renewed misery.

"You must make John understand that the betrothal to Sir Reginald was announced without your knowledge of it. You must make him understand your true feelings."

"How can I?"

"Merciful father in heaven! You haven't seen him since we returned from Foxmoor. Send him a message. Explain everything to him. Make him understand. This is not the time to be wailing about a lost love. It is not lost unless you let it be lost." Jenna was now standing over her friend, shaking her roughly by the shoulders until it seemed Elizabeth's head might snap from her neck. When Jenna released her, Elizabeth stared back at her in wide-eyed wonder.

"I fear it is much easier said than done. You have seen how Charles watches my every move. He has even refused invitations in my name, under the pretense of my illness. The only one he allows near is you, and only because of his feelings for you. I tried sending John a message. It seems I have his answer in his silence. He never responded."

"Did you take the letter to him personally?" Jenna persisted with growing impatience.

"I sent it with my maid," Elizabeth responded slowly.

"How can you be certain she took him the message? Your maid receives her wages from your father. Is it not reasonable to think that John may never have received your message?"

Elizabeth's fingers brushed vaguely across her brow. Clearly, it was a thought she had not considered.

"Surely Charles would not be so bold as to intercept a personal letter." Elizabeth struggled with her own doubts as she sought vainly to defend Charles.

"If Charles would decline invitations on your behalf, how can you think he would not do everything in his power to prevent any contact with John Whitmore? Elizabeth, can you not see? Charles is most determined in this; for reasons that are not clear. You know as well as I that Charles can be most intent on having his own way in matters. He will see you well married to Sir Reginald with hardly a thought to your true happiness. It only saddens me that your father would so willingly follow in his scheme."

"And what of you? Charles is equally determined that you and he shall be wed." Elizabeth was not unaware that Jenna did not return Charles's deep devotion.

"I know Charles's intentions. I am not so certain of my own," Jenna responded with complete honesty.

"And what of your feelings for Prince Kalinsky?" Elizabeth sniffled as she fought to compose herself.

"I think that of little import." Jenna tried to remain calm, refusing to admit how Elizabeth's question had startled her.

"What of his feelings for you?" Elizabeth persisted, knowing quite well she had struck a very delicate matter.

"Prince Kalinsky's reputation is well known. It seems he occupies most of his time with Madame de Stahl," Jenna answered evasively. Before Elizabeth could plague her with more questions for which there were no easy answers, Jenna pulled her friend from the chair and guided her to the small secretary desk across the room, gently shoving Elizabeth into the ornately carved chair.

"Write!" she commanded firmly.

"Explain everything to John. I will deliver the letter personally. This time you must leave nothing to chance."

Elizabeth picked up the feather quill uncertainly. She turned to stare pleadingly at Jenna.

"I am not certain what I should say."

"Tell him the truth. Everything. Leave nothing out. If

221

you love him, tell him you love him. If this letter fails, you know what the consequences will be." Jenna forced Elizabeth's hand down on the parchment paper.

Jenna waited patiently. Elizabeth began to write, the quill making faint scratching sounds across the paper. One page, two. Her thoughts gained momentum as the words filled the pages. By the time she finished, five pages of neatly scribed parchment lay before her. Elizabeth folded them neatly and tucked them inside an envelope and sealed it with heated wax. She handed the sealed letter to Jenna, her hopes filling the depth of her eyes.

"You will see that John receives it?"

"I promised I would. I shall deliver it this very afternoon. Be of good faith. I shall not fail you."

"Charles will be most angry if he should ever learn of this," Elizabeth warned tremulously.

"If John responds as I think he will, then all shall know of it, in time. But of course, by then it will be too late for Charles to do anything." Jenna tucked the letter into the fur pelisse. It would be quite safe there. A coach clattered across the cobbled drive and drew to a halt at the front of the large manor house. No matter that Mr. Flint had returned early. The weather had grown quite forbidding, and Jenna wanted to be certain that John Whitmore received the letter from Elizabeth that same day. She seized her cream-colored woolen coat, the rich sable fur that lined the high collar, matching the dark glow of her hair. Jenna bent to plant a loving kiss on Elizabeth's cheek, and whirling on her heel, left her friend to her silent hopes.

Jenna halted suddenly at the landing at the top of the wide staircase, as she heard voices from the doorway below. It was not Mr. Flint who had arrived, but Charles returning from some appointment. At that moment the last person she wanted to see was Charles Wingate. There was far too much at stake for him to find her there with Elizabeth. Jenna leaned over the balustrade and listened carefully. If Charles retired to the drawing room or the library, she might yet slip past to the front door with none the wiser as to her presence. Jenna pulled back suddenly, flattening herself against the far wall of the landing as Charles and his companion passed beneath her and entered the library. Jenna stiffened as their conversation continued. She had not seen Charles's companion, but she knew that voice that rose and then became fainter, as Charles stepped to draw the double doors closed against any interruptions. In those few moments Jenna had recognized a voice that she had heard many times before from her grandfather's library, when the prime minister and various members of his staff met to confer with Sir Avery. The man in the library with Charles Wingate was one of those men, of that she was certain. Jenna fought back her mounting fears. Charles was not given to political involvements. Indeed, he had often stated that politics were beyond his interests. What could his association with this man possibly mean, unless Stefan Kalinsky's warnings of Charles's involvement in the conspiracy were true. Jenna shivered with a sudden chilling dread of the truth. She retraced her steps back down the hallway past Elizabeth's chamber, down a long hallway in the west wing, toward a door that she knew led to a narrow stairway to the servants' quarters below.

Jenna hesitated as she passed Charles's chamber. Surely it was madness—but, more than proof of his involvement Jenna desperately hoped to find proof of his innocence. She pushed open the door to his chamber, closing it gently behind her.

The chamber testified to Charles's extravagant taste for the ornate. A large canopied bed dominated the room, hung all around with blue velvet hangings. A large armoire with gilt-edged scrollwork filled the opposite wall. A pitcher and washbowl sat atop an equally elaborate dressing table. The room was immaculate, with only a velvet robe laid neatly across the bed.

Jenna crossed the room to the desk that sat before the large paned windows. All was in perfect order. A gold inkwell, and quill pen, an ornate clock to mark the time. Jenna carefully pulled out the top drawer. There was nothing that might give her any information, only neatly stacked parchment and envelopes elaborately embossed with the Wingate family crest with Charles's initials beneath it. Jenna turned to gaze about the room thoughtfully. Her amber gaze swept the shelves of the bookcase on the wall behind the desk. She dared not linger to inspect Charles's taste in books. Like everything else in the room, the books that lined the shelves were all perfectly arranged, as if for decoration. It was as if no volume had ever been removed for reading; except for one book at the far end of the second shelf that protruded noticeably from the perfect line of bound volumes. Jenna reached to press the book into alignment with the other books, her fingertips brushing against a paper that had been inserted among the pages. As she reached to pull the book from the shelf, Jenna heard the sounds of someone approaching from the hallway. She quickly pushed the book back in line with the others. Whirling about, she darted across the room toward the heavy velvet drapes that hung to either side of the paned windows.

Charles Wingate crossed the chamber to the neatly arranged shelves of his favorite literary volumes. He immediately selected the same book Jenna had found only moments before, leafing through to the page he sought. It was a perfect selection; the collected verse and prose of Lord Byron, the literary lion of the season.

The silence in the room was unbearable. The frantic beating of Jenna's heart pulsed in her ears so that she feared the two men must certainly know of her presence. She fought back the rising panic that threatened to destroy the last of her composure. If she was found now, there would be no possible explanation that she might offer Charles that would be acceptable. Jenna fought the lightheadedness that set in from being unable to draw a deep breath of air. She forced herself to concentrate on what Charles and the unknown man were saying. Each word could well hold great importance.

Charles removed the piece of paper pressed neatly between the pages and turned to the man who had followed him from the library.

"This list of instructions is from Duvalier. Deliver it to our friend in Parliament. Make certain he understands that he is to do nothing until he receives further instructions from me. It is imperative that all instructions are followed precisely, if we are to be successful."

"What of Prince Kalinsky?" the man questioned.

Jenna strained to hear their words, which were muffled by the heavy folds of velvet that concealed her. Her faint breathing stilled in her throat at the sound of Stefan's name.

"You need have no fear of Prince Kalinsky," Charles answered confidently.

"After Dover, it would seem we have much to fear. He is most persistent. Some of the others fear you may not be able to stop him."

"You may tell the others, there is nothing to fear in Prince Kalinsky. He is only one, and no different than any royal weakling. He seeks only to preserve his royal station in life at the cost of others. His efforts will not succeed, I shall make certain of that. Napoleon will give us our advantage and we shall use it. England will be ours."

Jenna listened carefully, but any further conversation was silenced by the closing of the door to the chamber.

For several long moments, Jenna remained hidden in the voluminous folds of the drapes, only daring to venture forth when she was certain Charles and the other man had indeed left the chamber. Stepping out from behind the velvet hangings, Jenna drew her first deep breaths of air to clear her head. Surely it must all be some dreadful nightmare. Surely she had mistaken the words she had heard. Her presence in the dimly shadowed silence of Charles's chamber was mute proof that she was not dreaming. Gathering her composure, Jenna quickly crossed the room and listened carefully at the door. She heard nothing. She could only guess how long she might have been in the room. If she did not leave soon, Mr. Flint would be arriving for her, and all would be lost. Somehow she had to find a way out of Wingate Manor before Mr. Flint arrived.

Jenna returned to the bookshelves behind Charles's desk. Her gaze scanned the neatly lined volumes of books until she found the one she sought. Jenna quickly fanned through the pages. The list was gone, as she was certain it would be. Jenna replaced the book and listened again at the door. Satisfied that no one was about, Jenna quietly let herself out of the room. She glanced down the one end of the hallway toward the landing. She could not know if both men remained below, but she dared not risk being seen. She thought of returning to Elizabeth's chamber with the excuse of a prolonged visit, until she heard Charles's voice from that room down the hallway. There was now only one hope for escape.

Jenna turned back down the opposite direction of the hallway to the door at the far end just beyond Charles's chamber. It opened to a narrow, winding stairway that led to the servants' quarters below. As children, she and Elizabeth had often escaped from the governess down that same flight of stairs, from punishment for some misdeed. Those stairs now offered the only escape.

Jenna hesitated at the small door at the bottom of the stairway. She knew it opened onto the small hallway just beyond the kitchens. At the end of that hallway was a servants' entrance at the back of the large manor. Jenna opened the door barely enough to see into the shadowed hallway. She listened carefully for sounds of anyone approaching. When she was satisfied that all the servants were well occupied in other parts of the large house, she quickly stole out the door and down the short hallway.

Jenna didn't stop to look back. She darted quickly out the back door of the manor and stepped onto the cobbled pathway that wound through the private vegetable gardens that were maintained for the Wingate family. The sky had darkened, and a sharp wind had come up that sent icy fingers stealing through the folds of Jenna's coat. She buried her hands inside the pelisse and followed along the stone wall of the main house until she reached the cobbled pathway that led to the stables. She glanced quickly around the corner of the house and sighed her relief that

Mr. Flint had not yet returned for her.

Across the cobbled pathway a groomsman closed the stable doors against the coming storm. Jenna seized her opportunity and fled across the pathway just as the first drops of rain began to fall. Her flight across the extensive green of Wingate Manor was shielded by a long hedgerow along the far side that led to the heavy iron gates at the entrance. Jenna paused to catch her breath as she fought to maintain her footing on the rain-soaked green with only the thin slippers on her feet. She most certainly had not come prepared for cross-country escapes on foot. Her head shot up at the sound of an approaching team of horses. In one last frantic sprint in the shelter of the hedgerow, Jenna rounded the corner of the gate and practically ran headlong into the team Mr. Flint fought to control.

The rain had now become a torrential downpour, the cold wind quickly turning the drops of water into pellets of ice that stung Jenna's cheeks as she waved Mr. Flint to a halt.

Mr. Flint sprang from the top of the coach, and in one swift movement scooped Jenna into the shelter of his strong arms and deposited her inside the shelter of the coach. Not waiting for an explanation, he returned to the top of the coach and whipped the team into a frantic pace to reach Hallston House before the storm worsened.

Stefan Kalinsky read the brief message for the third time before slamming it down hard on the gleaming surface of the mahogany desk. All the frustrations of the last weeks showed clearly in the strained lines that formed the frown of his handsome lips. The muscle in his jaw tensed beneath the smoothness of his tanned skin. He turned to stare out the paned windows of the library at the leaden sky that had brought snow earlier, rapidly turning to stinging shards of sleet that pelted the glass as the wind gusted against the paned windows. Arms outstretched to brace his weight, Stefan leaned heavily against the window frame. Everything was moving beyond his control. The duke of Kent had insisted on this waiting game, which seemed to weigh more of a disadvantage with each passing day.

Dmitri had picked up the message that had arrived by courier earlier in the morning. The English words meant nothing to him. But Stefan's mood explained everything quite clearly. They had received one other such message the week before. The giant Cossack feared the message was the same.

"What of the man in Calais?" Dmitri questioned, breaking into the Russian language, which was much easier to understand than the French he had been forced to learn at Stefan's insistence.

"It is the same as before, my friend. Murdered. It seems our plans are known almost as soon as they are made. We must assume that someone we have trusted has betrayed us," Stefan admitted solemnly. His meaning was not lost on the giant Russian.

Dmitri knew well the doubts that haunted Stefan Kalinsky. "The little princess is innocent in this." There was a note of unshakable conviction in Dmitri's voice. He had never been wrong about anyone before. He refused to accept that he might be wrong now, especially when he had become so fond of the beautiful young girl.

"We must trust no one, until I have learned who has betrayed us. Do you understand? No one! Mademoiselle Randolph must be watched at all times; for her safety as well as for the success of our plans. Time grows short, my friend. We must stop the conspiracy. And now with the death of this second man in France, we must begin anew."

Dmitri watched Stefan Kalinsky with a practiced eye. He knew well the quietly restrained anger that rested just beneath the mask of perfect control. He had seen it countless times before. That anger was now fired by the mounting frustration and thwarted efforts of the last weeks and months. And by the possibility that the "little princess" had come to mean more to Stefan Kalinsky than he dare admit to anyone. The only news of hope in the last weeks had been of the French retreat from the bitter snows of winter across the Russian steppes. French losses had been heavy, and Napoleon had retreated to gloomy silence in his palace at Fontainebleu. Having failed to conquer Russia, Napoleon's concentrated efforts would probably be against England.

Stefan turned about suddenly as Alexei entered the library. Mr. Flint stood waiting in the hallway beyond, greatly resembling a great, bedraggled bear, weighted down by the sodden mass of the heavy woolen coat he wore. Stefan spoke briefly with Mr. Flint and then returned, crossing the room in long, even strides and quickly dispensing orders for his coach to be brought around to the front of the house. A fire glowed vibrant and menacing in the depths of his piercing blue eyes. It was as if he had suddenly been transformed into a wild, hunting beast, possessing a dangerous energy only barely contained within the form of a man.

Dmitri knew that look well. He had seen that haunting coldness before at Varykein, as the boy, forced to leave his mother, steeled himself against the pain of emotion. He had seen it again years later, in the man the boy had become, when they had been forced to leave Villandry, as Napoleon sent his brother to claim all private land holdings in the name of the Republic. Only Dmitri knew that the cold mask of reserve concealed a tormented soul. That look held only the promise of death and vengeance. He had pledged himself body and soul to Stefan Kalinsky, in a bond that only the two of them could easily understand. Without being told, he knew that the "little princess" had come to some harm. He shared Stefan's silent agony, for he greatly admired her fine spirit and fiery strength. He knew well that those responsible for bringing her harm would pay with their lives. If that included Charles Wingate, so much the better. Dmitri would gladly hold the blade to end his life.

The coach sped across London at a murderous pace, sliding uneasily across the cobblestones, which were now covered with a thickening layer of ice. Alexei heartily cursed the English coaches that were ill equipped for such weather as he cracked a whip over the heads of the horses. In the last light of day, darkened by the ominous stormclouds that crowded the late afternoon sky, it seemed their progress was painfully slow, as the horses struggled to maintain their perilous footing on the treacherous stones. Alexei had been given but one order, and he refused to slow their frantic pace.

Chapter Thirteen

Emma Kelly wrung her hands in mounting despair, as she kept her silent vigil over her mistress. She pulled another down quilt high over Jenna's shoulders as the chills returned to shake her slender body. The maid glanced uneasily at the clock, noting that Mr. Flint had been gone well over an hour. She cursed under her breath in a sudden outburst of Gaelic as she wondered what might be keeping him. She bent over to lay a hand across Jenna's forehead, her own coolness meeting intense heat in that flushed brow. She shook her graying head, silently wondering what might have caused her young mistress to run out into the middle of such a dreadful storm, rather than waiting for Mr. Flint to call for her. All Emma's persistent questions had failed to receive any satisfactory answer. Her mistress had been in a fine temper that Mr. Flint had returned to Hallston House rather than following her instructions to drive immediately to the waterfront along the Thames. Any further questions had been ignored as Jenna was taken with fever and chills. Emma Kelly had ignored all further protests and quickly sent her mistress to bed, dispensing Mr. Flint to return with the physician.

Emma Kelly looked up, the lines of concern in her rounded face easing as she heard the sounds of heavy boots down the hallway. She crossed the chamber, reaching the door a moment too late, as it was thrown open, the tall form of Stefan Kalinsky dominating the doorway.

Not waiting for approval from Emma Kelly, Stefan impatiently pushed the maid aside.

Emma Kelly sputtered and fumed at the sudden intrusion, turning her questioning glance back to the doorway, where Mr. Flint waited, his rain-soaked hat clenched firmly in his hands. A sudden dawning spread across her face. She turned the full concentration of her objections on Stefan Kalinsky, quickly scurrying around him with an agility that belied her advanced years, so that she stood like some fierce lioness, determined to protect her young.

"I'll not have you bothering her. She is ill enough without you coming here, and look at you. Practically soaked to the skin yourself. You'll be no better than she if you do not take yourself home and be rid of those wet clothes. And I'll thank you kindly not to interfere with Mr. Flint. He had his orders to bring the physician. Now we must wait all the longer, while I send him out again. It will be on your head if she comes to some greater harm for the delay," Emma Kelly fumed, drawing herself to her full meager height, as if she might hold back the towering man who stood before her. As Stefan removed the heavy woolen overcoat, tossing it aside and turning back to her with an expression of silent determination, Emma Kelly held her hands out before her.

"Nay, I'll not let you come any closer. 'Tis only harm you bring her. Go away and let the poor girl alone. Has she not suffered enough with the death of her grandfather?"

Before Emma could step back beyond his grasp, Stefan Kalinsky seized the short, stout woman about the shoulders and quite easily lifted her clear of the floor, setting her out of the way. A flood of Gaelic curses filled the air, as Emma became quite flushed in her efforts to gain her freedom, all to no avail. The fuming and sputtering halted only momentarily as Stefan deposited her beyond reach of the bed, near the hearth, suddenly jarring the breath from her lungs. In the next moment, Emma seized the iron poker from the hearth and launched herself at Stefan's back. Before she could strike her target, Emma found herself soundly grasped about her ample waist and lifted off the floor, so that she dangled helplessly in Dmitri's great, bearlike embrace. She struck out wildly, in an effort to hit anything within reach. Mr. Flint stepped forward, clasping her rounded wrist in his strong grip and easily removing the lethal poker from her hand.

"Cease, woman!" Mr. Flint commanded firmly.

Emma Kelly stared in stunned surprise at the authoritative command. Such outbursts were rare in Mr. Flint, and usually well heeded. Restrained but hardly defeated, Emma attempted a different tactic. She turned her arguments on Stefan Kalinsky, as she struggled to draw the slightest breath within the unyielding grasp of that great Russian bear.

"You will all be the death of her. A physician is what she needs. The longer the delay, the greater the harm. If you care for her at all, you will not interfere in this," Emma argued, helplessly pinned in Dmitri's grasp.

His patience countered by his concern for Jenna, Stefan whirled on the hapless maid, quickly dispensing his orders to Dmitri and Mr. Flint.

"Take her from here. She is not to be allowed to return until I give the order. Mr. Flint, I want hot water, enough to fill the tub for a bath. Dmitri, I want a roaring fire, a pot for brewing your special tea." Stefan's orders were fired in rapid succession, leaving no room for hesitation, as each man turned to see them carried out. Dmitri turned to see about more wood for the fire, a distraught Emma Kelly still hanging from his massive arms.

"You have taken complete leave of your senses. You cannot think to be exposing her to a bath, when she is already taken with a chill. If you have any caring for her at all, you'll not be doing this," Emma pleaded, drawing back instinctively as Stefan Kalinsky whirled on her.

"Cease, old woman!" Stefan ordered with menacing calmness. "You cannot possibly understand what I feel for her. Now go. Return only when you care to help. I know well what I am doing." Stefan's words carried a sharpness more commanding than any blade as he stared at the faithful old woman, who trembled visibly in Dmitri's grasp. When the burly Russian released her, Emma quickly fled the chamber. She doubted these barbaric Russians and their primitive ways, but she no longer held any doubts of Stefan Kalinsky's feelings for Jenna.

Stefan turned back to the large bed, which seemed to engulf Jenna's smallness. She lay beneath the mound of downy quilts, her violent shivering seeming to set the entire bed in motion. She seemed oblivious of Stefan's presence as he leaned over her, his long, lean fingers gently pressing against the molten heat of her cheek. A dreadful coldness closed about his heart. What could possibly have driven her out into the storm? Mr. Flint knew nothing more than her first orders to be taken to the warehouses that bordered the waterfront, hardly a reasonable destination. Had Mr. Flint followed those orders, instead of returning to Hallston House, Jenna's condition might have been far worse. Yet, watching the violent shaking of her slender shoulders, Stefan doubted that it could be much worse.

Maggie burst through the door of the chamber, quickly followed by two young maids and Mr. Flint. Emma Kelly reappeared, but remained in the doorway. The brass tub was quickly hauled before the hearth, and buckets of steaming hot water were quickly emptied from the buckets the maids carried. They retreated to bring more hot water from the kitchens below. Stefan could see that their efforts would be slow and costly. He quickly dispensed Mr. Flint to aid Dmitri in bringing sufficient wood to build a roaring fire on the hearth so that the water could be heated in the chamber. He dampened a linen cloth in the basin beside the bed and carefully laid it across Jenna's fevered brow, gently smoothing back the dampened tendrils of dark hair that clung to her skin. Stefan tenderly moistened her lips with the cloth, and Jenna opened her eyes for the first time with some sign of recognition. Her voice was shaky with the violent trembling that returned to wrack her slender body as she gazed at him uncertainly. His name was a faint whisper on her lips, and she again closed her eyes, certain she must be dreaming.

The fire on the hearth was fueled continuously with fresh logs, until the flames leaped high about the huge iron kettle filled with water. Steam drifted about the room, creating a vaporous warmth that seemed to ease Jenna's labored breathing. Emma Kelly had returned to stand quietly watchful at the foot of the bed. The remainder of the brass tub was filled with cold water from buckets the maids brought from the kitchens, cooling the water to Stefan's satisfaction. Stefan stripped the quilts back off the bed.

A horrified expression crossed Emma Kelly's face, as she guessed his intention. She flew to restrain his arm.

"You cannot be thinking to put her in there. The water is almost stark cold. You'll be killing her."

Stefan turned on the old woman with a menacing glare that silenced all further protest.

Dmitri crossed the room and quickly ushered the panic-stricken woman from the chamber.

In the delirium of her fever, Jenna felt a sudden coldness returning as the quilts were pulled away. Weakly she reached to retrieve that meager warmth as her slender body was possessed by another spasm of shivering. She felt only the gentle restraint of strong hands that easily brushed her hands aside and then reached to pull the gown from over her head.

"No!" Jenna's voice croaked from between fevered lips. The heat of the fever that consumed her slender body, distorting her thoughts. She saw only the figure of a man leaning over her, taking something from her. She could think only of the letter Elizabeth had given her. Someone wanted the letter. Jenna struggled with the myriad visions that swam before her blurred vision. She could not let him have the letter. She must get the letter to John. Jenna struck out at the man leaning over her, with feeble gestures that soon became impossible with her fading strength.

Stefan drew the muslin gown over Jenna's head and tossed it aside. He gently lifted Jenna and bore her to the tub of water before the hearth. She curled instinctively toward the only warmth she could feel, the lean, hard strength of his body. With infinite care, Stefan lowered Jenna into the cooling depths of the brass tub, cradling her head against his shoulder, the sleeve and shoulder of his shirt dampened beneath her slender weight. Jenna shuddered at the first contact with the cool water, too weak to struggle against Stefan's hold of her. She turned toward him, her wide amber gaze glistening brightly with the fever that raged through her. Stefan carefully pulled the waving mass of her long hair beyond the water. It was still damp from her flight through the storm. A score of questions filled his thoughts, but they would have to keep until later. He stared into the glowing depths of her eyes, seeing a momentary flicker of recognition there.

"Stefan?" Jenna whispered uncertainly, thinking she must be dreaming, unable to understand why he would wish to cause her harm, when all she wanted was the warmth of her bed. She reached to touch the line of his jaw with trembling fingers, so that she might know that he was indeed real.

"I will take care of you my little princess. You must trust me." Tenderly, Stefan pressed a kiss against the heat of her brow. Jenna relaxed within the curve of his arm in the water, and Stefan seized the linen cloth and gently bathed her, stroking her aching skin with a feather-light touch, the cool water slowly stealing the heat away from her skin. The unusual flush of color across her cheeks faded, and the violent trembling eased. Stefan gently lifted her from the tub and sat before the hearth, gently drying her with a linen towel, as one would a child. When she was sufficiently dried, he wrapped her in a linen sheet and seized a dry towel, fanning the thick length of her sable hair before the drying heat of the fire. When all traces of dampness were gone, Stefan lifted her gently and returned her to the bed, covering her loosely with the linen sheet and a light blanket. There was a faint knocking at the door, and Dmitri entered carrying a small kettle. Emma Kelly stole quickly through the doorway, hiding herself among the shadows.

Alexei quickly followed the maid, carrying an odd-looking urn crafted from the finest silver. Steam emanated from the spout of the urn, filling the air with a pungent aroma. Emma Kelly sniffed disapprovingly, yet maintained her silence as she noted Jenna had survived her cool bath, and indeed, seemed to be resting more comfortably. She watched Dmitri with a suspicious glare as the giant Cossack sat before the large urn. Taking a small, handleless silver cup, he tipped the urn until a dark liquid filled the cup. The pungent aroma was from the dark liquid he poured, and Emma crept forward to investigate the strange brew more closely. Dmitri nodded his great, bearlike head as he watched the woman in the shadows.

"You have nothing to fear in my remedies, old woman. It is a strong tea, made from the finest herbs. I carry them with me always. Many years ago, a Gypsy girl shared the secret of the herbs with me. We shared much more, but when she left she gave me the secret of the herbs that bring healing magic."

"Magic! Bah!" Emma retorted as she watched every move with growing curiosity.

"And I suppose next you'll be telling me you need that fancy silver pot to brew it in."

Dmitri considered the stout maid from behind the mask of heavy beard that covered his face. He handed Stefan the small silver cup of pungent liquid.

"The samovar is much like your teapot, but the brew it yields is far superior. One day I will show you," Dmitri offered stoically.

Emma Kelly huffed indignantly as she kept a vigilant eye on Stefan Kalinsky.

"I have no need of learning your barbaric Russian customs. A fine English teapot is far superior."

Dmitri continued undaunted. "The samovar brews the tea perfectly. Never too strong, never too weak, as with your English teapot. Always the same. For treatment of sickness, it is important that it always be the same."

Emma found his reasoning difficult to understand. She

didn't bother to argue that the strength of the mixture might possibly have something to do with the amount of tea, not the pot. She crept forward for a closer inspection of her mistress.

Stefan slipped his arm beneath Jenna's head and raised her from the pillow. He gently pressed the cup against her lips. Jenna groaned and tried to turn away, but Stefan persisted, speaking softly to her in a mixture of French and Russian that she could not have understood.

Stefan's words, gentle against her ear, washed over Jenna with tender persistence. Wanting only to sleep, Jenna found it impossible and responded to his gentle commands, taking a tentative sip of the liquid. Still Stefan persisted, not satisfied with her one sip of the tea. Jenna drank slowly, feeling a warming heat stealing through her body that lingered long after the tea was gone. Her entire body seemed to glow, all the aching coldness slipping away. The distant buzzing in her head silenced, and she looked at Stefan with returned sanity, just before uncontrollable sleepiness set in.

"Stefan, I must tell you," Jenna whispered, as Stefan cradled her gently in his arms.

He silenced her with a finger against her lips.

"We shall talk later, little one. For now, you must rest. And when the fever has gone, we shall speak of it."

Jenna could not fight the soft glow that stole over her senses, confusing her thoughts, making the words tangle on her thickened tongue. She resisted no longer, curling into the warmth of Stefan's embrace, the linen sheet falling away to expose her naked back. Stefan reached to pull the sheet over her shoulders, settling back against the corner of the bed. He would remain with her as long as necessary. He would trust her care to no one.

Emma Kelly suppressed a startled gasp to find that Jenna wore nothing beneath the sheet. She started forward to make her protests, and found her way soundly blocked by Dmitri. He seized her wrist in his great paw of a hand and guided her to the door.

"Come. I will teach you how to make the tea. Then, someday, you can make it for me. Eh?" His humor over his little joke filled the air as Dmitri escorted Emma from the chamber, his deep chuckling rumbling deep in his great chest. Emma could do little but obey. She cast a worried glance over her shoulder as she disappeared through the doorway.

Through the long hours of the night, Stefan remained with Jenna. When the fever returned, he again stripped away the linen covers and returned her to the cooling bath before the hearth. He repeatedly forced the steaming, pungent tea between her lips, and then built the fire on the hearth to maintain the warmth in the chamber while she slept.

Shortly before the first streaks of gray lightened the night sky, Jenna's fever broke, small beads of perspiration forming a film on her skin. Stefan tenderly drew the cool, dampened cloth across her body, wiping away the clamminess until her skin beneath his hand again felt normal.

Jenna drowsily turned her gaze to Stefan, the faint smile on her lips turning into a frown as she noticed the lines of fatigue and worry about Stefan's eyes. Her fingers sought his, drawing strength as they entwined.

Stefan drew her hand to his lips, pressing an impassioned kiss against her fingers, the fatigue of the last hours suddenly slipping away as he saw the sanity returned to her wide amber gaze.

"You have been here all this time?" Jenna whispered.

"I could trust your care to no other. I promised you I would keep you safe," Stefan responded huskily, with sudden emotion. "I could not know you were given to running about in raging storms. That was most foolish, little one. When you are recovered we shall speak of it again."

Jenna's memory of the day before cleared, a sudden uneasiness lighting the depths of her eyes. "The letter! I must deliver the letter. I gave my word." She spoke with sudden passion.

Stefan silenced her with a finger against her lips. "We shall speak of it later."

Jenna twisted her head from side to side in mounting desperation. "You do not understand; it is most important that the letter be delivered immediately. I promised Elizabeth."

Stefan smiled at Jenna tenderly as he comforted her with soothing words. "Where is this letter? I will see that it is delivered." His gaze followed Jenna's across the room to where her coat and fur pelisse lay across a chair. He quickly found the letter inside the fur pelisse, and soon recognized the name in neat lettering across the envelope. It explained Jenna's unsuccessful attempt to reach the waterfront warehouses in the midst of the storm.

"I will send Alexei to deliver your letter." Stefan returned to her side.

Jenna reached up to seize his hand imploringly. "Charles must not know. Please make certain he does not know."

Stefan smiled reassuringly as he bent over Jenna, his lips closing tenderly over hers.

"I promise you, my love, none shall know of it." Stefan lingered a moment longer, until Jenna relaxed, finally closing her eyes to rest. He left to give the letter to Alexei with his explicit instructions for secrecy. Returning to the chamber, he bent to place more wood upon the fire. He returned to Jenna's side, watching her face for any signs of the fever's returning. He saw none, only the soft glow of returned health upon her cheeks, her even breathing, the coolness of her skin beneath his fingers. She opened her eyes slowly at his touch.

"Your letter is being delivered at this very moment. You must think no more of it."

Jenna nodded obediently, sleep suddenly pushing all further thoughts from her mind. She struggled to remain awake, reassuring herself that Stefan was indeed near.

"Charles . . ." Jenna whispered faintly, as sleep crept over her.

"What of Charles?" Stefan leaned closer, again wondering what part Charles Wingate might have played the day before.

"Dangerous. So very dangerous," Jenna responded vaguely, as sleep finally returned.

Stefan held her slender hand in his, wondering what she had been trying to tell him. He could only wait until she was stronger. The exhaustion of the last hours had taken its toll. Beyond the warmth of the house, the storm had continued through the night, a light snow falling to lighten the dreary gray of dawn. Stefan removed his own clothes, carefully slipping beneath the covers, gathering Jenna's slender body beside him. He smiled gently as she curled toward him, entwining her slender legs with his. There would be other times, he vowed, when he could take full advantage of her softness beside him in bed. For now sleep was the best remedy. Very soon his own deep, even breathing matched hers.

Jenna stirred slowly, feeling the warmth of a heavier weight beside her in bed. She moved weakly, finding herself soundly pinned beneath an outthrust arm across her breasts. Her vision was filled with waving golden brown hair that framed a well-tanned profile. The rough golden stubble on Stefan's chin scratched her forehead as she snuggled against him, breathing in the masculine scent of his nearness. Her lips brushed the column of his neck, lingering to press a kiss against his skin. Drowsy, she had not the faintest idea how he had gotten there. She only knew an overwhelming pleasure at his warmth mingling with hers.

Stefan turned and gazed down at the exquisitely beautiful young woman beside him. His arms closed about her slender body possessively, feeling the coolness in her skin. The fever was gone. He smiled appreciatively. Dmitri's cure had worked healing magic. He luxuriated in the feel of her lips against his skin, marveling how her nearness could arouse such passion within him. She tilted

241

her lovely head back, and Stefan stared into the clear depths of her tawny gaze, alight not with fever, but with her own mounting desire.

"You are much stronger this morning," Stefan observed playfully, his fingers caressing the line of her jaw and continuing down along the curve of her slender neck to her well-rounded shoulder, his fingers fanning across the ample swell of her breast with tantalizing gentleness.

To Jenna, it seemed the fever returned instantly as his fingers ignited a molten path across her skin. She gazed at him with eyes that suddenly glowed with an intense inner fire. When Stefan thought better of their playing, not wanting to press her weakened condition, and removed his hand, Jenna quickly replaced his hand at her breast, breathing in with a sudden ragged longing that required no words.

"Jenna?" Stefan whispered uncertainly.

Her velvet gaze destroyed the last shreds of his will, drawing him into the depths of her own passion.

"Stefan . . ." Jenna whispered as she reached up, her fingers stealing softly across the lean, bronze smoothness of his chest.

Stefan grabbed her gently by the shoulders, turning with her in the covers, holding her away momentarily. Jenna reached up to stroke the tangled golden mane of his hair.

"You have created in me a need I never knew existed. Must I now beg you to fill that need?" Jenna whispered.

Stefan's embrace closed about her, drawing her into his warmth, his voice oddly muffled against the softness of her neck.

"I could bear any pain but yours, any loss, but not your loss. I would more easily forfeit my own life than see yours endangered." Stefan breathed passionately as his lips pressed kisses across the tip of her shoulder, up the column of her neck, until he held her head between his powerful hands, his fingers gently spreading through the silken masses of her hair. Stefan's mouth lowered over hers, feeling the exquisite warmth of her response.

Jenna reached up, her arms closing about his back, which was covered with lean, hard muscles that flexed and tautened with the strength that flowed through him like fiery heat as he pressed her into the covers.

Stefan's hands stroked the full length of Jenna's body as if he sought to satisfy all remaining doubts of her returned health. In spite of the fever, he felt the strength of her young body responding to his. Jenna arched against him as he moved over her, responding with abandon as she stroked her fingers through the golden thickness of his hair, her lips parting as she opened to him. Jenna breathed in deeply, her small tongue meeting his with silent longing, a ragged sigh escaping as his lips left hers to leave a heated kiss on her shoulder. She moaned softly as she stroked his hair, guiding him to her breast. She trembled as his lips closed over her, his tongue teasing the peak to taut hardness. Gently he kneaded that fullness, slowly arousing within Jenna a desire to match his own. Jenna's hands caressed the smooth skin across his ribs, down across the bone at his hip, inside the length of his thigh. With agonizing slowness her fingers closed around him, that exquisite heat searing through her where she touched him. Stefan groaned at that contact as he rose over her, his knee moving between her thighs. Slowly he entered her, closing the distance between their bodies, until she lay beneath him, no longer separate, but now part of him, in their joining. Tenderly he moved within her, luxuriating in her warmth mingling with his, feeling an overwhelming completeness with her body, as if two parts had joined to become one whole person. He stared into the depths of her eyes, knowing that with her, as with none before, he had found a passion to match his own. All pretenses were stripped away as they moved together, building within each other an equal pleasure. Their touching became a silent communication of the souls, questioning and answering, taking and then yielding, pleasing and then demanding pleasure. Stefan felt her release begin, beckoning his own with waves of passion washing over him, taking him with her. He bound her to him tenderly. There were no words, nor any need of them.

Stefan stroked the outline of Jenna's cheek, feeling the slow, regular pulsing beneath the tips of his fingers. Her eyes were now closed, the gentle sweep of long, dark lashes soft against her skin. He moved away from her side, only to find her awake, refusing to release him. Stefan smiled as he bent to press a quick kiss against her lips.

"There is a chill about the room. I will place more wood on the fire. I would not want to risk your recovery because of my carelessness."

Jenna's eyes glowed warmly as she watched him before the hearth, his lean body moving with a silent strength and power. She blushed as she thought she much preferred his golden nakedness to the dandified clothes that were the style of the day. She snuggled deeper into the covers as Stefan returned, pulling her possessively against him.

"Now, you will explain why you were running about in the storm," Stefan commanded gently.

Jenna closed her eyes and breathed in deeply with complete happiness at his nearness.

"Jenna!" Stefan insisted firmly.

Jenna explained her visit with Elizabeth and the letter her friend had entrusted her with. Stefan understood her frantic determination the night before that the letter be delivered immediately to John Whitmore. However, he greatly feared her involvement in the matter, when Charles Wingate seemed intent on an arranged marriage for Elizabeth. Jenna then described her search of Charles's chambers, calmly ignoring the disapproving frown that appeared on Stefan's handsome lips.

"You took a great risk," Stefan interrupted.

Jenna silenced him with a finger against his lips while she continued her story. Stefan grew silently thoughtful when she spoke of the instructions concealed in the book.

"You saw nothing of the instructions?"

"There was no time. Charles removed the list and gave it to the other man."

"Who was this man?"

"I dared not risk looking, but I am certain I know his

voice. I am certain he visited my grandfather many times. Charles told him to give the instructions to a man in Parliament.''

Stefan lay beside her, silently thoughtful. "It is as I suspected. The conspiracy reaches into the highest levels of the government, to those closest to the regent. When are they to act?"

"They are to wait for further instructions from a man called Edmund Duvalier. He is the same man I saw speaking with Charles, at Foxmoor. Elizabeth told me Edmund Duvalier has been to Wingate Hall on several occasions," Jenna added quickly.

Stefan stiffened noticeably beside her.

"Duvalier is their contact inside the French government. He is the man my friend warned me of. He has risked much to see the success of this conspiracy. He must be stopped. But he is only one man. Most certainly, Charles Wingate is part of the conspiracy, and this other man you heard, but unless we have the names of all the others, there is always the danger of their success.''

"I am certain I would know the man, if I were to hear his voice again."

"No! I cannot risk it. You cannot be certain Charles did not see you leaving after your visit with Elizabeth. Nor can we be certain of her loyalties. If her brother is capable of betrayal, she may well be part of it.''

Jenna suddenly twisted away from Stefan's side. "I believe in Elizabeth's innocence in all of this," she declared vehemently. "I can well believe Charles's involvement, though I little understand the reasons. But not Elizabeth's. Charles is doing everything in his power to make certain Elizabeth will marry a man of his choosing, regardless of her feelings in the matter. Somehow it is a part of all of this, though the reason eludes me. No, Elizabeth is risking much in defying Charles in this marriage. She is not part of the conspiracy.''

Stefan studied Jenna keenly. There was every possibility that she was right, but he could leave nothing to chance. He had been willing to see the letter delivered to John

Whitmore. Though he dared not speak of it to Jenna, there was no danger there. He sighed heavily as he tried to draw Jenna back into the warmth of the bed, noticing the goose bumps that rose across her skin.

"You have done your part in this. You must promise you will do no more," Stefan whispered against her shoulder.

Jenna gazed at Stefan, feeling herself mesmerized by the piercing blue of his eyes. "I cannot promise you that. It is important that we know who the other man is. Perhaps then we can find out the names of the others. I will know the man when I hear his voice."

"You must promise me that you will tell me before you do anything, I cannot protect you if you do not tell me," Stefan whispered softly against her cheek, realizing that for the moment further argument was pointless.

Jenna's promise was sealed with the heat of Stefan's lips against hers, drawing all further protests from her in a breathless sigh, as they lingered in the warmth of the bed. Stefan soundly turned away all concerned inquiries about Jenna's health, insisting with a wickedly handsome smile that a full day abed would certainly see her returned to good health.

Chapter Fourteen

The height of the royal season in London in most recent years had been the royal dinner and ball given at Kensington Palace by the prince regent, on the eve of Christmas. Invitations were highly prized by the privileged cream of society who were allowed to attend.

Jenna had not attended in previous years because she was too young. This season was quite another matter. Her invitation was hand delivered by Countess Lieven at an elaborate afternoon tea the countess had given for her favorite circle of friends. She could not know that the invitation had been extended at the insistence of Madame Lillian de Stahl. Seizing upon the opportunity presented her, Jenna made certain Charles Wingate would be her escort. She failed to understand the mood of the brief but clear message she received the following morning from Stefan Kalinsky. Under no circumstances was she to consider accepting Countess Lieven's invitation. Jenna promptly replied that the matter was none of his concern. She would be attending with Charles Wingate. The next message she received, on the morning of the ball, was from Stefan Kalinsky personally.

Jenna gave her final inspection to the score of small spice cakes that lined the countertop in the kitchens. The spice cakes had been a tradition in her grandfather's house, each filled with mixed pieces of fruit, nuts, and aromatic spices that were unique to the holidays. Emma Kelly had first learned to make the cakes when she was a small girl. She had taught Jenna how to make the fragrant cakes several seasons before, and she now stood aside watching with a proud eye as Jenna removed the pans from the ovens. Each was baked to a perfect golden brown, and removed from the ovens at the exact right moment. Emma nodded approvingly as she took a towel and helped remove the last pan.

"Aye, 'tis not the Christmas season without a fine batch of spice cakes. Was a favorite time of year for your grandfather. I'd not be surprised to find a cake or two missing. I'm certain he's watching over us now." Emma Kelly winked jovially at her young mistress.

Jenna was the picture of returned good health. There were no traces of the fever, which had disappeared so quickly that not a circle had been left beneath her eyes. Emma refused to acknowledge to Jenna that Dmitri's special tea might have aided her quick recovery, insisting her own fervent prayers had provided the necessary remedy. Jenna merely shook her head in resignation. When Emma had her mind made up about something, it was pointless to discuss the matter. In her own heart, she knew well that Dmitri's herbal tea and Stefan's tender ministrations were the balm that had made her well. Jenna turned as Maggie informed her that Madame Lessard had arrived for the final fitting of her gown for the Christmas ball. Jenna wiped her hands on a linen towel and brushed back a stray strand of rich, dark hair that waved enticingly about her ear. Her cheeks were flushed from the heat in the kitchens, from working before the large ovens. She might have left the baking to Emma, but it was a ritual she much enjoyed, and her talents were well noted in the line of perfect cakes that sat cooling on the marble sideboard. After a final inspection, Jenna fled the kitchens for her drawing room on the second floor of the large manor.

Jenna could not contain a certain excitement about the evening that awaited her. She had struck upon a bold plan and would set it into motion when Charles first arrived to escort her to the ball. More than anything, she was certain of Charles's deep feelings for her, and she fully intended to use that advantage to gain the information Stefan needed to expose the conspiracy. This was the first Christmas she would spend without her grandfather, and though the pain of that realization was deep, she also felt a sense of deep obligation to do whatever was necessary to expose the conspiracy that had taken his life. Jenna burst through the door to the second-floor drawing room, which adjoined her own chamber, and stopped in midstride. Indeed, Madame Lessard awaited her. However, the Frenchwoman's assistant had taken the form of Stefan Kalinsky.

Jenna stared in stunned surprise at Stefan. Their contact over the last weeks had been brief after her illness. Indeed, it had been limited to his strict orders not to interfere, and her bold declaration that she would be attending the royal ball. After that, she had seen Stefan only once, as usual in the company of Lillian de Stahl, and Jenna had chosen to ignore them both. But she could hardly ignore the man who now stood in her drawing room. Nor could she ignore the effect his presence had on her. She could feel a glowing warmth surging through her veins that had nothing to do with the morning spent in the kitchens. Madame Lessard quickly made her brief excuses and left the chamber. Jenna returned Stefan's appraising stare. He had come to her house in the disguise of a dressmaker's assistant, but underneath his plain costume were the garments of the prince. Jenna was silently angered with herself that she could respond so openly to his presence in the same room, as she felt the heated flush cross her cheeks. Stefan, too, noted the sudden rise of color in her face as he approached. He reached out a hand to gently caress the contour of her face.

"I hope the fever has not returned." He spoke softly, his words reaching out to caress her tenderly.

Jenna remained coolly aloof, knowing any response to his touch might well be fatal. If she yielded, Madame Lessard might well return to find her in complete surrender to Stefan Kalinsky. His harsh admonition to refrain from interfering further echoed in her mind.

Stefan was undaunted by her cool manner. An amused

smile pulled at the corners of his mouth. He knew her game, for it was a game he often played when in her presence, to restrain himself from bedding her whenever they chanced to meet. After all, there were certain proprieties to be maintained. And as long as they were to seem merely casual acquaintances, it was necessary that their contact be limited to that acceptable within certain social bounds. Otherwise, there was no knowing who might guess about their affair. Yet Stefan persisted in tearing down the barriers she placed between them. He gently caressed the slender column of her neck, his fingers disappearing into the thickly bound mass of her hair, until he found the combs and pulled them free, releasing the wild torrent of rich, dark hair until it cascaded freely about his hands.

"Please do not do this," Jenna pleaded unconvincingly. She stared into the ice-blue depths of Stefan's eyes, and her breath caught in her throat at the silent message she saw there. The truth of all their moments together, her innermost feelings, his tightly controlled desire for her, were carried in the flickering of white-hot flame that kindled there and held her fascination. Jenna responded as if in a dream, and yet she was not dreaming. She felt the last shreds of stubborn will being torn aside as Stefan drew her into his embrace. His mouth lowered over hers possessively, in a silent message of his will over her. Yet, had she been free to resist, Jenna would have remained in the safe security of his embrace forever.

Stefan slowly released her, and Jenna turned away as she fought to regain her composure. Damn Stefan Kalinsky! What was the game he played with her? His coming here was not merely to reaffirm her feeling for him. It was far too important that no one know of their meetings. No. Something of great importance had caused him to seek this meeting. Jenna gathered the length of her hair with a length of ribbon and turned back to face Stefan Kalinsky, her passion, her greatest torment.

"If you have come to speak against my attending the royal ball this evening, I shall hear no more of it."

"Not at all, Jenna. I understand the futility in that argument. I have come to give you a gift. It is also a custom in Russia, to give a gift of the heart. This is my gift to you." Stefan handed her a small package, neatly wrapped in silk cloth and bound with a strand of silver ribbon.

Jenna stared at Stefan uncertainly. She had thought of purchasing a gift for him and then decided against it. Nothing she found seemed appropriate to express the depth of feelings she had only just begun to know in herself. When she looked up at him, her wide amber eyes were filled with tears.

Stefan reached to take a single tear on his finger. "I had not thought to make you sad. I would have thought better of it, had I known it would bring your tears," he whispered tenderly.

"No. You do not understand. It is only that I had not thought that you . . ." Jenna's voice faltered as she gazed searchingly into that azure gaze.

"You had not thought that I cared as you cared." Stefan finished the thought for her. Jenna nodded slowly, staring at the package she held in her hands. Stefan reached beneath her chin, forcing her to look at him again.

"I have never spoken the words. I am not certain they are within me. But I have vowed my love for you in a thousand ways, dearest Jenna, and it will endure for as many years." It was a solemn promise, perhaps the most he might offer. It was more than Jenna had ever hoped for. She knew so little of Stefan Kalinsky that she could not know the struggle that he waged within himself to give her those few words. It was the struggle of the boy torn from his mother, her love replaced by the unfailing loyalty of the gruff Dmitri, in the northern wilderness of Varykein. It was the struggle of the young man denied a father, and then his only home in the solitude of Villandry. It was a thousand moments of anguish and pain, concealed behind the facade of casual caring. But in Jenna's exquisite beauty he had found a fire and a purpose to match his own. In her he had found his own soul, lost so many years before. He would fight to keep her, for her loss would again mean the

251

loss of his own soul. It was a loss he could not endure, at any cost. Stefan motioned to the package.

Jenna sat in the large upholstered chair before the hearth. Her hands trembled visibly as she unbound the satin ribbon. She pulled away the silk cloth to reveal a small, finely grained wood box. She lifted the lid of the box. Inside, carefully wrapped in velvet, Jenna found Stefan's gift. It was the elegantly crafted ring she had seen in the clockmaker's shop, weeks before. Five perfectly matched oval rubies glistened brilliantly from the shape of a single rose bloom. Jenna raised tear-filled eyes to meet Stefan's gaze.

"Had I known the gift would bring tears, I might have thought better of it," he teased tenderly.

"How could you possibly know?" Jenna whispered.

"I chanced upon a young girl admiring the ring in a shop. I admired her choice, and thought how you might care for it." Stefan suppressed a twinkle of amusement behind the sudden serious curve of his lips.

Jenna was not easily fooled. She reached out to gently silence his storytelling with a tender kiss. Stefan sat her back in the chair. He seized the ring from the piece of velvet and placed it on her finger, already certain of the perfect fit. A sudden thought returned to her, and Jenna lifted saddened eyes to meet his.

"I do not have a gift for you," she lamented mournfully.

Stefan reached behind her to retrieve the satin ribbon she had bound about her hair.

"This is all the gift I would have, for it is yours, and it holds all the more importance for me. I am bound to you, my lovely princess. Your life is my life, your happiness is my happiness. Never forget that you are mine—this is my vow to you." Stefan rose quickly, and turned toward the door, suddenly quite anxious to leave.

Jenna stared after him. Stefan turned back with a last thought.

"Charles Wingate is a very clever man. Always remember that the most dangerous enemy is the clever enemy. I will be close beside you this evening. Take great care, my little one." Stefan donned the plain woolen cape and hat and disappeared into the hallway. A moment later, Madame Lessard returned to the drawing room.

"We must begin immediately if I am to complete the gown for the ball this evening." Madame Lessard chatted idly as she took her large sewing basket and removed pins, scissors, needle, and thread.

"Mademoiselle?"

Jenna quickly removed her gown and took her position on the small footstool before Madame Lessard. The unfinished gown was quickly lowered over her head and pinned into place.

Madame Lessard made her final adjustments to the gown and then returned early in the evening to make certain all was perfection in her creation. She assisted Jenna in dressing, stepping back to give her masterpiece a critical inspection. After several long moments, she clapped her hands together in rapt delight at her handiwork.

"It is by far my finest creation, enhanced, mademoiselle, because you will wear it. There will be none more beautiful at the ball this evening. Everyone shall be quite envious of you," Madame said ecstatically as she walked slowly around Jenna, fluffing a sleeve, straightening the fragile lace border set within the bodice.

Jenna stared at her reflection in the full-length mirror that stood across the room. She hardly knew the girl she saw there. She had complete confidence in Madame Lessard's fine craft, but she hardly cared what the cream of London society might think of the gown. There was only one she cared to please, and she would find her answer in the depth of his blue eyes, later in the evening. But then her thoughts of the evening ahead dimmed the sparkling light that had sprung into the amber depths of her eyes a moment before. Charles Wingate would be arriving shortly to escort her to the royal ball. It would require all her efforts to remember the part she must play. Jenna turned around obediently as Madame Lessard straightened the line of the empire gown where it dropped away from the bodice. Indeed, it was the most beautiful the Frenchwoman had ever made for her.

The gown was cut from the finest velvet, in a deep, rich crimson color that contrasted perfectly with the soft-hued, pink of Jenna's skin. The empire cut of the bodice clung to the fullness of her breasts, pushing the ample swell alluringly above the delicate lace that was inset about the edge. The sleeves were full, and then gathered with a narrow band of gold braid just above her elbow, and each was elaborately decorated with the design of a delicate, large flower, made from the finest white satin and trimmed with gold thread. The fullness of the skirt was gently pleated at the bodice, flowing down the length of Jenna's lithe body, outlining the gentle curve of her bottom and then flaring into a wide fan of fabric at the floor. An elaborately woven gold braid flowerlet had been stitched just beneath the bodice, securing a wide band of white satin, hand-decorated in crimson thread, with small flowers to match those inset in the sleeves. At evenly spaced intervals, down the center length of the gown, two more woven gold, braid flowerlets were stitched into place, the last one securing a pleat in the gown that suddenly opened, just above Jenna's knee, to reveal the flowing skirt of a white-satin chemise she wore underneath. The gown was longer than those worn in recent years, and the cut of the bodice far more revealing. Jenna felt a sense of daring steal over her as she gazed at her reflection. Indeed, the gown was Madame's finest creation, and Jenna was certain the seamstress knew the reason for her selection of the crimson color. It matched to perfection the crimson of the first rose Stefan had given her.

Jenna's hair was swept back from her face, the fullness twisted and arranged in a mass of curls upon her head. Thin, wispy tendrils of hair were curled loosely about her face. Maggie finally stood back to check her work, just as Emma came in to inform Jenna that Charles Wingate had

254

arrived. Jenna donned white gloves, pulling them up the length of her slender arm. She daringly slipped the ring Stefan had given her over her gloved hand, the fit now quite tight. She cared not who might notice it. Only she and Stefan would know the meaning of it. Emma fastened a choker of several rows of small seed pearl about the slender column of her neck.

Jenna followed Emma down the sweep of the wide stairway. Emma draped the white satin shawl about her shoulders. It matched the design of the gown perfectly, hand-embroidered with an elaborate pattern of crimson and gold flowers. Jenna met Charles's appraising stare as she accepted his arm.

"How very beautiful you are tonight, my dear. This shall prove to be a most important evening. I am so pleased you will be there to share it with me," Charles greeted her sweetly.

Somehow Jenna could not believe his words. She gazed at him quizzically for a moment before he escorted her to his coach. Had Charles meant something more behind his casual pleasantry? Perhaps Stefan was right. Perhaps Charles somehow knew of her visit with Elizabeth. She smiled back at Charles confidently. She was certain he knew nothing of her visit to his chamber or of the conversation she had overheard. Jenna mentally sharpened her wits. Stefan had warned her of Charles's cleverness. She intended to be just as clever.

Jenna accepted Charles's hand as he assisted her into the waiting coach. Charles stepped in behind her, discreetly taking the seat opposite her, rather than the one beside her. Jenna refused to let his imperceptible change in manner shake her composure. She knew his purpose well. He had deliberately taken the seat opposite that he might watch her. Jenna smiled at him radiantly, her lips forming into a delicate pout.

"I fear this shawl is hardly meant for warmth, and the evening air is quite cold." She smiled invitingly, knowing the success of her plan depended on Charles's believing her sincerity.

Charles smiled, sudden concern marking his thin features. He accepted her unspoken invitation and quickly changed seats, settling into the thick luxury beside her.

"Will Elizabeth be joining us later?" Jenna ventured, knowing quite well the answer before she asked the question. She knew Elizabeth had made the excuse of illness to remain at home. With all in attendance at the ball, she had planned to meet with John Whitmore. Jenna smiled secretly. True to his word, Stefan had personally delivered Elizabeth's letter to John and had then carried a message in return.

Jenna forced her smile until her cheeks ached as Charles possessively seized her hand and tucked it through his arm, refusing to relinquish her hand, his fingers closing with surprising strength over hers. His fingers brushed across the polished smoothness of the ring Stefan had given her. For a brief moment, Jenna felt certain he would ask her about it.

"I fear Elizabeth suffers from a return of the malady she suffered at Foxmoor. It will all pass in a few days, and then I am certain she will call upon your assistance in making the plans for her wedding. It will be in the early spring." Charles hesitated, suddenly quite thoughtful, as he toyed with her fingers.

"My dearest Jenna, there has been so much distance between us since the loss of your grandfather. Tonight that will end. Indeed, tonight will be a most delightful evening."

The inside of the coach was fortunately bathed in darkness, hiding the sudden uncertainty that flickered across Jenna's face. She contemplated Charles's words as they rode the short distance to Kensington Palace in silence. She forced back a sudden coldness of fear about Charles's intentions. She could only guess what he had planned for the evening.

*   *   *

The royal banners of the prince regent waved from a score of poles high atop Kensington Palace. The darkness of night was suddenly dissipated by the glow of a multitude of lamps and candles, long before their carriage arrived at the wide expanse of steps that rose to the main entrance of Kensington Palace. A continuous flow of liveried footmen greeted each coach upon its arrival, giving assistance to each lady and gentleman.

Charles boldly refused the footman who rushed forward to assist Jenna from the coach, instead giving her his hand with an air of authority and maddening confidence.

Jenna smiled at him radiantly. To all who watched their arrival it must have indeed seemed that Jenna had deep affection for her escort.

Their arrival was announced as they entered the main ballroom inside the palace, and Jenna was immediately aware of the stares turned in their direction. They passed through the long receiving line to greet the prince regent, making their greetings to several royal guests. Jenna halted momentarily as she saw Stefan's handsome profile bending low over another lady's hand and greeting her warmly. He gave his formal greeting, and before straightening, cast a sideways glance in Jenna's direction. Her heart raced at the fire in the depth of his blue gaze. Beside her, Charles gave a formal greeting to the duke of Kent, oblivious of the exchange. Jenna nodded only slightly in acknowledgment of Stefan's silent greeting. He straightened, releasing the lady's hand, an amused smile playing across his handsome lips. Jenna longed to stand beside him, to feel the pressure of his arm against hers, the warmth of his body.

More greetings were exchanged, and Jenna finally approached Stefan and stood before him briefly. His greeting was no different than any he had given to anyone else. Only Jenna was aware of the sudden heat that flowed through her when he seized her hand. He lingered noticeably—to her—over the elegant ring she wore. His gaze locked briefly with hers, in silent communication, so that no others were aware of it. Stefan released her hand, and Jenna moved down the receiving line. She was unaware of the warning that flared briefly as Charles bowed stiffly before Stefan.

Stefan's gaze remained masked, yielding nothing as he looked beyond Charles to the next guest. He tightly controlled the anger that welled within him. He must not risk harm to Jenna or exposure for any retaliation now. He must wait for the perfect moment. The fire in the depths of his gaze instantly turned as cold as ice.

Jenna accepted Charles's arm as he led her out onto the dance floor. The gay, lively strains of music filled the air. Jenna longed for the warmth of Stefan's embrace as Charles's arm closed about her possessively.

The dinner was soon announced, and all the guests casually followed the duke of Kent as he proceeded to the elaborate dining hall. When all had taken their positions at the dining tables, the prince regent's arrival was announced. When he had taken his position at the head of the table, all the guests took their seats. A round of holiday toasting proceeded, as the first courses of the meal were delivered by an endless flow of servants from the vast kitchens of the palace. Bowls of steaming oyster soup were placed before each guest, followed by baked breads and fine wine. Roast baron of beef, was followed by legs of lamb, partridges, and pheasants, all from the royal hunting grounds. Vegetables roasted in a sweet honey sauce, the traditional plum puddings, and fruit-filled cakes filled every space upon the long tables. As the evening continued, the entertainers emerged to hold the rapt attention of the guests. A troupe of mimes performed their silent play before the royal audience, meeting with approval in the boisterous applause that followed the last act of their performance.

Jenna hardly touched the meal before her. She had no appetite for the knot that had formed in her stomach. Only occasionally did she dare steal a glance in Stefan's direction, to find him greatly absorbed in a lingering conversation with either Lillian de Stahl or the elegantly gowned matriarch to his left. She received no reassuring glances, only Charles's unwavering attentions, which soon set her nerves on edge.

When the dinner had finally ended and the guests returned to the ballroom, Jenna stole away for a breath of fresh air. Upon returning, she found Charles within a circle of acquaintances that included several well-known members of the prime minister's staff. The gentlemen were deeply involved in a discussion over the finest of their horses, which were to compete in the royal races the following spring. Their ladies were equally involved in conversation with Lillian de Stahl, who seemed like a royal bee holding court. Jenna approached slowly, quietly slipping her arm through Charles's in what must have seemed an intimate gesture. Lillian de Stahl noted the gesture with a perceptible raise of her painted eyebrow, and seized upon the moment.

"My dear, how very radiant you are tonight." Lillian de Stahl's voice fairly dripped with honeyed sweetness.

Jenna did not hear the woman's first greeting. She was concentrating on the conversation of the two men to her left. A certain tone in one man's voice had caught her attention. She listened attentively as their conversation continued. Jenna stared at Sir Robert Ludlow with mounting certainty that it was his voice she had heard in Charles's room. She felt an insistent pressure on her arm, and turned to gaze at Madame de Stahl.

"Ah, Charles, you are the fortunate one. Mademoiselle Randolph has certainly captured a great many hearts this evening, and such a grand evening it is. I wonder how you can refrain from celebrating. Surely, we can be allowed to drink a toast to the announcement of your betrothal to Lady Randolph?" Lillian de Stahl questioned innocently, her emphasis on the last words meant for Stefan Kalinsky as he rejoined her.

Jenna's head snapped around, her gaze locking with Lillian de Stahl's. She then glanced at Charles, noting well the hardened look that glinted in his gray eyes. She dared not look at Stefan. She had not been prepared for the possibility that Charles might seek to press the cause of their betrothal under such circumstances.

"Charles, please, I hardly think this the time or place to discuss such matters."

"My dearest Jenna, of course it is the time and place. What better time or place than the Christmas celebration with friends about? Friends and acquaintances, I am most pleased to announce that Lady Jenna Randolph consented some time ago to our marriage." Charles seized her hand in his and bent low to place a kiss on her gloved hand. Try as she might Jenna found she could not withdraw her hand from his unyielding grasp.

"You do me honor, Jenna. We shall all drink a toast." Charles turned toward the far end of the ballroom where elegant tables had been set for refreshments.

Jenna turned to stare into the icy blue depths of Stefan's gaze. She cringed at the hardness she saw in that gaze. She felt the white-hot rise of anger as she turned back to Lillian de Stahl. This had all been arranged. Jenna stared after Stefan as he stiffly followed Charles and his friends to the table. Their glasses were all filled with champagne, and Charles came forward to give Jenna her glass. Beside her, Lillian de Stahl smiled smugly as she too raised her glass in a toast. Jenna suppressed an overwhelming urge to toss the entire glassful of champagne in Lillian de Stahl's face. Somehow the witch was involved with Charles, and now Jenna was certain of the identity of the man in Charles's chamber—but at what a cost!

Lillian de Stahl set her empty glass upon the table and coyly slipped her arm through Stefan's.

"The music is delightful. We must not waste it," she cooed softly as she started to lead Stefan into the middle of the floor.

Jenna could not resist her moment of revenge. As the notorious courtesan moved past her, Jenna turned to Charles, firmly planting her foot in the middle of the length of gown that trailed the bold woman. A rending tear separated the skirt of the gown from the bodice. A satisfied smile pulling impishly at her lips, Jenna stepped back as Lillian de Stahl whirled around, her face suddenly drained of all color as she inspected the damage to her elegant gown. But in the crowd of people who stood about, it was now impossible to determine who the culprit might have been.

Lillian de Stahl quickly made her apologies to Stefan and fled the ballroom in search of one of the royal servants to repair the torn garment.

Jenna withdrew her arm from Charles's, as he seemed intent on resuming his conversation with his companions. Jenna whirled around at the feel of warm, strong fingers about her arm. Her gaze melted into Stefan's.

"May I also congratulate you on your betrothal, mademoiselle." Stefan spoke formally as he led her into the middle of the ballroom. It was an innocent gesture easily within the bounds of common courtesy.

"Stefan, you must believe I had no idea that Charles would make such an announcement."

"I can hardly believe that he made the announcement without your consent," he replied coolly. The unyielding strength of his body against hers was unmistakable.

Jenna's temper flared. "Madame de Stahl must also be congratulated," Jenna sniffed indignantly.

"Lillian is a friend of many years. How can you possibly consider her involved with Charles Wingate?"

"You would very easily accept my involvement. How can you be more certain of Lillian de Stahl?" Jenna retorted, her anger barely concealed as they stopped in the middle of the dance floor.

"Jenna, I do not doubt you." He spoke with a sudden passion that tore away at the anger that had come between them.

Across the ballroom, Jenna could see Charles watching them closely, and then slowly making his way to the center of the room as the musicians ended the waltz.

261

Jenna cast Stefan a warning glance. She tilted her head to him with stiff formality.

"I know the identity of the man in Charles's room," she whispered fervently, as she turned toward Charles, a welcoming smile upon her lips. There had been no time for her to say more. She joined Charles in the next dance, aware that Stefan watched every movement.

Jenna continued her flawless performance throughout the remaining hours of the evening. A toast was made to the prince regent as the massive clock in the ballroom struck the hour of midnight. Shortly thereafter, Jenna persuaded Charles of her fatigue. When Charles hastened to bring her shawl, Jenna's eyes searched among the crowd for Stefan.

"Charles Wingate is a very reckless man to leave you unguarded for even a moment."

Jenna whirled around to find Stefan standing before her.

"I thought you had gone. Madame de Stahl . . ."

"Unfortunately, Madame de Stahl found the damage to her gown quite substantial." A knowing smile pulled at the corners of his lips. "She accepted the use of my carriage to return home early. I had hoped we might continue our earlier conversation."

Before Jenna could respond, Charles had appeared at her elbow. She was immediately aware of his guarded manner as he wrapped the shawl about her shoulders possessively. His eyebrow raised arrogantly as he stared past her at Stefan Kalinsky.

"I do not recall your offer of congratulations, Prince Kalinsky, on the occasion of my betrothal to Lady Randolph. Are such matters of etiquette not recognized among the Russian aristocracy?" Charles taunted.

Jenna inhaled sharply at Charles's open rudeness, her gaze searching his face for some reason for his sudden maliciousness. Stefan waved off the biting remark with a casual smile.

"Even among the Russian aristocracy we recognize

rules of etiquette, and we have our own customs for such an occasion." Jenna was not deceived by Stefan's light-hearted manner. She knew well the hatred Stefan felt for Charles Wingate, though she hardly understood the reason for his performance. It was a role she had seen him playing over the countless weeks and months since they had first met. It guarded his cool purpose behind a mask of social inanities.

"With your permission, I but sought to give my congratulations to Lady Randolph, as is the custom in Russia," Stefan continued.

Not wishing to relinquish his supreme moment of conquest, Charles inclined his head agreeably.

Stefan seized Jenna's hand as if to place a kiss upon her gloved fingers. Instead of bending low over the captive hand, Stefan drew Jenna into the circle of his embrace, his fingers beneath her chin, turning her face toward his. In the next moment, Stefan's mouth lowered over hers in a searing, passionate kiss. A startled hush swept over the ladies and their escorts around them. When Stefan finally released her, Jenna stood back in stunned disbelief, thinking he must surely have taken complete leave of his senses.

"It is the custom in my country that all those wishing the betrothed couple good fortune are to receive a kiss from the lady." Stefan smiled arrogantly as he inclined his head toward Jenna.

"Indeed, I congratulate you, Sir Charles, on your bethrothal."

Stefan's obvious meaning was not lost on any of those who stood about them. It was an obvious insult to Charles, which he could not easily walk away from. A small part of Jenna died inside as she realized that Stefan had deliberately sought to provoke Charles, though for what reason she could not possibly understand. She noticed the sudden anger that sprang into Charles's eyes, and sought to calm him.

"Charles, please. Prince Kalinsky meant no harm.

Surely there is no reason to take offense."

"Prince Kalinsky has insulted you, and he has insulted me. I cannot accept such behavior." Charles ignored the restraining pressure of her hand upon his arm as he stared past her at Stefan Kalinsky.

"You have insulted me, sir, I demand satisfaction for your boorish behavior," Charles challenged, a menacing gleam lighting unnaturally in the depths of his eyes.

"Charles, no! You must not do this," Jenna pleaded in vain. Charles set her aside none too gently.

"This is a matter best settled between Prince Kalinsky and myself." Charles actually seemed to take great pleasure from his challenge.

Stefan's expression of mock surprise quickly faded as the challenge was given. Behind them, the duke of Kent pressed through the crowd of startled guests.

"Gentlemen, on behalf of the regent, I request that this matter be amicably resolved."

Charles refused to yield his advantage. "I apologize for the discourtesy of this matter. But a grave offense has been made against Lady Randolph. I cannot allow this to be forgotten."

Jenna's amber gaze searched Stefan's face for some meaning to his deliberate insult to Charles. Everything was moving beyond her control, and she felt a rising fear of the consequences.

"Very well, gentlemen. This matter must then be settled on a field of honor." The duke of Kent turned to Stefan Kalinsky, his manner calm and deliberate.

"You will have the choice of weapons."

Stefan's manner was calm. "I believe that Sir Charles prefers weapons of skill. I shall allow his choice of weapons."

Jenna stared at Stefan in stunned disbelief. She could not believe this was happening. She turned back to Charles. She drew back from the look of complete ruthlessness that had hardened his features. Charles nodded his agreement.

264

"Very well. I choose the rapier, a weapon of distinction and skill," Charles answered with smug satisfaction.

Stefan nodded his acceptance.

"Very well. The contest will be a duel, but not to the death. The regent disapproves of such practice. He has need of his countrymen, and his allies. Nor shall I permit such a contest to take place this night. The matter will be settled on a field of honor, on the third day of January, of the new year. Gentlemen, you will please select your seconds, in the event either one of you is unable to compete in the contest. The winner will be decided upon the first injury received by the opponent," the duke of Kent decreed. He turned to Charles and then Stefan.

"Do you both accept such terms?"

Both men nodded their acceptance. The duke of Kent turned and approached Jenna.

"I regret this entire matter, Lady Randolph. I request the honor of escorting you home," the duke of Kent offered authoritatively. It was a request that could not be ignored.

The ride to Hallston House seemed unbearably long. When the large front door of the manor closed behind her, Jenna gathered her gown and raced up the wide sweep of the stairway, past Emma Kelly, who regarded her with an expression of complete surprise.

Jenna stepped out of the velvet gown and pulled the elaborate combs from her hair. As if possessed by the devil, she tore through the dresses that hung in the rosewood armoire. None suited her purpose. Clad only in the satin chemise, Jenna flew down the hallway into the small chamber Maggie occupied just opposite the stairway to the servants' quarters below. The young maid sat up groggily as Jenna burst into her room. Jenna quickly found the plain garments she sought. Returning to her own chamber, she quickly donned the soft gray woolen skirt and white blouse. She gathered the waving length of her hair with a length of ribbon and pulled on her own black woolen cape with a hood to hide her features. She pulled on riding boots and turned toward the doorway. A determined Emma Kelly stood in her path.

Jenna quickly brushed past the stout housekeeper and bounded down the wide stairway. There was no time to summon Mr. Flint; she would saddle her own horse. Instead of the front entrance, Jenna left the large house by way of the servants' entrance at the rear of the house. It was the nearest to the stables. A single lantern glowed outside the stables. She knew Mr. Flint often worked late into the night.

The clear night air stole icily through the billowing folds of the long cape as Jenna quickly crossed the green that separated the stables from the manor house, the thin film of ice upon the greensward crunching underfoot. Jenna lifted the latch and entered the stables. In a matter of minutes she had saddled the gray stallion and led him into the cold night air. The gray nickered softly at the intrusion, blowing a stream of hot, moist air against Jenna's cheek as she adjusted the cinch of the saddle. Behind her Emma Kelly trotted across the green, struggling to keep her nightcap in place as she approached, a lantern swinging wildly with her rolling gait. The dear woman halted a few paces away, unable to speak or draw an even breath. Jenna swung easily into the saddle as Mr. Flint finally emerged from his quarters to see what the noise was about.

"Mr. Flint, you must stop her. She has taken complete leave of her senses." Emma Kelly struggled to keep her words together so they might make some sense. Mr. Flint looked from the stout housekeeper to Jenna.

"What is this about?" he asked gruffly.

Jenna could see his objection in the firm line of his grizzled jaw. She whirled the gray about toward the gate at the front of the house. She gave Mr. Flint only a brief explanation before sending the gray headlong down the cobbled pathway that led to the main entrance of Hallston House. She had to see Stefan. Now that she knew the identity of the other man, perhaps Stefan could expose the conspiracy. Somehow there had to be a way to stop this madness. Charles's reputation with the rapier was well known about London, indeed throughout the whole of England. More than a few men had suffered serious injury, even death, from his skilled blade. She hardly doubted the outcome of such a duel. She had lost her grandfather because of the conspiracy. She could not bear to lose Stefan as well.

Chapter Fifteen

Jenna guided the gray stallion down the icy cobbled street at a treacherous pace. She slowed her pace until she approached the park at the center of Grovesnor Square. Here the dirt pathway that bordered the park provided more secure footing. The night was crystal clear, the darkness lighted by a brilliant glowing moon that added its light to that of the gas lampposts that lined the streets. The soft glow of light spread into the darkness, bringing shadows to life as she passed by. Jenna passed one coach and then another as she held a firm rein on the gray. She knew well the folly of riding alone into the night with no protection. Down the next street, she was certain the shadows on the far side of the street moved with stealthy silence. She urged the gray to a faster pace as the imposing facade of the Georgian town house loomed before her.

Jenna quickly dismounted. Several lights shone through the windows. She mounted the stone steps to the main entrance. Her frantic knocking was answered as Alexei opened the front door. Jenna pushed back the hood of her cloak in greeting. The sound of voices came to her from the library as she breathlessly asked for Stefan. Without waiting for Alexei to announce her unexpected arrival, Jenna pushed open the double doors of the library. She stopped abruptly as Stefan whirled around to face her. Across from him, Lillian de Stahl stood before the hearth, clad only in a sheer chemise with a silk wrapper drawn loosely across her matronly form. Jenna's amber eyes widened in shocked surprise.

For an agonizingly long moment, the crackling of the logs at the hearth was the only sound in the library. Alexei quickly entered the room, in a vain attempt to give Stefan warning of Jenna's arrival. Lillian de Stahl was the first to recover from the intrusion.

"Dearest Stefan, I was not aware we were expecting guests." There was a maddening, unmistakably intimate note in her voice, as she slowly drew the wrapper about her thickened body, as if Jenna had indeed interrupted some private moment between them.

Jenna's senses seemed to fail her. It was as if everything about her had taken on the eerie quality of a nightmare. She backed away uncertainly as Stefan approached her. She felt as if she were smothering, as if something had been drawn very tightly about her, preventing her from drawing a deep breath to clear her thoughts. Jenna felt the solid frame of the doorway at her back, and that somehow jolted her senses. Her one thought was to flee the house, to run as far as she might from Stefan Kalinsky, that she might escape the pain that tore through her like a finely honed blade.

Jenna fled the library. She was oblivious of everything about her, except her need to be very far away from Stefan. Tears of anger and pain filled her eyes as she brushed past the startled Alexei, out the front door, and into the darkness beyond the house. The crisp night air suddenly cleared her thoughts. Damn Stefan Kalinsky and his lies. She heard her name shouted into the night air as she whirled about in search of the gray stallion. Untethered, the gray had wandered to the small carriage house that stood behind the town house. Jenna dashed at the tears that coursed down her cheeks as she crossed the cobbled pathway and quickly retrieved the reins that dangled to the ground before the stallion. The gray sidled nervously, snorting a cloud of steam into the crisp night air as Jenna's foot missed the stirrup. Her curses were sobbed into thickness of the cloak as she tried again to mount the nervous stallion. Gaining a foothold, she struggled to pull herself into the saddle.

Whirling the gray about, Jenna seized the riding crop and raised her arm to bring it down hard across the stallion's rump. Her target became empty air as Stefan's hand closed around her wrist with bruising strength. Jenna struggled to maintain her seat in the saddle as the gray snorted wildly and sidestepped. Twisting her wrist free of Stefan's grasp, she raised the riding crop with deadly intent.

Before she could strike again, Jenna was roughly hauled out of the saddle. Stefan's arm closed about her waist. Undaunted, Jenna struck at Stefan blindly, her blows falling far short of the target as Stefan reached to grab her arm, twisting it painfully behind her back, forcing her into submission.

"Jenna, stop this!" Stefan's voice was rough and commanding against her ear as he held her against him, trying to halt her struggling.

"Jenna! It is not what you think!" Stefan tried to reason with her.

Jenna twisted her head from side to side, refusing to accept his shallow excuses. For months she had ignored what was common knowledge about all of London. A sob broke in her throat as she struggled with renewed effort against Stefan's hold of her. She felt his tightening grasp about her waist, yet still she refused to submit.

"Jenna, you must listen to me." Stefan drew her tightly against the firmness of his chest, his strong, sinewed arm like a band of steel about her. Again she struggled to free herself, like some wild creature. Still Stefan's grasp tightened about her, until her breathing came in shallow, ragged gasps.

Jenna ceased struggling as she realized it required all her effort to draw the faintest breath. A buzzing began somewhere in the back of her head, and her thoughts were disoriented. Jenna felt herself losing control of her senses. A thick fog seemed to engulf her, and she felt herself falling.

Stefan gathered Jenna into his arms. He whirled around toward the stables, kicking open the large planked doors. A young stableboy immediately emerged half-dressed from an adjoining room.

"Leave us!" Stefan commanded roughly in Russian. The boy immediately donned a heavy, woolen jacket and fled in the direction of the main house.

Stefan carefully deposited Jenna on a pile of straw in a vacant stall. She moaned softly as she drew her first even breath of air, and her senses cleared slowly.

Jenna struggled to her feet. She tried to lunge past Stefan, but found her way blocked by the unmovable strength of his lean, muscular body.

"Release me!" Jenna spat from between tightly clenched teeth, her pain of the moment before now giving way to mounting anger.

"Jenna, you must listen to me. You will listen to me," Stefan commanded.

Jenna struggled to twist free of his hands and found her arms soundly pinned behind her back. She was completely helpless. She threw back her head and stared at him in the meager glow of a lantern at the far end of the carriage house, the amber depths of her eyes glowing with a feral light.

"I do not care to hear any more of your lies. Release me. You cannot hold me against my will. You have no authority over me!"

"Jenna, you must listen to me. You have caused your own pain by coming here unannounced. You should not have come," Stefan tried to reason with her.

"Should not have come?" Jenna stared back at him incredulously. "I came to tell you the man I heard in Charles's house that night was Sir Robert Ludlow. I came to warn you; no, I came to *beg* you not to go forward with this duel. To think I actually cared that you might be injured." Jenna stared at him through the flood of tears that threatened to return. "Bastard! I would gladly see your blood upon his blade!" she cursed him, trying again without success to loosen his hold on her.

272

Stefan only drew her more tightly into his embrace. How he had feared this moment. How he had guarded against it. And now all might be lost. Jenna might be lost to him forever. Stefan turned his face into the softness of her neck, trying to comfort her pain. He felt the stiff, unyielding strength of her young body full against his. He dared not release her until she had heard his words. Tenderly, Stefan kissed the saltiness of her cheek where her tears had fallen. She tried to twist away from him, as if she had been touched by something evil. Still he persisted, though she would not listen to his words. Somehow he had to make her understand. His lips brushed against her neck. He felt the wild pulsing beneath his touch.

"How can I make you understand, my little princess? Would you believe the truth if you heard it? Yes, it is true that once, a long time ago, Lillian and I were lovers. I was but a boy of fifteen, and she was worldly, wise, and beautiful. Always it is so the first time, when a boy becomes a man. Nor would I try to make you believe there were no others, for I have known other women, but their faces, their names are a memory, all but forgotten. Whatever my past before you, it is nothing. It was only the path I traveled to the final destination, my love for you. I vow this to you; since the first time I saw you there has been no other woman in my life. It is as if from that first moment, you became my life, my very soul, bound to me by some unseen force that I could neither ignore or escape. There is no other life for me, but you—this I promise," Stefan whispered against her ear.

His words stole over her like a healing balm. She didn't want to believe him, but she needed to believe him. Something deep within fought against all reason, all logic. She leaned heavily against the firmness of his chest beneath the formal waistcoat and closed her eyes, closed her mind against her pain. Jenna felt the warmth of his lips against her cheek. He offered her no further explanations. She must accept what he had given her. A gentle sob escaped as Jenna drew in a deep breath. She longed to forget everything that had happened. She longed to be far away from the war. She longed only for Stefan, in spite of the pain and the anger he had brought her. Jenna turned toward the warmth of his kiss. His lips closed over hers with agonizing tenderness.

Stefan felt the last of Jenna's resistance flow from her. "I did not want to love you," she murmured into the soft wool of his tunic, her voice full of her misery.

Slowly Stefan released her wrists. "Nor was it my choosing, little princess. But, I fear, my fate was sealed the moment I first saw you."

Stefan drew her full against him as his lips sought hers with growing urgency, their warmth becoming one. He had no right to hope that she would believe him, and yet he knew that she had. Gently, he lifted her slender weight and bore her to the soft mounding of hay in the empty stall. He lowered her gently, joining her there and pulling her within the warmth of his embrace. He was content merely to hold her, to soothe her sobbing, to ease the hurt he had caused her. Her breathing became even, the sobbing gone. Much later Stefan felt her breathing deep and even against his chest.

They remained within the carriage house until the first light of dawn filtered through the paned windows.

Stefan gently roused Jenna from sleep. He tenderly kissed the tip of her nose as she gazed at him uncertainly.

"It is the Christmas Day, little princess. My gift to you is my love, for always." Stefan stared into the wide, glowing depths of her amber eyes.

"Stefan . . ." Jenna's questions were silenced beneath the gentle pressure of Stefan's finger against her lips.

"You must ask nothing more, for I can say nothing more. Believe in my love, for it is strong." Stefan gently kissed her parted lips, then stood, pulling her from the hay to stand beside him.

"You must return home. It would be unwise for anyone to find you here." Stefan drew her with him as he opened the wide doors of the carriage house. The gray stallion stood in the shelter of the long building, his ears pricking forward at the possibility of finding shelter within. Stefan led Jenna to the gray stallion.

"Dmitri will see you safely home. From today until the duel there must be no contact between us. The duel will determine the outcome of many things."

Jenna leaned forward from the saddle, an expression of concern suddenly replacing the sleepiness. "I fear for you. You do not know Charles. He excels with the rapier, and takes great pleasure in the duel. He has never been known to lose a match."

Stefan seized her hand, passionately kissing her fingertips.

"I shall heed your warning, my princess. But be not deceived by the outcome of such a duel." Stefan turned as Dmitri approached from the main house. There was no further opportunity to question him as to his meaning.

Jenna glanced back over her shoulder as she followed Dmitri. The new sun cast a golden glow that glistened brightly off the softness of Stefan's hair as he watched her leave. She shuddered as golden light suddenly reflected red in the gray of dawn, casting an ominous crimson across the front of Stefan's tunic. For an instant it glowed blood-red, and then was gone.

For Jenna there was no solitude to be found in the celebrations of Christmas Day. Upon her return to Hallston House, Emma Kelly deluged her with a constant round of questioning as to her whereabouts the night before. Dmitri's imposing stature soon silenced her questions behind her wary regard for the giant Russian.

Jenna's head ached from lack of sleep and her concern for Stefan, yet there was no rest to be found in the merrymaking of the holy day. She joined Emma for early morning services at Westminster Abbey and then assumed her role as hostess, together with Elizabeth, at Wingate Hall. The elaborate manor was open to all who would come to offer their greetings and a gift to their host. Charles was the essence of gentlemanly behavior, fairly doting on Jenna's every movement until she thought she might scream for one moment to herself. She wanted very much to speak with Elizabeth, to hear about her evening with John Whitmore. Through the entire afternoon, Elizabeth seemed to be glowing with some inner happiness that Jenna could only guess at. Stealing a moment of privacy late in the afternoon, in Elizabeth's second-floor chamber, Jenna pressed her friend for details of the previous evening. Elizabeth's happiness seemed to bubble forth into the room.

"John has asked me to marry him." Elizabeth clasped her hands together in complete happiness, a warm glow lighting her plain features, so that she seemed very beautiful.

"And of course you accepted." Jenna answered for her. The light in Elizabeth's eyes suddenly dimmed.

"Jenna, I did not give him my answer," she replied morosely.

Jenna stared at her friend in disbelief. "Do you love him?"

"Of course, I love him."

"And does he love you?" Jenna persisted.

"Oh, yes." That soft glow returned to Elizabeth's pale eyes.

"I can see only one answer you can give him."

"But how can I? You know well how father and Charles feel about John."

"Charles be damned. And I think Lord Wingate will accept the idea when he realizes that you are quite determined in the matter. Elizabeth, you must not turn away the chance to love completely," Jenna added almost wistfully.

Elizabeth stared at her friend, suddenly aware that the words had not been entirely for her alone.

"You do not love Charles," Elizabeth stated with sudden certainty, as she gazed into the depths of Jenna's amber eyes. She often found it difficult to understand the depth of their friendship, since they were so very different. Now, as she saw the sudden sadness in Jenna's face, she knew they were very much alike.

"You know well that Charles often takes it upon himself to speak for those about him." Jenna avoided answering Elizabeth's question directly.

"Perhaps in time, I may grow to share a mutual caring for Charles."

"And what of Stefan Kalinsky?"

Jenna's head snapped up at the mention of Stefan's name. Elizabeth was far more astute than she had given her credit for. Jenna's silence was her answer.

"Then I offer your own advice, my dear friend; do not turn away from the opportunity to love completely."

Together they rejoined those gathered below, as Lord Wingate offered the Christmas toast.

Jenna declined Elizabeth's fervent offer to remain at Wingate Hall the next few days, preferring instead the quiet solitude of Hallston House. She quietly bid her friend good-bye after the celebrations had subsided and only a few guests remained. They planned to meet over the next days, to further discuss what Elizabeth should do.

Jenna readily accepted Charles's offer to see her home, seizing upon the opportunity to plead with him against the duel. If she could not dissuade Stefan, she might convince Charles of the folly of such a contest, if for no other reason than their impending marriage. Charles poured out his heartfelt love for her, pleased that she was so concerned for his well-being, but his manner changed abruptly, when she brought up the duel, refusing to consider withdrawing from the match. He insisted it was a matter of honor, and no matter her feelings, he would see it through.

Upon arriving at Hallston House, Jenna pleaded fatigue against Charles's insistence on spending the evening in her company. Instead of a casual kiss upon her hand, Charles leaned forward, seizing her about the shoulders, and planted an impassioned kiss upon her lips. Jenna recoiled from his touch, wondering that she had once cared deeply for him.

In the solitude of her own chamber, Jenna called for steaming hot water, to ease the tension in her tired body and to cleanse herself of Charles's touch. For hours afterward, Jenna lay in the darkness of her room, sleep refusing to release her tortured thoughts of the day yet to come. The ornate clock on the mantel over the fireplace struck three before Jenna finally dozed fitfully, tormented by recurrent dreams of the duel and Stefan's blood-soaked body lying at Charles's feet. Shortly after dawn she awoke, unable to drive the haunting nightmare from her thoughts.

Over a cup of steaming hot tea, she quickly penned a letter for Mr. Flint to deliver to Stefan. She was not surprised when Mr. Flint returned within the hour, with her letter, unopened.

Three more such missives over the next seven days were returned in the same manner, each unopened. Stefan had warned her they must have no contact. With each passing day, the circles of worry and fatigue beneath Jenna's eyes grew more obvious. Her nights were plagued with nightmares of Stefan's injury, or possibly worse. Her days were brightened only by Elizabeth's presence and the plans they made. Charles had retired to the sports' club to practice for the coming contest.

January 3rd dawned cloudy and ominous. A persistent wind had come up off the Thames the day before, filling the sky with the threat of a storm.

Ladies were not allowed to attend such contests; therefore Elizabeth spent the night at Hallston House, offering her support to Jenna by her presence. The contest was to begin promptly at three in the afternoon. A long, agonizing day lay before them.

Unable to sleep, Jenna had risen well before the first gray light entered the paned casement of her chamber. Elizabeth joined her in the drawing room, where Maggie had built a roaring fire against the aching cold of the day. Jenna tried to concentrate on the stitchery design she had begun days before. Never one of her greatest interests, she cursed heartily at the unfinished sampler as she pricked her finger for the third time, a single crimson droplet of blood staining the sampler. In mounting frustration, she cast the sampler aside. She dared not admit how that one crimson droplet unsettled her. It was as if Stefan's blood flowed across the fabric. Elizabeth stared at her friend. There were now no words of comfort she might give her. Together they waited.

When Jenna had begun the same pattern in the same place on the heavy linen fabric yet one more time, she finally cast the framework away from her with mounting impatience, and paced the width of the drawing room. The breakfast tray had been removed, untouched, to be replaced by a light midday meal, as nerves wore thin. When the clock struck the hour of two, Jenna could bear the confines of the house no longer. Seizing a heavy woolen shawl, she wrapped herself against the bitter cold of the winter afternoon and sought release of her mounting fears and frustrations in a brisk walk about the barren gardens that surrounded Hallston House.

An hour later, when Emma had begun to fear for her health, Jenna burst through the large double doors of the drawing room from the gardens beyond. Her wide amber eyes were ablaze with the fire of sudden purpose, her cheeks vividly flushed from the cold air that swirled in about her. The heavy woolen shawl had pushed back from her head, and her long hair was loose and waving from the dampness of the light mist that had begun to fall. Emma thought her suddenly seized with a return of the fever from weeks before as she flew to Jenna's side.

"Dear child, your hands are as cold as ice. What can you be thinking wandering about with the weather so dreadful? I was about to send Mr. Flint after you," Emma scolded gently, as she looked into the impassioned gaze that turned to her.

"Send for Mr. Flint at once. I want the coach brought to the front of the house immediately," Jenna ordered with complete calmness.

Emma could only stare at Jenna, as if she thought she might have taken complete leave of her senses.

"The coach is ready, mistress."

Jenna whirled around and stared at Mr. Flint's

imposing height in the doorway of the drawing room. Instinctively he had known she could not bear to stay away from the coming contest. Jenna fled the drawing room for her own chamber, returning in a matter of moments wearing her heavy woolen coat which covered the silk morning dress with ample, warm folds. It was lined with the finest fox fur about the hood and sleeves. Elizabeth quickly joined her.

"You did not think I would remain behind? You are my dearest friend; I could not bear that you face this alone."

Jenna understood the silent meaning behind Elizabeth's words of loyalty. Though they had never spoken of it, Elizabeth understood that Jenna's fears that day were not for Charles. Jenna reached out and affectionately squeezed Elizabeth's hand. They both ignored Emma's heated protests about venturing out on such a dreadful day, quickly entering the coach that stood waiting for them. There was no need for Jenna to give Mr. Flint their destination. He knew well the purpose of their ride.

That third day of January 1813, Vauxhall Gardens was a park of barren trees, stripped of their lush, summer foliage by the colder climes of winter. Countless rows of elegant blooming plants were now frozen back to the ground, only a lingering memory of the rich, abundant flowers that would once again appear with the warmth of spring. Divergent pathways, used during the summer months for rides in open carriages, were now empty. Mr. Flint urged the team of horses on at a faster pace as he guided them around the next bend that converged with another pathway that led to a cobbled promenade. In warmer months, fashionably dressed ladies and their escorts often wound their way through Vauxhall Gardens, strolling along this same pathway while musicians played from the bandstand. There were no such festivities this day. Indeed, the mood was quite somber. Mr. Flint reined the team to a halt beside the long line of coaches.

Several men stood along the perimeter of the green beyond the promenade. None seemed to take notice of the arrival of yet another coach. Jenna strained to see from the window of the coach. She saw nothing but the warmly clad figures of others who had come to witness the duel. In the silence that surrounded them, Jenna shivered as she heard the distant sound of blade meeting blade. She reached for the door handle, feeling Elizabeth's restraining hand on her arm. She firmly pulled free of Elizabeth's grasp, alighting from the coach before Mr. Flint could stop her.

Slowly, Jenna pushed her way through the line of men. She was oblivious of the disapproving stares cast in her direction. She stopped as she reached the edge of the spectators, disbelieving the scene before her.

Coats removed, both Stefan and Charles seemed unaware of the biting cold of the winter's day. The heavy mist that had fallen throughout the day had soaked their shirts, until they clung like second skins molded to their bodies. Stefan's golden-brown hair lay plastered to his head, whether from the mist or from the strain of his efforts, Jenna could not know. It was not the condition of Stefan's garments that caused Jenna to pull back in sudden horror, but the spreading crimson stain down the length of his left sleeve. The fabric had been neatly sliced through, revealing a wound of equal length on his arm. Another stain of blood had formed at the lower left side, and Jenna could see the result of another slash across the back of his right hand, which slowly dripped blood.

Jenna's wide amber gaze sought his, but found no recognition in the icy blue coldness she saw there. His concentration was complete, as he parried Charles's thrust and circled wide before him, the tip of his blade seeking some point of vulnerability in his foe. He found none. As they both circled again, Jenna's gaze locked with Charles's. He was the essence of control and deadly calm, as yet untouched by the blade. Charles moved with the quiet stealth of a practiced hunter, taking great pleasure in the torture he brought his prey. It was no contest. It was an exhibition of the worst form of sportsmanship. Jenna turned her head from the look of keen pleasure upon Charles's sharp features. Her heart ached. Somehow she had dared to hope that she might stop the duel. Failing that, she had thought perhaps to find Stefan not unskilled with the rapier. She saw now that it was not to be.

Vainly, Jenna searched among the men for the field judge. The duke of Kent had ordered it was not to be a duel to the death. Surely someone must see that the duel had to be stopped. A murmur went through the spectators. Stefan had lunged at Charles, and they were now locked in a desperate battle of strength as Charles blocked Stefan's move, their blades locking at the hilts. Though Stefan was of greater stature, Charles seemed to possess the greater strength. She cringed as she saw the twisted expression on Charles's face, very near Stefan's, as they struggled in their match, each refusing to yield.

Charles seemed to draw on some inner strength as he moved against Stefan, suddenly throwing him off balance. With one twisting motion of his blade, Charles wrenched the rapier from Stefan's grasp, his blade quickly returning to rest with deadly menace against the column of Stefan's throat, as Stefan's blade fell to the ground beyond his ability to recover it. Everyone stood in stunned silence at Charles's sudden intentions.

Jenna stared at the men about her. It was the thrill of the sport. They longed to see complete defeat. Jenna pushed through the circle of men who surrounded Charles and Stefan. She felt a restraining hand like a great paw close firmly over her wrist.

"Do not interfere in this, little princess."

Jenna turned to stare at Dmitri in stunned disbelief.

"You must do something. You cannot allow this to happen." Jenna's voice caught with her emotion as she mutely appealed to the giant Cossack. He merely shook his great, shaggy head.

"This is a matter of honor. It would be his disgrace if anyone were to intervene."

"It will be his life, if someone does not."

"You are wrong, little princess. Charles Wingate will not be the cause of my master's death. He seeks only humiliation."

Jenna struggled to free herself. She could not believe what she was hearing. From Dmitri, of all people, she had expected unfailing loyalty. It was beyond her capacity to understand, that he would willingly stand by while Stefan was slowly cut to pieces. Jenna turned back to stare at Stefan. Her heart constricted at the sight of his blood-soaked shirt, the ugly cut across the back of his hand, the look of defeat in his lifeless blue eyes. She had thought Charles oblivious to her presence. She gasped as Charles's gaze suddenly locked with hers. She saw nothing but cold brutality, and she realized that Stefan had been right. Charles Wingate was a most dangerous man.

Charles briefly acknowledged her presence, the cold look of death suddenly disappearing before the smile of the victor. He lowered the blade. Stefan Kalinsky's defeat was now complete.

Dmitri relinquished her arm to Mr. Flint. "Take her from here."

Jenna resisted, turning back toward Stefan. "No!" She cried angrily, trying to twist free of Dmitri's grasp.

"The duel was fought because of you. You will only cause him more harm, if you do not leave now. It is important that the others believe your concern to be for Charles Wingate." Dmitri's dark eyes glistened with a hard light. Jenna stared at Stefan with mounting confusion. For a brief moment his eyes met hers, as Dmitri reached him, supporting Stefan's body against his massive shoulder. For the barest moment, Jenna saw recognition, and Stefan's silent command that she not interfere.

Jenna obeyed Mr. Flint's gentle commands as he led her back to the coach. She responded not with a will of her own, but like a sleepwalker who can only partially return from the nightmare. Mr. Flint helped her into the coach, drawing down the shade at the window. Charles appeared beside the coach, laying a restraining hand on the door, so that it was impossible for Mr. Flint to close it. Charles reached inside the coach, seizing Jenna's hand in an impassioned grasp.

"My dearest Jenna, I regret that you were subjected to

283

this. I had hoped to spare your worry and concern. Now you see, my love, all was for naught." Charles bowed smugly before her. In his other hand he still held his rapier, moist with Stefan's blood.

Jenna choked back the anger that welled within her. Beside her, Elizabeth cautioned her with a hard squeeze of her hand. How she longed to scream the truth at him. How she longed to tell him it was not fear for his life that had brought her to the park. Jenna's eyes glowed feverishly with the anger she suppressed. Silently she vowed that if Stefan failed to recover from his wounds, she would see Charles dead for it. Inhaling deeply, to quiet the torment that raged within her, Jenna pulled her hand from his grasp. Her gaze lowered, as she could not trust herself for the lie she must speak.

"Please, Charles. I must return home. I should not have come."

"Of course, my dear. I see you are feeling faint. Elizabeth will see you home." Charles seized her hand again.

"I shall call upon you on the morrow. We shall put this unpleasantness behind us, and begin making the plans for our marriage." Charles spoke confidently.

Jenna nodded faintly as Charles moved to close the door. He stepped back from the coach and gave a signal to Mr. Flint. Jenna clung to the handle near the door of the coach, as if it were a lifeline to reality. She heard nothing of Elizabeth's words, spoken to comfort her. She was aware only of the lurching motion of the coach, and the haunting vision of Stefan standing before Charles's brutal onslaught. A coldness surrounded her heart, as she silently vowed that Charles Wingate would pay for his cruelty.

Beyond Vauxhall Gardens, Jenna ordered Mr. Flint to stop the coach. She instructed him to see Elizabeth home first. Though her friend heartily objected, fearing Jenna to be more deeply upset than either of them realized, Jenna calmly but firmly refused her friend's entreaties to remain yet another night at Hallston House.

Elizabeth hesitated and then yielded to Jenna's decision. She knew no amount of arguing or pleading would change Jenna's mind when she had made a decision.

They arrived at Wingate Hall some time later. Jenna quietly and calmly bid her friend good-bye, with the promise that they would meet in the next few days.

The leaden sky that had threatened the entire day now darkened visibly with the last light of day. A light snow had begun to fall as Mr. Flint turned the coach onto the cobbled lane that wound before the large doors to Hallston House. Jenna gave her instruction that he was to await her, as she quickly stepped from the coach, not waiting for him to assist her. She was determined to see Stefan, no matter what Dmitri or Mr. Flint might say of the matter.

Before Jenna reached the top step, the door was thrown wide open. Maggie stood in the doorway, her face ashen as she stood aside for Jenna to enter.

"Maggie, what is it?" Jenna demanded briskly. The maid swallowed with great difficulty, not knowing how she might tell her mistress. The girl broke into tears and reached for her apron to dab at her eyes, suddenly overcome with emotion.

For the first time in her life, Jenna felt the greatest temptation to strike someone.

"Maggie!"

"Oh, Miss Jenna. It is dreadful. They had to bring him here. And he was all covered with blood, and as pale as a ghost. I do not know how a man could live having lost that much blood." Maggie sobbed with renewed effort into her apron. Jenna seized Maggie about the shoulders and shook the girl until her teeth rattled.

"You will tell me now! Who is here?" Jenna demanded with a threatening edge to her voice Maggie had never heard before.

"The Russian prince. That big man, Dmitri, brought him here. He said he feared he would not live long enough to reach home."

Maggie was roughly shoved aside as Jenna suddenly released her and fled up the sweeping stairway to the second-floor chambers, the wide sweep of her coat billowing out behind her in a flurry of snow and cold air.

It could not match the coldness of fear she felt about her heart.

Jenna burst through the door of the large, second-floor chamber across the hall from her own. Three pairs of eyes briefly acknowledged her presence. Emma held a basin of water and clean towels, while Dmitri cut away the stained remnants of Stefan's shirt. Alexei had straightened when she first came in, his hand firm upon the pistol he wore in his belt. His face relaxed when Jenna pushed back the hood of her coat as she rounded the foot of the bed.

Stefan's face wore a deathly pallor. His golden hair was still damp and matted against his head. His eyes were closed, his breathing shallow and ragged, and he seemed oblivious to anyone's presence in the room. Jenna sighed her relief that he still lived. She pulled off her warm gloves and unbuttoned the heavy woolen coat, casting both carelessly aside. Almost fearfully, she moved closer to the side of the bed. Dmitri stripped away the last of the shirt, and Jenna could well see that, indeed, he would never have survived the remainder of the journey to the town house.

Emma stood aside as Jenna leaned over Stefan, her cool fingers pressing gently upon the skin at his neck, already flushed with fever. His eyes opened slightly at the softness of her touch, and he smiled faintly at her in greeting. Jenna could not know that he had bargained with the devil to be able to look upon her one more time.

Chapter Sixteen

For three days, Stefan fought back the evil specter of death. During those days Jenna assumed the role of complete authority over his care, and none dared question her. Dmitri, loyal friend of many years, refused to allow a physician to be summoned. He trusted no one to care for Stefan, except Jenna, and reaffirmed his mistrust of everyone else except his own men.

Jenna had cringed at the first sight of the deep blade wound in Stefan's side. She swallowed back her nausea at the sight of the gaping flesh, and nimbly applied her needle to closing the outer skin to aid healing. More than once she had stopped, fighting back the tears that threatened to break her composure. Each time Dmitri's strong, large hand reached to comfort and steady her. When the wound was finally closed, Dmitri had mixed some of the same herb leaves he had once mixed for Jenna in warm water, grinding them to a thick paste, and then packing the pungent mixture against the wound, binding it with clean linen strips about Stefan's waist. The long gash on Stefan's arm and the cut on his hand were not deep wounds. Jenna cleansed both thoroughly, spreading Dmitri's salve across the skin before binding both loosely to aid healing. Then they waited, while the fever from the wounds spread through his body.

Through the long hours of the days and nights that followed, Jenna refused to leave Stefan's side, insisting that she change the bandages for clean ones. Her worst fear was of internal bleeding from the deep wound in Stefan's side. She constantly tormented herself that had she more knowledge of such matters she might have cared for him differently. Dmitri refused to accept such self-doubts, and together they kept their silent vigil.

Dmitri brewed his magic healing tea from more herbs, and together he and Jenna forced Stefan to drink down the steamy liquid. Circles of fatigue prominent beneath her wide eyes, Jenna refused Dmitri's gruff suggestion that she rest, finally curling up on the upholstered chaise near the bed to doze fitfully, suddenly coming awake at the slightest change in Stefan's breathing to reassure herself that he had not slipped away from her.

Beyond Hallston Hall, time seemed to have stood still. The storm of those first days persisted, blanketing everything in a layer of snow, buffeted about by the wind. The third day the snow ceased, replaced by rain that quickly froze into thickened shards of ice that rattled against the paned windows. Heavy velvet drapes had been drawn across the windows, and every hearth in the house blazed with a roaring fire to drive back the cold. Those who dared to venture out quickly returned, seeking refuge from the storm before those inviting flames. Jenna was unaware that in those three days Charles Wingate had sent a servant to inquire after their needs. Mr. Flint carefully intercepted all such missives, sending the messenger back to Wingate Hall with word that all was well.

Charles Wingate's efforts to learn of Stefan's condition had received no results. As far as he was able to determine, no physician had been summoned to treat the wounded prince. Indeed, the London town house remained darkened and closed. His efforts to gain some knowledge of Stefan's condition through Lillian de Stahl had met with the same dismal failure. She had received no word from Stefan since the day prior to the duel. Eventually a well-placed rumor reached Charles Wingate that Stefan Kalinsky had not survived the first night following the duel. Charles was hailed as a masterful sportsman among his circle of friends, but as a dangerous and worthy adversary among others. It was a rumor that would serve both men well.

The morning of the fourth day Jenna roused from her fitful slumber and stared about the darkened chamber groggily. Her eyes adjusted slowly to the meager light. She was not certain what had awakened her. She listened again, and then sat up stiffly upon the chaise. Stefan's breathing was different this morning. No longer shallow and rapid, he now seemed to sleep deeply for the first time in days. Jenna felt his forehead. His skin was cooler. She jumped as Stefan weakly seized her hand.

"Stefan?" His name was a faint whisper on her lips, and she thought she must surely be dreaming. And yet the faint pressure of his fingers about hers was no dream.

Jenna's voice caught in her throat as she fumbled with the lamp beside the bed, turning the wick up with one hand as Stefan refused to relinquish her hand. She would not have broken that contact for any price.

The soft glow of the lamp illuminated Stefan's pale features. Already a faint glow of color had returned to the high cheekbones, but if Jenna had any doubts of his recovery, they were banished forever by the brilliant blue of his gaze as he stared at her with complete recognition.

All Jenna's fears and doubts of the last days disappeared in a torrent of uncontrollable tears. She buried her face in the thick covers of the bed, her fingers entwined with Stefan's as she gave herself completely to a flood of relief. Stefan pulled weakly at her hand, and Jenna looked up at him, crying and laughing at the same time. She clasped his hand against her cheek to reassure herself that he was really there. He would be well again.

Stefan's hand shook visibly as he reached to caress her cheek. She was indeed real. He had not been dreaming. He had bargained with the devil, and won. He buried his hand in the softness of her silken hair, untying the ribbon that bound it away from her face. Jenna turned to press a tender kiss in the palm of his hand. His fingers behind her head, Stefan insistently pulled her to him. His lips sought hers, briefly, tenderly. His hand slipped to her shoulder limply. Jenna gently rubbed her cheek against the back of his hand. Stefan's eyes closed in sleep.

Jenna turned toward Dmitri as he returned to the chamber, a light he had not seen in days burning brightly in the depths of her amber eyes. The radiant smile on her lips was answer enough.

The morning of the fifth day, Jenna returned to Stefan's room to find a large tub of steaming water before the hearth. Her gaze flew to the large bed, where Dmitri stood over Stefan, his mammoth arm about Stefan's waist as he assisted him from the bed. Jenna immediately descended on both men, a look of stubborn determination on her exquisite face.

Two pairs of eyes, one brilliant blue, the other as black as onyx, raised to meet her defiantly.

Before she could loose all her objections on the two men, Stefan held up a bandaged hand.

"Do not interfere in this, Jenna. I am determined to bathe, however briefly. I am sincerely grateful for your care of these last days, but I cannot endure another day in that bed. I shall grow as soft and weak as a young maiden, although I swear I hardly smell like one." Stefan cast her a warning look, which could not conceal a sparkling of humor in his blue eyes.

Jenna could see that her role of authority over the last days had effectively been replaced. She could not repress a faint smile. It was a role she gladly relinquished. A badly needed full night's sleep the night before had virtually erased the weariness from about her eyes, and a brisk morning walk about the grounds had returned a healthy glow to her cheeks. Staring at the two men, she could well see that all her objections would be wasted. She had learned quite early the futility of arguing with Stefan. Her point was more easily won by other methods of enticement. Jenna joined Dmitri in assisting Stefan from the bed.

Stefan cast her a wary glance, wondering at the game she played. He quickly decided it would be well worth any

290

price just to have her near. He leaned heavily on her shoulder, inhaling the fragrant scent from her hair. He promptly decided the last days had been small price to pay for his enjoyment now. The linen sheet fell away as they slowly moved away from the bed, exposing Stefan's naked body. Jenna concentrated on their destination rather than on his state of undress, as wide, crimson patches of color spread across her cheeks. Even with the purplish marks of the wound at his side, Stefan Kalinsky was quite magnificent.

Dmitri supported Stefan's weight as he stepped into the brass tub, Jenna quickly coming around to take his arm, as Dmitri announced they would need more firewood for the hearth and left the room.

The muscles in Stefan's arm tautened as he braced his weight on the rim of the tub, the effort requiring no small amount of will as he slowly lowered himself into the steaming liquid. He released his hold on the tub, suddenly slipping into the water. His grip about Jenna's shoulders tightened deliberately, pulling her with him.

Jenna shrieked as she felt herself pulled off balance by Stefan's greater weight. She helplessly grabbed at the rim of the tub, her hand slipping off the wet brass. Any further effort to save herself ended abruptly as Jenna fell forward into the warm water, her shoulder grazing Stefan's knee as she vainly tried to break her fall. Jenna came up coughing and sputtering from her unexpected dunking, her dark hair hanging in wet tendrils about her face. Her eyes flew wide open in startled surprise as Stefan's laughter filled the chamber.

Jenna fumed as Stefan's hand landed with a firm smack across her bottom, causing her to lunge forward for a second dunking. Seeking some leverage to push herself back out of the water, Jenna's hand brushed intimately between Stefan's thighs. All the fury quickly faded from her startled face as she turned to stare at him warily.

"Oh no," Jenna warned as she noted the devilish gleam that had sprung into the brilliant depths of his blue eyes. She knew that look quite well. Invalid he might be, but

Stefan Kalinsky certainly seemed less hindered by his wounds than any man Jenna had ever seen. Before she could react, Stefan's hands had closed about her waist, nimbly turning her over and pulling her across his lap. Only the hem of her gown remained dry as she struggled in the clinging, sodden mass of fabric that weighted her down, as if in support of Stefan's playfulness. She sat back and raised her wide amber gaze, suddenly breaking into uncontrollable laughter at her predicament. Further struggling only continued to soak the gown completely, as Stefan's arms closed about her, pulling her full against him, his fiery blue eyes suddenly turning the color of smoke as he stared down at her with a sudden passion.

"Had I thought you would come to me so willingly, my dearest Jenna, I would have taken advantage of my confinement to that bed much earlier," he whispered huskily against her ear.

"I fear your condition did not allow for such activities, your highness," Jenna responded softly beneath the warmth of his lips against hers, her hand reaching behind his neck to hold him near. It was a tender moment, as Jenna's last fears slipped away. She could feel Stefan's strength in his arm about her waist as he bound her to him. Their playful moment was gone, at the sound of light knocking at the door. Dmitri would not have bothered to announce his arrival. It was not his custom to adhere to such formality with Stefan. Jenna moaned with sudden misery as she realized Emma might well enter the chamber to find her in Stefan's lap. She struggled out of the tub, only to return with a sudden splashing as her foot slipped on the polished wood floor. The knocking came again.

Not the least embarrassed about Jenna's plight, Stefan calmly acknowledged the knocking. Jenna threw him a murderous glare as she finally struggled free of the water that seemed reluctant to release her. She stood before the hearth, soaking wet, attempting to wring the water from her gown when Maggie entered the chamber.

The young maid's eyes widened in shocked surprise as she glanced first at Stefan, submerged barely to his hips in the tub before the hearth, and then at her mistress, an obvious flush of color spreading wide across Jenna's cheeks as she vainly attempted to restore some order to her sodden appearance. Maggie averted her gaze, coughing loudly, trying to suppress a smile behind her hand. She moved across the chamber, busying herself with throwing the heavy velvet drapes wide to allow more light into the room.

"Sir Charles and Elizabeth Wingate are in the drawing room. They have asked for you. I told them I would see if you were about yet this morning," Maggie informed Jenna politely.

Jenna's gaze flew to Stefan's with sudden apprehension. She could well imagine the repercussions if Charles were to discover Stefan Kalinsky's presence in her house. Her thoughts raced as she bent to scoop the soggy skirt of her gown into one hand. Stefan caught her by the arm. The sudden, cold look in the depths of his eyes spoke of his hatred for Charles Wingate.

"I shall send Dmitri."

Jenna could well imagine the assumptions Maggie had already made about her relationship with Stefan. Surely finding her in his bath, fully clothed and sharing an intimate embrace, had confirmed any doubts that remained. Jenna cast all pretenses aside as she bent low over the tub, her lips brushing his briefly.

"No, you must not. It would only cause more harm. Charles must not know of your whereabouts," she argued as she stared into the depths of that haunting azure gaze. She shivered as she saw only the look of death there.

"I want his death, more than I want my own life," Stefan whispered fiercely.

Jenna reached to take his face between her slender hands. "Another day, this will be settled between you and Charles Wingate. For now, you must yield the moment. To take up the sword again, so soon, would surely mean your death. And I fear I could not bear it." Jenna spoke softly against his lips. She pulled back and gazed at him with a sudden mischievous light leaping into the golden

293

depths of her amber eyes.

"In any event, you can hardly take up the battle in your present attire," she observed pointedly, her gaze raking the length of his naked body. "Dmitri has removed your clothes for cleaning, and I fear my silk wrapper would hardly provide a suitable garment." Jenna smiled wickedly. "As to your weapon, I fear the only 'sword' in your possession, though of sound strength and a fine instrument, is hardly sufficient for such a contest." She winked at Stefan with a coquettish tilt of her head. "And I could hardly allow you to risk damage to the 'blade' I speak of. It is intended for other, finer tasks."

At the window Maggie suppressed a fit of giggling as she divined Jenna's meaning. She averted her gaze, as Jenna turned about to move the fresh linen towels beyond Stefan's reach.

Stefan cast Jenna a warning frown for the game she played. She quickly darted beyond his grasp, and his hand closed on empty air.

Jenna quickly darted across the chamber, giving Maggie instructions to set the bolt in place after she left. She would send Dmitri to make certain that Stefan did not yet decide to settle the matter of the contest in her drawing room. With no clothes, she was confident he would not quickly leave the chamber. It was more her purpose, though, to keep anyone else from entering the chamber.

Jenna pulled off the clinging, wet gown, and quickly donned a morning dress of deep blue silk. She brushed through the length of her dampened hair and handily twisted it tightly, winding it about the crown of her head. It would have to do. She was certain Charles would not notice. She gave her hastily contrived appearance one final inspection and then quickly departed her chamber. Dmitri was nowhere to be found. She silently prayed the giant Cossack would not blunder upon Charles in the drawing room. It would precipitate an unavoidable confrontation that might well end only in death.

Jenna inhaled deeply as she reached the final step of the sweeping stairway, her footsteps falling softly on the woolen rug. Nervously, she smoothed the silk of her gown and brushed back a tendril of hair before entering the drawing room.

Charles Wingate turned about at the sound of her entrance, a mask of pleasant cordiality falling into place as he approached her. Elizabeth sat before the hearth and rose to greet her friend, a silent message passing between them.

"My dear, how very lovely you are this morning. Maggie had been so long, I feared we might have come at a bad moment," Charles commented pleasantly.

"It is quite early for calling, and I had not expected anyone. The weather has been so dreadful, I fear I have developed a severe laziness these last few days."

Charles stood back for a moment, holding her hand wide as he took a better inspection of her. "You have not been ill, after your venture to Vauxhall Gardens? Though I was deeply touched by your concern for me, I would not have risked your health."

Jenna smiled radiantly to hide her growing vexation with Charles, that he might actually believe her concern to be for him. She turned at the sound of the double doors of the drawing room being opened wide as Emma entered carrying a silver tea service, and smiled her gratitude for the woman's diligence.

Emma Kelly smiled with polite rigidity at Charles Wingate, her dark eyes conveying a sudden urgency to Jenna. Then she efficiently informed Jenna of an early appointment at the banker's, an appointment that existed only in the scheming mind of the faithful servant.

A sudden look of surprise lit Charles's aquiline features. "I had not realized you possessed an interest in such matters, my dear. Surely after we are married, you will no longer be troubled with such matters. I had intended to visit with business associates this morning. I would be delighted to see you to your appointment, and then perhaps we may enjoy a bit of luncheon."

The light in Jenna's gaze dimmed as she saw no easy way out of accompanying Charles. When they arrived at the bank, he would realize she had lied.

"The appointment was not definite, and I had thought to do a bit of shopping if the weather permitted. Madame Lessard has several adjustments to make to a gown I have ordered," Jenna responded lamely.

"I am not one to be bored with such events. Elizabeth and I shall accompany you, and perhaps you will make some selections for your wedding gown."

The cup in Jenna's hand rattled badly in the saucer as she attempted to pour tea. She glanced up to catch Elizabeth's steady gaze. Her friend nodded slightly as Jenna handed her a cup. Elizabeth turned to her brother, an innocent expression lighting her face.

"Dear Charles, you know quite well that such matters of women's fashion are far beyond your interest. I shall accompany Jenna, and thereby accomplish two purposes in one afternoon. I must, after all, make the selections for my own wedding gown. It will take hours, and perhaps require several trips to Madame Lessard's shop. You have promised to meet with your friends, and I will not allow you to disappoint them. Mr. Flint will see us to the dressmaker's, and Jenna will promise to dine with us this evening." Elizabeth quite efficiently maneuvered Jenna out of a compromising situation with her plans for the afternoon. When Charles made to object to their sudden arrangement of plans, Elizabeth innocently waved aside all his arguments.

Jenna joined in Elizabeth's game, whirling about with sudden excitement and proclaiming that she heartily needed a day at the dressmaker's, and that it was hardly proper that Charles should accompany her for such an important selection as the fabric for her wedding gown.

Charles stood in the center of the drawing room, a scowl darkening his features. His plans had effectively been overruled, and he could not easily persist in the matter, when Jenna had spoken of their forthcoming marriage for the first time with a note of anticipation. He was not certain of the reason for her change in mood, but he wished for nothing to change her attitude. He sighed heavily as he acquiesced to the greater will of two

296

determined women.

"Very well, but only with your promise to dine with us this evening, as Elizabeth suggested." Charles seized Jenna's hand possessively, and then as if Elizabeth might not have been there, leaned forward to press an impassioned kiss against Jenna's lips. His kiss brushed the corner of her mouth, and Jenna received his emotional display with a sudden shyness.

"Of course, I will accept your invitation," Jenna murmured softly, with as much control of will as she could gather.

When Charles had gathered his heavy coat and hat and finally departed, Elizabeth turned to Jenna with sudden urgency.

"Where is Prince Kalinsky?"

Jenna continued at her game of hostess, dutifully refilling the empty teacups.

"I have not the slightest idea where Prince Kalinsky might be. I have heard from the servants that he has left London."

Elizabeth rounded the table to confront Jenna directly.

"You know as well as I that he was gravely injured, and hardly in any condition to leave London. The weather of the last days has made most roads to the country impassable. Yet no physician has been summoned to attend his wounds. I pray he still lives."

"I had not known of your great concern for Prince Kalinsky," Jenna ventured with sudden surprise.

"I am indebted to him. I should like to repay that debt, if he has a need of it. I can only think that he still remains in London for the time to recover from his wounds."

Jenna stared at her friend with sudden curiosity.

"How might you possibly be indebted to Stefan Kalinsky?"

Elizabeth returned Jenna's even gaze. "I know that you asked Prince Kalinsky to carry my letter to John Whitmore."

"How could you possibly know of it?" Jenna set the teacup down with sudden alarm. Even with the announcement of Elizabeth's arranged marriage to Sir Reginald Guilford, Jenna had not felt entirely certain of her friend's loyalties.

"I know of it because Prince Kalinsky personally carried John's reply back to me."

"But how could he, without Charles's knowing of it?"

"Through Madame Lessard—he knew of my plans to visit her shop. After Charles had left, Prince Kalinsky approached me with John's message. At first I dared not believe him, but the proof was in John's letter. I could not deny his handwriting. If not for his kindness, my dear John might have been lost to me forever. The debt I owe Prine Kalinsky is John's love."

Jenna did not know how to answer her friend. A thoughtful silence fell between them, suddenly interrupted by a loud thumping overhead. Jenna rose uncertainly to her feet. She had every reason to suspect that Stefan might well have gained his freedom and be on his way to the drawing room at that very moment. She well realized the danger of involving Elizabeth further. Being under Charles's direct control, she was far too vulnerable.

"Jenna . . ." Elizabeth looked at her uncertainly.

Jenna knew her friend would not easily accept a lie.

"I know only that he lives, and will recover from the wounds he received. More than that I cannot tell you."

"I will gladly do whatever I can to help him. He has made it possible for John and me to be together. It is a debt I fear I can never repay."

Jenna suddenly forgot her apprehensions for Stefan as she turned to her friend.

"What are you saying?"

Elizabeth smiled bravely as she tilted her small chin defiantly. "I shall not be marrying Sir Reginald Guilford," she proclaimed with complete confidence.

"I do not understand. Have you managed to convince your father to allow your marriage to John?"

Elizabeth shook her head sadly. "I fear Father hears only Charles's continuing accolades of Sir Reginald's glowing qualifications as a husband. And the fact that Charles is greatly interested in acquiring a claim to Sir Reginald's vast estate in Sussex. I cannot fully understand the bond between Charles and Sir Reginald. Indeed, Sir Reginald is very near the same age as my father. Surely he and Charles have little in common, except perhaps their devotion to the same gambling clubs.''

"Then how is it possible that you intend to marry John?''

"John is making our plans now. He has sold his company to a buyer, from Virginia, in the American states. There was an opportunity for John to purchase an interest in a shipping company there. As soon as the weather permits, later in the spring, John will sail to Virginia. I have persuaded Father to set the date for the wedding the first week in May. Before that can happen, I shall be well on my way to Virginia with John. Once we have left England, none shall stand in our way.''

Jenna stared at her friend in shocked surprise. "Aren't you the sly one!'' she exclaimed with amazement.

"I shall have a need of your help in this. I dare not see John before the day we sail from England. Until that time, it must appear that I am agreeable to this marriage with Sir Reginald. I will make all the plans, as would be expected. I hate the deception I must play against Father. But I cannot marry Sir Reginald. Perhaps in time, Father will understand.''

Jenna put a comforting arm about Elizabeth's shoulders. "I shall help you whatever way I can. You know I want only your happiness.''

"What of your happiness, Jenna?'' Elizabeth questioned honestly. "You cannot make me believe that you love Charles. I know you too well. I can see it in your eyes. Jenna, you are free to say who you will wed. I know it is dreadful of me to speak against Charles. But he frightens me, and though I believe in his own way he does love you, I fear for that love. It is destructive. You must take great care, or it will find you.''

"I will take great care, my dear friend.'' Jenna pressed her friend's hand confidently as Elizabeth rose to leave.

"Are you leaving so soon?"

"I must see that all is made ready for dinner tonight. I regret there was no other way to be rid of Charles. I am certain you have much to keep you busy until this evening." Elizabeth leaned forward and planted a sisterly kiss on Jenna's cheek.

"John will be in touch with you."

"I will give his message to you as soon as I have it," Jenna promised faithfully.

Elizabeth hugged her with a sudden fierceness.

"You must see to your own happiness, Jenna."

Jenna smiled with more confidence than she felt as she bid her friend good-bye.

Jenna knocked lightly on the door to Stefan's chamber. Maggie quickly unbolted the door when she heard Jenna's voice. The maid then scurried out of the room, slamming the door behind her with a loud thud, a well-soaped cloth landing in the middle of the floor, where the maid had stood a moment before.

Jenna whirled about to find Stefan still submerged in the brass tub. The water had cooled considerably since she had left him under Maggie's guard, although his temper had not.

"She threatened me with boiling water if I merely tried to move out of the water," Stefan growled with mounting anger.

Jenna handed him a linen towel, easily sidestepping his hand as he reached for her arm.

"You have ruined one gown this day; you shall not ruin another. I shall call Dmitri to help you."

Stefan waved Jenna back with mounting irritation.

"I shall do this myself. I have no need for treacherous women or weak-minded fools," he grumbled unhappily.

"I should have liked very much to meet with Charles Wingate."

Jenna whirled on Stefan with a sudden feral vengeance glinting in her amber eyes. She had little tolerance for his foolishness.

"And yet have your life taken for his cruel pleasure? I will not allow it. Allow Charles to wonder about your whereabouts and your health. Would it not be of greater advantage for him to believe you gravely wounded, or fled the country, according to the rumor? What purpose would your death now serve, except to give Charles the final success of his conspiracy? My grandfather gave his life to uncover the conspiracy. Yours has very nearly been taken also. I will not lose again," Jenna threatened with mounting passion as she stood before Stefan, her slender hands clenched into tight fists at her sides.

Stefan chuckled softly at the vision of the fiery young woman who stood before him. Had she descended on him at that moment he would not have possessed the strength to defend himself, much less take on Charles Wingate. He nodded his acceptance of her authority for the time being. Suddenly feeling very weak, he leaned back upon the edge of the brass tub.

In an instant, Jenna was beside him, her concern for his health in the faint lines that formed into a frown about her mouth.

Stefan's fingers gently raised her chin until her gaze locked with his.

"I much prefer to see a smile upon your lips," he coaxed.

Not that easily won over, Jenna strengthened her frown. It quickly disappeared beneath the assault of Stefan's lips against hers. Her eyes flew open in sudden wonder.

"It would seem you are not in such great need of help. I shall send Dmitri." Jenna twisted out from beneath his arm.

Stefan was momentarily set off balance, and he grabbed for the edge of the tub. His face paled noticeably at the pain caused by that effort. In an instant, Jenna had returned to his side, her slender arm about his waist.

"I had hoped you might be convinced to give me your personal care. I fear Dmitri's skills are greatly lacking in certain matters," Stefan whispered against her cheek.

Jenna's head shot up as she realized the game he played

301

with her. Though a smile pulled at his handsome lips, Jenna could see that he suffered considerable pain behind the mask of his humor. He leaned heavily on her shoulder as she guided him to the bed. He slumped wearily into the downy softness of the bed, while she finished drying him.

"I fear I might have taken a chill from an overlong bath. I have a need of your warmth, little princess."

Jenna stared at him warily. She knew very well the game he played, however there was no denying his shivering beneath the heavy covers. She turned toward the hearth to set more wood upon the fire, Stefan's fingers closing gently about her wrist as he drew her toward the edge of the bed.

Stefan pulled her across the width of the bed, one arm firm about her waist as he reached with the other hand to turn her face toward his, his lips moving over hers with an unexpected hunger.

Jenna moaned softly under the assault of his passion. It was madness, a madness that she gave in to willingly. Too many days, and nights she had longed for the feel of his hands upon her body, the warmth of his lips possessive upon hers. Now, when everything around them seemed determined to tear them apart, they had been granted one more moment together. Jenna felt the buttons at her bodice unfastened beneath Stefan's insistent fingers. Her breath caught in her throat at that first searing contact of his mouth against the swelling mound of her breast as he reached gently to free her. Her words of caution against hurting himself died on her lips as she arched against him, feeling the exquisite pleasure of his teeth gently nibbling at the firm, taut peak. Her slender fingers raked through his tawny hair as she moved away from him momentarily, her lips seeking his with a sudden urgency.

Her name was a harsh whisper upon Stefan's lips as she moved away, her hands shielding her gaping bodice. Stefan reached out with unexpected quickness, his lean bronzed fingers closing over her slender wrist. Slowly he drew her hands away, reaching to softly knead the ripe fullness of her breast. Again he whispered her name.

Jenna leaned forward, giving him a kiss of promise. She moved quickly about the chamber, pulling the heavy drapes across the paned windows and setting the heavy bolt at the door. In the golden glow of firelight that played across the walls in the chamber, Jenna quickly stepped out of the silk gown and the chemise she wore underneath. Reaching back, she pulled the combs from her hair, letting it wave about her shoulders and tumble wantonly down the length of her back to her hips.

Jenna sat down beside Stefan, carefully checking the bandages, her ministrations suddenly halted as Stefan seized her hand. He raised her fingers to his lips, gently kissing each delicate member until he had arrived at the palm of her hand. He lingered there for a moment and then continued his casual assault of her soft skin, placing a chain of lingering kisses up the entire length of her arm, pulling her closer with each kiss, until she lay across his uninjured side, their bodies separated only by the bandages.

Jenna pulled back, fearful of causing him further injury. When Stefan moved to resist, she firmly pushed him back against the pillows. She leaned over him, her lips seeking his reassuringly. Slowly, as he had done, Jenna gently traced a path of kisses down his neck, across his muscular shoulder, and down across the gleaming expanse of his bronze chest, where the muscles tautened and relaxed beneath the touch of her lips. Jenna moved lower over Stefan with deliberate slowness, as he had once showed her. She wanted to prolong their moments together, that they might savor the full measure of passion to be found in each other. With feather-light softness her tongue flicked across the surface of his skin as she savored the sweet taste of it. Her hand brushed across the prominence of the bone at his hip and caressed the length of his thigh.

With a sudden urgency, Stefan drew her to him, his lips demanding hers in a feverish kiss that dispelled any doubts of his strength. Their kiss unbroken, Stefan turned with her in the covers, pressing her into the softness of the bed.

"You are a witch, a Gypsy temptress who has stolen my heart and my soul until I am not my own man," Stefan murmured against the hollow of her throat, his eyes closing with the ecstasy of the pleasure of touching her.

Jenna's arms entwined about his neck, binding him to her until their bodies seemed to mold into one, incapable of life without the other to make them whole.

"And who are you, Stefan Kalinsky? Are you prince, highwayman, soldier of fortune, lover?" Jenna whispered passionately, as Stefan drew back to gaze into the depths of her uncertain eyes.

"I am whatever you would have me be, dearest Jenna. But above all, lover and protector. Our fates are now one. There is no changing it. I think it all began many years ago, when you were but a child and I a reckless young man. One day I will tell you of it, when the truth cannot harm you. For now, you must accept the safety of innocence. What you do not know cannot harm you."

Jenna reached up tenderly to stroke the lean, hard line of his cheek, her doubts not easily assuaged.

"What is it that you fear, little princess?" Stefan wrapped his hand about hers and turned to gently press a kiss into the palm of her hand.

"I have grown to fear the dawn," Jenna whispered softly. "The moments we share are found in darkness. Always you must leave, when the dawn comes; almost like a dream, so that what we share does not seem real."

Stefan smiled softly, tiny lines crinkling in the bronze skin about his eyes, which had suddenly darkened to a smoky hue. "Then I must make certain to bed you in the full light of day, so that you will know it is no phantom come to haunt you." He leaned forward to kiss the gentle curve of her shoulder, and lower, at the ample roundness of her breast. "Be assured, little princess, no phantom will ever love you as I love you." Slowly Stefan's greater weight lowered against her, his warmth melting into hers as he sought to destroy the fears that welled within her.

Jenna abandoned herself to the fire of his touch against her skin as his hands stroked away the fear of the moments before. For a time she lay pliant beneath his hand, luxuriating in the fiery warmth he kindled within her, heightening her pleasure with each moment, each touch, each lingering caress, until she cried out with longing and urgency to be released from the lingering torture. She reached up, molding Stefan to her, kissing his neck with mounting passion, opening to him, whispering his name until it seemed she begged for release. Slowly Stefan answered her silent pleas, turning with her in the soft tangle of bedcovers, pulling her down over him, his need for her more important than life itself. Once again he found fulfillment in the passion he gave her, as a slow, gentle stroking began. In the moments they now shared there was no tomorrow, no morning after, only the exquisite agony of the moments that were theirs, for now.

Chapter Seventeen

Stefan Kalinsky watched the departing coach from the window of the second-floor chamber. A deep frown creased his lean, handsome features as he drew back the heavy velvet drape. His warmth against the frosted glass fogged the panes, until the coach was blurred and then disappeared completely into the darkness of night, except for the distant glow of the lanterns that swayed gently with the rocking motion. When the last glow of those distant lights had disappeared like the last glimmering of distant stars, he turned back to the desk. He rubbed his hand over the thick bandages beneath his shirt and winced at the tenderness of the wound. All his arguments had failed to persuade Jenna to refuse this latest invitation. She insisted they dare not risk suspicion with her continued absences from social obligations. Though he well knew that she was right, he could not bear the thought of Charles Wingate's attentions to her.

The last weeks had been a special gift of time that he knew they might never experience again. It seemed as if the heavy winter storms had closed about them like a protective cocoon, keeping the world at bay beyond the shelter of the heavy walls and doors of Hallston House. He had known a peace and contentment here that he had never before experienced, as if he had first come alive when he was with her. His soul was like that of the poor pauper who for a moment possesses the rarest jewel, which will bring him all of life's greatest riches, only to feel it slipping beyond his grasp. Having once possessed the rarest jewel, he knew that all others would be worthless by comparison. Stefan's fingers traced the intricate gold design of the music box upon the dressing table. He knew how Jenna valued the box. It was part of her, and somehow his fears were eased some small measure as he touched the glowing gold that had known her warmth only a short time before. It was as if the essence of her presence was in the gold.

Stefan's gaze returned to the heavily embossed gold seal upon the latest communication from Vienna, which had arrived nearly three weeks earlier. In recent weeks, reports of the war had been vague and unchanged. All of Europe seemed to have stood still for a brief moment in time as winter descended with resounding fury, on the continent as well as on England. Considering the lack of news of the war in London, Stefan was far better informed than most. He well appreciated the advantage of everyone's believing he had left London in disgrace following the duel with Charles Wingate. During his recovery, Dmitri and Alexei had been his eyes and ears. They often left early in the mornings and returned well after darkness had fallen, after carrying some message for him to the duke of Kent, or perhaps Lillian de Stahl, who remained his contact with their allies beyond England.

Stefan responded briefly to the knocking at the door, glancing up only after Emma Kelly had entered the chamber and stood stoically before the large writing desk. Her first hostility toward him had mellowed to grudging acceptance. Stefan respected her unfailing loyalty to Jenna, which he knew well extended beyond the bounds of mistress and servant. He nodded gruffly as he leafed through the papers on the desk.

"There is someone here to see you," Emma announced with great formality. She watched the lean, hard line of his body braced against the desk. She knew that the wound still caused him great discomfort, although he would never admit it. He was strong, for few men could have survived the wounds he had sustained. But he had borne his pain in silence, spending long hours in that chamber when Jenna was forced to keep a social engagement, always pacing back and forth like a lean hunting animal, demanding to be on his feet before his strength had fully returned. Demanding that she assist him down the stairs when his men were not about to give aid. But more than his strength and stubborn will, Emma had seen the expression that crossed his face when Jenna entered the room. All the pain and fatigue seemed to leave him when she was near, as if he gained some inner peace and comfort from her presence. Emma was not unaware of the lingering glances from those haunting blue eyes, or the smile that seemed to pull at his handsome mouth when her mistress was about. It was a special look, a very private, intimate look, shared between two people deeply in love, though neither dared to admit it. Emma Kelly's round gray eyes widened in wonder at the discovery she had made. She had once shared those same private messages with Jamie Kelly. Her heart was suddenly filled with a great sadness for the truth she had discovered. The frown that had formed at her rounded mouth relaxed into a gentle smile. Somehow, the saints could not be so cruel again. She offered up a silent prayer for her mistress and Prince Stefan Kalinsky.

Stefan was immediately wary. He had sent both Dmitri and Alexei to accompany Jenna at a discreet distance. He was certain there were no weapons in the house, and sincerely doubted his ability to use one.

"Who is it?"

" 'Tis a lady. Madame Lillian de Stahl." Emma watched as the sudden tension of the moment was suddenly replaced by a look of anger.

Stefan followed Emma, at a much slower pace, down the wide stairway to the drawing room below. Lillian de Stahl stood before the inviting warmth of the fire at the hearth. The look in Stefan's eyes hardly returned the same warmth.

Lillian de Stahl rushed forward in greeting, a radiant

309

smile upon her lips at seeing Stefan indeed seeming to be recovering from his wounds.

"My dearest Stefan, you don't know how I have worried these last weeks, with only vague words from Dmitri or Alexei. Only their strict instructions prevented me from visiting you before this."

"Why have you come? I have made it clear that it is far too dangerous for you to come here." Stefan winced visibly as Lillian embraced him intimately.

Lillian de Stahl's finely curved lips made a slight frown. "How have I angered you that you must be so cruel, after all we have meant to each other? Surely the moments of the past are not all so easily forgotten."

"How can you be certain you were not followed?" Stefan persisted as he moved slowly before the fireplace.

"If anyone should ask of it, I shall explain that I was calling socially on Lady Randolph. But I see she is not present this evening. In truth, my dearest Stefan, I would not have come unless it was a matter of grave importance. Our cause is still the same, my love. More than ever, I wish to see the arrogant little emperor stripped of his throne and his power. We each have our own reasons to see Napoleon's reign ended. I bring an urgent message from Czar Alexander. It arrived only this evening by courier from Dover. It seems the English conspirators against the Crown have relaxed their vigil, now that they believe you are dead. The man slipped through quite easily after arriving by schooner from Rotterdam. He had ridden continuously since crossing the frontier of Austria." Lillian de Stahl smiled confidently as she handed Stefan the sealed packet. She knew she had brought a message of great importance.

Stefan glanced briefly at the seal. It bore the imprint of the imperial crest of Czar Alexander of Russia. He quickly broke the seal and scanned the neatly penned message.

"Where is the man who brought this letter?" Stefan continued reading the document.

"He is taking a well-deserved rest at the town house. He will deliver your response, when you are ready."

"There will be no response. We shall leave at first light for Vienna."

Lillian de Stahl watched the strong line of Stefan's jaw and the muscles that played beneath the skin. How many times had she watched him as she watched him now, or more intimately, when they had once shared the more private moments that all lovers share. She reached to tenderly caress his lean cheek. Stefan's gaze met hers. He took her hand gently in his own and kissed it. A long moment passed before Lillian de Stahl trusted herself to speak. She had seen something in his brilliant blue eyes, something she had prayed she would never see. Where she had hoped to see the loyalty of love first known many years before, she had seen only the loyalty of remaining friendship. Stefan had meant more to her than any man. She had known him as friend as well as lover, and she realized in that one look that she had lost him forever. She had lost him to a dark-haired young beauty with a will and a passion to match his.

"You are not yet strong enough to travel," she murmured softly.

"This is what we have waited for these long months."

"Is Alexander in Vienna?"

"Lillian, it will be safer for you if you know nothing more. We shall speak no more of this."

"I shall not remain in London. I shall return to Vienna with you."

"Lillian, it is impossible. The path we take will be dangerous, hardly possible for someone traveling by coach."

A strange, somber light filled Lillian de Stahl's eyes as she gazed at the young man who had once been her lover. Vainly she hoped there might be other moments, however few.

"I want to be with you in Vienna. As it was in the beginning for us." Gently, she rested her hands against his chest, feeling the vibrant beating of his heart beneath her fingers.

Stefan gently took both her hands in his. "Lillian, it

cannot be. Do not ask it. When this war has ended, when it is once again safe, you shall return to Vienna. I go but to fulfill a promise to Alexander."

"Do you love her so completely?" Lillian de Stahl bit back the words almost as soon as they had been spoken.

Stefan tenderly stroked the softness of her golden hair, pulled back from the soft oval of her face, which was considered by many to be the fairest face among the courtesans. "Do not torment yourself with these questions."

"Do you love her?" Lillian de Stahl persisted, as if by his word alone she might be released from the torment of the love they had once shared.

Stefan sighed heavily. "I love her as I never thought I could love anyone. How can I make you understand, that it will not cause you pain?" Stefan continued slowly, as he sought the words she might understand.

"She is the light in the morning that brings the day; she is strength when I have none. She is the air I breathe. She is my soul." Stefan reached to gently hold Lillian as he felt the warmth of her tears against his cheek.

"I love her as you once loved me, long ago."

Lillian de Stahl pulled back from Stefan's embrace. "I pray she loves you as well."

Stefan smiled solemnly. "I pray you are right."

"Will you tell her you are leaving?"

"She will know soon enough."

Donning her heavy woolen cape, Lillian de Stahl reached out a gloved hand.

"Be careful, my darling. There are many who would see you fail in this."

Stefan smiled at her, a golden light springing into the depths of his blue gaze as he leaned forward to kiss her cheek.

"They will find that I am very determined. If one blade could not strike me down, neither will Napoleon have his victory. Monsieur Bonaparte will be stopped. I have no intention of failing."

Lillian de Stahl tenderly touched his cheek. It was a

312

loving gesture, a brief reminder of the time they had once shared in his youth. She turned about abruptly, no longer trusting her emotions.

"Shall I contact the captain of the schooner for your return to Rotterdam?" Lillian fastened the closures of her coat for warmth against the cold of the evening.

"There is too much danger the man may have been seen. My own yacht lies safely at anchor near Hastings. We shall sail for Boulogne on the first tide."

"My darling, you dare not risk it. There is too much danger in traveling through France."

Stefan chuckled softly at Lillian's concern for his safety. "For Prince Stefan Kalinsky perhaps, but for a ghost, I think not. The quickest route to Vienna is through France. None will suspect homeless peasants, wandering about the countryside. Do not forget, dear Lillian, France was once my home. I know it as well as any Frenchman."

"Stefan, please allow me to come with you. There is nothing left for me in London. My home is in Vienna. If Alexander is in Vienna, I must be allowed to return."

Stefan patiently held both Lillian de Stahl's gloved hands in his own. He could see she would accept no argument.

"Once we reach the coast of France, we will travel fast. There will be no stopping for rest until we have reached Vienna. It is far too dangerous for you to cross the frontier. Stay here in London, where you will be safe. When it is possible, I will send word for you." Stefan reached to smooth back a stray blond curl. "Will you promise me you will remain here?"

Lillian de Stahl stared back into the brilliant blue depths of Stefan's gaze. Though she longed to see a lover's concern there, she saw only the caring of long friendship. She nodded resolutely.

"I will await your word," she promised.

"You must go now, before anyone learns of your visit. The fewer who know of it, the greater the chances for our success."

Lillian de Stahl hesitated as she reached for the handle

of the door, which stood ajar.

"You must give me your promise, you will be careful."

"You have my word." Stefan smiled gently.

Lillian de Stahl turned back abruptly, placing an impassioned kiss on Stefan's lips. She whirled about, brushing past Emma Kelly in the hallway before slipping silently out into the darkness of night. The coach moved quietly down the pathway toward the main road, away from Hallston House.

Jenna glanced at the clock in the hallway of the grand house. It seemed impossible to her that she had arrived only an hour earlier. Charles was temporarily occupied with a circle of business acquaintances, and Jenna had welcomed the respite from his tedious questions about their forthcoming marriage. Thinking Charles had returned, Jenna inhaled deeply at the gentle pressure upon her arm. She turned, and with great relief gazed into Elizabeth Wingate's solemn face. Her dear friend had been forced to endure yet another evening in the boring company of Sir Reginald Guilford, who seemed quite content to occupy her every moment, posturing like some dandified fool with his powdered wig and satin brocade jacket of another age and generation. Jenna heartily pitied her young friend, as Sir Reginald seemed intent on playing the part of the enamored suitor. Elizabeth had finally gained a moment of freedom from the dinner party, pleading a lady's need for privacy, quickly seeking Jenna among the guests of the earl of Herfordshire.

Jenna smiled sympathetically at her friend, thinking herself perhaps more fortunate in the game they both played. At least Charles Wingate was a young man. Had their roles been reversed, Jenna might well have planted a foot where it might be of most benefit to Sir Reginald. He was certainly the most pompous, insufferable idiot she had ever met.

"I have only a moment. I fear Sir Reginald shall soon be upon me. Jenna, you must take word to John that I cannot

314

bear this much longer. And now Charles is talking of moving up the date of the wedding. It is almost as if he suspects something. Oh dear, I don't know what I shall do if Father consents to changing the date. John insists we cannot possibly sail before the end of April." Elizabeth Wingate clung to Jenna's hand with desperation.

Jenna tried to comfort Elizabeth, realizing her friend was very close to tears.

"It will only be a few more weeks. You must try very hard. Think of your future with John. You must be convincing when you are with Sir Reginald. If Charles were to suspect anything, all would be lost. He would surely set up the date for the wedding, and it would be impossible for anyone to stop him. I shall speak with Charles and see what may be done about keeping the date that is set. Perhaps he will listen to me."

Elizabeth slipped a folded piece of paper into Jenna's gloved hand. "Will you deliver this?"

"Of course, I will deliver it." Jenna smiled gently, and then her smile froze as she saw Charles and Sir Robert Ludlow approaching. She quickly slipped the note inside her glove as she leaned forward to whisper encouragement to her friend.

"You must be brave, Elizabeth. Think of your future with John," Jenna whispered fiercely as she turned to give Charles a welcoming smile.

"My dear, I do believe you have met Sir Robert. He was an acquaintance of your grandfather's," Charles reminded Jenna politely.

Jenna smiled carefully, wondering at Charles's game.

"My grandfather had many friends, many who were not known to me. It would be impossible for me to remember everyone," Jenna responded casually.

"Your grandfather was a very fine and dedicated man. I know the prime minister valued his services highly."

"You are very kind," Jenna said innocently as she accepted Sir Robert's arm and allowed him to lead her out onto the floor for the next dance.

"I did not know you were well acquainted with

Charles," Jenna ventured casually as she executed the intricate steps of the dance with precision.

Suddenly caught off guard by that innocent amber gaze, Sir Robert studied her intently, his thick lips twisting into a secretive smile.

"I have known Sir Charles for a long time. Because of our friendship, he asked me to see what I might be able to learn of certain political matters," Sir Robert answered benignly, watching the wide sweep of Jenna's eyes for any sign of recognition. He saw none, only a widening of that amber gaze with feigned curiosity about matters that held little interest for women.

"I was not aware of Charles's interest in politics," Jenna responded, with only mild curiosity.

"Oh yes, my dear. This nasty business of a conspiracy has everyone quite excited. With your grandfather's work, I am quite surprised he never mentioned anything of it to you. But then, it would be quite like Sir Avery to keep the entire matter to himself."

"Sir Robert, you must tell me more of this conspiracy. I fear everyone will know of it except myself. I find it all quite exciting." Jenna smiled at the old gentleman from under the sweep of her long, dark lashes. He puffed up like a preening peacock under the assault of her undivided attention. Jenna played her little game expertly, slipping a slender hand into the crook of his thick arm and smiling at him demurely, pleading sudden warmth and requesting a glass of champagne.

Sir Robert leaned forward discreetly, as if about to share some great secret, and handed her a glass of chilled champagne. "Several months before his death, Sir Avery was rumored to have uncovered some sort of conspiracy to overthrow the monarchy. With the Whigs and the Tories at each other's throats politically, one can only guess the advantage such a conspiracy might offer Napoleon, should he attempt to launch an assault against England. If the conspiracy were successful, England would be left completely vulnerable. It was thought that Sir Avery died without learning the identity of the conspirators. But it

316

seems Sir Charles has uncovered certain documents disclosing the identities of the conspirators."

Jenna's smile of moments before seemed frozen upon her face as she stared at Sir Robert. This was complete madness. The last thing she had expected was for Sir Robert to approach her openly about the conspiracy. Her thoughts raced over her conversations with Charles during the past days. Did he possibly suspect she might know something of the conspiracy? Was it all some elaborate scheme to learn what her grandfather might have told her before his death? If the documents Sir Robert spoke of did indeed exist, she knew where Charles had obtained them. Jenna took another sip of champagne to calm her shaken nerves. The smile never wavered as she accepted the challenge.

"Please continue, Sir Robert. I find this all quite fascinating."

"I suppose there is no harm in your knowing of it now. Especially with this nasty business about Prince Kalinsky over with."

Jenna could feel the crimson heat of color rising in her cheeks at the mention of Stefan's name.

"I can see this is upsetting you. I should have known better, after his crude behavior toward you."

"Please do continue. It is nothing. I am quite all right," Jenna pleaded sweetly, struggling with an inner desire to drag the man's words from him if he hesitated again.

Sir Robert leaned discreetly forward again, his gaze lingering over the ample swelling above Jenna's bodice. She was aware of the direction of his gaze. She felt as if her garments were suddenly being stripped away from her. Had she not wanted the information about the conspiracy so badly, Jenna would have emptied her champagne glass in his face. It might have cooled him in some small measure. Unfortunately, to gain that information, she was forced to play his lecherous games.

"It seems that Prince Kalinsky was the leader of the conspiracy, together with several dispossessed royal emigrés, and had formed the conspiracy to assassinate several members of the royal family."

Jenna pulled back with a look of stunned surprise that was not completely contrived. "But to what purpose?"

"To eventually gain England for themselves. It seems the members of the conspiracy are of similar background: bastard sons, blackguard renegades, mercenaries, each cast out of his own country, and now seeking to take England for their own."

Jenna stared at Sir Robert with a look of amused surprise.

"But it is not possible. Such a plan could not possibly succeed," she responded finally.

Sir Robert shrugged his rounded shoulders.

"Who may say it is not possible? It is rumored that the entire conspiracy was Napoleon's scheme to gain control of England. These last years, England has remained an insurmountable island fortress, which he cannot conquer. But if the conspiracy began within England, with a group of men, highly respected, all with access to influential circles of power, it might all be done quite easily. And England would lie vulnerable to French domination. Who knows what our fate might then be?" Sir Robert shrugged his shoulders, as if the answer eluded him.

Jenna was not so easily fooled. She knew Sir Robert had deliberately sought her out; but to what purpose? Was it merely to discredit Stefan? What better way to divert attention away from their own actions? Her anger was not for the simpering man who stood beside her, but for the man who had sent him. She had no doubt that Charles had devised this little charade. He was making a great effort to insure his own innocence, and Stefan's guilt. It was quite easily done. Charles had called Stefan out in public, in defense of her honor. He had sought to prove Stefan a coward and a blackguard. He seemed to have accomplished that purpose. It would now be quite easy for everyone to accept that Stefan had led the conspiracy against the English monarch, allowing Charles to move about unhindered to see the matter done.

Jenna endured the remainder of the evening with the

318

greatest of skill, and none was aware of the fear that seemed to have possessed her. At the end of the evening, Jenna retreated to the safety of silence as Charles escorted her home. She sat in the coach in relief that the evening was very nearly at an end as she felt the familiar lurching of the coach up the incline of the cobbled pathway that wound before the large doors of Hallston House, the soft, freshly fallen snow squeaking softly under the horses' hooves. She quickly reached for the door handle, as the coach came to a stop, moving a bit too slowly as Charles's hand closed over her arm, drawing her back.

"Jenna, must you leave so quickly? It seems I am forever doomed to sharing your company with others. I had hoped we might share more intimate moments—like two people who are to be married."

Jenna stiffened under the pressure of Charles's grasp, and sought to divert his attention to other matters as she remembered her promise to Elizabeth to speak with Charles about the date of the wedding. The coachman made no attempt to assist her from the coach, and she could only assume the man acted on Charles's instructions. The interior of the coach glowed softly with the golden light from a single lantern at the opposite door. Jenna smiled at Charles politely. He seemed to accept it as her willingness to linger a moment longer. He drew her closer, a sudden firmness in his grasp. His one arm encircled her waist as he pulled her closer.

"Charles, I had hoped to speak to you of Elizabeth's wedding," Jenna ventured hastily, hoping to divert his attention.

"Ah, yes. I suppose Elizabeth has told you that I had hoped she would consider moving the date closer. It is only with thoughts to our own wedding that I even suggested it," Charles lied, with amazing believability.

Jenna attempted to move away from his confining embrace, but found herself soundly caught.

"Charles, surely you must realize that there are a great many plans to be made for such a large wedding. Elizabeth is quite upset that there will not be enough time for all the details to be exactly right. Charles, please, it is a most important occasion for Elizabeth. Can you not allow her to make the plans as she would prefer them?" Jenna pleaded, a sudden softness in her voice.

Charles seemed to consider her words as he gazed down into the golden depths of her eyes that reflected the glowing light from the lantern. His thin face softened with a sudden smile that caused a sudden rippling of fear in Jenna. It was not Charles's habit to yield a cause so easily.

"You seem forever to take Elizabeth's cause in the matter of this marriage. It would almost seem that the two of you scheme at some plan," he ventured, with a touch of sarcastic humor.

Jenna forced her most dazzling smile, as she turned to Charles. "Not at all. It is only that I realize how much easier it will be to devote my full attention to making our own wedding perfect, if I know that Elizabeth is happy." Jenna watched Charles carefully from under the wide sweep of her long, dark lashes. She hated herself for the lies she had spoken, but realized she would have told many more to help her dearest friend.

Charles's dark mood seemed to disappear before his pleasure at her attention. "Very well; I shall speak to Elizabeth about it in the morning. It would seem that I cannot fight both of you in this matter." Charles's embrace of Jenna tightened intimately as his thoughts returned to his earlier intentions.

"Charles, please. It is quite late, and there is a terrible chill in the air," Jenna objected as she felt herself drawn into an unyielding embrace, her hands flattened against his waistcoat. She turned away as Charles's face lowered very near hers, his hot breath burning against her skin. He seemed not to have heard anything she had said.

"Charles, no." Jenna struggled against his grasp, alarmed at the sudden strength she felt in his arm about her shoulders. Charles pulled her back into the softness of the upholstered seat, her cape falling open to expose the gleaming mound of her breasts above the cut of her gown.

320

Jenna saw immediately the direction of his gaze as the meager light from the lantern played across the pale surface of her skin. Charles persisted, pinning her against the seat with one arm, while his other hand freely roamed the silken softness of skin across her shoulder and up the curve of her neck, until he held her chin firm against any struggling. Her one arm pinned beneath her, Jenna vainly pushed against Charles with the other hand. With a sudden, sickening awareness, Jenna felt a hardened pressure against her thigh and knew his intent.

"Charles, no . . ." All further protests were muffled beneath the pressure of his mouth against hers, hard and brutal as he fought to possess her, his tongue invading the softness of her mouth until she was certain she would wretch. With a sudden fury born of desperation, Jenna twisted away, pushing against Charles with all her strength. Breathing heavily against her shoulder, Charles was far from surrender. Jenna shuddered violently as she felt the sickening wetness of his mouth against the mounding of her breast. Her strength rapidly failing, Jenna felt a sudden, dizzying coldness stealing over her as she struggled to draw a deep breath beneath his greater weight. In the next moment the coach was suddenly filled with a rush of cold air that filled her lungs and cleared her senses as the door was roughly pulled open. With a loud curse, Charles moved a discreet distance away as the shadow of Mr. Flint's imposing stature blocked the light from the doorway.

"It is quite late, mistress," Mr. Flint intervened gruffly. Only Jenna was aware of the deadly intent in his eyes masked behind the subservient demeanor.

Jenna pulled her cape tightly closed against prying glances. She dared not let Stefan know what had passed between her and Charles. Jenna had no doubt of the outcome, should Stefan Kalinsky and Charles Wingate again take up the blade in contest. She weakly smiled her gratitude to the loyal servant as she accepted his assistance.

Charles leaned forward in the coach. "Do not forget you promised to accompany Elizabeth to the seamstress's shop. Though I have given you my word, be certain there will be no delays in these wedding plans."

Without a backward glance, Jenna mounted the steps to the front door. Confident that Charles would not press his cause before Mr. Flint, Jenna quickly entered the manor house and collapsed back against the tightly closed portal.

Inhaling deeply to steady her nerves, Jenna looked up. Emma Kelly stood in the hallway, a heavy woolen shawl pulled tightly about her shoulders. Jenna avoided the woman's prying gaze as she moved past her toward the drawing room. Warming her hands before the hearth, Jenna fought to control their shaking as she folded them behind her and sought to warm other parts, as well. If Stefan were to see her now, he would surely know what had passed between her and Charles. His anger toward Charles had deepened to an unrelenting hatred, and she could not risk his knowing of it. Jenna accepted the cup of steaming tea Emma had poured for her.

"Dear child, what has happened? You are as cold as death and shaking like a leaf in the wind." Concern lined the old woman's face as she gazed at her mistress.

"'Tis nothing. It is only a chill from the cold of the evening," Jenna lied.

Emma Kelly watched her with a steady gaze. She was not fooled. Something or someone had frightened her young mistress. Emma hesitated to tell Jenna of the woman who had visited Prince Kalinsky earlier.

Jenna was aware of Emma's sudden nervousness. "What is it? Has something happened?"

At the woman's continued silence, Jenna turned on her, a sudden fear rising within her.

"Emma, what is it?" Jenna seized the old woman by the shoulders. "Is it Stefan?" she whispered with rising panic. She knew he had not wanted her to leave this evening, and yet she had insisted.

Emma shook her graying head. "There was someone here this evening, asking for Prince Kalinsky. A woman."

"What woman? Emma!" Jenna whirled on the faithful servant with mounting frustration.

Jenna felt a tight constricting in her chest, as if a steel band had closed about her. She described Lillian de Stahl to Emma.

"Aye, that is the one. I could not remember her name. Do you know her?"

"Yes, I know her." Jenna answered quietly, her voice suddenly strained.

"She brought an important message for the prince," Emma added, attempting to ease the pain that had appeared in Jenna's face.

"What sort of message?"

"I could not say. The prince seemed to be expecting it, though," Emma answered carefully.

Damn Stefan Kalinsky. Damn him. He had been so very convincing in not wanting her to leave, knowing well she would go, giving him the perfect opportunity to meet his mistress. She wished she had let him die. How could all their moments have been a lie? How was it possible? For her they had been the only truth she had known the last months—and yet what did she know of Stefan Kalinsky? Perhaps everything Sir Robert had suggested was true. Jenna whirled around, slamming the teacup down upon the table. She reached for a decanter of brandy and poured herself a hearty draught in the cup. With one swift flick of her wrist, Jenna downed the entire amount. Unaccustomed to anything more than an occasional glass of wine with dinner, she was seized with a fit of coughing as the liquid burned through her like molten heat. Her dark eyes watered, tears appearing as she tried to draw an even breath, blurring her vision as she vented all her anger.

"Jenna, you must never drink alone. Had I known you had returned I would have joined you," a rich, vibrant voice penetrated her misery. "There is too much sadness in the world. The drink makes it seem as if it is all yours."

Jenna whirled about and stared where Emma had stood a moment before. Stefan's towering height filled the doorway. Her wide amber gaze locked with his piercing blue one.

Seeing the fire that glowed in the depths of Jenna's eyes,

Emma retreated to safety beyond the drawing room.

"Get out of here," Jenna commanded in a hoarse whisper.

Stefan crossed the room, Jenna backing away beyond his reach as he continued to approach her.

"Go to Lillian de Stahl; go to your mistress. It is of no concern to me." Jenna whirled around and tried to move past him. She felt Stefan's hand closing about her arm.

"Jenna, you must listen to me. Lillian brought me a message of great importance. Surely you are aware that Dmitri and Alexei have carried a great many such messages for me these last days. The message she brought tonight could not wait. There was no need for you to know of it. It only brings you greater danger."

Jenna whirled on Stefan. "Do you think I will believe your lies now? I will not warm your bed and play the whore. If you choose your mistress, then so be it. I will not await your pleasure until she has had hers." Jenna bit off the last words with a startled gasp as Stefan seized her roughly about the shoulders.

"You seem intent on believing what you think to be the truth. By God, you will listen to me."

"I will not." Jenna struggled out of Stefan's grasp, passion overruling all reason as she fled for the doorway. Stefan was beside her in quick even strides that belied the pain of the wound in his side. Before Jenna could pull away, his arm encircled her waist, his other arm slipping beneath her as he lifted her in an unyielding grasp. With little regard for the pain she caused him, Jenna pushed against his chest with all her strength.

"Put me down!" Jenna ordered as she continued to struggle within his grasp.

Ignoring her protests, Stefan whirled through the doorway and carried her toward the stairway. Hovering beyond the doorway, near the kitchen, Emma started forward, uncertain how she might best defend her mistress. Dmitri's imposing shadow fell across hers in the hallway, halting any further assistance. He gently but firmly escorted the maid back to her chamber. It was much wiser to leave these matters alone.

With mounting frustration that she was powerless to stop Stefan Kalinsky, Jenna doubled her small hand into a fist and pummeled the broad expanse of his chest. Stefan silently ignored all her protests as he bore her up the wide sweep of the stairway. Gaining the landing, he reached her chamber in long, even strides, kicking the door open with such force that it threatened to splinter from its hinges. Crossing the chamber, Stefan tossed Jenna into the middle of the large bed. Slamming the door shut, he turned to face her anger once more.

In that one brief moment when he turned away, Jenna quickly scrambled off the bed. She knew his intentions, and would have none of it. This would not be so easily settled as other matters. Jenna warily backed toward the dressing table, looking about frantically for something she might use as a weapon. The fireplace poker was far beyond her reach. Warily, she watched as Stefan turned back toward her.

"Jenna, we will speak of this. Now!"

"There is nothing you can say that I will believe. Everything you have told me has been lies." Jenna felt the firm pressure of the dressing table at her back, blocking any further retreat. She glared at Stefan warily.

"You came to me after my grandfather's death with a story of your involvement in his work to uncover the conspiracy. But it was all a lie. You were trying to protect yourself, to keep anyone from learning the truth. Did you merely give the order for my grandfather's death, or were you in the library the night he died, and then again later searching for his documents, so that you might destroy the evidence of what he had found?" A sob escaped as Jenna confronted Stefan with all her doubts, all her fears.

Stefan approached her slowly. She was very near hysteria, though hardly from the effects of the small amount of brandy she had consumed. He had expected her anger upon learning he had been with Lillian de Stahl, perhaps even cool indifference to mask her pain. But this was not anger. Stefan had seen her anger. What he saw now in the depths of her wide, dark eyes was more than anger. It was fear, a deep, haunting fear, which wrapped around his heart. Something had frightened her tonight, something she had not spoken of. Slowly, Stefan reached out to her.

Jenna shook her head vehemently. "No! Please, go away."

"Very soon I shall go away, but not while this pain tears at us," Stefan said softly.

Jenna stared at him warily. Her emotions were raw. She had fled Charles, seeking the haven of Stefan's love and tenderness, only to find that Lillian de Stahl was still very much a part of his life. It was a truth she had chosen to ignore. It was part of the world beyond Hallston House that they had retreated from. Now that world had come to them.

"I must return to Vienna. I leave at first light, it is most urgent. But I will not leave you in anger," Stefan whispered hoarsely as he continued to tear down the protective wall Jenna tried to place between them.

Slowly Stefan approached her. His heart ached for the pain and anguish he saw in the vast dark pools of her eyes. It tore at him that he had caused her pain. There was now so little time to bridge the anger that flowed between them. Tenderly, he reached to caress her cheek.

Jenna tried to back away from his touch, knowing well her vulnerability. The dressing table prevented her escape. Everything within her cried out that she resist him. She turned, a torrent of denials dying upon her lips as she gazed into the haunting blue depths of his eyes. The mesmerizing warmth of that gaze wrapped around her, stripping away her resistance.

"No, I do not want your love." Jenna whispered sadly. "I fear I cannot pay the price you ask."

"I ask only for your love Jenna, nothing more. It is all I have ever desired," Stefan breathed against the softness of her cheek. Gently his fingers touched her chin, turning her face toward him.

"Look at me!" he commanded softly. When she

326

hesitated, he spoke again, his fingers fanning with deliberate tenderness across her cheek down over the line of her jaw to the slender column of her neck. He breathed her name among words that were unintelligible, an odd mixture of French and Russian, words that stole quietly into her soul, filling her senses with the essence of her need of him. Slowly he traced her lips with his fingers, warm and vibrant against her skin.

Jenna inhaled sharply at that most innocent contact that sent a rivulet of molten heat coursing through her veins. When she breathed her lip trembled, at the conflicting emotions that raged within her. With agonizing slowness, Stefan's lips lowered over hers. All her protests were silenced beneath the tenderness of his kiss, and she responded with a desire born of her desperate longing to believe him. She moaned softly as his lips left hers, seeking the softness of the skin across her shoulder about the cut of her gown.

Jenna closed her eyes tightly, forcing everything from her thoughts, except the exquisite pleasure of his touch. Carefully, he bent to pick her up, this time finding no resistance as she clung to him breathlessly, her lips seeking his with a ravening hunger.

Gently Stefan lowered Jenna to the bed, his hands slipping behind her to loosen the fastenings of her gown. When her silken chemise lay on the floor beside her other clothes, he joined her, leaning across her to kiss the soft curving of her hip, his hand fanning across the taut surface of her belly, causing her skin to ripple beneath his touch. It was as if he had touched the finest satin that glowed with an inner fire that seemed to reach for his touch. Stefan cradled Jenna in his arm, his lips tearing away the last shreds of her resistance. He stroked the silken surface of her thigh, causing her sudden gasp of surprise as his fingers wandered more intimately. Tenderly Stefan caressed her, with an agonizing slowness as he sought to remember each curve, each softly hidden pleasure of her lithe, young body, as he built a hunger within her.

Jenna murmured his name as she reached to unbutton

327

his shirt. Her eyes glowed golden as she stared at Stefan, the light from the hearth flickering across the smooth expanse of his bronze skin. It was as if a wild, untamable beast had come to her, a beast capable of taking her life or giving her life. Jenna reached for the lean, hungering beast, drawing his warmth to her with a longing that grew from within. Her skin flamed beneath his touch. It was as if he had released within her a need that only he might fill. Jenna pulled Stefan to her, as her lips sought his.

Stefan molded her to him, drinking in the tantalizing pleasure of her warmth against him. He lingered over her, wanting to prolong their time together against the loneliness of the days to come.

Jenna's soft whisperings of his name became impassioned pleas for him to take her, and she arched against him, seeking to lose the pain of her doubt in the exquisite pleasure of his warmth deep within her.

Slowly Stefan closed the distance between them as he entered her, the promises she longed for spoken silently in the love he gave her.

Jenna lay tightly curled beneath the warmth of the heavy coverlet, a frown turning the lovely curve of her lips in sleep. Stefan watched her, as he had watched her the last hours, unable to sleep as dawn approached. He drew strength from her presence. It was enough for now just to watch over her. He leaned forward and drew the warm coverlet high over her shoulders against the chill that had invaded the chamber.

Quietly he closed the door behind him as he left her chamber. He turned to find Dmitri waiting patiently in the hallway. Beyond the house, the darkness of night provided a cloak of secrecy.

"Alexei is ready. The horses are saddled," the giant Cossack informed his master. Dmitri thrust a thick leather pouch at Stefan.

"The herbs will provide comfort against the pain of the wound."

Stefan gratefully accepted the gift. He grabbed his loyal companion firmly by the shoulders. Head to head, they were of equal height, but Dmitri's greater width dominated his prince.

"Dear friend, I know you would like to ride with me. But you are needed here. You must stay with her and see that no harm comes to her."

Dmitri nodded, his emotion at their parting obvious in his suddenly gruff manner.

"No harm will come to her, while I live. I vow this to you."

Stefan embraced his friend, and then released him just as quickly. There were no more words to be spoken. Everything between them was known, with an understanding born of many years together. In quick, even strides that fell silently on the carpeted stairs, Stefan Kalinsky disappeared into the darkness beyond Hallston House.

Chapter Eighteen

Jenna strolled slowly through the organized clutter of Madame Lessard's fashionable shop. A vast array of luxurious fabrics was displayed across cutting tables. Still more fabric had been rolled tightly, layer after layer, around long wooden rods, each neatly stacked on a display counter, with only the ends left unbound so that a customer might admire the quality of the fabric. Jenna was amazed that when most goods were difficult to obtain because of the war's greatly curtailing trade activities, Madame Lessard always maintained a vast array of fine fabrics to create elegant gowns for London's most fashionable ladies. Jenna stopped to admire a brilliant blue velvet of such a rare color that she was certain there must be no other like it.

"A gown made of such fine fabric would be perfect for mademoiselle." Noticing Jenna's admiration of the fabric, one of Madame Lessard's young seamstresses had come forward to give assistance.

"No, I think not," Jenna answered abruptly as she turned away. How could she possibly explain to the young girl, that the color would only remind her of someone she had chosen to forget. If Stefan could leave her so easily, then she must forget him, just as easily. Jenna softened the harshness of her words with a faint smile as she waited patiently for Elizabeth.

A small bell tinkled merrily at the glass-paned door as a

woman entered the shop with her young maid. Jenna immediately recognized Countess Lieven as the woman emerged from the heavy woolen cape wrapped closely for protection against the chilling wind, in spite of the sun that had warmed that morning late in February. Countess Lieven smoothed back a fat golden curl as she removed her cloak and handed it to her young maid, her eyes lighting with genuine pleasure to have found an acquaintance while shopping.

"My dear Jenna, how nice to see you, and how very lovely you are. But, of course, you are here for the fitting of your wedding gown," the countess surmised.

"Not at all," Jenna quickly corrected her. "I promised Elizabeth I would accompany her for the final fitting of her own gown."

"Oh yes, of course." The countess seemed to remember. "I must say, I find this marriage to Sir Reginald quite difficult to understand, what with all the difficulty he has experienced of late. But then, I suppose, Lord Wingate does have his reasons. Still, it is quite strange that he would seek such an alliance when Sir Guilford seems to have such an appetite for gambling, and Lord Wingate disapproves of it so highly."

Jenna could not disguise a certain curiosity. "I was not aware that Sir Reginald cared for gambling."

"Oh, my dear, yes. His reputation at Watier's and White's is quite well known, though, I must admit, more for his losses than his winnings."

"I am certain Sir Reginald can well afford such losses."

Countess Lieven's eyes widened with a knowing glance. "With his marriage to Elizabeth, I am certain he will be able to afford his habits for quite some time. Although such pastimes can become quite tedious for a new bride," the countess responded, with a wink of her eye.

"Surely you are not suggesting that Sir Reginald would seek this marriage for monetary gain." Jenna stared at Countess Lieven with surprise at what the woman seemed to be implying.

Warming to a welcome bit of gossiping, the countess

leaned forward discreetly as another elegantly dressed customer entered the shop.

"It is well known about London that Sir Guilford is entirely without resources. Though his first marriage brought him substantial wealth, it has been gone for some time. A close friend of mine has said the dear man is living entirely on the generosity of his friends. And who knows how long that may continue? His affections for Elizabeth may be quite genuine, but none can deny the opportunity for financial gain. It is quite well known that Elizabeth will inherit a substantial fortune from her mother's family upon her marriage. It is a pity it will go the way of everything else. I cannot help but think that dear Elizabeth is destined for unhappiness. Though I wish it were not so."

"But Sir Reginald has his family estate in Sussex, and his London town house," Jenna responded, with growing concern. She had heard rumors of Sir Guilford's careless regard for money lost betting on horse races and sporting events, but out of her loyalty to Elizabeth she had paid them little heed. Though Countess Lieven was a known gossip, there was none who could deny the accuracy of her information.

"I have learned from certain acquaintances that his country estates are heavily mortgaged to pay his gambling debts. Surely you are aware that your own dear Charles has made him a substantial loan in order to keep the London town house. The creditors were quite ready to seize the house and take poor Reginald off to prison, had not Charles intervened. But certainly you knew of this. Certainly Charles had spoken of it to you." Countess Lieven cast Jenna an inquiring glance.

Jenna smiled at her reassuringly. "I am quite certain he mentioned it. I must have forgotten. Such matters hold little interest for me."

Countess Lieven patted Jenna's hand as she turned to greet the young seamstress who had come forward to help her with the selection of fabrics for her new gowns. "I shall be expecting an invitation to your wedding, of course, my dear. It will prove to be one of the grandest occasions of the season. I have heard whispers of the gift Charles intends to give you, but of course I would not dream of telling." The countess seemed somewhat disappointed when Jenna did not press her for hints of the gift. She quickly sought to lure Jenna into further conversation. "It will be a grand surprise. Have you thought of your other guests?"

Jenna shook her head absently as she thought about Sir Reginald and Charles's loaning him a substantial sum of money. She found it quite difficult to understand that Charles would press so feverishly for Elizabeth's marriage to a man who owed him money. She turned back to Countess Lieven with a careful smile.

"I really have not had the time as yet, countess. I have promised Elizabeth to give her whatever assistance I can with her own plans. I could not possibly think of anything else right now," she answered truthfully.

Countess Lieven selected several of Madame Lessard's finest fabrics, giving instructions for each piece to the young seamstress before she coolly acknowledged the presence of the woman who had entered the shop. Jenna watched the exchange with mild curiosity, sensing a certain coolness in the countess. When the woman tilted her head in icy response, Jenna felt a tightening inside as she recognized the elegant patron.

Lillian de Stahl pushed back the hood of her cape, revealing the gleaming golden smoothness of her pale blond hair pulled gently back from the oval of her face. Her skin was as smooth as the finest alabaster, with the faintest glow of pink across her high cheekbones, and her eyes glistened pale blue from the cold of the afternoon air. Powder and rouge had been artfully applied to disguise the lines that had begun to form about her eyes and mouth. She was the type of woman Emma Kelly disapproved of openly as wanton, and she had made no pretenses that she enjoyed the reputation she had acquired as a courtesan to the Austrian court. She possessed a mature beauty that would not yield for a good many years to come, and Jenna was certain that in her youth she had been quite dazzling,

dazzling enough to entice a young Russian prince to her bed, for the first lessons of his manhood. It was even rumored that Lillian de Stahl was of royal birth, by virtue of a titled Prussian grandfather, and thereby received many invitations to fashionable parties and balls within socially prominent circles. Though the titled ladies of English nobility quietly and discreetly snubbed her, the men of London seemed to find her fascinating, and therein Lillian de Stahl enjoyed a certain notoriety. She was beautiful, worldly, and possessed of a carefree spirit that a great many men found irresistible. And if rumors were to be believed, she enjoyed the pleasure of several notable lovers.

Jenna gave her the barest acknowledgment, desperately hoping to avoid a confrontation with the notorious courtesan. Vainly she hoped Elizabeth would soon be ready, so they might leave. She heard Lillian de Stahl's animated conversation and tinkling laughter as she shared some news with Countess Lieven. For all their pretenses, it would have seemed to the casual observer that they were the closest of friends, hardly adversaries in an unspoken contest to gain the most popularity among London society.

It was not Jenna's good fortune to escape the courtesan. Countess Lieven had engaged Lillian de Stahl in a lively conversation as they approached the draped dressing room.

"My dearest Jenna, here is the only person who will not be able to attend your wedding. Madame de Stahl has told me she will be traveling to Vienna very soon. I think it very brave of her, considering the entire frontier is still controlled by the French."

Jenna forced a strained smile, trying to suppress her sudden shock that Lillian de Stahl would be traveling to Vienna.

"I had not thought to be leaving London quite so soon, but I have been assured that it is quite safe. I am most anxious to return to Vienna. I have many loved ones there. I shall be leaving in the next few days, and Madame

Lessard has promised me several new gowns. I do hope she will have them ready." Lillian de Stahl smiled slyly at Jenna, conveying an undeniable message of challenge.

Jenna fought back the tightening pain that tore through her as she reached out a hand to steady herself from the trembling that suddenly seemed to possess her. She was painfully aware of the confident smile on Lillian de Stahl's face. In the weeks since Stefan had been gone, Jenna had received no word from him. The silence, perhaps more than any hastily written message, tore at her. She had been haunted by recurring nightmares of his death on the long and dangerous journey to Vienna, and Dmitri had been unable to relieve her fears as he attended his own responsibilities with gruff silence. If he had received any message from Stefan, he had not spoken of it. And perhaps with good reason; Lillian de Stahl's meaning was unmistakable. She fully intended to join Stefan in Vienna.

Jenna turned with sudden relief as she heard Elizabeth's voice from the dressing room, but her hopes for escape quickly disappeared as Countess Lieven and Lillian de Stahl gathered to give their admiration for Elizabeth's wedding gown. Jenna leaned heavily against the edge of a cutting table, everything about her seeming suddenly to have taken flight. She felt a wave of nausea from the oppressive warmth in the small shop. The doors opened momentarily, and Jenna inhaled shakily, the cold morning air clearing her head. She had not eaten that morning in her rush to accompany Elizabeth to the dressmaker's, and now realized her foolishness. She smiled wanly as Elizabeth pirouetted before her, in grand display of the elegant gown. To all who watched, it seemed that Elizabeth Wingate wore the excited blush of a young bride deeply in love, eagerly anticipating her wedding. None could possibly know that Sir Reginald Guilford would never see Madame Lessard's exquisite creation.

Elizabeth rushed forward in sudden excitement so that only Jenna might hear her words.

"Do you think John will be pleased?" she whispered excitedly.

Jenna smiled reassuringly as the color returned to her cheeks.

"How could he not be pleased? It is most elegant. This time, Madame Lessard has made her finest gown for you."

"Is there anything wrong?" Elizabeth wondered at Jenna's suddenly quiet mood and pale color.

Jenna smiled to reassure her friend. "Do not forget we have another appointment to keep this morning," she added with hidden meaning.

If it were at all possible, Elizabeth's face seemed to glow more brilliantly. She giggled behind her hand, and then her mood suddenly sobered at the secret they shared.

"I shall be only a moment, and then we shall leave. Madame Lessard has said she can have the gown ready in three days."

Elizabeth squeezed Jenna's hand affectionately. "I have asked that it be delivered to you. I dare not have it delivered to the house, or Charles will know of it and become suspicious," Elizabeth whispered excitedly as she left to dress.

Always the essence of discretion, entrusted with countless secrets from her elite clientele, Madame Lessard could be trusted for her confidentiality. Jenna made her polite farewell to Countess Lieven, nodding coolly at Lillian de Stahl as she left to await Elizabeth in the coach.

Jenna hardly heard Elizabeth's excited chatter as they crossed Grovesnor Square and turned down the long street where Jenna had lived as a child. The coach halted before the small but imposing brick facade of her grandfather's house. They waited until Mr. Flint made certain they had not been followed.

Jenna accepted Mr. Flint's hand as she alighted from the coach. Elizabeth fidgeted impatiently as Jenna twisted the large key in the lock and entered the foyer of the house.

Jenna hesitated a moment as her eyes adjusted to the darkness of the house at that late hour in the afternoon.

337

From the outside the house had seemed the same as she remembered it, with hardly a trace of the fire that had driven her away months before. Her memory of the fire and its destruction was vivid, but inside there remained little trace of the damage. Vague shadows were outlined in the darkened drawing room as Jenna moved across the hallway. Behind her Elizabeth gasped suddenly, and Jenna whirled about to see a soft glow from the opened doorway to the library. Jenna paused uncertainly as she pushed the door open cautiously, the glow in the room becoming larger, casting eerie shadows across the empty chamber. She halted at the sight of someone crossing the chamber, the light from a single lantern carried in one large hand.

"Dmitri!" Jenna breathed with a sigh of relief. The giant Russian loomed before her in the dimly lit chamber. He smiled broadly, his black eyes glowing from the light of the lamp.

"I could not allow you to come here without first making certain it was safe," Dmitri replied with a shrug of his broad shoulders.

Jenna cast him a wary glance. It was difficult to know what Dmitri's responsibilities were. When Stefan had left for Austria, Dmitri had remained in London. He occupied one of the rooms in the stables and took his meals at the long table in the kitchen, often disappearing for the remainder of the day before returning for the evening meal. Dmitri seemed to know everything she did; therefore she was not greatly surprised to find him there. Indeed, over the last weeks, it seemed Dmitri had become her constant, if not always apparent companion.

"Has Mr. Whitmore arrived yet?" Elizabeth asked breathlessly as she brushed past Jenna.

"Indeed I have, my dearest Elizabeth," John replied from the hallway where he had just entered from the back entrance to the house.

Elizabeth rushed across the entry into the waiting arms of John Whitmore. The long days and weeks of waiting had come to an end. All the secretly conveyed messages could now be given in intimate conversation. All the endearments of two who loved deeply could now be given freely without the fear of anyone's eavesdropping. Jenna turned aside as Elizabeth reached to welcome John with a long-awaited kiss. It was a moment only two could share.

Quickly forgotten by the young lovers, Jenna quietly slipped up the newly finished stairs to inspect the second-floor rooms. Dmitri followed close behind, a second lamp lighting the way.

Jenna went quickly to her own chamber. Here the damage had not been so severe. The Aubusson carpet had been cleaned and lay neatly rolled against the far wall. Cotton cloths draped the furnishings against gathering dust. Indeed, the room seemed but to await her presence. The outside of the house had seemed unchanged. Inside there was more evidence of the fire that had driven her from her grandfather's house months before. But now, instead of smoke and charred walls, the house smelled of fresh paint and new wood. It was no longer a house of ruin, but a house of promise, and Emma Kelly's meticulous care for detail and cleanliness could be seen everywhere. The faithful servant had spent long hours supervising the extensive cleaning, so that all would meet with Jenna's approval upon her inspection. It was the suggestion of such an inspection that had given Jenna the idea for Elizabeth to accompany her. It provided the perfect, discreet opportunity for Elizabeth to see John Whitmore. She had dared not arrange a meeting at Hallston House, for she could never be certain when Charles might decide to pay an unannounced visit. It was a risk she and Elizabeth dared not take, though she knew well how the long wait had weighed heavily on her friend. She, too, had come to understand emptiness and longing over the last weeks, like a need born deep within her that had suddenly awakened. Jenna wiped angrily at the hot tears that suddenly spilled from her eyes. Damn Stefan Kalinsky!

"The damage is not so great, little princess. Already it seems as before," Dmitri offered gently, misunderstanding the reason for her tears.

Realizing that he little understood her misery, Jenna brushed past the large Russian. Her grandfather's room lay at the opposite end of the hallway. Jenna opened the heavy wood armoire. All his clothes had been removed. Jenna suspected Emma Kelly's efficient hand was responsible for removing painful reminders. Here, as well, the furnishings had been draped. A brief inspection of three more rooms on the second floor revealed that the fire had not reached much further. The hall carpet had been badly burned. It had been removed, and the wood floor beneath replaced. Jenna smiled as she thought of Emma's penchant for order and cleanliness. Hallston House required the diligent efforts of a sizable staff. But here, Emma could reign as supreme mistress, overseeing all the smallest details with great pleasure.

Jenna returned to the drawing room, to find John and Elizabeth involved in serious discussion. Elizabeth glanced up at the sound of Jenna's footsteps.

"John says we may be forced to delay our departure for America." Elizabeth cast Jenna a wistful glance.

John tried to comfort Elizabeth as he gathered her hands in his. "The weather does not seem to favor our plans. The continued storms have delayed any shipments leaving Liverpool."

"Surely by the end of April, the weather will be more favorable," Jenna suggested hopefully, as she noticed Elizabeth's sudden tears.

John glanced solemnly at Elizabeth, before turning to Jenna.

"We have decided that whatever the weather may provide, Elizabeth will leave London April twentieth for Liverpool. It is a two-day journey. My ship will be waiting to take us to America at the earliest possible date. We shall be married aboard the ship. If necessary, we can remain aboard at Liverpool harbor until weather permits our departure."

"That is only three days before the wedding," Jenna said thoughtfully.

"But how shall I be able to leave the house? Charles will surely suspect something."

Jenna smiled confidently. "Not at all. It will be necessary for you to visit Madame Lessard for the final fitting of your wedding gown. With that excuse, we shall arrange for you to leave for Liverpool immediately. It will be several hours before you are missed, and by that time you shall be well on your way, with none the wiser for your destination."

"But how?" Elizabeth twisted her hands with mounting despair. "Mr. Hodge, father's driver, will never consent to driving me to Liverpool. And Charles would know of it immediately."

"There will be no need for Mr. Hodge to drive you. I shall call for you early in the morning with the excuse that we will be shopping late in the day. Dmitri will take you to Liverpool in my coach." Jenna smiled devilishly, considering the plan to be perfect. A wide, radiant smile spread across Elizabeth's face as she rushed from John to gather Jenna in an excited embrace.

"You are my dearest friend. None of this would be possible if it were not for you."

"I shall remember that, and call upon you to return the favor someday. But let us first make certain that we are successful. We must say nothing of this to anyone. No one must suspect what we are about, or Charles will surely put an end to our plans."

John Whitmore rose from the covered settee and gathered his cloak and hat. He glanced down solemnly at Elizabeth as he folded her hand in the crook of his arm. "I am quite prepared to deal with Charles Wingate in whatever manner is necessary to insure Elizabeth's happiness. I shall not leave England alone."

Elizabeth reached out pleadingly as she rested her hand against his chest. "You must promise you will do nothing. Our plan will work. I know it will." Elizabeth looked to Jenna for confirmation.

Jenna returned a confident smile, and then her manner grew more serious. "I fear we dare not even risk your meeting again. There is too much danger that Charles will learn of it."

Elizabeth cast Jenna a sorrowful glance, but she knew well the truth of her words. They had dared this one meeting to make their final plans. They dared not meet again as the date of the wedding drew closer. Elizabeth clung to John in silent farewell as Mr. Flint announced they should be leaving. John gave Elizabeth an impassioned kiss, then turned to leave by the back entrance to the house. All Elizabeth's misery at their parting was evident in the soft oval of her face.

"You must not think of the moments apart but look to your moments together. I promise you the time will pass quickly." Jenna spoke encouragingly as she hugged Elizabeth comfortingly.

The hour was late as Mr. Flint guided the coach onto the road that led to Wingate Hall.

"And what of your happiness, Jenna?" Elizabeth said from the secluded darkness, where she sat across from Jenna.

"You must not concern yourself with such matters. The most important thing is that you and John will be together," Jenna reassured her friend from the shelter of darkness that hid the startled expression on her lovely face.

"I am not a fool, Jenna. I know full well you do not love Charles. Why have you accepted this betrothal?"

"Elizabeth, please. You do not understand." Without success, Jenna tried to change the subject of their conversation.

"I am not blind. I have seen you with Charles countless times. You do not love him."

Jenna laughed nervously at her friend's accurate assumption. She lifted the flap at the windows to see their location, desperately wishing they might arrive at Wingate Hall soon.

"Whatever are you talking about?"

"It's a certain look I've seen in your eyes, like some sudden fire glowing inside you. It is not there for Charles."

"Elizabeth, please, you are speaking in riddles. I think

342

love has made you think everyone should feel as you do."

The coach turned down the cobbled path that circled before Wingate Hall and stopped. Mr. Flint alighted to assist Elizabeth, holding the door open as he waited for her. She reached across the distance that separated them, seizing Jenna's slender hands in her own.

"There is only one man who brought that light to your eyes. I have seen only sadness since Prince Kalinsky has been gone," Elizabeth said boldly. Jenna's head shot up at the undeniable truth in her friend's words. Any protest she might have offered died on her lips as Elizabeth stepped down from the coach.

Returning late to Hallston House, Jenna ordered a hot bath, refusing the tray of hot food Emma Kelly delivered to her chamber. When she had finished bathing, Jenna donned her silk wrapper and tried to find some warmth before the large fire that roared at the hearth in her chamber. The truth of Elizabeth's words haunted her. Her friend had known better than she the truth of her feelings for Stefan. Elizabeth had spoken what she had tried to deny. She could not possibly go through with her marriage to Charles, and to let him continue to believe it was the greatest falsehood, though she easily recognized that telling him of it now might endanger Elizabeth's plans.

Unable to sleep, Jenna rose early and brushed the tangles from the silken mass of her hair that hung loose about her shoulders. Pulling on the silk wrapper against the chill in the silent house, Jenna quietly made her way to the kitchen, where she knew Maggie would already have hot tea brewing.

The kitchen was warm and inviting, with the embers of the fire the night before still glowing brightly at the hearth. As she had expected, a kettle simmered over the fire. Jenna rubbed her hands together against the cold morning as she reached for a cup and saucer.

"Weak tea will not put fat on your bones. You must have food."

The fine china cup slipped from her grasp and tumbled

to the floor, shattering on the gleaming wood floor, as Jenna whirled around. She stared in stunned silence at Dmitri's imposing height.

"I did not mean to frighten you. I always take my breakfast early. The girl, Maggie is good enough to leave fresh pastry. Come, join me. You must eat," Dmitri continued insistently.

Jenna shook her head firmly as she bent to pick up the pieces of the shattered cup. In an instant Dmitri was beside her, gently brushing her hands aside as he picked up the splintered pieces of china.

"You must eat." Dmitri spoke again firmly, almost as if he were handing some order that she must follow.

Jenna knew that Maggie's pastries were among the finest to be found anywhere. She had learned the fine art of making the finely layered dough for the croissants from a French maid she had befriended. Indeed, the light, flaky pastries filled with any assortment of jams and jellies had been her grandfather's favorites. Nor could she deny that on many occasions when she had already downed one for her morning meal she had stolen another from the tray in the kitchen. Now, however, the idea of the rich, fruit-filled pastry seemed anything but appealing. Jenna forced back another wave of nausea as Dmitri held a plate before her. She hastily pushed the plate away, preferring the strongly brewed tea. She reached for another cup.

"The child cannot grow strong if the mother does not eat," Dmitri observed somberly.

Jenna whirled about, very nearly losing her grip on the second cup in her hand as she stared in stunned disbelief at Dmitri.

"Did you think to keep this secret from Dmitri?" he asked gruffly, and then his deep voice rumbled into a gentle chuckling. "So, I have guessed correctly. Always it is so with one as innocent as yourself. I think you will not keep this secret very long. Knowing the father, the child will grow long and very strong. You are not wide and fat enough to conceal the extra burden of the child. It will show soon enough on your slender bones."

A sudden warmth spread across Jenna's cheeks as her mouth flew open in quick denial of Dmitri's assumption. She stopped suddenly, as she realized she could not deny what she had known for several weeks—that she was carrying Stefan's child.

Jenna slowly approached the wide breakfast table, where Dmitri sat silently, popping another pastry into his mouth, his glistening dark eyes never leaving hers as he wiped his mouth and beard with a cloth.

"You are wrong, and I will hear no more of it. I have never cared for a large meal at breakfast," Jenna responded evenly as she fought to control the panic that rose within her.

Dmitri guffawed his delight at the game she played with him. He slammed his hands down flat on the hard surface of the wooden table, studying her carefully.

"It is not only the breakfast that you push away. You have no appetite now, but in the months to come that will change. It is always so."

Jenna slammed the cup and saucer down on the table with such force that Dmitri pretended to shield his face from more broken china.

"It is surprising that you seem to have so much knowledge of such things," Jenna fumed with mounting irritation at the truth he had so easily discovered.

"It is not so surprising. I was the first of eleven children. The last child was born when I was already a man. On the Russian steppes, life is simple. There are no physicians to attend a woman when she is with child. Whenever my mother found herself with child, we all knew of it quickly. When there are eleven children, in a small house, these things are easily known. When my father thought I was old enough to understand, he explained such things to me. There is a certain look in a woman when she carries a new life within her. I know. I have seen it before. I see it in you, little princess." The lines about Dmitri's eyes softened as he gazed at her. "In time, all will know of it. But that will be some months from now, I think. It was to be expected, of course."

345

"Expected!" Jenna's eyes flashed with anger as she whirled on Dmitri.

Dmitri returned her gaze evenly. "Always it is so with one who is young and innocent. You had not considered such possibilities," Dmitri stated with certainty, and then, seeing the tears that threatened, he rose abruptly, seizing Jenna gently by the shoulders, drawing her to the chair before the table.

Jenna sat down slowly. "Most certainly, a woman like Madame de Stahl would never allow such a thing to happen." Jenna spoke bitterly.

"Lillian de Stahl is a courtesan. She has made her life with many men. But there was a time when she hoped to bind a man to her with a child."

"What are you saying?" Jenna stared back at Dmitri uncertainly.

"You must have no fear of this, little princess." Dmitri thumped his broad chest with confidence. "A child is a blessing from God, and a child made of the love between a man and a woman is the richest gift."

"You do not understand, Dmitri. There is no acceptance for a child that is born a bastard," Jenna whispered sadly. "I think it would be better not to be born at all."

Dmitri nearly upset the large, heavy table as he rose suddenly, a fierce, golden light gleaming in the depths of his dark eyes, seizing Jenna by the wrists and drawing her out of the chair. Jenna cringed, knowing well the strength he was capable of.

"You think I do not understand," Dmitri whispered harshly, holding her in an unyielding grasp. "I know the pain suffered by the child who is born a bastard. I have lived with it. You must believe me when I say there is no shame in the child you carry. I have heard of women who would easily rid themselves of a child. It is common among certain courtesans in the royal courts. I have no patience for such actions." He spoke gruffly.

Jenna stared at Dmitri in stunned disbelief at what he had assumed.

"The child is innocent, whatever the deeds of its

346

parents. You need have no fear, Dmitri. I could never take the life of an innocent babe." Jenna spoke honestly.

Dmitri's grasp about her wrists eased as he seemed to believe he might trust her. He watched her carefully as he returned to his chair and downed another pastry.

Jenna rubbed her bruised wrists where Dmitri had held her a moment before. "You spoke of your parents. How could you possibly understand what a bastard child is made to suffer?"

Dmitri gazed at her steadily as he considered what he would tell her. He had never spoken of it to anyone, and yet as he watched the beautiful girl who sat before him, he realized that she above all others needed to know. It might help ease the doubts and fears he knew she carried.

"It is not of myself that I speak. I speak of a boy many years ago, who came to my village. He was sent by his mother because she knew he would be accepted in my family, as his father had lived among us. It was not safe for the boy to remain with his mother, and the father had been sent far away. The child was a bastard child, but he carried the blood of Catherine the Great, the empress, and the greatest Cossack general to fight beside the Czars. But he was a bastard child, and he was made to suffer because of it. We rode together across the steppes. Together we learned the ways of the Cossacks. He became strong and brave. When he played among the children in the village, they teased him with their cruel jokes about his mother and father. It was difficult for a small child to understand, but he learned well the lessons they taught him, until the day that he refused to run from their ugly words. I found him surrounded by boys from the village, all brave in their many numbers. They were not quite so brave when they faced him one by one. When darkness fell in the village, none remained to fight him, though many were taller and stronger. Out of the darkness and sadness of his pain, he had learned a valuable lesson: that a man must have cunning as well as strength."

Jenna gathered her knees beneath her and wrapped the silk robe around herself more closely for warmth as she

347

stared back at Dmitri with a sudden overwhelming sadness for the boy who had been made to suffer so much for his birth.

"What happened to the boy?" she whispered.

"In time, the mother sent for the boy. She decided he must have other education; the education of books. He was sent to school in England and France, only returning to the land of his birth for brief visits."

"If she loved her child, how could she bear to send him away?"

Dmitri lifted a cup of thick, strong tea and drank slowly, letting the steaming liquid warm though him.

"She sent him away because of her love for him. Had she chosen to keep the boy with her, he would have suffered more from his stepfather. In time the boy grew to be a man, and came to understand the circumstance of his birth, but he never forgot the cruelty he suffered. There are some wounds that can never heal completely. You must be very careful, little princess. You must say nothing of this, not even to your friend, Elizabeth. Charles Wingate is a very dangerous man. You must trust no one."

"No one?" Jenna cast Dmitri an amused smile. The gruff man who had held her in such a threatening grasp a moment before, rose from the table and stood over her, his dark eyes sparkling from beneath the shaggy mane of his unkempt hair.

"I fear I might not always be near when you need me."

Jenna tilted her lovely head to one side, silently contemplating the man who stood before her. There was much more he had left unsaid, and yet she knew well if she pressed him further, he would retreat to stony silence as he had in the past weeks. Jenna sighed heavily as she turned to leave the kitchen.

"I shall heed your warning, my friend. Have no fear for the babe. It is a life I hold most dear."

Jenna returned to the haven of her chamber, sighing shakily as she leaned against the closed door. She smoothed her hand across the firm, flat hardness of her belly beneath the silken chemise. Jenna thought of the child that rested within her, so new that it hardly seemed real to her, and yet it was a truth she could not deny. She dared to wonder if the babe would be a son, with golden hair and brilliant blue eyes to mark its sire, or perhaps with dark hair and amber eyes, like the Gypsy her grandfather had spoken of. Jenna wiped back the tears as she thought of Stefan, and what his thoughts might be about their child. Jenna quickly drove the thought from her mind. Stefan was far away, and might well never know of his child. He had given her no promises, only the brief moments they had shared, and she had asked for none, convincing herself it would be enough.

The small rowboat bumped against the wooden pillar of the quay and slipped noiselessly up against the last step of the landing. The thick fog heavily shrouded the empty dock in murky dampness as a man stepped ashore, quickly followed by two more. A fourth man emerged from a safe vantage point and quickly reached to secure the boat. They exchanged no words as they moved quickly along the dock to the safety of the brick warehouse, following the fourth man inside to a small storage room at the far side of the warehouse where a single lantern glowed faintly.

"Did you have any trouble?" the fourth man asked as he turned to his companions.

The first man from the boat pushed back his heavy cap, the meager light sparkling in the brilliant depths of his blue eyes.

"None. The French grow careless. There was only one ship this morning, and we used the fog as a cover to outrun them."

"What news have you?" The fourth man had now removed his coat, revealing a well-tailored waistcoat and breeches.

"There is now an armistice between Austria and Russia. The Austrians have joined us to form a coalition against the French. The Czar has given the orders for the Russian army to immediately move against Hamburg. I have brought a request from Czar Alexander for the English army to move against Napoleon in the south. I must see the duke of Kent immediately. Time is of the essence."

"It is far too dangerous for you to be seen in London," the fourth man replied solemnly. "Think of the harm if you were to be seen. There is too much danger, not only to you but to others."

"I must return, my friend. I gave my solemn oath the papers would be delivered. And there are other matters I must attend to." Stefan Kalinsky accepted a glass of brandy, downing it quickly to drive back the aching cold from their journey across the channel.

"You must take care. The conspirators have grown bold in your absence. They are more confident than ever of success. Charles Wingate was heard speaking openly against the regent only a fortnight ago. The matter was blamed on heavy drink, but he was quickly escorted home by his friends. There is word that they will move soon."

"Who told you of this? Dmitri?"

John Whitmore regarded Stefan evenly, knowing well that he had returned for other reasons as well. "Dmitri has been able to learn nothing. His presence alone is suspicious. They guard well against all men. Charles Wingate is a clever man. He trusts no one. I made an unexpected trip to Dover last week. A sleek, fast schooner lies at anchor in a secluded cove. There is word that her owner is a rich gentleman from London, though none could remember hearing his name. The ship is well guarded. I was not able to get close. You should know that Charles Wingate has forced Jenna to set the date for their marriage." John saw the sudden tensing of muscles beneath the bronze smoothness of Stefan's jaw. He laid a restraining hand on Stefan's arm.

Stefan's head had shot up, a sudden menacing gleam lighting the depths of his gaze. "That day will never come, my friend."

"Easy, my friend. Do not be foolish in this. For the moment, Jenna is safe, and there are other matters of greater importance."

John Whitmore could see that his arguments mattered

little. "I know your thoughts, Stefan, but you must not risk going to London. I will see the papers are safely delivered to the duke of Kent. I have business in London. No one will be suspicious of me, but you cannot easily hide among the shadows."

Stefan reluctantly nodded his agreement. "Have you seen Jenna?"

"I fear Charles Wingate occupies much of her time. And I am not allowed to call at Wingate Hall," John replied wryly.

"Have you completed your plans to leave England?" Stefan downed another glass of the amber liquid, thinking how the shimmering dark color reminded him of Jenna's eyes.

"There is going to be a ball at Wingate Hall, Friday next, in celebration of Elizabeth's wedding. Jenna has arranged for Elizabeth to join her for a last bit of shopping the following day. Elizabeth will leave for Liverpool that morning, in Jenna's coach, so that none may be the wiser. It is arranged that Dmitri will accompany her."

Stefan leaned upon the heavy wooden table. If the ball was to be in four days, and Charles hoped to leave England shortly thereafter, it could only mean that the conspirators hoped to complete their own plans very soon. There was no time to be wasted. If they were to stop Napoleon, the conspiracy had to be broken and an army sent against the French from the south.

Stefan handed the leather-bound packet of papers to John Whitmore. "These must reach the duke of Kent as soon as possible. No one must know of them. Alexei will ride with you. You realize the risk if you are caught?" Stefan replaced the cap on his head.

John Whitmore nodded solemnly. "I owe you a great debt, my friend. And though I leave England, I could not live with myself if the conspiracy were to succeed."

Stefan nodded his understanding. "We need horses."

"You will find horses at the stables at the far end of the street," John answered as they emerged from the warehouse.

Stefan and his men followed John to the waiting coach.

"Thank you, my friend. I know I can trust you to see the matter done." Stefan turned to his men and gave his orders in Russian. Alexei joined John Whitmore in the coach.

"How will I be able to find you?" John Whitmore asked as he leaned to bid his friend farewell.

"Do not look for me. I shall find you." Stefan Kalinsky closed the door behind them, latching it securely.

"Be most careful. It seems Charles Wingate's friends are everywhere." John warned in parting.

"Do not worry my friend. I have no intention of letting anyone know I have returned; not yet. It would spoil the hunting." A feral gleam sparkled in the depths of Stefan's gaze, and then he was gone, the curling wisps of fog closing about him, as if he were indeed some soulless phantom of the night.

Chapter Nineteen

Jenna smiled faintly at the young solicitor who returned to escort her with great formality into the dark, wood-paneled offices of her grandfather's lawyer.

With maddening indifference, Sir Lawrence Renfield continued to read through the document before him on the ornate mahogany desk, as if she might not have been there. Jenna inhaled deeply to calm her growing aggravation with the man before her, reminding herself that she must remain calm if she was to obtain the information she sought without arousing the lawyer's suspicions of her true purpose in asking for the appointment. Miraculously, the nausea that had plagued her for the past weeks had failed to materialize that morning, replaced instead with a ravenous appetite, which had heartily pleased Emma Kelly. After an ample breakfast, and careful selection of her attire, Jenna felt confident of her plans.

Standing patiently in that office where she had stood months before, Jenna remembered the sadness on that last occasion. The vivid green silk of her dress rustled faintly as she took the chair before the desk. She was not about to be put off by Sir Lawrence Renfield's solicitous attitude that masked his abiding loyalties to Charles Wingate.

Sir Lawrence looked up, as if suddenly aware of her presence for the first time. "My dear Lady Randolph, how very nice to see you once again."

"Good morning, Sir Lawrence." Jenna replied warmly.

"I must admit I was somewhat surprised to receive a request for this meeting. However, as I always sought to accommodate your grandfather in all his needs, how may I now serve you?"

Jenna was not fooled by his solicitous manner, which concerned a certain curiosity. It was rare, indeed, for a woman to seek out the services of a lawyer. It was a matter usually of concern to the husband, or a man of close relation. Jenna was subtly aware of a glimmer of curiosity in Sir Lawrence's manner. She hardly doubted that the entire subject of their conversation would quickly reach Charles Wingate.

"I am most grateful that you agreed to see me on such short notice. I know you must have other clients with far more important matters whom you must see. But I had hoped perhaps to get some more information about my grandfather's estate and his will," Jenna began sweetly.

"But surely, you need not be concerned with such matters at this time. Certainly Charles will be more than happy to handle all matters of your grandfather's estate. Since you are planning to be married before your next birthday, it will be quite a simple matter to have all details taken care of by your husband," Sir Lawrence offered, responding warmly to her radiant beauty. Charles Wingate was indeed a most fortunate man.

"It is with thoughts to my marriage that I sought a better understanding of my grandfather's estates. As you are well aware, I am currently allowed limited funds from the estate. There are a great many expenses for a young bride. These past weeks as I have helped Elizabeth Wingate prepare for her own wedding I have become more aware of it. There are several items I would like to purchase before my own wedding."

Sir Lawrence Renfield smiled with sudden understanding. "I am quite certain, Lady Randolph, that you have only to make Sir Charles aware of these needs, and all will be taken care of."

"I couldn't possibly let Charles know of this!" Jenna exclaimed with apparent alarm. "It is most important that

354

a lady not burden the man she is to marry with such matters. I could not bear for anyone to think that I was without finances.''

Jenna reached inside her embroidered silk reticule for a lace handkerchief. She sniffed with sudden emotion and dabbed at her eyes as she seemed to crumble with the emotional burden of her financial plight.

Sir Lawrence Renfield immediately sprang from his seat and quickly rounded the desk in an effort to comfort her. He could ill afford for a valued client like Charles Wingate to think he had upset the suddenly distraught young woman in his office.

"Please, Lady Randolph, certainly there is no need for such sadness. I am certain something can be arranged to alleviate this situation.''

Jenna sniffled again loudly into her handkerchief as she looked up at Sir Lawrence Renfield with wide, soulful eyes that seemed to mirror all her misery. Sir Lawrence was quite defenseless when he thought he might possibly offer a solution to aid a lady in distress, especially a lady of such position.

"I would be most greatful for any assistance you might offer. I simply dread telling Charles that I am without funds. I fear he would be most angry.'' Jenna folded the handkerchief after wiping her eyes one last time.

Sir Lawrence Renfield blanched at the thought of what Charles Wingate's reaction would be. He could ill afford offending a man with wealth and temper. Sir Lawrence smiled at Jenna with a sickening air of benevolence.

"Now, how may I help you?''

Jenna smiled at him gratefully as she realized he would probably have been willing to turn over the entire wealth of the royal treasury, had it been at his disposal, to avoid the wrath of Charles Wingate. She had not been wrong about the man's loyalties. She warmed to her little scheme as she fastened him with a dazzling smile of gratitude.

"I have found several items I should like to purchase, including one very special gift.''

"Of course, I understand,'' Sir Lawrence responded,

convinced the very special gift most assuredly was intended for Charles Wingate, as a gift from his bride.

"If you will but give me a list of your intended purchases, I will arrange for the necessary funds to be advanced from your grandfather's estate funds."

Jenna hesitated suddenly. The arrangement was hardly what she had planned for. She smiled demurely at Sir Lawrence as a thought suddenly seized her.

"I owe a substantial amount to Madame Lessard, for my trousseau. The woman can hardly be expected to bear the expense for all the fabrics I have chosen. I had hoped to give her the entire amount. I am certain it will inspire her greatest efforts. And Charles is most conscious of my wardrobe." Jenna turned an innocent smile on Sir Lawrence.

The lawyer quickly returned to his desk and took a leather-bound ledger from one of the bookshelves that lined the wall behind his desk.

"Of course. I am certain we can handle whatever amount is necessary. After all, the funds are there. It is merely a matter of advancing them. Upon your marriage to Sir Charles, the entire estate will immediately be available to you."

Jenna inhaled deeply as she thought again of the amount she had decided upon, not knowing what reaction she might receive from the lawyer.

"I think ten thousand pounds should cover everything for now. That will also allow me to purchase that very special gift I spoke of."

Sir Lawrence Renfield scanned the neatly penned columns of the book before him. From his continued silence, Jenna thought he might not have heard her reply. And then, quite suddenly, he glanced up from the thick ledger before him and smiled secretively.

Jenna could feel the heavy pounding of her heart as she held her breath, certain that he must know of her scheme. In one quick motion he slammed the heavy volume closed on top of the large desk and rose from his high-backed chair. With slowly measured steps, he rounded the desk and crossed the room to the door. He returned a few minutes later to stand before her.

"My dear Jenna. I have asked the maid to bring tea. Mr. Dunleigh, my assistant, will prepare the draft for the amount you requested, and bring it along presently."

Relief flooded through Jenna as she fixed Sir Lawrence with an appreciative smile. At that moment, she might have been willing to bargain with the devil for the money she needed. When the tea had been poured, Jenna sipped from the delicate cup.

"I trust I may rely on your discretion in this matter," she suggested demurely. "The gift I have planned will be a grand surprise, and I shouldn't want Charles to know of it before it is ready."

Sir Lawrence gathered her gloved hand in his and bent low, pressing a brief kiss against the soft leather.

"I give you my promise of complete confidentiality. I take great pleasure that I may be of some assistance in such a matter. Sir Charles is a valued friend and client."

Jenna smiled warmly with the success of her scheme. Now all she required was a little information.

"My grandfather's will mentioned land that he owned in the United States. I believe it was in Virginia," she mentioned casually.

"Yes, he acquired the land as payment for a debt some years ago. He seemed pleased enough with the transaction, although I heartily advised him against it. Now this bloody war with the United States had made the land an unattractive investment." Sir Lawrence shook his head sadly.

"But now that the war has ended, surely the land might be of some use," Jenna suggested.

"The land is of substantial use, my dear Jenna. It is my understanding that much of the land has rich soil. For several years your grandfather received sizable revenues from the sale of crops and livestock. Although he continuously reinvested capital to improve the crops and horses bred at the farm, I urged him against it. Even with the help of his overseer, it is most difficult to maintain such property at this great distance. I strongly urged him to sell the farm on several occasions, but he would not hear of it. I am certain that with your marriage Sir Charles will see the folly of maintaining the farm in Virginia and seek a buyer at the earliest moment." Sir Lawrence glanced up as his assistant entered the office, the draft for Jenna's funds in his hands.

Sir Lawrence accepted the draft, glancing over it quickly before handing it to Jenna.

"I believe this was the amount requested."

Jenna forced her smile of gratitude as she accepted the draft.

"I am most grateful, Sir Lawrence. Now I must be leaving. I fear the hour is quite late, and I should like to give Madame Lessard the payment she requested so that she may begin her work. Charles will be so pleased, when he learns how you have helped me." Jenna cast him a grateful smile. Indeed, Charles would be quite surprised to learn how Sir Lawrence Renfield had helped her. But by then it would be too late.

Jenna returned late to Hallston House, patiently submitting to Emma's reprovals for the late hour, with so little time remaining before she was expected at Wingate Hall for the party to celebrate the forthcoming wedding of Elizabeth and Sir Reginald. She bathed quickly, eating sparingly of the tray of food Maggie set beside the dressing table. She must not be late and arouse Charles's suspicions. So much depended on everything's being perfect.

Jenna let the sheer silk chemise slide easily down the length of her body, unaware that Emma had returned with her gown, freshly pressed.

"How long do you think you can keep your secret from Sir Charles?"

Jenna whirled about, clutching her silk wrapper against the length of her body to conceal the obvious curve of her stomach beneath the revealing chemise. She stared at Emma Kelly in stunned disbelief, thinking that she had kept her secret well over the last weeks.

"Did you think I would not know? You are like my own

daughter. I have cared for you since the day you were born."

"When did you guess?" Jenna breathed shakily.

"Almost from the beginning. There was hardly any preventing it. I could see that from the very beginning. Is Prince Kalinsky aware of the babe he has given you?"

Jenna shook her head firmly.

"No, and you've not had a word from him, either. And where is he now, when you and your unborn babe have a need of him?" Emma huffed indignantly.

Having heard enough of the woman's tirade, Jenna tossed the silken wrapper aside, as there was hardly any reason to conceal the truth any longer. She turned on the maid with a feral gleam sparkling in the depths of her eyes.

"I will say this now, and we will speak of it no more. Yes, I carry Stefan Kalinsky's child, but I will tolerate no disapprovals from you or anyone else for it. Whatever else, this child will have a mother, and it will be loved. Never again speak against Stefan Kalinsky. He gave me no promises, and I asked him for none. I will not accept your scorn. The child was made of two people. I went willingly to his bed. I willingly accept the responsibility for my child."

Emma swallowed uneasily. Never in all the years they had been together had Jenna ever spoken against her. But the beautiful, determined, young woman she saw before her was no longer a child. Her mouth twisted into a slight frown as she looked down at the gown in her arms and smoothed the gold silk with a worn hand that trembled visibly.

"I have made you my life, dear child. 'Tis not likely that I would turn from you now. Nor is it proper for me to criticize you. I will help you whatever way I may, and care for the babe as I have always cared for you."

Jenna rushed across the chamber, wrapping Emma Kelly in a frantic embrace. "I could not bear your loss. I thought you, more than anyone, would understand. But I feared telling you, because I didn't want to hurt you."

"Dear child, you could not be closer to me if we were of

the same blood. I accepted you long ago; I'll not turn from you now. And I do understand the love you have for Prince Kalinsky. It is only that I wanted more for you than I had." Emma reached up to gently stroke Jenna's cheek.

Jenna smiled lovingly at the old maid. "I would not wish the child away. I love Stefan Kalinsky more than my life. If it is fated that we shall never meet again, I will always have the memory of his love. And I will have his child."

"What of Sir Charles?" Emma questioned earnestly as she held the gown out for Jenna, carefully arranging the capped sleeves over Jenna's shoulders before buttoning the gown. She adjusted the skirt of the empire waistline in a long flowing line to the floor. The cut of the gown completely concealed the slightly rounded curve of Jenna's waist.

"Even if it were not for the babe, even if I had never met Stefan Kalinsky, I could never have married Charles Wingate. These past months I have learned a great deal about Charles. So much that I chose to overlook can no longer be ignored. Charles is cruel, caring only for his own gain. I fear Grandfather was right in not trusting him."

"He will press you for marriage as soon as Lady Elizabeth has wed."

"He may do whatever he likes. We shall be long gone from England."

Emma Kelly stood suddenly and stared at Jenna with wide, quizzical eyes.

"What are you up to?"

Jenna smiled at the maid confidently. "Elizabeth will not be marrying Sir Reginald Guilford. More I cannot say, except that she will be leaving within a few days' time for the colonies, and we will be leaving with her."

"Saints alive!" Emma Kelly exclaimed, clapping her hands firmly over her mouth as she stared aghast at her young mistress. "But what of the war between England and the colonies? There'll be no way of reaching there safely."

Jenna smiled confidently. "The war is quite well ended.

There is no danger. Trade between England and the colonies has already resumed. We shall be traveling on a merchantman, and quite safely."

"But how shall we live? Where shall we live? I have heard stories of indians and pirates," Emma said, her voice rising with more excitement at each moment.

"Grandfather owned a farm in Virginia. Each year he has received substantial revenues from the farm. Upon his death, the farm is mine. We shall go to Virginia."

"Leave England?" Emma Kelly stared at Jenna in wide-eyed wonder.

Jenna smiled indulgently at the old maid. "I shall need you, Emma, and Maggie and Mr. Flint. But if any of you should decide not to make the journey I will understand. I do not easily leave England. It is something I must do."

Emma squared her well-rounded shoulders. "I'll not be letting you go off into a strange, foreign place with no family to care for you. You'll have a need of care when the babe comes, and I could hardly allow anyone else to see to the babe. Maggie might be better off finding herself a husband in Virginia, and I know Mr. Flint will go. He has nothing to hold him here. But where will you get the funds for such a journey?"

Jenna smiled confidently as she reached inside her reticule and produced a receipt for the ten thousand pounds, which she had deposited to her bank account.

"I convinced the lawyers to advance me the funds against the estate. We have more than enough to insure our passage to Virginia, and to cover our costs for at least one year. By that time, we shall know the true status of the farm, although by all reports it is rich in crops and livestock. But for tonight, I must attend the party for Elizabeth. On the morrow our plan will be set in motion."

Emma Kelly stared aghast at Jenna. "Tomorrow? That is not enough time. We must pack." The maid wrung her hands in mounting despair as she mentally noted all the details to be completed before they could leave.

"It must be done tonight. We will take only our personal belongings. Everything else stays. On the morrow we shall follow Elizabeth to Liverpool, and all must be done with none the wiser for it, or all shall be lost." Jenna gave one final inspection of her gown before turning toward the door.

"You must have everything ready by morning," she called over her shoulder, as Emma Kelly stood in the middle of the chamber wondering where she might begin with the packing.

Through the long evening, Jenna forced her composure. If she felt the strain of the game they played, she could only guess that Elizabeth suffered much worse. Elizabeth was deceiving both her father and her brother in her determination to be with the man she loved.

The large clock in the ornate drawing room of Wingate Hall struck nine o'clock as Jenna sought Elizabeth as a partner for a game of hazard. She noted the fevered glaze in Elizabeth's eyes as she found her friend hopelessly immersed in conversation with a maiden aunt. Jenna politely stole Elizabeth away from her torment.

"I thought I might never escape. If one more old maid corners me to explain a woman's intimate responsibilities to her husband, I think I shall scream," Elizabeth threatened.

Jenna quieted her with a comforting squeeze of the hand. "Be patient. Everything depends on this evening's being perfect. It is only for a few more hours, and then you and John will have the rest of your lives to laugh about the entire matter."

"I pray you are right. Oh Jenna, I could not bear for anything to go wrong now."

"You must believe that everything will be fine." Jenna smiled confidently. She stopped suddenly, staring at Elizabeth uncertainly. She felt it again, a faint fluttering, like the gentle brushing of butterfly wings within her. Jenna inhaled deeply, with sudden wonder at the movement of the child inside her.

"Jenna, are you quite all right?" Elizabeth clutched her

hand with sudden concern.

Jenna smiled back at her friend. "I am quite all right. And I thought to tell you now that I should like to come to Virginia with you and John."

"Oh Jenna, I can't think of anything that I would like more," Elizabeth breathed with sudden joy. "It will be so wonderful to have you near." Elizabeth's mood suddenly grew more solemn. .

"I always knew you did not love Charles, even before Prince Kalinsky. Loving John as I do helps me understand that we have little choice in the matter of whom we love, or why we love. What of Prince Kalinsky?"

Jenna smiled bravely at her friend. "I cannot know where he might be, or if he will ever return. My only certainty is that I cannot marry Charles. There are so many other reasons that I cannot say."

"I know John will be pleased that you have decided to sail with us. We both owe you such a great debt that we could never hope to repay, and John is quite fond of you." Elizabeth hugged Jenna encouragingly.

"Well now, dear ladies. What is this—certainly not tears?" Charles ventured as he moved between Jenna and Elizabeth, possessively taking Jenna's hand and tucking it through his elbow.

"Not at all. Elizabeth and I were merely talking about the final plans for her wedding," Jenna lied convincingly. Elizabeth flushed crimson with her mounting fear that Charles might have overheard their conversation. Jenna coolly accepted a glass of champagne as Charles led them to a nearby table.

"I shall leave you ladies to your card playing. I have some matters to discuss with business associates. I fear it would all be quite boring for you." Charles pulled out the chair for Elizabeth, and then Jenna, lingering over her, his gaze raking the swell of her breasts above the gold silk of her gown. Jenna's cool gaze never wavered as she reached her gloved hand to pick up a deck of gilt-edged playing cards. Charles quickly seized her other hand, imprisoning it in his stronger grasp as he lifted it to his lips. With slow deliberation Charles kissed the tips of her gloved fingers, his fingers closing over the ring Stefan had given her. It was as if he played out a silent game of challenge with his ardent attentions. As if he sought to establish his claim to her before everyone.

Jenna coolly retrieved her hand. "Charles, you must not keep your friends waiting."

Charles bowed stiffly before her, his lips twisted into a confident smile. "I yield the moment, milady. We shall have a lifetime to play out our little charades."

Jenna calmly concentrated on the cards she held in her hand, but all her tightly held composure could not still the shaking in her hands. She quickly placed the cards on the table before her, lest her sudden quavering betray her. Elizabeth stared at her solemnly.

"I fear for you, Jenna. Charles is determined to possess you. I think he might easily overlook my leaving tomorrow, but he will never allow you to go. You must be careful."

Jenna smiled bravely as she tried to still the shaking that had overtaken her. She felt as if she had looked upon the devil incarnate. "You need have no fear Elizabeth, I am most determined to be free of Charles."

When the clock had struck midnight, Jenna bid Elizabeth farewell for the evening, promising to send Dmitri with her own coach early the next morning. Elizabeth promised to be ready. She would take nothing except the clothes she wore and her wedding gown from Madame Lessard. They bid each other goodnight, with a solemn pledge for the secret they shared.

Stepping into the waiting coach, Jenna was forced to turn back as Charles refused to release her hand.

"My dearest Jenna, I fear I have neglected you this evening. There are matters of importance that must be attended to. I apologize. In three days' time Elizabeth will be wed, and we can look to our own marriage." Charles's hand slipped beneath her elbow, cleverly pulling her closer.

"Charles, please. It is very late, and I am quite tired."

Jenna pressed the flattened palms of her hands against the soft wool of his waistcoat as Charles pulled her close, his arms slipping about her waist, his cheek brushing against her as his lips sought hers with sudden urgency.

"Jenna, my darling, surely you must know how I desire you." Charles's breath was hot against her ear as he pulled her closer. Jenna recoiled from the intimacy of his hands at her back, holding her as only one other man had held her.

"Charles, no! What will everyone think?"

"They will think that I desire you, which is true. And none would dare interfere," Charles whispered confidently.

Jenna finally pulled away, turning quickly and scrambling into the waiting coach, slamming the door abruptly as Charles started to follow.

"It really is quite late, Charles. I must be going," Jenna called, as Mr. Flint immediately cracked the whip over the heads of the horses, sending the coach lunging away from the cobbled driveway.

Jenna pulled the woven shawl more closely about her shoulders trying to drive away the coldness that had suddenly taken hold of her, which had nothing to do with the night air. She shuddered at the thought of Charles's hands upon her, as if something sinister and evil had touched her. She sank back into the softness of the cushions, wrapping her arms about herself as she fought back the fear and misery that threatened to overcome her.

Her emotions betrayed her as her thoughts filled with the memory of Stefan. Her eyes filled with tears, and she felt an overwhelming loneliness and longing. The sound of the wheels was oddly muffled, and Jenna was vaguely aware that the coach had slowed. Certain they had not yet had enough time to reach Hallston House, Jenna leaned forward to peer out the shade that had been drawn over the window. She drew back suddenly at the sight of several mounted riders surrounding the coach. Though it was dangerous for highwaymen to attack a coach within London proper, it was not completely unheard of. Jenna pounded on the roof of the coach in a desperate attempt to signal Mr. Flint. She knew he carried a pistol at all times. She knew, as well, that she was completely defenseless inside the coach. Her grandfather had never felt the need for a pistol, always relying on the stalwart Mr. Flint for necessary protection. As she heard voices beyond the coach, Jenna momentarily regretted her hasty words to Charles Wingate. His protection would have been better than none at all, though she knew that had she allowed him to accompany her home, it would have been questionable where there was greater danger—in being attacked by highwaymen or by Charles's groping hands. Realizing there would be no easy escape, Jenna reached for the handle of the door. A gasp escaped her lips, as the door to the coach was opened from the outside and she was pulled forward. Vainly she attempted to prevent her fall as she grabbed for the edge of the door, feeling it slip beyond her grasp as it swung wide. Jenna had only a moment to glimpse the riders that surrounded the coach as she tumbled through the doorway. Instead of the cold hardness of the cobbled stones in the street, Jenna felt a strong arm about her waist, preventing her fall as she was gently pushed back into the cushioned seats, the door of the coach slamming shut, closing her in complete darkness once again. A command was given, and the coach moved off slowly.

Disoriented, Jenna struggled to sit up. The wheels of the coach no longer clattered loudly over the cobbled street, but were softly muffled as they turned onto a dirt pathway. Finally regaining her seat, Jenna brushed back the tangled mass of her hair, and sat upright. Slowly she reached toward the lantern near the door. She gasped as her hand was seized in a firm grasp.

Darkness disappeared as the wick in the lantern glowed more brightly, casting a soft, golden light inside the coach. Jenna pulled back with mounting fear of the shadows that formed before her. The confines of the coach barred further retreat from the menacing shadow that held her, refusing to release her arm, now closing the distance between them. Jenna cried out as she was dragged across the inside of the coach, but her voice was muffled beneath a gloved hand clamped firmly over her mouth. Any thoughts she might have had of calling out for Mr. Flint quickly silenced. Her mind was suddenly filled with horror of the arms that closed about her with unmistakable intent. Her vision was filled with the sinister mask of her assailant as she was drawn toward the man who held her.

With one arm pinned behind her, Jenna beat frantically with her one free hand doubled into a small fist. She closed her eyes in silent desperation as she struggled against the unyielding grasp that imprisoned her. She felt the last of her strength rapidly fading.

"Jenna!"

Somewhere in the depths of her awareness Jenna was aware of her name being called. Her struggling stopped, and she thought she must surely be dreaming. Again Jenna heard her name hoarsely whispered. Her amber eyes wide with terror, she stared back at the masked figure. A memory stirred faintly. Jenna felt the hand across her mouth loosen as she continued to stare at the faceless black silk mask. When the hand was drawn completely away, Jenna drew a deep, even breath as she stared with dawning realization at the man who held her.

"Stefan?" Jenna whispered faintly, reaching to draw away the silk mask. Her breath caught in her throat, as her gaze locked with his brilliant blue eyes.

Stefan reached out to touch her trembling lip with his finger as Jenna stared at him disbelieving.

"I did not mean to frighten you," Stefan whispered. "There was no other way I could dare to see you now."

Jenna stared at him incredulously. "All this time, there was no word from you. I didn't know if you were dead or alive. Not one letter, not one brief message, except to be informed that you had sent for Lillian de Stahl. Damn you!" Her temper flared as she struggled to free herself from Stefan's embrace.

"What are you talking about? Jenna!" Stefan commanded firmly, refusing to release her.

"I am talking about your mistress. She made very certain that I knew you had sent for her. As if that would have made any difference to me. You are quite welcome to your royal whore. My only regret is that you both escaped the French. I should think they would have enjoyed such prizes," Jenna spat venomously, her temper raging beyond control. The episode with Charles had only served to fuel all her doubts and fears of the last months.

"Jenna!" Stefan warned.

"Save your words for her. I am certain she will welcome you when you are ready to return to her bed. As for me, I have no such intentions. May the devil take you and your damned conspiracy." Jenna was very near tears as she tried again to twist free of his grasp. His hands about her arms tightened with bruising strength.

"I am not certain what this is about, but we will speak of it now. Whatever you have heard of Lillian de Stahl, know that you cannot believe it. Yes, Lillian de Stahl is in Vienna, but only after taking great risk to bring me important news of the conspiracy. As to her occupying my bed, I once explained that it did not concern you. I say it again. It is of no concern to you. I have known Lillian de Stahl many years. Whatever existed between us happened many years ago, long before I met you. More than that I will not explain."

Jenna tossed her wild mane of dark, sable hair as she returned his stare. Only the wide, dark depths of her eyes, flashing with golden light, betrayed the anger that grew within her. "I have no use for your excuses. I demand that you release me immediately." Jenna's lip trembled faintly as she faced him bravely.

"Do you believe that I would have returned if all I wanted was Lillian de Stahl? She has always been a willing partner. I had only to ask. I could have easily sent Alexei or Dmitri to put an end to this conspiracy. I chose to return to England, and for only one reason."

"Why didn't you come to Hallston House? I waited for you. All those weeks, I waited for you," Jenna responded bitterly, fighting back the tears that threatened.

"It was impossible to return before. Were you aware that Charles has had you watched constantly? I could not come to Hallston House. There was too much risk that we might be seen. Dmitri had informed me that you would be traveling this road. I thought it the best way to meet you." Stefan smiled at her devilishly. "I thought certain you would remember that first time, on the road to London. No one could have been more surprised than I, to find such a skilled marksman in a woman."

"Damn you! Yes, I remember. And I remember other moments." A sob escaped Jenna as she turned away angrily, suddenly unable to trust her emotions. Stefan's unyielding hold barred further retreat. Slowly he reached to turn her face toward his.

"I, too, remember other moments." Fiery lights sprang into the depths of that blue gaze, as Stefan held her close. "It was the memory of the moments we shared that brought me back to England, and you." He reached to gently caress her cheek, mesmerized by the golden flames that flickered in the depths of her dark gaze. He saw anger, but he also saw something he had never known her to possess. He saw fear in the wide depths of her eyes. Something, or someone, had frightened her very badly, and her fear tore at his heart. He ignored her feeble protests, pulling her closer as he brushed her hand aside. Tenderly Stefan's lips lowered over hers, claiming her as he had that day, so many months before. In spite of her anger, he felt her sweet response, faint at first, and then stronger, as he invaded the sweet softness of her lips, releasing within her all the emotions of the last weeks that she had kept tightly controlled.

Jenna's hands were flattened against the firm, hard expanse of Stefan's chest as she tried to push him away. His warmth invaded her soul. Jenna reached up to draw him closer, yielding to the ravening hunger that ached within her, her small hands twisting in the silk of his shirt, binding him to her. All her doubts and fears dissolved under the assault of Stefan's lips against hers, searing, bruising, demanding as he sought the truth of her own

369

desire. Jenna sighed shakily as his lips left hers and traced a path across her bare shoulder, while he pressed her back against the seat.

"No," Jenna protested unconvincingly, vaguely aware that the coach had stopped. Indeed, it seemed as if everything about them stood still as they crossed the barriers of doubt and fear.

Stefan pressed Jenna back into the depths of the cushioned seat, his desire overruling all caution as he reached to push down the silk-capped sleeve of her gown, revealing the gleaming fullness of her breast. Her skin gleamed softly in the golden light from the lantern and seemed to beckon his touch.

Jenna's breath stilled in her throat as she felt the exquisite torture of Stefan's lips against her breast. She moaned softly as her fingers stroked through the golden waves of his hair, binding him to her with a growing need she had convinced herself no longer existed. It existed within the very depths of her soul. It mattered not that they took great risk of being discovered. All that mattered was the feel of Stefan's hand upon her skin, his warmth lighting a fire within her that threatened to consume them both. Jenna's eyes closed in silent wonder at the light stroking of his fingers along her thigh, up the curve of her hip, his hands seeking the warmth of her bare skin beneath the gown. Her heart seemed to still as Stefan gently caressed the firm hardness of her stomach, his hand slipping beneath her hips as he drew her beneath him. Fearing the words he might say, Jenna reached out to Stefan with growing urgency, her hands hungrily seeking to free him from the restraints of waistcoat and breeches. Feverishly, she stroked her hands beneath the soft cotton of his shirt, feeling the magnificent heat of the skin across his back beneath her fingers. A deep aching rose within her, a haunting emptiness that demanded fulfillment. Silence surrounded them as Stefan sought the warmth of her young body. Each delicate curve was renewed within his memory as he built a fiery passion within her. It was as if their weeks apart had redefined their need of each other, so that each stroke, each caress brought new discovery of pleasure.

Stefan pressed Jenna deeper into the velvet softness of the cushions, moving slowly against her, luxuriating in the joining of their bodies as the fiery heat spread through them like quicksilver invading all the secret places of their beings. Stefan's hands closed over the ripe fullness of her breasts, gently kneading, caressing, his arms entwining to pull her more fully into him. His lips sought the taut peak, closing over it tenderly. He felt the growing urgency deep within Jenna as she met each thrust equally, demanding pleasure as she gave it. Almost imperceptibly, Stefan felt the release beginning within her. He reached up, his hands, closing over hers, their fingers entwining, as a cry escaped her lips, only to be silenced beneath his. Fiercely he bound her to him, as the fire seared through her and reached to consume him.

Jenna shivered faintly, and Stefan reached to pull a lap robe high over her bare shoulders as she snuggled deeper into his embrace. He tenderly kissed the fragrant softness of her hair, which tumbled loosely about her shoulders. Jenna sighed heavily, her lips brushing against the smooth, bronze surface of the skin across his shoulder. Stefan reached to tilt her head back so that he could gaze into the wide, dark depths of her eyes.

"How could you think I would not return? You are mine. It is a promise I gave you from the beginning."

"To some people, promises are not meant to be kept," Jenna murmured softly.

Stefan chuckled at her foolishness. "Ah yes, I break so many promises that I leave Dmitri to watch over you in my absence."

Jenna pulled back from Stefan in sudden surprise. "But that is impossible. These last weeks, Dmitri has hardly been around. It seems he is always called away on some matter of importance. This very evening he . . ."

Stefan silenced Jenna with a gentle kiss. "Though Dmitri might not always be visible, you must believe he has always been near. This very evening, he left to bring me an important message from John Whitmore before he returned to make certain you came to no harm from Charles Wingate."

Jenna laughed softly, thinking he must be joking. It would be impossible for Dmitri to steal among the shadows at Wingate Hall to watch her. His size alone made such a feat unthinkable. Jenna stared at Stefan, realizing he was quite serious.

"My little princess, these many weeks since I left England Dmitri has been your silent companion. His sole responsibility was your safety. I knew I could trust no other. I also knew of your plan to aid Elizabeth Wingate." Stefan reached up to tap lightly on the roof of the coach. Mr. Flint immediately drew the team to a halt. Stefan retrieved his hat and the black silk mask he had worn as he reached for the door handle.

"Must you go? Return to Hallston House with me. You will be safe there. No one will suspect." Jenna pulled the blanket close about her shoulders as the cool night air rushed through the opened door. Stefan turned back briefly. He reached to caress the softness of her cheek as his lips brushed hers in farewell. Beyond the stand of trees that lined Grovesnor Square, Jenna could see a mounted horseman waiting, a second, riderless horse carefully secured.

"In the morning, send Mr. Flint with the coach for Elizabeth, as planned. He will see her safely to Liverpool. Remain at Hallston House. Do not leave for any reason. It will be several hours before Charles realizes what has happened. By then, I feel certain his fellow conspirator, Sir Robert Ludlow, can be convinced to give me the information I seek. By this time tomorrow the conspiracy will be broken, and Charles Wingate will pay for his crimes against the Crown." Stefan closed the door carefully and nodded silently to Mr. Flint, atop the coach.

Jenna reached out her slender hand, briefly feeling the strength of Stefan's fingers before their grasp was broken. Mr. Flint urged the team of horses beyond Grovesnor Square, to Hallston House. Jenna watched as the shadows

372

of the trees closed about the riders until they were hidden by darkness. She released the shade at the window, settling back into the depths of the seat. She could still feel the warmth of Stefan's touch upon her skin, but it was not enough to hold back the terrible foreboding that closed about her heart.

Chapter Twenty

Jenna scrawled the hastily written message and thrust it into Mr. Flint's hand. She had given instructions that he deliver the message to Elizabeth Wingate when he called for her later that morning. Jenna prayed Elizabeth would accept the letter without question. For the first hour after Mr. Flint had gone, Jenna paced the floor of her chamber nervously. When the faithful servant failed to return after two hours, Jenna grew confident that Elizabeth was safely on her way to Liverpool, and John Whitmore.

Jenna occupied the remainder of the morning in the gardens. The only task that seemed to calm her nerves was tending the flowers and plants that had sprung forth with the warming days of late April and now grew in abundance. The day was quite advanced when she heard Maggie calling from the main house. She continued cutting the yellow daffodils and crocus that would adorn the drawing room. She heard Maggie calling again as she reached to brush aside a stray tendril of dark hair that tickled against her cheek beneath the wide straw hat that protected her from the warming sun. She looked up as Maggie's voice came louder and more urgent. She pocketed the small clipping shears in the muslin apron she always wore when gardening and straightened as Maggie finally reached her.

"It's the most dreadful thing. You must come quickly," Maggie announced breathlessly.

Jenna's heart leaped into her throat. "What is it? What has happened? Has Emma returned from market?" she asked anxiously. Whatever the latest news was in London, it traveled quickest among the servants of the nobility. There was no better or more accurate source of information. Jenna quickly headed toward the side entrance of the large house, with Maggie struggling to match her strides.

Tossing aside the wide-brimmed straw hat in the kitchen, Jenna found Emma Kelly brewing a pot of fresh tea.

"You were certainly gone long enough. What kept you so long?"

Emma Kelly whirled about with a start. She clenched her small, rounded hands together to calm her shaking, pressing them over her heart. Seeing the maid was quite distraught, Jenna brushed aside her shaking hands and poured her a cup of the calming brew, fearing the china might not survive if she allowed Emma to pour her own. Jenna had long since learned that when greatly distressed over some matter, Emma sought comfort first in a steaming cup of tea. Jenna quickly lost her patience as a multitude of thoughts raced across her mind, though she realized it was quite futile to press Emma for information before the woman had calmed sufficiently. When greatly excited or nervous, it was not uncommon for Emma to lapse into an unintelligible mixture of English and Gaelic, and Jenna had never learned much of the latter. Gently she reached to pat Emma's hands reassuringly, wishing she might have truly felt so confident. She could not rid herself of a sudden uneasiness, after Stefan's parting words the night before.

"Emma, you must try to tell me what you have found out this morning." Jenna tried to keep her voice calm.

Emma stared at her with eyes suddenly filling with tears. "Oh mistress, it is most dreadful. Especsially after your poor, dear grandfather and all."

Jenna's patience was wearing desperately thin. She fought to control the uneasiness in her own voice. "What did you hear this morning?"

"'Tis Sir Robert Ludlow; oh dear, it is most horrible."
Emma sniffled into her handkerchief before sipping from
the cup of tea.

"Emma, if you do not tell me exactly what has
happened, this very moment, I swear I shall drag the words
from you," Jenna threatened.

"I heard it this morning from a young maid who's been
keeping company with a stableboy in Sir Robert's employ.
They found Sir Robert this morning, murdered at his
home in the country. Supposedly, several horsemen were
seen very near the house. One of the other maids was
supposed to have heard a terrible fight at the house. Sir
Robert was a friend of your grandfather's; they worked
together a great deal those last months before your
grandfather died. I simply cannot understand any of this.
And there is the rumor about also, that the duke of Kent
only narrowly escaped injury, or worse, when his coach
was attacked by riders, evening last, when returning to
Kensington Palace. I heard it said that Napoleon has
promised to take London in a fortnight. It is all quite
dreadful. Dear child, what can this all mean?" Emma
dabbed at her eyes with the corner of her handkerchief.

Emma continued mournfully from behind her handkerchief. "Sir Robert was a kind man and well liked. I
cannot imagine how this could have happened. And now
the authorities are determined to find the murderers. They
think there may be some connection with the attempt on
the duke of Kent. Oh dear, I shouldn't say anything more."
Emma blotted at her reddened eyes, realizing she had said
more than she had intended.

"There is more! What is it you aren't telling me?" Jenna
pressed, a sudden fear possessing her heart. "You must tell
me everything."

Emma stared at Jenna from behind the linen handkerchief. She reached to hold Jenna's slender hand in her
own, their roles now reversed as she sought to give her
mistress comfort. "I could not believe it when I heard it.
Not after knowing Prince Kalinsky, and seeing him with
you in this very house. And you carrying his babe. Dear

377

child, it breaks my heart to tell you of it," Emma sobbed.

"Tell me now, or I swear there will be more broken than just a heart," Jenna threatened earnestly.

"The lad saw the riders leaving. He is certain they spoke in Russian. He gave a description of a large man, and another riding a horse as black as night. Indeed, the boy was quite frightened. He was telling tales of the devil astride that horse, breathing fire and wailing like a banshee."

Jenna pulled her hand from Emma's grasp with sudden horror. "No, it is impossible. How could you so easily believe these superstitious tales. Surely, someone must be mistaken," Jenna cried out in sudden anguish as she remembered Stefan's words the night before. He had hoped to learn valuable information from Sir Robert. Indeed, he had said that if Sir Robert cooperated, the conspiracy might soon be broken. Had Sir Robert refused to cooperate and paid for his misguided loyalties with his life?

"I must find out what really happened. Where is Dmitri? He will give me the truth and not invented tales."

"I have been here all morning, little princess." A gruff voice startled the two women. Jenna turned to face the giant Cossack, who filled the doorway to the kitchen.

"Is this true, Dmitri?" Jenna whispered hoarsely with growing fear.

"Stefan will tell you about it when the danger has passed," Dmitri answered gruffly.

Jenna stared at the large man before her, not at all certain she wanted to know the truth. Yet, she was certain in her heart that Stefan would never have committed murder. He desperately needed the information Sir Robert had about the other conspirators, in order to expose their deadly scheme. It would have been foolish to kill the man. Jenna shuddered with a sudden cold dread as she realized there was only one person who might gain by Sir Robert's death. Especially if that person feared Sir Robert might be persuaded to reveal information about the conspiracy. Charles Wingate dared not risk anyone's connecting him

378

to the conspiracy. Jenna felt suddenly very weak at the thought that Charles Wingate might commit murder.

"Where is Stefan?" Jenna whispered.

Dmitri seized Jenna by the elbow, his strong arm firm about her waist as he saw her suddenly grow very pale.

"He has ridden for Dover this morning. He learned from Sir Robert that Charles Wingate planned to sail for France on the next tide. We have known for some time that he kept his ship at anchor there."

"What of the names of the other conspirators?" Jenna pressed anxiously.

"Sir Robert died without being able to give us any of the names."

Jenna shook her head as she gripped Dmitri's hand with an unnatural strength. "I will not believe that Stefan would do such a thing."

Dmitri patted her slender hand reassuringly with his large paw, roughened by years of hard riding and fighting.

"You need have no fear of it, little princess. We found Sir Robert in the stables, already very near death. He did not die by Stefan's hand. This I promise you."

Jenna stared at Dmitri, the dark depths of her amber eyes glowing with a sudden feverish light. "Was Charles the murderer?" she whispered shakily.

"Sir Robert was unable to name his murderer. Stefan found this in his hand. Sir Robert tried to defend himself, but he was struck from behind. Only a coward would wait in the shadows. A man would face his enemy evenly and accept the consequences of his challenge." Dmitri opened his hand to reveal a gold stick pin, used for decoration in the lapel of a waistcoat or to secure the cravat of a man's shirt.

Jenna reached for the pin and studied it carefully. It was ornately decorated with small rubies set all around a large diamond. She remembered it well, for Elizabeth Wingate had given it to her brother the previous Christmas. Charles greatly treasured the piece, though more for its monetary value than for any sentimental reason.

Dmitri watched her carefully, his dark eyes missing

nothing. She seemed to suddenly grow much paler.

"Do you know this pin?"

"Yes. I helped Elizabeth Wingate select it. It was a gift for Charles."

Dmitri swore under his breath in a mixture of French and Russian.

"There is much danger, little princess. If Charles Wingate is responsible for the death of Sir Robert, then it was to silence him. The jackal knows when the hunter closes in for the kill and can be a most dangerous adversary. In this final hour of the conspiracy, Charles Wingate is a dangerous and desperate man. I have made a vow to see to your safety. Now the risk is even greater. You must stay inside the house and never alone. Someone must be with you at all times, until Stefan has returned."

Jenna turned wistful eyes on the large Cossack, all her fears mirrored there.

"I do not fear for myself. But I fear for Stefan without your strength beside him."

Dmitri smiled encouragingly. "He rides with the finest Cossacks, all good men. They have been with him many years; since Varykein. I trained them all myself. They will not fail him." He spoke confidently.

Jenna smiled wistfully. "I pray you are right. Still, I would feel more at ease if I knew you were with him."

Dmitri chuckled, his voice rumbling like distant thunder in his broad chest. "I have ridden with Stefan Kalinsky many years. Always together, never separated. I remain here because he asked it. He would entrust no other to protect the little princess, and the son she carries."

Jenna's head snapped up, and she stared at Dmitri with stunned surprise. "But he could not possibly know of the babe. I said nothing to him. Unless . . ." She looked up at Dmitri with sudden certainty.

"How could he know, except that you told him," Jenna accused him with mounting suspicion.

Dmitri shook his great shaggy head. "I told him nothing. I would have told him only if he had been foolish enough to turn from you. He could easily have remained with the Czar in Vienna, but he risked returning. It was not the conspiracy that brought him back to England. He might easily have resumed his life as it was before. England is not his cause. You brought him back to England. As for the child, he knew after last night. These are not things that can remain a secret between a man and woman, eh, little princess?"

Jenna felt the rise of crimson warmth across her cheeks as Dmitri chuckled loudly and with good humor at his observation. She cast a wary eye toward Maggie lest the entire household soon know of her condition.

"I suppose you are quite right. Very soon, everyone will know of it. Already my shape has become quite well rounded. If not for the style of my gowns, all of London would know of it. At least I can thank Napoleon for one accomplishment—fashion."

"As I have said, my little princess, there is no shame in the child you carry," Dmitri reminded her gently. "He will be strong like his father. And I will teach him to ride like his Cossack grandfather. He will know his heritage and always be proud."

Jenna sighed as she smoothed her hand over the slight roundness of her stomach, as if to reassure the child that rested there. "But will his father be proud, Dmitri, or will he turn from the child he has made, because it is a bastard?"

"The child will be no bastard, little princess. You have my word on this. But for now, you will rest, and soon this danger will pass. Stefan will be successful. He will find Charles Wingate."

Jenna smiled at Dmitri affectionately as she turned to leave the kitchen. "Stefan must accept his child because it is what he wants, not because it is his obligation."

Dmitri smiled as he watched her disappear down the hallway toward the stairway. He knew well what Stefan Kalinsky wanted. He had known it from the first moment, when they had found the granddaughter of Sir Avery Randolph in that coach so many months before.

Jenna pushed the luncheon tray aside, having barely

picked over the ample meal Maggie had brought her. She was far too uneasy to eat. Weary from a sleepless night, Jenna curled beneath the downy comforter spread across her large, postered bed. It seemed she had dozed only a few minutes before she was startled from sleep.

Jenna sat up sleepily, wondering what had awakened her. She heard it again; a loud crashing sound from downstairs. Her thoughts were suddenly filled with another time she had awakened from sleep, to find her grandfather's library engulfed in flames. A sudden uneasiness seized her as she became more alert. Pushing the heavy comforter aside, she opened the door to her chamber and started down the carpeted hallway toward the stairway. She halted abruptly as she heard the sounds of heavy footfalls on the carpeted stairs.

"Dmitri?" Jenna called uncertainly. When there was no answer, she backed away, a tingling of fear creeping down her back. The heavy footsteps increased, becoming louder as someone mounted the stairs with great urgency. Unable fully to comprehend the warning that flared in her brain, Jenna whirled about and fled into her chamber. She closed the door quietly behind her, quickly sliding the bolt into place as someone approached from the stairway. She drew back from the door fearfully as she heard someone searching each of the chambers down the long hallway. Each door was opened and then slammed shut. She quickly realized Dmitri would have had no need for such measures. He knew very well which chamber was hers.

Jenna's heart raced wildly as she turned and quickly crossed the room to the window. From the hallway beyond she could hear the sound of doors being opened and then slammed shut as the intruder searched each chamber. She turned back to the large bed, realizing that very soon the intruder would try to search her room. She had once escaped a burning house through a window with a rope made of bed linens—she might escape that same way once more. Jenna reached for the heavy satin coverlet just as she heard the rattling of the doorknob to her chamber. She backed away fearfully as she realized there was no more time for escape.

Jenna cringed as the door to her chamber held briefly under the force of the first blow and then splintered with the next one, swinging wide. Charles Wingate stood in the doorway like some demon, his face contorted with anger and rage.

"Dear Jenna. So beautiful, so foolish. Did you really believe I would not learn of your and Elizabeth's plan? All these months, while the two of you appeared to be making plans for her marriage to Sir Guilford, you were planning her escape with John Whitmore."

Charles advanced into the chamber, a pistol clenched in his right hand. His hair was tossed wildly, and an ugly bruise spread across his cheek. The wound was fresh, and Jenna backed toward the windows instinctively as she realized Dmitri had undoubtedly tried to stop him. A cry rose in her throat at the thought of Dmitri's fate. The huge Russian had warned her that Charles Wingate was a most dangerous enemy.

Charles moved toward her slowly, realizing there was no escape for her. He moved with the quiet confidence of the wolf who has finally run its prey aground. With her back to the window, Jenna was soundly trapped. Charles reached out, seizing her wrist with painful brutality.

Jenna winced as she tried to twist free of his grasp. She felt as if her bones were being crushed as his fingers closed about her wrist like a band of steel. Her thoughts were full of fear for Elizabeth as she realized there was no doubt that Charles had discovered their plan.

"Where is Elizabeth? What have you done?" she cried out in pain.

"Elizabeth is home, where she will remain until her marriage can take place as planned. I think Elizabeth has now learned the price to be paid for her deceitfulness. Now *you* must learn the price, my lovely Jenna." Charles laid the pistol aside on a nearby table.

Seeing her advantage, Jenna momentarily twisted free of his grasp and fled in the direction of the doorway. Charles was upon her in an instant, seizing her from behind as his hand closed over the soft muslin of her gown. The fabric separated with a rending tear as Jenna lunged away from him, falling heavily against the dressing table, its contents crashing to the floor as she struggled to maintain her balance. She gasped as she felt the coolness of air against the bare skin across her back. Her brief moment of surprise was her doom. Charles closed in with lightning swiftness, seizing her arm, whirling her about and pinning her against the wall beside the doorway that a moment before had offered her freedom.

His hands firm about each slender wrist, Charles pinned them behind her back as he leaned heavily against her, the full line of his body pressed against her intimately.

"Lovely Jenna, always elusive, always the proper lady. Your grandfather refused to allow our betrothal. When he could no longer object, you gave your weak excuses of mourning his death, until I forced you to accept the betrothal. But there was another reason you refused me. Do you think I did not know of your flirtation with Stefan Kalinsky? How long did you think it would be before the whispered rumors would reach me? Lillian de Stahl made certain I knew of them. She is to be congratulated for being a woman of many resources. Her only cause is herself, and that made her a worthy ally."

Jenna turned back to stare at Charles. Stefan had been so certain in his trust of the courtesan. Could it be that Charles was telling the truth, that Lillian de Stahl had provided just enough information to thwart Stefan's efforts to expose the conspiracy? The unnatural light in Charles's pale eyes warned her of the danger she was in. Charles was capable of uncontrollable anger. Indeed, she had seen the results of such anger before. She shuddered as she tried to twist her head away from his nearness. She easily realized that Charles's anger seemed to feed on fear. Her only hope was to show him no fear.

"Charles, you are hurting me. Please release me at once." Jenna spoke with a calmness that belied the wild racing of her heart. She returned his gaze boldly.

"Lovely Jenna, do you think me a complete fool? Do

you think I do not know that you would run immediately to your lover and tell him of this? He would then have everything he needed to expose the conspiracy." Charles leaned intimately against Jenna, his knee pressing boldly between her thighs.

Jenna fought back a wave of revulsion at his movement against her, refusing to surrender to the fear that threatened to reduce her to hysterical tears.

"Your lover cannot save you now, my lovely Jenna. He has followed a fool's errand on some wild rumor to Dover. He will find an empty cove, and dead men can tell him nothing." Charles breathed against the bare skin of her shoulder as the gown gaped away, exposing the rounded fullness of her breast beneath the sheer silk of her chemise.

Jenna fought to remain calm as she pulled away from the touch of his lips across her shoulder, as if she had been burned by something evil. "You are wrong, Charles. Do not do this. I but sought to help Elizabeth find some happiness. She would never have been happy in a loveless, arranged marriage." Jenna tried to reason with Charles. His demented thoughts refused to hear her words.

"How many times did you welcome him to your bed? How many times did you give him willingly what you always denied me?" Charles accused her through the fog of his madness, his hands reaching to caress the bare skin of her breast.

"Charles, no!" Jenna's cry of desperation was torn from her throat as Charles seized her about the waist and pulled her across the room, shoving her roughly down onto the postered bed. Her scream of terror was oddly muffled against his shoulder as he lay across her, his hands tearing at her gown. The voice that responded was the voice of some crazed animal, and Jenna struggled with the last of her strength.

"You shall give me what you gave him so willingly. You were promised to me. By God, you will not deny me now!"

"Charles, no! I carry his child." Jenna cried out with a sob as she desperately tried to push him away. It was a full, long moment before she realized that Charles lay still across her.

Charles moved away from her as if he had been jerked from behind. He stood staring at her, that look of crazed madness giving way to bitterness. His face was contorted with hatred as he glared down at her.

"How fitting; a bastard for the bastard." He smirked viciously.

Jenna crawled backwards away from him across the bed, trying to hold the shreds of her gown together across her breasts.

"He leaves his mark on you with his bastard child, and now he returns to England to destroy me. He will not succeed. Even now it is too late. Already the final steps are being taken to insure the success of the conspiracy. The attempt on the life of the duke of Kent was merely a ruse to divert the attention away from the regent. By the time Prince Kalinsky and his men discover their mistake, it will be too late. He cannot save England now, and by God, he will not save you!" Charles screamed, turning toward the doorway as more footsteps could be heard from the hallway.

"Fix your gown, Lady Randolph," Charles hissed maliciously. "We leave now, and you will be leaving with us. I think it a perfect final touch to my victory over Prince Kalinsky." Charles turned and disappeared through the shattered doorway.

Beyond the destroyed portal Jenna could hear the sounds of voices, and then Charles retreating down the hallway. A young man appeared in the doorway, her guard, to prevent any attempt at escape. Jenna scrambled off the bed to the far side of the chamber, realizing her only hope now was to gain time. She quickly searched through the armoire for another gown. Her fingers trembled as she removed the tattered remnants of the muslin gown and quickly donned a modest silk one with a high neckline that gathered with a velvet tie about her neck. She realized that a more daring cut would only encourage Charles. She shuddered at the thought of his hands upon her and choked back a sob of misery.

At the sound of Charles shouting orders below, Jenna quickly finished dressing. She pulled the pins from her long hair, releasing the disheveled mass into a long cascade. There was no time for more than a ribbon to bind it back. Jenna searched among the scattered contents of the dressing table for a ribbon, finding one beneath the shattered glass of the gold music box her grandfather had given her. Jenna picked up the box, which suddenly tinkled a melody from the movement. Tears filled her eyes as she noticed that the tune was oddly changed, the mechanism inside the box apparently damaged from its fall. Jenna shook out the last shards of splintered glass that had once protected the inside of the box. A small piece of paper fell to the floor at her feet. Jenna picked up the small piece of paper and unfolded it. She stared in disbelief at the small, perfect lettering on the paper. The strokes of the pen were unmistakable. The last time she had seen that same lettering was in a brief letter her grandfather had sent her the summer before. From beyond the grave her grandfather had sought to insure that the conspiracy would never succeed. Somehow knowing he might not live to prevent it, he had secreted the names of the conspirators on that small slip of paper inside the music box. So simple, and yet so clever. Jenna read each of the names again, recoiling in horror as she recognized each one, all either prominent members of Parliament or titled lords of the peerage. Each man possessed enough power that together they could easily insure the continuation of the government after having disposed of the regent. Jenna was startled back to reality at the sound of Charles's voice from the landing at the top of the stairway, issuing his final orders. Her life would be worthless if Charles suspected her capable of identifying the conspirators. Jenna glanced about the room quickly, her gaze resting on the hearth where a few live embers still glowed from fire Maggie had built late that morning. Jenna quickly thrust the paper into the hearth. She watched as the edges of the paper darkened, a tiny trail of smoke rising as the embers found the meager fuel. Jenna turned abruptly as Charles entered the chamber.

"Come along, my beautiful prisoner. Now you will see the price to be paid for betrayal," Charles threatened cruelly as he seized Jenna by the arm and guided her out the door to the stairway. She cast one last look over her shoulder to see the paper burst into momentary flame, which died away as it was consumed.

Jenna stumbled as she tried to keep up with Charles. He brought her up sharply, his steely fingers bruising the softness of her flesh beneath the fabric of her gown. They halted at the foot of the stairway. Jenna stared in mute horror at the sight of Dmitri's crumpled form at her feet. A long gash bled profusely at the back of his head, and his spotless white tunic was covered with crimson from an indiscernible injury. Jenna cried out as she pulled free of Charles's relaxed grasp and knelt beside the fallen Cossack. She seized his giant hand and gently stroked the shaggy mane of hair from his eyes, fearful of the deathly pallor he wore.

"We have no time for this," Charles growled impatiently, as he again seized Jenna by the arm.

Before he could pull her away, Jenna leaned forward and whispered a desperate last message that she could not be certain Dmitri could hear. Time allowed her only to give him one of the names from the message, hoping he might live to give the message to Stefan. Jenna was roughly hauled to her feet. Across the foyer she found Maggie, carefully attending Emma Kelly. A dark, ugly bruise swelled across the maid's cheek. Emma warned her to silence and glanced away. Jenna could easily see that any protest she might make would only bring greater danger to those who remained behind. Charles's hand firmly at her back, Jenna was pushed out through the front door of the house and into a waiting coach. Charles had cleverly chosen to use the coach she had sent for Elizabeth. She grimly wondered what Mr. Flint had suffered at the hands of Charles and his conspirators, if indeed he had survived. Jenna sought a solitary corner of the darkened coach, and Charles settled into the seat across from her. There would be no chance for escape as long as he remained watchful. And Jenna knew she must somehow escape. Charles was completely mad. It would be futile to try and reason with him. The babe she carried had given her a momentary reprieve. So great, so unreasoning was Charles Wingate's hatred of Stefan, that she held no doubt that the child would also seal their fate. Jenna folded her arms across the roundness of the child that grew within her. As long as she lived, she would fight to give her child life. As long as she lived.

Stefan Kalinsky led a murderous pace as he returned to London. He had foolishly believed that Charles would leave for France from Dover. Instead of the yacht moored within the cove as John Whitmore had informed him it would be, they found two of John Whitmore's men cruelly murdered as they had stood watch at the mouth of the cove. Stefan had no doubt that they had died as Sir Robert Ludlow had died, struck from behind. He found it difficult to believe that Charles had sailed for France without attempting to take Jenna, and indeed even as he thought it, Stefan knew that Charles Wingate had no intention of leaving England without Jenna. Something had caused Charles to alter his plans; perhaps the two men he had found watching the yacht. Stefan would never be certain. His only certainty was that the jackal was about to slip through his fingers, and with a prize Stefan valued more than life itself.

The black stallion labored beneath him to cover the distance to London before first light. Alexei and the remainder of his men struggled to keep pace. It seemed, indeed, as if the devil rode at Stefan's heels, taunting him, tormenting him with his fears for Jenna's life. He knew Charles Wingate's cruelty, and he also knew Jenna would never submit to him. She would die before she allowed it to happen.

Stefan was not surprised at the lights that glowed like a

beckoning beacon through the last darkness of night before the dawn as he approached Hallston House. Not bothering to secure the black stallion, who stood lathered with sides heaving, Stefan gained the front steps two at a time, charging through the door to meet a formidable Mr. Flint, pistol aimed in one hand, a small cutlass in the other, and a deadly gleam in his eyes.

"In the name of God, put that down," Stefan ordered as he quickly searched the main rooms of the house.

"Where is Dmitri?" Stefan asked briskly.

"Dmitri is upstairs. He has lost much blood, but not before he delivered several good blows. Emma is certain he will recover. Had he not feared for Lady Randolph's life he might have stopped them," Flint answered.

"Where is Jenna?" Stefan turned on the older man, already knowing the answer.

"Charles Wingate and his men descended on this house like demons from hell. He suspected something was wrong when I called for Miss Elizabeth this morning. His men caught up with us on the road outside London bound for Liverpool. There were at least eight of them, but I managed to take two of them with me. They seized the coach. I finally managed to find a horse and return here. By that time Sir Charles had already been here. Dmitri put up a good fight, but there were too many of them. They fight a good game when the numbers are in their favor. They run like scared dogs when the numbers are more even. Had I been here, I doubt they would have been able to take her," Mr. Flint added soberly.

"Had you been here, my friend, I have no doubt you would have paid with your life for your bravery. I have a greater need of you now," Stefan comforted the loyal servant.

"Wherever you must go, I will ride with you. I owe a great debt to Sir Avery from many years past. I'll gladly repay it by saving his granddaughter."

Stefan nodded grimly. "I fear, my friend, that Charles Wingate and his men have already left England."

"You are quite right, Stefan. I have word that his yacht

was seen just beyond Southend. She set sail at sunset and struck a southerly course."

Stefan turned about as John Whitmore slowly descended the wide stairway, his height dwarfed by Dmitri who leaned on his shoulder heavily. Stefan quickly crossed the foyer to give assistance as they led Dmitri to a large chaise in the drawing room. Emma Kelly followed quickly behind, fussing over the large Russian as if he were a child with a bruised knee.

"You were supposed to be well on your way to Liverpool." Stefan nodded to John Whitmore.

"I would have been had I not chosen to await Jenna's coach and accompany Elizabeth myself. When the coach was delayed I became concerned. I doubled back along the postroad from London. It was I who found Mr. Flint. We rode back here together."

"What of Elizabeth?" Stefan asked, his face lined with concern.

John Whitmore smiled conspiratorially. "Evidently, Charles assumed I had already left London. He arranged for Sir Reginald Guilford to stand guard over Elizabeth. The old fool was hardly a good match for Mr. Flint and myself. I have had Elizabeth taken to an inn, where she is well protected by two of my men, until my return."

"And what of Lord Wingate?"

John Whitmore sighed heavily. "I fear Lord Wingate is dead. I found him in his room at Wingate Hall. He had been badly beaten. Elizabeth is unaware of it, and Sir Reginald claims complete ignorance. From what I was able to learn from a maid we found hiding in the kitchen, Charles and Lord Wingate had quarreled violently. I will tell Elizabeth of it later, when she has had time to recover from all of this."

"It would seem Charles Wingate has a great deal of blood on his hands," Stefan observed grimly.

Dmitri grumbled his discomfort. "We must go after them. The little princess is in great danger. They are bound for France. I heard them speaking when they thought I could no longer hear them. Indeed, I think they thought me dead." Dmitri winced as Emma leaned over him, pressing against the thick bandage at the back of his head to make certain it was secure.

"Where were they headed, my friend? Did you hear anything else that might tell you their destination? Was it Calais? It is the quickest route to France." Stefan pressed Dmitri for an answer, realizing well that each moment they delayed might well mean the difference between life or death for Jenna.

Dmitri shook his great, shaggy head, wincing again. The movement caused him no small amount of pain. It seemed as if a score of demons were doing battle within his head.

"I think it was not Calais. One man with a French accent spoke of others who would be waiting at Deauville." Dmitri brushed Emma Kelly's hand aside as if it were a bothersome insect. When she persisted in checking the bandages, fearful he might have started the bleeding again, he grumbled at her fiercely.

"Cease, woman!" Dmitri roared, sending the demons colliding once more within his great head. "Cease, or I swear by all the saints I shall thrash you until you cannot move," he swore heartily. Emma backed a safe distance away, but kept a watchful eye on the unpredictable Russian, thinking that he indeed greatly resembled a great, grumbling bear.

"Is it possible they would take such a route? There are others that would land them in France much more quickly." Stefan looked up at John Whitmore.

John Whitmore nodded his agreement. "That would explain their southerly course. They have chosen a less obvious route, with less risk of encountering an English man o' war. They will probably follow the English coastline, under an English flag, until they have passed through the Strait of Dover. None will suspect what they are about. When they are well beyond Portsmouth, they will probably come about and take advantage of the tide and favorable winds for a quick run across the Channel. Deauville is less obvious, and therefore more desirable.

There, Charles Wingate can await the completion of the conspiracy. When the regent and the family have been eliminated, he will merely await his rewards in safe seclusion and then return to London to collect the spoils of war," John Whitmore concluded, an edge of bitterness in his voice.

Stefan stood before his trusted friend of many years. He affectionately seized Dmitri by the shoulders, taking great care not to cause him more pain.

"What of Jenna?" Stefan whispered, the strain in his voice obvious as he fought to control the feeling of dread that had possessed him. The depths of his blue eyes glistened dangerously, and the muscle in his jaw tightened perceptibly.

Dmitri reached his great pawlike hand to seize Stefan's with an affection and understanding born of a lifetime together.

"She was unharmed when they left. The little princess is brave. She will try to escape. I know this." Dmitri spoke with great effort.

"I fear you are right, my friend. And it may mean her death," Stefan answered hoarsely.

"She is without fear. In parting, when the others were certain I could bring them no harm, she gave me a message."

Stefan's gaze locked with Dmitri's. "What message? Can you remember what she said?"

"It means nothing to me. It was a name. She said you must find a man called Worthington." Dmitri looked at Stefan for some sign that the message held some significance.

Indeed, the message held a vague meaning. Stefan looked to John Whitmore for confirmation.

"Lord Harold Worthington is one of the leaders of the Whig party. He has aligned himself with the prince regent, but is openly outspoken against the monarchy. It is no secret that Lord Worthington has enjoyed a certain camaraderie among Charles Wingate's inner circle of friends. It is rumored, with strong foundation, that he has manipulated the prince regent against the old king on several occasions. Worthington would be a dangerous adversary if he chose to be part of the conspiracy."

As if he had suddenly made a grave decision, Stefan looked to John Whitmore. "I will have need of a fast ship, and an able crew."

John Whitmore nodded. "The *Celeste* lies at anchor at Portsmouth. She's the fastest and finest ship in my fleet." He winked at the secret he shared with Stefan Kalinsky. "I am certain the 'new owner' will have no objections to your use of her. She stands manned and ready to sail. I know the crew well. They are the finest to be found, and loyal to the last man."

"Thank you, John."

"There is no need to thank me yet, until we are successful."

Stefan shook his head firmly. "Not this time. I will take Mr. Flint, Alexei, and the remainder of my men. You must make certain that the duke of Kent knows of Lord Worthington's involvement. Jenna risked much to give us the message. We must see the matter taken care of. And I would not wish to face Elizabeth Wingate to explain that I have allowed you to sail off with me on this dangerous journey. She is a formidable lady. I now understand her friendship with Jenna. It is a trait they share."

John Whitmore nodded regretfully. "God speed, Stefan, and good journey."

Stefan turned to Mr. Flint. "We must have fresh horses for the trip to Portsmouth. We ride immediately."

Dmitri struggled out of the chaise and approached Stefan with careful steps. "I will not remain here with these women, while my little princess is in danger. I ride with you."

"It is madness. Your highness, you cannot allow it. It will mean his death." Emma Kelly had drawn herself up to her meager height and crossed the room with quick, bold strides, as if she fully intended to stop Dmitri herself.

Stefan looked from the determined housekeeper to his

injured friend. He quickly dismissed Emma's hearty objections.

"I fear it would be a graver injury to deny him revenge. He cares for Jenna almost as much as I."

Dmitri sighed his gratitude that it was not necessary for him to do battle to have his way. His thirst for revenge against Charles Wingate and his men was stronger than the pain that threatened to separate his head from his shoulders. As long as there was breath in his great body, he would travel the ends of the earth to make certain the little princess was safe. It was a vow that came from his heart.

Chapter Twenty-One

Jenna tossed the bowl of watery, grayish gruel out the porthole of the small cabin she had occupied for the last two days. It went the way each previous bowlful had gone, momentarily confusing the gulls that followed the ship, until it disappeared in the frothy foam that formed a gurgling trail behind the sleek schooner. Even those scavengers of the sea thought better than to sample the fare served aboard the ship. For a moment Jenna luxuriated in the damp coolness of the sea spray that seemed to clear her senses. She watched the coastline, as she had watched it the day before as the white cliffs of Dover slipped past them with amazing swiftness. She remembered the stark beauty of Dover from a childhood visit there with her grand-father. Their amazing height seemed to rise straight out of the sea, like a sudden point of safety in that wide expanse of blue ocean. With great effort, Jenna reached with her bound hands to close the porthole as she felt a sudden shifting in the ship. She watched as the coastline of England disappeared from view, replaced by the vast emptiness of the sea. At last she knew Charles's course: the coast of France. Jenna leaned heavily against the edge of the small bed, her fears engulfing her as the schooner came about, heeling into a strong crosswind that quickly filled the sails and sent them swiftly across the English Channel.

Hunger gnawed at Jenna, as she eyed the thick slice of bread that had been brought with the gruel. She trusted the cook aboard the schooner no more than she trusted Charles Wingate. But her fears that Charles might have put something in her food had passed quickly. If he intended to kill her by poisoning, he would have done it already. And though something might easily be disguised in the vile-looking mixture she had thrown out, hiding something in a piece of bread was quite another matter. Jenna quickly downed the crust of bread, paying little heed to its stale, dried condition, as it helped ease the aching hunger within her. She drank sparingly of the water, having made one concession to Charles's generosity aboard ship. She might live for a while without food, but water was quite another matter. Jenna drew back suddenly as she heard the rattling of the heavy key in the lock at her door. She followed obediently as the guard escorted her topside onto the heaving deck. The salty sea spray blew across the deck, and Jenna reached for a more secure hold as she squinted into the midday sun. Each day she had been allowed a small amount of freedom from her prison below decks, always under the watchful eye of Charles Wingate. Though her cabin was small and cramped, her hands tightly bound until they bled, and her moments of necessary privacy few, Charles had not pressed his cause with her further. Indeed, except for their brief moments together on the deck of the schooner, Charles had remained quietly aloof. It was his quiet manner that frightened her more than any of his rages. In anger, Charles could be intimidating, but the secrets he hid behind his cold, gray eyes were more frightening than she dared admit. With his stony silences she could never be certain of his thoughts or his schemes.

Jenna leaned far over the carved wood railing at the bow of the schooner. Again, as on several occasions over the last two days, she wondered at the chances of reaching shore. She readily admitted to herself that though she was a strong swimmer, the distance was forbidding. It would merely be a matter of choosing a quicker death by drowning than awaiting Charles's plans for her. As if he perhaps feared she might choose that fate, Charles's hand closed about her arm with numbing pain, as if to remind her of his superiority.

Jenna turned on him, the crisp breeze from the ocean lifting the sable-colored streamers of her long hair like banners in a brilliant blue sky. She could not know of the pain that twisted within Charles as he gazed upon her exquisite beauty knowing with sudden clarity that he could never hope to possess her. Jenna's amber gaze met his defiantly as she started to move past him. His hands locked about her arms, halting her flight below deck. He reached out to stroke the satin softness of her cheek, brightly hued from the cold sea air. Jenna jerked away from his touch, intense hatred burning like a live flame in the depths of her dark eyes.

His anger rising at her bold defiance, when she was no more than a prisoner and completely at his mercy, Charles drew her to him, his arms locking her in an unbreakable embrace. Brutally, his lips crushed against hers as he sought to prove his power over her. Instead of fiery defiance, Charles received only cool indifference as Jenna stood impassively locked in his unyielding embrace. He would gladly have met her anger, but her coolness only infuriated him. Charles buried his hand in the long mane of her dark hair, twisting it about his fist until he held her securely. Cruelly he pulled, bending her back over his arm until she was forced to meet his gaze. Again, he saw only her indifference as she seemed to gaze past him at some distant point. Roughly Charles shoved her from him, ordering the crewman to take her back to her cabin.

Jenna went down badly on the hard deck, bruising her knee. Defiantly, she refused the crewman's assistance as he rushed forward to give her aid. She cast Charles one last look as the crewman escorted her below deck once more. The seaman shuddered at the look of death he saw in that dark gaze.

Once more within the relative safety of her cabin, Jenna examined her bruised knee. The pain hardly mattered. She sighed heavily as all her hatred and anger was quickly replaced by an overwhelming fear that Charles might well see her dead. Jenna's eyes closed with silent agony as she felt the strong movement of Stefan's child deep within her. She inhaled deeply as her resolve strengthened. Fear was her worst enemy. Charles hated weakness of any kind. It seemed to release an uncontrollable anger within him. Jenna fought back her tears as she examined the rope that had been bound around her wrists. Already ugly red welts had raised where the rope had chafed her skin. Jenna immediately knelt on the floor beside her small bed and resumed working the rope back and forth against the sharp corner of the wood bunk. She hardly felt the pain as the rope cut deeper into her soft skin.

That night Jenna slept fitfully, as the sleek schooner cut through a roughened sea. Mercifully, she was not bothered with nausea from the constant rising and falling of the ship. Finally dozing, just before dawn, she was abruptly awakened by the sound of something bumping against the side of the ship. A few moments later her guard had arrived to inform her they would soon be going ashore. Jenna rose quickly, splashing cold water against her face and raking her fingers through the length of her hair to remove the tangles. Once ashore, she might well find her opportunity for escape.

The dinghy rocked unsteadily as Jenna was assisted ashore by one of the crewmen. Charles had already gone on ahead to make arrangements for the last part of their journey. Jenna's gaze swept the buildings that lined the small coastal port for something that might tell her the name of the town. She was silently grateful her grandfather had adhered to the English custom of education in both English and French languages. She easily read the storefront signs that denoted a baker, an apothecary, and a fish merchant, who would have been known by the smell alone. The smell of the day's catch, glistening in the sun, accomplished quite nicely what a heaving ship had not managed in the last three days. Jenna paled as she was suddenly overcome with nausea. She reached to steady herself as she fought to control the sickness that threatened. She opened her eyes when she felt a gentle pressure against her arm.

"Mademoiselle? Are you feeling all right?"

Jenna opened her eyes to stare into the wide blue gaze of a boy who couldn't have been more than ten years of age. His face was smudged with dirt, his shirt torn, as well as his trousers, and his feet were bare. But there was an honest look of concern in his eyes, which peered at her from under the fringe of matted, unkempt hair. He spoke to her again in French, and Jenna sighed gratefully for a friendly face. She had not seen Charles returning down the dock.

In the next moment the boy was flattened to the dock by a crushing blow from Charles. The boy cried out, covering his head with his arms as he attempted to protect himself from the next blow.

"Charles, no! The boy meant no harm." Jenna cried out in anguish as she quickly knelt beside the boy to defend him. The young lad stared aghast at the ropes that bound her wrists and her raw and chafed skin. His gaze raised to hers, and his breath caught at the sight of her exquisite beauty. Certainly, she was the most beautiful woman he had ever seen. His heart melted as he gazed into the depths of her dark gaze, wishing there were some way he might help her. He pulled back with a yelp as the Englishman threatened another blow.

The English lady was roughly dragged to her feet and cruelly jerked down the length of the dock in the direction of the inn.

In the orphaned years of his youth, the nameless French boy had easily survived worse that a mere beating. He quickly scampered to his feet and followed the elegantly dressed gentleman with the cruel temper and the beautiful English lady. Though her French had been flawless, her outcry for his safety had been spoken in English. Since the war, it was uncommon to see an Englishman on French soil. Warily, the boy darted around the corner of the inn to a rear entrance, where he knew the innkeeper's daughter might offer a crust of bread and a little information about the unexpected guests. He had seen the ropes that were tightly bound about the beautiful lady's wrists and wanted

401

to know more of these people newly arrived from across the sea.

The *Celeste* cut easily through the heaving waves that tossed the English Channel, her wood decks gleaming in the midday sun. Every bit of sail had been furled aloft, snapping in the brisk May breeze and then billowing full and taut as the halyards were drawn tight by muscular crewmen accustomed to a fast run before the wind. Her skipper was a robust Spaniard who had spent the better part of his years far from the plains of his birth. The call of the sea had come early, and he had soon given his allegiance to the owner of the finest ships in the world. To some he might have seemed a pirate, a man with no country or loyalty, except to the magnificent ship that rolled beneath his feet. To Stefan Kalinsky he was a friend of long standing, a man whose life he had once saved, and who, in return, had made it possible for Stefan and his men to leave France years earlier when Napoleon had begun his bloody purge for power. Now they returned to France together.

Stefan Kalinsky gazed up the mast, the brilliant blue of the sky reflected in his gaze. He sought an elusive prey, one of great cunning and skill. His hand rested easily on the rapier fastened to his side as he grew restless with the length of their journey, anticipating the moment when he would again meet Charles Wingate.

As the sun slipped from the sky, on the second day, they made landfall. They lowered three small boats and slipped silently ashore. The golden lights of Deauville glistened in the night like so many watchful eyes. Darkness protected her secrets like a dark veil across the shoreline.

The first boat bumped gently against the dock, quickly followed by the second and third. Captain Villega and Dmitri remained with the boats, and Stefan went ashore. Disguised as a common seaman, he approached a nearby inn, the noise and the aroma of food promising easy conversation, with the aid of a good wine.

Stefan gazed across the small inn. A fire crackled at the hearth to drive away the damp, evening chill of the sea air. He ordered a bottle of the finest burgundy, in fluent French, from the young girl who approached with a tray and an inviting smile on her full lips. She sidled between Stefan's casually sprawled legs, rubbing intimately against his thigh. She knew all the men of the village, most of them intimately, but this one was a stranger. She silently mused about the number of strangers to visit their village over the last days. She returned with the wine, bending low across the table to place a goblet before Stefan, sending him an unmistakable invitation as her soft cotton blouse gaped away from the fullness of her young breasts, unencumbered beneath the thin fabric. Stefan laid out the necessary coin for the wine and another gold piece for the girl. She cast him a knowing smile as she set her tray aside, and then slipped her hand into his, pulling him from the chair toward the narrow stairway that led to the second-floor rooms. Stefan emptied the goblet of wine and then followed the young girl. Had his thoughts not been of a fairer, dark-haired beauty, he might have taken advantage of her youth and eagerness. He closed the door quietly and turned. In those few moments the girl had stripped away her simple garments and stood before him unadorned, except for her waving, auburn hair. Her smile promised him much. Stefan reached out to take her hand, carefully placing several more coins in the palm of her hand. She stared at him uncertainly.

"I do not understand. Most men are reluctant to pay before they have taken their pleasure." The girl spoke huskily as she regarded him, thinking that here was a man she might have lain with for nothing more than the pleasure to be found. She circled him carefully, admiring the lean, muscular line of his body beneath his garments. She slowly slipped her hand beneath his shirt, feeling the magnificent hardness of his chest and the taut muscles across his stomach.

Stefan gently seized the girl's wrists and pulled her around before him.

"I want information, mademoiselle. If you give me the right information, there is much more gold for you. Lie to me and I shall return to make certain you never tell your lies again." In one easy, fluid movement Stefan twisted her arms behind her back and drew her against him with quietly controlled strength. The fear in her eyes suddenly turned to glowing fire as she moved her body against him sensually, thoroughly enjoying his little game with her.

"You shall have your information, and anything else you wish. I do not ask for your gold," she breathed huskily against the fabric of his shirt, biting gently at his skin beneath the fabric.

Stefan folded the girl's fingers around the coins before turning to leave the room. She frowned at him disappointedly, and then smiled as she opened her hand to count the gold she had earned for little more than a few words. Stefan quickly descended the stairs, seizing the bottle of wine as he returned to the docks.

"What did you learn my friend?" Dmitri stepped from the shadows at the end of the dock, his hand firm on the deadly cutlass sheathed at his belt.

"There is a boy who may know something, a street urchin, an orphan. Finding him will be the hard part."

"Perhaps a boy dressed in rags, with scraggly hair and bright blue eyes?" Dmitri questioned. Stefan returned his gaze, as if he thought his friend suffered more than just a great bump on his head. Dmitri reached into the shadows, retrieving a struggling, clawing lad with torn clothes and sparkling blue eyes that rivaled Stefan's for color. Dmitri chuckled good-naturedly at the look of stunned surprise on Stefan's face.

"My friend. While you are asking questions, my men are also asking questions. The boy does not respond well to either Spanish or Russian." Dmitri chuckled with humor at his own jest.

Stefan gently seized the boy, who regarded him warily from behind the ragged mane of hair that shielded his gaze.

"What do you know of a ship that arrived here two days

ago, with an Englishman and lady?" Stefan questioned in flawless French. The boy remained silent as he contemplated the man who held him from behind the mane of thick hair that spilled across his forehead. When he received no answer, Stefan repeated his question.

"There are no English here. France is at war with England. No Englishman would be foolish enough to come here," the boy answered unconvincingly.

Stefan described Charles Wingate, and then he described Jenna. He noticed a sudden flickering of recognition. Stefan removed a small pouch of gold coins from his pocket and dangled it before the boy's eyes.

"What will you do to the lady when you find her?"

Stefan sighed heavily, not knowing if he might trust this orphan of the streets, yet realizing the boy was his only link to Jenna.

"The lady carries my child. She is being held prisoner. If I do not find her soon, she will die." Stefan spoke bluntly.

The young boy's eyes clouded as he remembered the beautiful young woman and the heavy ropes that cut into her skin. He brushed aside the small bag of gold. "She was kind to me even when she was bound with ropes that cut her painfully. If it means her freedom, I will gladly give you the information you seek. There were men waiting for them at the inn. One man had too much wine, and he spoke freely of the Abbey at Mont St. Michel; that all was in readiness. The Englishman struck the man and sent him to check on the horses. They traveled in two coaches toward Caen, but Caen is not their destination." The boy tugged on Stefan's arm insistently.

"Will you go after the lady?"

"Yes, I will go after her."

The boy smiled sadly. "My mother died when I was born. I never knew my father. I have lived in the streets all my life. Please find the lady, so her baby will not be orphaned like me."

Stefan squeezed the boy's shoulders reassuringly. "I shall find her, and the child she carries. It shall have both mother and father," he promised.

Stefan turned to Dmitri and Captain Villega. "St. Michel is more than eight days' ride on the fastest horses. I fear we may be too late."

"Perhaps eight days on horse, but my lovely lady shall carry us swiftly." Captain Villega smiled wickedly in the gleaming light from one lantern that glowed from the bow of the small boat nearby.

"There is much danger in sailing off the coast. We might easily be spotted by a French frigate," Stefan warned.

Villega guffawed his delight at that thought. He would have liked very much to lend his own efforts to the waning war with France. "Ah yes, my friend, but first they must catch us." His dark eyes sparkled merrily as he called orders in Spanish to his first mate. Within an hour they were aboard the *Celeste*, slipping silently through the water beyond the harbor of Deauville, under minimum sail in the evening breeze. Out on the open sea, the mainsail fluttered loosely and then caught the stiff breeze that swept toward the coastline. Captain Villega brought his sleek schooner about as they ran before the wind. Their destination: the island fortress of the Abbey, Mont St. Michel.

Jenna shifted her position in the closed coach. Five days of bouncing over uncertain roads across the French countryside, constantly eluding the French who patrolled the roads with keen wariness, had made every bone in her young body ache. If she had doubted Charles's sanity, she was now certain he must be completely mad. He had set a pace after they had left Deauville that neither man nor beast could long endure. At Caen they had exchanged their exhausted team for fresh horses and then continued their frantic pace. Jenna was never left alone, even for moments of privacy, and she was forced to remain in the coach with the shades drawn against the possibility of her knowing their location.

On the sixth day Jenna was startled awake by the sound

406

of pounding surf. She sat up, fighting to clear her muddled senses. She had not been mistaken. The distinctive sound of waves breaking could be heard beyond the coach. From the sound of the wheels Jenna knew they had left the dirt road and now traveled over a cobbled street. The coach had slowed noticeably, and Jenna was certain they must have reached their destination. The coach came to a complete stop, and she could hear voices. The door of the coach was yanked open, and Charles leaned inside, the fading, gray light of day silhouetting him like some ghostly apparition. Jenna drew back momentarily, realizing there was hardly any corner where she might retreat.

"Come my dear, see your new home," Charles grinned with malicious intent as he grabbed her arm with brutal strength and pulled her from the coach.

Without the freedom to steady herself, Jenna struggled to prevent herself from falling. She leaned heavily against Charles as she alighted from the coach, immediately pulling back from that brief contact, as if she had touched something loathsome. Charles's sudden laughter was cruel and evil.

"Behold, Jenna, surely a castle worthy of any lady and her bastard child. Behold, the Abbey Mont St. Michel."

Jenna gazed past Charles at the imposing stone fortress that loomed beyond the small town, where houses clustered along the street that wound up to the abbey. It was a well-fortified monastery, seeming to grow out of the rock of an island surrounded by ocean and shifting sand. Fortified walls, gates, and towers rose directly from the edge of the ocean, reinforced by enormously thick retaining walls to protect against the sea. Indeed, the entire north wing of the abbey extended out from the upright line of the rock, supported by massive buttresses. Far below, a narrow causeway connected the village with the abbey. But the tide was already turning and was already flooding the sandy lowlands that dropped away to the sea. In a short while the entire causeway would once more be under water. It was an impregnable fortress that had withstood centuries of assault. It would now be her prison.

Charles helped Jenna back into the coach and quickly followed, giving his orders for the driver to proceed across the rapidly disappearing causeway. The second coach followed, as well as Charles's men. Soon no one would be the wiser for their presence. All trace of their passage was washed away by the encroaching sea.

The vaulted ceilings, ribbed and cross-ribbed, the elaborate work of eleventh-century artisans, echoed with forbidding coldness. Jenna shivered as she was led past the cloister, the refectory, and the monks' dormitory to the guest hall, where an elaborate meal had been prepared and awaited their arrival. Several places had been set at the long dining table, and Jenna could only assume that others were expected very soon. It was the first decent meal she had seen in days, but her appetite was greatly lacking after an enforced diet of water and crusts of bread. Jenna looked away indifferently. Her coolness only infuriated Charles. Cruelly he jerked on the ropes that bound her wrists painfully. When her head snapped around her gaze met his defiantly. Charles drew back his hand and slapped her cruelly, the force of the blow sending Jenna to her knees.

"By God, you will humble yourself. You are no more than a whore. You will gladly accept what is given," Charles raged at her.

"Like a dog, to do your bidding? I think not." Jenna turned on him.

Charles advanced on her menacingly. There was death in his eyes as he fought for control. He shouted at his two men, who stood silently in the doorway. "See that the lady is made comfortable in one of the guest chambers. Have her well guarded. I want no mistakes. If she makes trouble, call me immediately." He turned to Jenna.

"There are ways to force your cooperation. Think well of the child you carry, lest you meet with some accident. It means nothing to me if the child should be lost before its time. Remember this, Jenna. The child means nothing to me."

One guard came forward and seized Jenna about the arm. His touch was surprisingly gentle, as if he somehow felt some measure of pity for her.

Once inside her solitary chamber, Jenna sank wearily down on the narrow bed against the far wall. She gazed at the shuttered windows. A quick inspection revealed that although they were not barred, escape would be impossible. Beyond the window, the wall of the monastery dropped three levels to the crashing surf below.

Jenna huddled deeper into the softness of the straw mattress, pulling the one woolen blanket high over her shoulders to protect herself against the chill from the stone walls. She winced as she gingerly felt the swelling skin of her lip. Her entire cheek felt as if it were swelled to twice its normal size. She fought back the misery that threatened to overcome her. Deep within the island fortress, her hopes for escape seemed more remote than ever. Eyes wide with the fear she could no longer hold back, Jenna yielded to the sadness within her. And yet the tears that fell were not for herself. Her greatest fear was for her unborn child.

Stefan watched the jutting coastline of France with a keen, practiced eye. Through the long hours of the night, darkness had concealed their presence. Now, as the dawn illuminated their sails in a pale sky, he glanced skyward, a sudden smile creasing the hard line of his face. Instead of the Union Jack snapping crisply in the wind, the French tricolor fluttered noisily. His gaze met Captain Villega's across the deck, and he saluted his friend for the deception. Stefan turned back to the railing as he continued his scrutiny of the coastline. Just before sunset the night before they had rounded the Cape de Hague and entered the Channel Islands, which were held by the English. Even these small outposts had managed to repudiate attempts by the French to gain control. They had passed the night anchored off the Jersey Island, and three hours earlier had begun the final leg of their journey. Ahead lay St. Malo, and just beyond, Mont St. Michel.

They spent the remainder of the day anchored in a remote cove. Guards were posted aboard the schooner, while Stefan and Dmitri went ashore. Returning just before sunset, Stefan motioned Dmitri and Captain Villega into the cabin.

"What have you learned in St. Malo?"

Stefan unrolled a map that outlined the coast of France. He pointed to a small, secluded bay.

"Mont St. Michel is here. It could easily be reached in no more than an hour's time with a favorable wind. A French frigate patrols the coastline between these two points. She is well armed, with sixteen cannons. She returns to St. Malo every three days. Tomorrow is the third day." Stefan gazed solemnly at Captain Villega.

"Then we must sail tonight for Mont St. Michel, or return to Jersey until the French have gone," Villega answered.

"We have not the time to wait. It must be tonight."

Villega gazed at his friend, a wide grin splitting his swarthy face. "She must be beautiful, for you to risk so much my friend. I never thought I would see the day when you and this great bear, Dmitri, would be chasing after a broken heart. You are much better to make the girl your mistress."

Stefan leaned across the table, his lean, strong fingers closing about the linen of Villega's shirt as he drew the stout captain across the width of the table.

"This once I will overlook what you have said. From now on you must never speak of her in that way again. She has risked her life for me. She has lost her grandfather, and her home. She is without fear, indeed braver than most men I have known. And now she is captive of a madman who would easily see her dead, because she carries my child. It goes beyond making her my mistress. She is my

410

very soul," Stefan whispered fiercely. Abruptly he released Villega.

"I could not expect you to understand." Stefan spoke from between tightly clenched teeth, the firm, hard muscles in his jaw outlined beneath his dark skin.

Villega stared at the man he had known since he was a young lad. "I apologize, my friend. I do understand. Once there was such a woman for me. I would have sailed into hell to be with her. There were others who thought better of it, and kept her from me. She took her life rather than be forced to marry against her heart." Villega smiled sadly beneath the thick coverage of his dark beard. "Do not look at me so. Once I was young and handsome, and full of life, and love for this woman. Her death has made me what you see now. I shall carry my sadness until my last breath. We shall find your princess. I could not bear to carry the burden of her death also. We shall sail this night," he promised, a sudden passion in his voice.

Stefan embraced the Spanish sea captain. Their eyes met in silent communication. Then the captain brushed past Stefan to give his orders to the crew.

"I will go with you to St. Michel." Dmitri spoke gruffly. "There is a score to be settled with Charles Wingate."

Stefan gazed across the map at Dmitri, their friendship born of years together, their understanding of each other like that of brothers who carried the same blood.

"I would not try to prevent your coming, my friend. But remember, Charles Wingate is mine."

The somber silence aboard the sleek schooner during the next hours was broken only by the sighing of the water as the bow slipped through the blue-black depths of the sea. A gentle, caressing breeze carried them to their destination. A few distant, soft-hued lights twinkled from the coastline. Captain Villega pointed out the village of St. Michel. Carefully, the schooner was brought about, and the last of her sails lowered as they slipped into a secluded cove. With the cover of darkness, Stefan, Dmitri, and a full score of his men slipped over the side of the schooner and

411

made their way to shore.

Once they had reached the secluded, sandy stretch of beach, just beyond the island and the abbey, the small boats returned to the sea. They lingered, caught momentarily on the crest of a new wave that seemed intent on returning them to shore. Muscles strained at the oars, and first one boat and then the other breached the crest of the wave and then slipped across the cove to the waiting schooner.

It was now very near dawn, and it had been arranged for Villega to take the *Celeste* out to the open sea. There was too much risk they might be seen and those within the abbey alerted to their presence. Villega was to return for them the following night, under cover of darkness. If all went well, they would be in the cove awaiting the boats.

The brilliant glow of a full moon illuminated the abbey, perched like an impenetrable citadel on its rocky promontory. The shadows of clustered rock outcroppings along the sandy stretch of beach shielded them as they moved quickly along. A softly sworn oath mingled with the gurgling of the seawater among the outcroppings, frustration quickly turning to panic as a man ordered ahead to check their path found his feet being dragged beneath the surface of the soft sand. All efforts to pull himself from the clinging sand only pulled him deeper. Vainly the young Cossack looked for something to grab hold of. He dared not cry out lest he be discovered. He dared not let the others venture forth into the uncertain footing of the quicksand that closed around him with deadly purpose.

Stefan grew uneasy as the young Russian failed to return. He motioned to Dmitri, and then moved ahead in the direction the young Cossack had gone. Stefan stopped after a few paces and listened. He heard only the sound of the waves on the beach. His muscles tensed as he sensed that something was very wrong. He whistled softly, calling the sound of a thrush. Again he listened, and moved ahead cautiously, his hand resting on the deadly blade concealed in the belt at his waist. Stefan whistled the signal again. He heard a faint reply. Moving along the beach, his boots sinking softly into the sand, Stefan rounded the last outcropping. Here the sand was much softer. A warning flared in Stefan's brain, just as he saw something ahead in the sand. He moved back instinctively, until he felt firmer footing. He whistled again. The object in the sand moved, and the whistling response came again. Stefan moved ahead slowly, until he felt the sickening softness of the shifting sand beneath his boots; quicksand.

"Easy. You must not struggle. I will return with Dmitri and the others. You must not move, it will draw you down more quickly if you try to free yourself," Stefan called to the young man as he turned back up the beach.

Within moments Dmitri and the remainder of Stefan's group of men had joined them. With one of the ropes they had brought they formed a loop and tossed it across the sinking sand toward their companion. Submerged nearly to his shoulders, he struggled to loop the rope about his body. When the rope had been secured around a nearby rock, Stefan and his men pulled as one. With painstaking slowness they retrieved the young Russian. When the sand àt last yielded, making a gurgling sound as he was pulled free, Stefan and his men sat down wearily. They resolved to proceed with more caution, in groups of two men each. The young Cossack smiled gratefully at Dmitri, humbling himself before his prince. Stefan clapped him on the shoulders.

"I think had you not eaten so much aboard the *Celeste*, you might have escaped with little difficulty. You should think better, of challenging Dmitri to a contest of appetites." Stefan laughed good-humoredly.

"Are you strong enough to continue?"

Vasily nodded. "I am strong enough. I will not be left behind to await your return. You will have need of each sword."

Stefan nodded curtly at the unspoken loyalty that shone in the young Russian's eyes. He would not have traded one of his men for all of Napoleon's ill-fated grand armée. The French had failed to conquer Russia. Charles Wingate and his traitorous alliance would also fail.

413

Chapter Twenty-Two

Jenna stared warily at Charles Wingate across the width of the long dining table in the great hall of the Abbey Mont St. Michel. Painfully she rubbed the swollen, red welts on each wrist where the ropes had rubbed her skin raw. She found his sudden kindness in removing the ropes difficult to understand after his cruelty of the last days. Indeed, in the two days since they had arrived at the abbey, Charles had left her alone, in her locked and well-guarded chamber, perhaps to contemplate her uncertain fate. She was more than aware of her soiled and disheveled appearance. She wore the same gown she had worn that last day in London. She had cared to take nothing more. She had pulled back the length of her hair and bound it with a length of cloth. Indeed she felt as pitiful as the boy she had seen at Deauville, though she cared little for her appearance at the moment. Charles approached from around the end of the table, and Jenna immediately backed away the same number of measured steps.

"My dearest Jenna. I asked you here because I have something of importance I wish to tell you. Later today, three other gentlemen will be joining us to await our moment of triumph. In four days' time the world will be stunned to learn of the deaths of the prince regent and the entire royal family, obviously at the hands of mercenaries. A trilateral commission will be formed to enable the English government to function. All members of the commission will be men of great power and foresight. It was necessary that we leave England for a time, in order to divert suspicion away from our little group. When the deed is done, we shall quickly return and establish ourselves in key positions of government."

"Why are you telling me this? Aren't you afraid that I might tell someone?" Jenna spat back at him.

"How would that be possible, my lovely Jenna? When I return to England, you shall remain here at the Abbey, under safe protection. I could hardly allow you to return with me and take the risk of your telling everyone. No indeed, you will remain here, until the joyous occasion of the birth of your child," Charles jeered maliciously.

Jenna released a momentary sigh of relief as she realized he did not intend to put her to death. Her relief however, was only momentary, as Charles approached and he stood before her. Slowly he reached for her hand. Jenna tried to pull away from his hold, but Charles's fingers closed around hers with painful strength that threatened to break her bones. She winced as he crushed her hand in his mercilessly.

"As I have said, my lovely Jenna, you will remain here until you are no longer burdened with the bastard that grows within you. When the child has been born, you will be allowed to return to London, where you will join me," he explained simply.

Jenna cast him a suspicious glance. She found his generosity difficult to understand. There was only one part he had failed to explain thoroughly.

"What of my baby?" Jenna whispered uncertainly.

"I will not be burdened with the bastard leavings of another man. Certainly you can understand this, Jenna. The child will be cared for."

"No!" Jenna backed away, aghast at what he was suggesting. "I could never leave my child."

Charles's face contorted with barely controlled rage at her outburst of defiance. He halted her retreat, drawing her toward him and twisting her wrist cruelly.

"The choice is not yours, my lovely Jenna. The choice is

mine. And for now, I have chosen to allow your child to live. Only you may guarantee that your child will continue to live. Your cooperation will be the assurance of its life. If you betray me again, if you speak against me, be assured my revenge will be swift and sure."

"You are surely mad!" Jenna whispered hoarsely as she stared disbelieving at Charles Wingate.

"That may be, my dearest, but I will surely have you, as it should have been from the beginning. Your grandfather objected to our betrothal. He cannot object any longer."

"Is that why you had him murdered? Or was it because of the conspiracy? How could you believe that I would ever accept you, knowing what you did to my grandfather? Did you think I would not know?" Jenna responded boldly.

Charles halted all further retreat, as his arm encircled her waist and drew her intimately against him, his hips pressed against hers, his passion undeniable. He breathed heavily against the column of her throat as his lips sought hers. His hand reached to stroke the satin softness of her long hair as he released it from the ribbon, and it spilled over his hands like a live, wanton creature. His greatest torment was the thought of another's having possessed her as he had longed to, a man who had taken her innocence and left his seed within her, to taunt him now, as she grew rounded with the proof of their love.

"You will assume your role this very evening. You will be hostess to our guests, and you will do so gladly. You know well the consequences for your refusal," he murmured huskily against her ear.

Jenna fought the nausea that welled within her, which had nothing to do with the child she carried. In vain she tried to push Charles away, twisting her head away from the vile smell of his hot breath, heavy with the wine he had been drinking.

"I will not play hostess for your group of murderers," she cried out from between tightly clenched teeth as she shoved at Charles with all her strength, throwing him off balance. As he lunged for her, Jenna quickly darted beyond his grasp. She stood, feet apart, warily considering her next move.

"Jenna!" Charles bellowed warningly.

"No. And there is nothing you can say that will make me change my mind. You have blood on your hands. My grandfather, perhaps Dmitri, and many others who died to stop you. From the moment you first took me from London, I knew my life was worth nothing. You may do what you will, but I will never be part of your madness. If that should mean my death, then so be it," Jenna swore passionately.

Charles felt a momentary uncertainty as he stared into the depths of her amber eyes, suddenly afire with a light that seemed to burn from her very soul. He knew a deepening hatred for the bastard who had taken her from him. He swore under his breath as he reached for a crystal goblet on the table and poured himself a healthy draught. Quickly swallowing the contents, he whirled around, smashing the goblet against the hearth across the room. Even the wine seemed to have become bitter and unsatisfying. He whirled on Jenna, seizing her by the arm, striking her cruelly as blind rage reached to consume him.

"Return to your chamber, milady. And await my pleasure," he taunted her cruelly. He motioned to the guard and quickly gave his orders.

Jenna sighed shakily as she returned to the temporary safety of her chamber. She collapsed wearily on the narrow bed, feeling suddenly drained of all strength, all hope. Warm tears slipped down her cheeks, into the new cut at her lip. The saltiness stung painfully, causing a torrent of tears as she yielded to the misery of her fear and pain. She pulled the woolen blanket higher over her shoulder to warm herself against a sudden chill that seemed to invade the stone chamber and set her to shaking violently. Only after a while did she drift into exhausted slumber, dreaming of another time and place, of moments of love stolen in the seclusion of a woodland cottage or the walled safety of Hallston. Her heart cried out with silent longing for gentleness and warmth, but most of all for the passion that had released hers. Instinctively, Jenna curled protectively around the roundness of her child. It might well be the only happiness she would know in the days to come.

Stefan Kalinsky waved back one of his men, posted as lookout, as the distinct sounds of an approaching coach were heard over the pounding of the waves on the rock foundation of Mont St. Michel. Within moments, the coach came into view at the other end of the causeway. Stefan watched from his secluded vantage point as the driver halted the team, sending one of several outriders ahead to check the depth of the sea water that washed across the causeway as the tide began its return. When it was determined that the depth was not enough to hinder passage, the rider signaled to the driver.

Stefan turned and quickly signaled to Dmitri, safely hidden in a clustering of rocks nearby, as the coach continued across the causeway without the additional guards who had ridden with them for protection. The horsemen turned back toward the village to spend the night in the comfort of the local inn, with willing female companions. It would be necessary for the coach to stop at the end of the causeway in order to negotiate the sharp turn in the narrow dirt road that wound precariously up the side of the rock island. That brief stop would give Stefan the opportunity he had sought all day to gain entrance to the abbey. Their only other alternative was to scale the sheer stone face of the fortress, a task that would have been impossible, except in the full light of day. And without the cover of darkness, the chance of discovery would be too great. Stefan smiled broadly as Dmitri clambered down from his rocky outpost.

"You have a plan?" Dmitri asked in Russian, recognizing the glint of light that sparkled in the depths of Stefan's blue gaze.

"Yes, my friend, a plan that will gain us entry to the abbey. In order for the driver of the coach to safely negotiate the turn onto the road that leads up the mountain, he must slow the coach to a stop." Stefan unbelted the scabbard of his sword and handed his friend the lethal weapon, tucking a pistol in the belt of his breeches.

"I shall take advantage of that moment, and ride with them through the gates of St. Michel." Stefan smiled wickedly with the brilliance of his plan.

Dmitri laid a restraining hand on his friend's arm. "There is too much danger that you might be discovered. I shall go. If I am found, then you still remain to lead the others," Dmitri decided firmly.

Stefan shook his head. "I appreciate your loyalty and your wisdom, my friend. But I must be the one to go. This is my quest. If we fail, if we do not find her alive, then there is only myself to blame. I would not share that blame with anyone."

"At any rate, you are far too large, old friend." Stefan teased with returned humor. "I fear the horse might not be able to pull your ponderous weight up that hill. When the driver stopped to find the cause, imagine his surprise to find a great Russian bear weighting him down."

Dmitri eyed his prince with pretended injury. "Then you will not listen to my arguments?"

Stefan nodded. "I will not listen. You will remain behind with the others. When darkness has fallen, make your way to the main entrance as quickly as possible. I will find a way to open the gates. Listen for my signal."

Dmitri nodded reluctantly as Stefan carefully crept through the rocks toward the sudden turn in the road at the end of the causeway. Dmitri waited with the others, well armed against the possibility of any trouble as the coach slowly approached across the causeway.

As Stefan had predicted, the driver of the coach slowed the team of horses to a stop before turning them sharply up the road that wound up the side of the rocky island. In that brief moment, Stefan stole quietly from his secluded hiding place among the rocks and dove under the rear of the coach. He had barely enough time to grab onto the frame of the coach and pull himself clear of the ground before the driver called to the team and urged them

420

onward. The coach lurched and rocked over the uncertain terrain of the seldom-used road, loosening Stefan's perilous grasp on the frame. The wheels of the coach sank suddenly into a deep rut, momentarily dislodging his feet, which were entwined about the shaft that ran the length of the undercarriage. Beads of perspiration poured down the sides of his face as he struggled to regain his uncertain perch. The coach lumbered up the steep incline of the island as Stefan kicked and strained to regain his footing. He clung, helplessly dragged as the driver continued. Around the next turn, the driver slowed once more, and Stefan kicked one more time, his foot wedging over the top of the shaft. One more kick, and he brought his other foot up. Clinging to the shaft, like a castaway clinging to a lifeline, Stefan continued his uncertain journey to the top of Mont St. Michel. The coach slowed as it finally gained the summit of the island and passed through the massive double gates of the abbey, which led to a small inner courtyard. From his seclusion beneath the coach, Stefan could see rows of outlying wooden buildings. When the driver finally reined the team of horses to a complete stop, Stefan seized his opportunity and lowered himself to the ground, quickly rolling clear of the coach before the driver alighted. Hidden in the shadows of the massive retaining wall of the abbey, Stefan darted inside the nearest building, which served as a granary. The door stood ajar, and Stefan listened intently as the passengers in the coach also alighted and walked the rest of the way toward the main entrance of the nave. He was not surprised that they spoke the King's English, indeed, he had expected it. Stefan watched their retreat and smiled coldly at the irony of their selection of the Abbey of Mont St. Michel for their haven to await the success of the conspiracy. The abbey had served centuries of monastic orders until the French Revolution. When Louis XVI had been deposed and replaced by the order of the Grand Republic, the abbey had fallen onto hard times, serving the new order as a prison. Only in recent years had the abbey stood empty. His smile deepened, with deadly intent. The prison of Mont St.

Michel would serve his purpose well. Far below, Dmitri and his men awaited darkness.

Stefan watched the brilliant blue of the warm afternoon fade into the gray mists of evening as a fog rose from the sea to surround the island fortress. Lights glistened from within the abbey, and Stefan left his hiding place. The front gates had been bolted from within. The driver of the coach had long since retired to a warm meal inside the abbey. The team of horses had been unhitched and stood quietly in the rambling stables at the far side of the yard. Stefan stole quietly to the front gates and slowly moved the bolt back across them. The dampened wood gate creaked complainingly, the sound oddly muffled in the dampened fog that encased the island like a shroud. Stefan listened, his gaze searching the darkness for some sign of Dmitri. He whistled a signal, and listened again. Without warning a large, forbidding form loomed before him. Stefan instinctively reached for the pistol tucked in his breeches. The form took shape, and, in the meager light of a torch that flickered at the gate he saw the bearlike head of his friend. He patted Dmitri on the shoulder in silent greeting as the giant Cossack slipped through the gate, followed by first one man and then another, until Stefan's small but deadly band of men stood within the imposing shelter of Mont St. Michel.

Without a word spoken, they followed Stefan's silent footsteps across the yard to a small door beyond the main entrance to the nave. Stefan tried the latch. It moved freely. Silently Stefan and his men slipped through the narrow side entrance that ran beside the main entrance, and then turned sharply to the right, passing along the tiny unoccupied chambers of the cloister. Stefan halted in the darkness of the shadows as voices echoed through the vaulted monastery. His gaze followed the soft glow of lights that could be seen just beyond a series of storage rooms. Two men suddenly emerged from the main guest hall, and Stefan and his men flattened themselves in the shadows only a few paces away. Stefan turned and nodded his silent command to the last two of his men, who quickly dropped back and disappeared into the shadows of a large vertical column. An oddly muffled gasp was the only sound to be heard as the two guards dropped unconscious to the hard stone flooring. They were quickly bound and gagged and dragged into a nearby storeroom. A few moments later Stefan's men rejoined their small group, dressed in the garments of the two guards.

Stefan gave orders for his men to break into three groups. The first would check the outer chambers for any other guards. The second would return to the yard, to make certain there would be no surprise visits by any of Charles's men left to guard the perimeter of the abbey. The remainder would follow Stefan.

In rapid succession, four more guards yielded their posts and their garments, Stefan's men quickly replacing them. A thorough search of the remaining chambers of the cloister and monk's dormitory revealed that Charles had brought only a few, select men to guard the abbey. They waited until they were rejoined by Stefan's other men, sent to search the outer chambers. All but two were dressed similarly to the others, in the guards' garments. Vasily nodded his silent message that all was secured. Now all, except those in the main dining hall, had been replaced with Stefan's men, and the one thing Stefan had hoped to find had not been found. Jenna had not been in any of the chambers they had searched.

Stefan accepted his sword from Dmitri and checked the pistol tucked inside his belt. He gave a silent command, and two of his men moved ahead and casually entered the dining hall, taking up discreet positions in the shadows at the far side of the room. Stefan dispersed the rest of his men to other points within the main hall and then followed Vasily to a small hallway that ran along the far wall of the dining hall. It ended at the vast kitchen that had been built adjacent to the dining hall for ease of serving meals. Stefan, Vasily, and Dmitri drew back inside the narrow hallway as two young women returned from the hallway to take more platters of food to the hungry guests. The platters and bowls were amply filled by a stout, gray-haired woman who called her instructions in French. Both girls scurried about to follow her orders.

"We cannot risk the women alerting Charles Wingate," Dmitri whispered from the shadows.

"When the two girls return, we shall relieve them of their duties," Stefan replied lightly, his eyes sparkling with a certain deadliness as he grew eager for the final confrontation.

Within minutes the two girls had returned to the warm kitchen. They glanced about uncertainly, as the cook was nowhere to be seen. One girl crossed the kitchen to check the pantry, while the other one checked the hallway that led to the cloister. Their outcries of surprise were silenced beneath strong hands, and they quickly joined the bound cook on the mounding sacks of flour and grain in the storeroom. The door was carefully closed, and Dmitri turned to Stefan with a wicked gleam in his sharp black eyes.

"Now for the final prize."

Stefan laid a cautioning hand on Dmitri's arm.

"Easy, my friend, only if I should fail. Remember, Charles Wingate is mine. I have a score to settle."

"What of the little princess?" Dmitri growled his mounting concern at not having found Jenna.

"Before we can free the dove, we must destroy the jackal," Stefan whispered harshly, the coldness of death in his voice.

Dmitri nodded his silent agreement, patting his large hand over the hilt of the deadly blade he carried. He trusted in Stefan's skill with the blade; indeed, he had taught him all he knew of the weapon. What he had not been able to teach him, Stefan had learned from the most skilled swordsmen in all of France. If by some chance or trickery Stefan failed to kill Charles Wingate, then he would see the matter done.

The sounds of revelry and of hearty appetites being well satisfied reached them from the dining hall beyond. Stefan stole silently along the short passage from the kitchens. He hesitated a moment in the shadows, his eyes narrowing as he carefully scrutinized the large room. Two men sat on each side of the long dining table. He recognized one as a high-ranking member of Napoleon's elite military cabinet. The other three men conversed fluently in French, and were unknown to him, but they were obviously important members of the conspiracy. Charles Wingate sat at the head of the table, impeccably dressed in soft gray breeches and waistcoat. Indeed, he was the essence of the perfect host, as he rose slowly from the high-backed, carved wood chair and seized a crystal wine goblet.

"Gentlemen, friends. Today we join in celebration of the success of our mutual cause. Within a matter of days, we shall see the fruits of our labors. England will be ours. I congratulate you all." Charles lifted the goblet to toast the four who sat at the table, the crimson liquid gleaming iridescent from the golden light of a multitude of candles in the heavy, ornate silver candelabrum that adorned the center of the table. A self-satisfied smile crossed his thin lips as he sipped from the dark wine. The four around the table raised their goblets in homage to their host before tasting the wine. A second toast was offered, to Napoleon of France. Charles Wingate's grasp of the delicate goblet tightened perceptibly, his manner suddenly guarded and cautious. He smiled condescendingly to his guests to hide his true thoughts.

"Of course, gentlemen. A toast to Napoleon of France." Charles smiled secretively over the rim of the goblet, his true thoughts known only to one other man in the room.

"I believe your celebration is a bit premature, gentlemen." Stefan stepped from the shadows of the hallway that led to the kitchens, an amused smile playing across his handsome face as he leaned casually against the framed entry, his left hand resting easily on the pistol tucked in his belt.

Charles Wingate's head snapped up in sudden alarm. Almost as one, each of his guests reached for his weapon, only to remember they had chosen to dine unarmed, relying on the protection of their guards within the abbey.

They stared at the stranger who had emerged from the shadows, a single man dressed in doeskin breeches and linen shirt opened at the neck, and spotless black Hessian boots. Indeed, he looked more like a pirate. The three Frenchmen stared questioningly at Charles Wingate, more confused than alarmed, as the stranger seemed to concentrate on their host. The fourth man had no such confusion, for he immediately recognized Prince Stefan Kalinsky. He felt a sudden prickling of fear down the back of his neck, as he remembered their last meeting years before at Villandry, when Emperor Napoleon Bonaparte had given his orders for the confiscation of all royal lands. Prince Kalinsky had sworn his revenge.

Charles Wingate stared at Stefan Kalinsky in stunned disbelief, his face suddenly ashen, his mouth dry. He rose from his chair with such force that it was sent over backwards, clattering loudly on the stone flooring, the sound echoing in the vaulted hall.

"Behold, Lord Wingate. I am no ghostly apparition sprung from the grave to haunt you. Not at all." Stefan's gaze narrowed, the blue of his eyes as cold as ice as he straightened and approached the table.

"I have come to welcome you to France. You see, France was once my home, before it was taken from me."

Charles's face flooded crimson with growing anger as he stared across the table at Stefan Kalinsky.

"How is it you are not dead?" Charles's voice strained with his effort. Stefan's relaxed manner only grated against his tightly restrained composure all the more.

"Let us say, you were merely careless in your skill with the blade. I'll admit the injury was severe, much more severe than I intended, but as you can see, I have recovered completely," Stefan ended with a flourish of both arms, spread wide mockingly.

"But to what purpose?" Charles stared at Stefan, all his hatred glowing in the pale depths of his gray gaze, as he refused to believe that it was he who had been the pawn in his duel with Stefan Kalinsky.

"It was essential that you win the duel, a public display

426

of my humiliation, perhaps even injury, to serve my purpose. It was only a matter of letting you believe that I had not recovered," Stefan replied evenly. His gaze rested on Charles Wingate, but he was completely aware of the growing discomfort among the other guests.

Charles Wingate's laugh was full of derision as he refused to believe his part in the scheme.

"And I suppose you would have me believe you yielded the match, also to serve your purpose. My own physician checked the wound. The victory was clearly mine. That you escaped death is indeed regrettable, although hardly important," Charles sneered.

Stefan quickly seized the pistol in his belt as the Frenchman cautiously moved away from the table with some thought to alerting the guards. He immediately stopped as the pistol was raised and pointed directly at his heart.

"As I have said, Lord Wingate. It was essential that you win the duel. You had been aware for some time of my work with Sir Avery Randolph. You and your fellow-conspirators knew that Sir Avery had uncovered the conspiracy, and you feared he might know the identities of those involved. It was for that reason that Sir Avery was murdered. You could not risk the possibility that I might have learned those identities also. During those last weeks, it had become impossible for me to learn more of the conspiracy. I was aware that my every move was constantly watched. If you believed me to be dead, then there was the possibility that you might become careless in your confidence. Indeed, you became very careless." Stefan smiled confidently. "Sir Robert Ludlow revealed much before he died."

Charles's gaze sharpened to hardened steel. "You are a fool if you think you can stop me now. You will never leave the abbey alive. And, more than that, I hold a valuable prize. Would you also cause her death?"

The unwavering smile of complete confidence on Stefan Kalinsky's face was maddening. Charles Wingate slammed his fist down hard onto the surface of the wood table as he roared for his guards. His entire body trembled with barely controlled rage as he waited for the guards to appear. Long moments of silence only added to the unyielding anger that welled within him. By God, he would have Jenna brought forward and then see how brave this arrogant Russian bastard was then. Two guards appeared from the large double-doors that opened into the nave beyond. They stood silently at either side of the doorway, their hands resting easily on the hilts of their swords as they awaited further orders. Charles's fury flew to new heights as he again bellowed for the guards to come forward, the truth only a vague suspicion that had begun to gnaw at his composure. He grew increasingly uncomfortable at Stefan's confidence, which never wavered. Indeed, that arrogant smile deepened.

"Behold, Lord Wingate, your guards." Stefan waved his arm wide in introduction of the two men who now stepped from the shadows of the doorway and stepped to the side. Two more well-armed guards entered behind them and took up their positions along the far wall. More of Stefan's men emerged from the hallway that led to the kitchens, followed by Dmitri, whose great size and bulk were unmistakable. A low murmuring went up from the group of men at the table, who had just begun to realize the truth of their predicament. Charles Wingate's smoldering gaze burned through Stefan Kalinsky. With one sideways motion of his arm, he sent goblets and platters crashing to the floor with unrestrained rage.

Stefan merely continued to stare at him calmly. "You will find my men now control the abbey. It seems your guards were somewhat derelict in their duties. But that is to be expected when loyalty is purchased with gold."

Charles's anger seethed as he slowly rounded the table, like a wary animal that has been driven to ground and turns for the final battle. "You have failed, Prince Kalinsky. Your efforts here are futile. Even now, my final plans are being carried out. Within days the world will know of our brilliant conspiracy. But by then it will be too late."

"You have left a bloody path, Lord Wingate. You became careless in your desire for power. You should have taken greater care that Sir Robert Ludlow could not divulge your secrets. As it is, he told much before he died. He knew he had been betrayed. His final revenge was his betrayal of you. Before he died, Sir Robert gave the information we needed to stop the attempt against the prince regent. For complete success your plan required the assassination of the entire royal family. Now there will be no success. You have failed," Stefan concluded simply.

Undaunted, Charles shook his head, like a great, menacing beast. "He lies! He guesses at the truth because he does not know it. He comes here to cause dissension among us, as a last, desperate act, when he knows he has already lost."

The brilliant blue of Stefan's gaze suddenly darkened, his manner at once more threatening as he waved Dmitri back.

"I do not come because of the conspiracy. I have come to take back what is mine," he breathed warningly, his face like a mask of death as he turned to meet Charles evenly.

"Ah yes, you have come for the lovely whore. I wonder if you will want her quite so badly when you see her," Charles taunted him savagely. In one quick movement, he lunged toward the nearest of Stefan's men, quickly throwing him off balance with his sudden movement, seizing the man's sword as he went down. The silence in the hall was shattered by a full score of blades drawn from their sheaths and half as many pistols immediately turned on Charles Wingate. The Frenchman seized his opportunity and immediately drew a small blade concealed in his belt. The breath was knocked from his lungs as he was hit from behind, his hand slammed repeatedly down on the top of the table until he yielded the blade. He was roughly cast aside as Stefan's men moved forward.

"Stand away!" Stefan ordered his men as he slowly approached Charles Wingate, his steady gaze never leaving that menacing blade as Charles circled away from him warily. "He is mine!" Stefan's gaze narrowed with

429

deadly purpose as he carefully set his pistol aside and drew the finely tapered sword from its sheath.

"Perhaps you would care for a rematch, to settle the question of victory, once and for all," Stefan challenged.

Charles Wingate circled away from him warily, his gaze never leaving Stefan's face. He halted a few feet away, a cruel smile twisting his lips. "Very well, a final contest of skill, to determine the fate of Lady Randolph."

Stefan nodded his acceptance of the terms of the contest as he watched his adversary warily. When there was no longer a place to hide, a trapped animal was the deadliest of enemies.

"I should like to remove my coat."

Stefan nodded his head, never taking his eyes off Charles Wingate. Charles cast the coat aside and turned with cool confidence to meet the challenge.

"You risk much for a common whore and her unborn bastard, who shall carry my mark. The lady grew lonely in your absence, and sought her pleasure with me. But if you live, you are welcome to her," Charles taunted cruelly, seeking to break Stefan's composure.

Stefan well knew the game Charles Wingate played. It was a game of desperation. Though the words tore at him, and he could easily have ripped the man apart for what he said against Jenna, he kept one thought in the forefront of his mind as he prepared to deliver his opponent to his death: Jenna was alive.

Both men saluted with their swords as they stood apart contemplating the contest that would determine the victor. Seeing that his cruel remarks had gained him little advantage, Charles pressed his attack, lunging for the first strike against Stefan. His blade carved empty air as Stefan carefully sidestepped, circling his own blade with a casual indifference that had a maddening effect on Charles Wingate. Again he slashed at Stefan, their blades locking at the hilts as each man leaned his weight into his stance, attempting to throw the other off balance. Stefan backed away easily, releasing his blade, slashing through the air to neatly sever the buttons from Charles's vest. They scattered across the floor as Charles halted for a moment, staring down at the vest that gaped away from his shirt. A crimson flush of anger rose across his cheeks, and he again pressed his challenge, jabbing at Stefan, his blade finding empty air with each jab.

Stefan met each renewed thrust with the strength and agility of a lean, graceful animal that moved quickly and warily, always eluding death at the tip of that lethal blade. Again and again he met Charles's thrusts, their blades locking momentarily as they leaned into each other. Slowly, almost imperceptibly, Stefan could see Charles beginning to wear as they parried and returned thrust for thrust. For Stefan it was a game, a game he had once yielded for a cause. Now the game had become the cause. His other hand resting casually at his back, Stefan moved with catlike grace around the perimeter of the dining hall, evading Charles's thrusts with energy that seemed boundless. He watched as perspiration beaded across Charles's forehead and streamed down his cheeks. Again Stefan moved against Charles, his blade easily carving through the latter's slowed defenses to slice a long gash down the length of Charles's forearm.

Charles Wingate yelped with stunned surprise as he sprang away from Stefan's attack. He stared in disbelief at the crimson stain that appeared down the length of his sleeve. When his gaze returned to his opponent, he saw that self-confident smile deepen and a golden light spring into the depths of that blue gaze.

"That is repayment for your treatment of Dmitri," Stefan coolly informed Charles.

His awareness heightened by the pain that pulsed in his left arm, Charles Wingate now became more deadly, the wounded animal struggling to survive. Again he lunged at Stefan, quickly turning about and pressing his attack at Stefan's back as Stefan whirled about to meet the challenge.

Dmitri immediately moved forward as he saw the coward again strike at Stefan's back. Stefan quickly waved his friend away.

"I shall win this contest fairly, so that none may question it," Stefan swore beneath his breath, as he returned Charles's parry and defended against the menacing blade that carved through the air, very near his face. Stefan blocked another thrust, and then spun away from Charles, to gain better advantage, his blade returning to carve another opening in the silk of Charles's shirt. Now a brilliant crimson arc curved across the white shirt that covered Charles's chest. A scream of death tore from the man's throat as he pressed his attack with renewed vengeance.

"That is repayment for your murder of Sir Avery Randolph," Stefan informed his opponent with chilling conviction as he moved easily away from another thrust. Indeed, he seemed much like the cat that merely plays with the mouse, before ending its life.

The loss of blood from the wound in his arm and his chest began to have an effect as Charles Wingate's movements became more conservative and guarded. He moved haltingly, his eyes warily concentrating on his opponent, his breath coming in ragged gasps from his efforts. He lunged, slashing uncertainly in Stefan's direction as sweat blurred his vision. In vain, he wiped at his dampened brow as he slashed again, his sword contacting a heavy iron sconce, quickly sending the fixture crashing to the stone floor. He shook his head, to clear his vision as well as his thoughts. Now, only blind rage strengthened him as he pressed his attack. Stefan's delays only seemed to infuriate him further.

"Aren't you man enough to meet my attack? Will you run from me now?" Charles screamed at Stefan Kalinsky, attempting to goad him into hasty retaliation.

Stefan's cool gaze never left his quarry. Slowly they circled, one slow and stumbling, the other wary and controlled.

Charles Wingate's eyes gleamed with deadly intent as he moved against Stefan Kalinsky. Boldly he thrust forward, quickly deflecting Stefan's block and then thrusting again, his blade barely grazing Stefan's shoulder. Pressing his advantage, Charles lunged again, the deadly tip of his blade plunging unchecked toward Stefan's heart.

Stefan's counter move was checked only momentarily as he felt a tingling of pain in his shoulder. His blade was quickly deflected, and then just as he suspected he would, Charles stepped back and prepared to lunge again, before he had time to recover. Stefan moved backwards several paces. Where Charles's blade would have pierced his heart a moment before, it struck only air. Stefan quickly countered the lunge, his arm straightening to take Charles's full weight as the blade sank deeply into his chest.

For a full, long moment, Charles Wingate stared wide-eyed, with disbelief, as he felt the blade slicing through him. The next moment he lay crumpled on the cold stone floor of the hall as Stefan pushed him away, retrieving his blade. Their fierce struggle ended, silence echoed in the vaulted chamber.

Stefan's men quickly crossed the room and secured the other prisoners. Dmitri knelt beside Charles Wingate and felt for a pulse in his neck. Charles's eyes opened briefly, a cold smile twisting his lips.

"You will never be certain of the child," Charles whispered hoarsely. His crazed laughing was broken by wracking coughs that produced flecks of crimson spittle on his lips, his smile contorted with the pain of his death.

Stefan stared down at Charles Wingate's lifeless form. Unlike in other confrontations, he felt no remorse for the life he had taken.

"You must not believe his words. They were the words of a dying man, to leave you with doubts when there should be none." Dmitri spoke solemnly.

Stefan refused to acknowledge what his friend said. In his heart he knew Charles's words to be lies, and yet they tore at him, as Charles Wingate had hoped they would. It had been his legacy. Stefan kicked at the lifeless body with the toe of his boot.

"We must search the abbey. In a few hours the tide will be out, and we must make our escape before the soldiers from the village return."

Stefan turned about as Vasily crossed the hall.

"There are several chambers beyond the nun's cloister. One of them is locked."

"What of the guards?" Stefan asked as he quickly motioned Vasily to lead the way.

"There was only one guard. He quickly yielded when he saw our greater numbers." Vasily grinned widely as he led Stefan and Dmitri past the cloister and the refectory. Several meditation chambers lined the opposite wall, which more recently had been used to hold prisoners. The last one at the far end stood locked and heavily chained. Vasily quickly produced a large key that had been taken from the guard.

The chamber was darkened, with only the meager light of a high window casting pale shafts into the cold dampness. Dmitri quickly appeared with a torch. He muttered a horrified oath in Russian at the sight of the slender girl sprawled across the damp stone floor.

Stefan quickly brushed both men aside as he entered the chamber and knelt beside the prostrate girl. The gown she wore hung in shreds across her back, where welts were raised in the soft flesh. Tenderly Stefan turned her over, his heart constricting at the pale, seemingly lifeless beauty he held in his arms. Fearing they might have come too late, Stefan's hand trembled as he reached to smooth back a tendril of her hair. His fingers brushed gently across her bruised cheek and dry, parched lips. Frantically, he looked for some sign of life, at last feeling a faint pulsing in her neck beneath his fingers. He breathed her name as he gathered her into his embrace, cradling her as he would an injured child, trying to comfort her with whispered endearments as he tried to break through the veil of death that had closed about her. Stefan looked down at her, and he felt a faint response. Her eyes fluttered weakly and then opened as he called her name over and over.

"Stefan?" Jenna whispered faintly.

"I am here, my princess. I am here," Stefan replied hoarsely, gathering her protectively in his embrace.

"Charles? You must be careful. Stefan, he is mad. He will kill you." Jenna struggled feebly as she fought to make him understand.

Stefan kissed her forehead tenderly, the soft oval of her cheek, and then her lips, as he sought to reassure her the only way possible, when she seemed not to hear his words.

"Please don't leave me again. Charles will hurt my baby," Jenna cried softly, still unaware that Charles couldn't harm her at all anymore.

"I will never leave you again. I promise you, I will never leave you again," Stefan vowed, gently lifting Jenna from the cold floor and bearing her from the chamber.

When Jenna awakened, she recoiled in sudden fear at the large, dark shadow that loomed over her. Dmitri's gruff but gentle voice quickly sliced through her fear and confusion. In a moment Stefan was beside her, his lean, strong hands, closing over hers. Jenna stared at him, disbelieving, for a long moment, and then dissolved into tears as he pulled her against his shoulder.

"I was so afraid you were dead. Charles said no one would be left to tell of the conspiracy. He left men to make certain." Jenna pulled back weakly, her hands gently cupping the handsome face that was more dear to her than life itself. Her arms stole around Stefan's neck as she melted into his embrace, oblivious of the pain it caused in the tender flesh across her back. Tenderly Stefan settled her back on the narrow but comfortable bed, turning her onto her side to ease her pain.

"We must leave in a few hours. Do you think you are strong enough?"

Jenna nodded with confidence. "As long as I know you are with me, I could go anywhere," she whispered, rubbing the back of Stefan's hand against her bruised cheek. Stefan seemed to recoil from her touch as he abruptly rose from her side. Jenna clung to his hand, uncertain of his mood.

"I know the names of the conspirators," Jenna whispered, thinking that perhaps the uncertainty of the conspiracy had caused his sudden thoughtfulness.

Stefan's blue gaze returned to hers. "We learned the name of one man before Sir Robert died. More than that he was not able to tell us, though it was enough to keep the prince regent safe."

Jenna shook her head. "There are near a full score of men involved in the conspiracy. I found a list inside the music box, that day Charles came to the house. Grandfather must have placed the list there. He must have known he might not live to complete his work." Jenna sighed heavily as she leaned back against the pillows.

"Can you remember the names?"

"I can remember them all. They are all people I know. Some of them were close associates of Grandfather. Stefan, he worked all those months, knowing what they were doing, and able to tell no one, except you."

Stefan gently gathered her slender hand in his, unable to resist the soft glow in the depths of her amber eyes. It was as if all the lies were being torn apart by a greater truth that lay behind that gaze, as if she were reaching into the very depths of his soul, giving him back life. And yet he was not ready to acknowledge the life that grew within her. For now it was enough that she was safe.

Jenna gave Stefan the names of the conspirators, names of important men, influential in every corner of power within the English government. Many of them had indeed been associates of her grandfather, many of them trusted by the regent, and by Parliament, as well. The conspiracy had indeed been far-reaching and dangerous. And when she had told him all that she knew of the conspiracy, she slept soundly for the first time in many days, her fingers gently entwined with Stefan's, drawing strength from his nearness, feeling completely safe, even within those very walls that had held her prisoner only hours before.

Stefan remained by Jenna's side through the long hours of the night. His men remained at guard until the last hours of darkness, when Dmitri returned to the small chamber to remind Stefan that they must leave soon or risk

436

being found within the abbey. Stefan nodded his silent agreement as he bent over Jenna to try and awaken her.

Comforted by Stefan's nearness, Jenna had surrendered to the exhaustion of the last days. She murmured softly in her sleep, never coming fully awake, as Stefan lifted her gently from the small bed and carried her from the abbey.

The horses that had drawn the two coaches were quickly harnessed. Dmitri gently lifted Jenna into Stefan's waiting arms and then swung up on another horse. Several of Stefan's men mounted the other horses, and the rest went on ahead on foot, to carefully guard the road against any surprise visitors. Slowly they descended Mont St. Michel, reaching the craggy bottom just as the first gray light of dawn paled in the western sky.

Jenna stirred at the sudden chill from the morning air feeling Stefan's warmth slip away from her. The warmth quickly returned as Dmitri's great, bearlike embrace closed about her. She sat up in the saddle in front of the giant Cossack, and Stefan's voice penetrated her drowsiness.

"Stefan?" Jenna mumbled uncertainly.

"You must go with Dmitri and my men." Stefan reached to take her slender hand in his, drawing her fingers to his lips for a farewell kiss.

"Where are you going?" Panic began to rise within Jenna as she suddenly realized Stefan did not intend to come with them.

Stefan nodded a silent message to Dmitri before looking once more to Jenna. "You are not strong enough to travel far. Dmitri will take you to Villandry. It is not far, and the French will never expect to find any of us still within France."

"I will not leave without you." Jenna clung to Stefan's hand with fevered desperation.

Stefan smiled down at her tenderly. "I must go to England. If the conspiracy is to be stopped completely, it is imperative that the duke of Kent knows the names you have given me. I can trust no one else to the matter. If one of these men escapes, no member of the royal family will be safe." Stefan tried to explain so that Jenna might understand. "Your grandfather gave his life to stop the conspiracy, and I must go to England now and make certain it is ended, or everything that he worked for and gave his life for will have been wasted."

"But how will you reach England?" Jenna whispered plaintively.

"In a cove very near here, a schooner lies at anchor, waiting to take me to England. But I must leave now, or she will sail without me."

"You promised you would not leave me again." Jenna's voice broke with her weak effort to keep him near, even though she knew well it was in vain.

Stefan leaned forward from his saddle, his lips closing tenderly over hers. He felt her trembling and tasted the salty sweetness of a tear that rolled down her cheek to her mouth. It stirred a desperate longing within him, to remain with her.

"Know that you are mine, Jenna. You have been mine, from the first moment I saw you. Because you are mine, we can never truly be parted. You must understand this is something that goes beyond our love. We cannot fail in this. We must not," he whispered passionately. Stefan kissed her again briefly, his face suddenly grim and hardened at the thoughts of the task before him. He glanced up at Dmitri.

"Take good care of her, my friend. Protect her as you would me. If I should not return, you have your instructions."

Dmitri nodded solemnly as Stefan turned his horse about. Jenna's fingers slipped through his as he urged the horse through the quickly receding water that washed across the causeway and along the length of the beach. A moment more and he disappeared completely among the sheltering rock formations that lined the coast.

Dmitri turned his own mount in the opposite direction, heading inland, the gently lapping waves washing away all traces of their passage. Jenna leaned sadly against Dmitri's massive shoulder. She had not asked about

438

Charles or his men. Though she had seen several men bound and gagged as they left the abbey, Charles had not been among them. She felt no remorse for his certain death as they carefully picked their way through the rocks along the shoreline.

Jenna cast a long, last look at the sheltering of rocks where Stefan had held her briefly. She shuddered at the nagging fear that she might well not see him again. Hadn't he spoken of the orders Dmitri had been given if he did not return? Sadness stole over her, dulling her meager spirit, and she quickly dozed against Dmitri's broad chest, lulled into deeper slumber as she was borne further and further away from Stefan.

Chapter Twenty-Three

The grandeur that had once been the Chateaux Villandry nestled in the verdant seclusion of the Loire Valley. It had not been diminished, either by the order of the Emperor Napoleon, or by his Grand Armée, sent from France to conquer the entire world.

Trees and vines, overgrown from lack of the practiced hand to manicure their shapes, and the magnificent gardens that surrounded the Chateaux, all had survived to cast forth their magnificent harvest season upon season, unattended. Villandry had been built during a time when royalty and others among the privileged had preferred the quieter ambience of the Loire Valley to Paris. The glory of Villandry had never been seen before. It would never be seen again.

As with many fine houses owned by the titled and the wealthy, the chateaux of the Loire had been vandalized during the first years of the Revolution. In the years since, Villandry had stood empty and forlorn, like a grand lady of the French court, dressed in her finest and awaiting the audience of her subjects. A handful of loyal servants had returned to Villandry and had managed to live off the bountiful harvests produced in the orchards and gardens. They awaited the return of their master, and were neither surprised nor frightened when Dmitri and his loyal Cossacks arrived there in late May. Several smaller rooms on the ground floor of the chateau were opened to

441

accommodate the new arrivals. Conversations that were exchanged were a mixture of French and Russian. These were the people of Stefan's youth. These were the loyal servants who had come with the young boy to France and who had served the royal princess, his mother, when she had fled her father, the Czar, and a cruel and loveless marriage.

During those first days at Villandry, the names and faces of the people were a blend of confusion for Jenna. Weakened by her ordeal at Mont St. Michel, she ate only sparingly of the simple but abundant fare, often nodding into slumber before the meal was finished. Rest seemed the healing balm that she needed, and yet Dmitri fussed over her like a mother over an ailing child. Always slender, her cheekbones seemed more defined in the soft oval of her face. The only fullness to her was the child she carried, which seemed to cling to life with Jenna's determination of will.

For nine days, Jenna had slept on a faded satin chaise that had been made into a bed, waking only to eat or to be bathed by the kind old woman who fussed over her with as much concern as Dmitri. Having ventured from her bed, after several days, for a walk into the overgrown gardens, Jenna napped soundly, undisturbed by the sounds of an approaching rider. Nor was she awakened a few minutes later when Stefan entered the sitting room, newly returned from England.

Not fully trusting Dmitri's hasty reassurances of Jenna's returning good health, Stefan quietly strode into the sitting room that he might see for himself that Jenna was indeed recovering from her ordeal at Mont St. Michel. The heavy velvet portieres to the windows had been drawn against the warmth of the afternoon sun, allowing only a faint light into the chamber. Stefan knelt beside the chaise, watching the rise and fall of her breasts with her even breathing. A faint glow spread across her cheeks, replacing the ugly purplish bruise that he remembered. Unable to resist the softness of her skin, Stefan reached out, tenderly stroking the delicate curve of her cheek, his fingers brushing back a stray tendril of long, dark hair. The thick sweep of her dark lashes rested against her cheeks, and her lips were slightly parted. In her hand she still held a brilliant crimson rose she had picked earlier in the garden. He fought against the doubts that had haunted his journey to England. Now, as he gazed down at her, he wondered about the child that grew within her. So long they had been apart. And yet it was impossible for him to believe Charles Wingate's taunting lies, spoken in death. Stefan reached out hesitantly, resting his hand lightly on the gentle swell of her stomach. As if in answer, he felt the child move strongly, and he wondered again about its father. Finding no answers by gazing at the exquisitely beautiful girl before him, Stefan rose wearily, straightening against the growing stiffness in his back. There would be time enough to know the truth of the child.

Jenna stirred faintly, as Marya, the old maid, entered the chamber. It seemed as if she had slept for days, instead of just a few hours since early afternoon. Her appetite seemed to have returned as the smells of the simple stew Marya had prepared filled her senses. She ate heartily, finally accepting a second glass of wine that the maid pushed into her hand. Jenna relaxed back against the chaise as Marya straightened the linens.

"Where is Dmitri?" Jenna questioned groggily, already beginning to feel the effect of the wine. She had come to enjoy the quiet moments when Dmitri visited her and stayed to relate some story of Stefan's childhood. It had been his custom to take the evening meal with her, and she wondered what might have kept the giant Cossack away that evening.

"He is with the others. They have gone into the woods nearby in search of game," Marya replied.

"I miss his company," Jenna sighed, feeling a soft glow from the wine stealing through her. "I had hoped he might share one of his stories tonight."

Marya scoffed gently. "That great Russian bear always tells his stories a little bit differently. I have heard all the same stories, and they are never the same twice."

443

Jenna nodded sleepily, trying to resist the sudden heaviness in her eyes. "Please tell Dmitri that I insist on a story in the morning."

Marya turned about to remove the dinner tray and shook her graying head as she gazed at the sleeping girl. For the first time in all the days since they had arrived, she had eaten a substantial meal. Marya sighed heavily as she removed the tray. She knew from Dmitri that Prince Kalinsky had sent them to the safety of Villandry. She knew also of the child the girl carried. From the protection and respect the girl received from each of Prince Kalinsky's men, she had no doubt who the sire might be. She shook her graying head as she closed the door of the sitting room behind her, at a loss to understand the young man she had helped to raise from a boy.

Jenna stirred at the sounds that came through the open windows of the room, thinking at first that she had been dreaming. As the noise of horses and riders persisted, Jenna came fully awake and rose from her bed. The heavy portieres had been drawn back to allow the cooling morning breeze in to enter the chamber. The delicate lace curtains lifted gently as the breeze returned. Jenna stared out the window at the riders in the yard beyond the gardens. Stefan Kalinsky sat astride his magnificent black stallion, leaning forward to give Vasily some last minute instruction before riding off to join his men. Jenna seized a light shawl, wrapping it about her shoulders as she fled the chamber barefoot. The garden lay just beyond her chamber, and she reached them in a matter of moments, her dark hair long and flowing down the middle of her back. Vasily and Dmitri stood in the center of the yard watching the departing riders.

"Why wasn't I told that Stefan had returned?"

Dmitri turned abruptly at the sound of Jenna's voice, taken aback by her radiant beauty, completely unadorned, in the soft glow of early morning light. Vasily coughed uneasily, quickly excusing himself to some task in the stables. Dmitri faced her uncertainly.

"He returned last night, and he asked that you not be

disturbed," Dmitri responded simply.

"Not be disturbed! After all these days, and countless reports of French patrols about the countryside; how could you not tell me of his arrival?" Jenna stared at Dmitri, suddenly understanding that his first loyalty was to Stefan.

"I was given my orders, little princess. Do not think harshly of him for this." Dmitri tried to ease the pain he saw in the wide, dark eyes that stared at him uncertainly. In vain, he tried to protect her from the coldness and aloofness that he had sensed in Stefan from the moment he had arrived.

Jenna sighed heavily as she turned back to the chateau. All the past days she had lived for the moment of Stefan's return, and when that moment was at hand, he had not even awakened her. Taking no time to rest, Stefan had quickly ridden out with his men, seeming to take more ease in their company than hers. Jenna fought back the nagging uncertainty that welled within her at his mood, which seemed so greatly changed since their parting at Mont St. Michel.

Over the next days and weeks it became increasingly difficult for Jenna to ignore the coolness that had sprung between them, like an insurmountable barrier that neither could cross over. Stefan had taken the room across from hers in the main house, leaving her to her silent tears behind the heavy door that closed each night. He rose early, taking his morning meal quickly in order to join his men for a full day's ride about the valley, returning late each evening long after the evening meal had been served. Late in the night, long after the last candle had burned low, Jenna could hear him moving about in the solitary seclusion of his own chamber, and she wondered at the silence that had sprung between them, her tears flowing down her cheeks as she hugged herself tightly, finding temporary comfort in the child that grew within her, Stefan's child.

When she could tolerate the silence no longer, Jenna rose early one morning and followed the well-worn path to the stables, drawing the thin woven shawl close about her shoulders against the morning chill. As she knew she would, Jenna found Stefan saddling the black stallion he had brought back from England. The magnificent animal nickered softly in greeting as she entered the stables. Reaching out, Jenna stroked the velvet softness of the outthrust muzzle as the black searched for some treat. Jenna retrieved one of the small red apples she had brought from the kitchen. She gazed uncertainly at Stefan from behind the wave of her hair that flowed loosely over her shoulder, trying to guess his mood. Stefan grimly continued tightening the cinch strap about the stallion, seeming oblivious of her presence as he roughly slapped the sleek beast when he moved forward, stepping too close to Stefan's booted foot. The black snorted, rolling his great dark eyes warily at Stefan's uneven temper.

Jenna gathered her courage, which threatened to rapidly disappear in the presence of his dark mood. "You are gone so much. We have hardly had a moment to speak," she began uncertainly.

"I do not have time for idle chatter. There is much that must be done here if we are to remain safe from the French," Stefan bit off sharply.

Jenna stiffened at his harshness, but continued along the uncertain course she had begun. "It seems you have little time for anything of late, and I do not want to be a burden to you. I came to tell you that I want to return to England, as soon as possible. There is no reason for me to remain here."

Without the slightest indication that he had heard anything she had said, Stefan finished buckling the cinch strap and lowered the stirrup into place.

Jenna waited impatiently, uncertain whether to persist or forget the entire matter. Stefan swung easily into the saddle, the sun warming the golden streaks in his hair, the dazzling blue of the summer sky reflected in the depths of his eyes. Jenna was uncertain of the anger she saw in that brilliant gaze, uncertain of what she might have done to cause the harshness in his manner.

"It is impossible for you to go to England now. There is too much danger between Villandry and the coast. Napoleon's men are everywhere. I cannot be bothered with this now. You will remain here," Stefan replied curtly, avoiding her startled gaze as he swung the black stallion about and quickly urged him across the field toward the distant hill where his men waited. Stunned by his unexplained anger, Jenna whirled around, nearly colliding with Dmitri as she wiped at the tears that blurred her vision.

"Easy, little princess. You must take greater care, that you do not cause yourself harm." Dmitri reached to steady her, but she twisted away from his grasp.

"Why is he so angry with me? What have I done to warrant his hatred?" Jenna choked back a sob.

"He is not angry with you. He is angry with himself. He bears no hatred for you. He carries a great burden inside, a burden that cannot easily be lifted. He blames himself for what happened to you at Mont St. Michel." Dmitri spoke gently, trying to make her understand.

"But that is past, if only he would let it be. And I am well. I have recovered completely. I think I have never been healthier, and yet still I find him looking at me sometimes as if he cannot bear the sight of me." Jenna's voice broke off in a whisper.

"It is the fear within him that makes him uncertain. You must try to understand."

Jenna laughed, thinking surely Dmitri made some jest. She stopped when she saw his grim frown. "Stefan has never been afraid of anything. What does he fear in me?"

"He carries the scars of the tormented child, born a bastard, sent far away from his mother, never knowing his father until years later. The scars are deep and not easily healed," Dmitri answered vaguely.

"Does he hate the child I carry because it will be born a bastard?" Jenna asked with brutal honesty.

Dmitri sighed heavily as he swung atop his own horse. He realized that he dared much in speaking so openly of his friend and master. Yet as he stared down at the slender

447

girl who clung to the reins of his horse insistently, he saw only love in the depths of her dark eyes. Jenna spoke the words that Dmitri could not find the strength to say.

"He does not believe the child is his." Jenna said quietly.

Dmitri leaned from the saddle, covering her small hand with his larger one, comfortingly.

"I know that the child is his. I know exactly when the child was made," Dmitri replied with a sudden twinkling in his eye. He seized the reins from her hand gently. "I think it is not long before he knows it is true. Until that time, you must be patient. You must help him to understand."

"How can I make him understand, when he does not speak to me?"

"Over many years he has learned to close out pain; but with you it is different. He has never loved completely before. Now he must learn to choose whether he will have love in his life or only sadness. He will make the right choice." Dmitri nodded confidently as he turned toward the distant field where Stefan had ridden moments before.

Jenna watched Dmitri disappear over the hillside and then turned back toward the chateau. She was surprised to find Vasily in the kitchen, thinking that all of Stefan's men had ridden out that morning. He smiled shyly at her sudden appearance.

"You are not aware, but each day when the others ride out, one of us remains behind. It is merely as a precaution, should the French venture this far," Vasily explained good-naturedly as he took a last slice of fresh, hot bread from the platter, before Marya could pull it beyond his reach.

Vasily disappeared in the direction of the stables, and Marya was soon bustling about the large kitchen, having much to do with so many to feed, now that Stefan and his men had returned. Jenna finished the glass of milk Marya had set before her and then quickly retreated from the kitchen before the old woman could criticize her for the meager meal she had eaten. She quickly found solace in the gardens beyond the chateau. The living quarters were on three sides of a court, which provided a sweeping view of the valley. With its abundance of turrets, esplanades, and moats, the chateaux was indeed impressive, but the finest part of Villandry, by far, were the gardens. Planting patterns that included vegetables and flowers had been intricately arranged with great care. The beds for the gardens had been framed by box hedges, forming geometric patterns. Pathways led between the beds, and here and there were fountains and yew trees that had once been pruned into shapes similar to those of the balusters of the chateau's balcony railing. Viewed from a higher terrace the garden's pattern reminded one of an oriental carpet, or perhaps a fine embroidery.

Waterways and reflecting pools, some enormous, had once added another dimension of splendor. Trellises supported vines that were now overgrown, along the walkways. Pergolas provided an accent at each walkway corner, seeming to invite a visitor to pause. It was sad to realize the beauty and magnificence that had once been Villandry, and to look at it now in such sad neglect. Yet beyond the overgrown gardens and now empty reflecting pools she could see the beauty that might again be Villandry. She wondered what it had been like for the young Russian prince, exiled to France because of his birth. She wondered, too, of the woman who had defied both father and king to give Stefan life. Jenna sighed heavily as she realized that her meager prunings of the last weeks had hardly made any visible difference in the gardens. Still, she continued her cutting, finding some solace for the restless thoughts that wandered through her mind.

Faintly Jenna heard Marya calling from the chateau. When the old woman's calling became more insistent, Jenna glanced up to see Marya frantically waving a cloth to gain her attention. She could hardly understand the woman's words as she called out in an excited mixture of Russian and French. Realizing that something was indeed very wrong, Jenna set aside the basket that she had nearly

449

filled with flowers. She sped down the long row and cut across the overgrown lawn that surrounded a large pool in the center of the garden. When she reached the steps of the side entrance to the chateau, Marya was nowhere to be seen. Jenna glanced across the yard as Vasily came running from the stables.

"What is it?"

"Go with Marya, to the woods. She will take you to a gamekeeper's cottage. Do not leave until I come for you."

"What has happened?" Jenna tried to free her arm from Vasily's grasp.

"A French patrol is on the main road from Toulon. They will be here any moment. You must go now. It would be very dangerous for them to find you."

"I will not leave you." Jenna succeeded in pulling her arm free of his grasp as Marya appeared from the kitchen with a heavily laden basket.

"We must go now." The old woman wrung her hands nervously. In the distance they could hear the sounds of approaching horses, from the lane that lead to the chateau. A sword in one hand and a pistol tucked in his belt, Vasily motioned them toward the woods as he disappeared around the corner of the north wing.

"I will not leave him to face them alone." Jenna spoke firmly to Marya as she ran into the kitchen, down the hallway toward the room Stefan had occupied across from hers, during the past weeks. Behind her, Marya followed, frantically trying to persuade her to leave while time remained. Glancing through the heavily draped windows that opened out on the gardens, Jenna could see there was no more time for escape. Three French soldiers approached the front entrance of Chateaux Villandry.

Jenna searched among the drawers of the desk, at last finding what she sought. Her hand closed calmly over Stefan's pistol. She would be allowed only one shot. It would have to be enough. Behind her Marya gasped, as she realized Jenna's intentions. Jenna hid the pistol in the folds of her apron. Both women jumped as the heavy latch to the front door of the chateau was broken and the door sent back hard on its creaking hinges. Through the windows, Jenna could see one of the soldiers approaching the stables, obviously in search of horses. A deafening roar exploded the silence of the warm afternoon as a pistol was fired. Another soldier quickly gave orders in French, and a second soldier left to give assistance The third soldier remained just inside the main entrance of the chateau. Jenna waited and listened. She could hear the sounds of struggling from the stables beyond. Inside the chateau she could hear only the sound of her own heartbeat, which seemed to echo like a resounding drum. And then she heard it: the sounds of heavy footsteps on the wood floor just beyond the chamber. The door was pushed open slowly, and then the figure of a man in a soiled uniform appeared in the doorway. His wary expression quickly turned into a smile of keen surprise as he calmly returned her gaze. His hand on his pistol, the soldier motioned Jenna out into the foyer. The soldier glanced uncertainly out the door toward the stables. When he saw neither of his men, he glanced back at Jenna, a keen light springing into his dark eyes. Here was greater fortune than he had expected. He would take his pleasure of this dark-haired beauty, and then they would take whatever else of value might be found.

Slowly the soldier approached Jenna. She backed away warily, until she felt the wall of the foyer at her back, barring further retreat. The soldier reached out a scarred and dirty hand to brush back the mass of Jenna's hair, which had fallen loosely over her shoulder. Jenna jerked her head away defiantly, only to feel that hand twisting in the length of her hair, as the soldier pulled her against him, laughing his pleasure at her spirit. Her hands flew up to push him away as his one arm encircled her waist and pulled her intimately against him. His breath was sour with a sickening warmth against her skin, as he tried to taste the soft skin across her bare shoulder. Jenna struggled to twist free of his grasp, panic rising within her. In vain she tried to call out for Vasily, and a grimy, calloused hand quickly clamped down over her mouth.

Jenna twisted her head away, biting down on the man's hand. He howled in pain as he drew back, and then struck her, sending her back against the wall. Across the foyer, Jenna could see Marya, a long carving knife clutched desperately in both hands. The old woman's strength would be no match for the man who held Jenna pinned against the wall. Desperately, Jenna tried to warn the woman back, momentarily drawing the soldier's attention away from herself. Jenna twisted away, bringing the pistol up sharply. The soldier roared with laughter as he saw the old woman poised to do him harm. One strike of his arm, and Marya crumpled to the floor. The Frenchman turned back to Jenna, his amusement at the old woman quickly fading as he stared down the barrel of the pistol. The smile returned faintly and then broadened into a wide grin as he considered the foolishness of a mere girl's handling a pistol. The French soldier descended on Jenna, a lustful gleam lighting his eyes. The roar from the pistol sounded like that of a cannon as it echoed against the walls of the chateau. Jenna was pinned against the wall behind her as the French soldier fell forward, his greater weight falling against her. She closed her eyes against the horror of the lifeless eyes that stared from the face beside hers. Panic welled within her as she tried in vain to push the man's heavy body off her. Through the confusion and fear, Jenna could hear the unmistakable sounds of more riders approaching. She could only fear the worst.

Jenna struggled to her feet, her knees threatening to buckle beneath her. She retrieved the pistol and then leaned heavily against the wall, trying desperately to remember where Stefan might have left more powder and shot. But there was no more time, as the riders dismounted and quickly entered the chateau.

Jenna stared in stunned disbelief as Stefan appeared in the doorway. She was unaware of the blood smeared across the front of her gown, which presented a ghastly sight, as Stefan quickly crossed the hall and gathered her in his arms, while shouting orders at his men. She could not know the terror that had filled his heart at the sight of one soldier slain in the yard and a second lying across Vasily, the front door of the chateau standing wide open. They had returned as soon as they had received word that soldiers had been seen on the road to Villandry. Now, as he held her against his heart, he realized how easily he might have lost her.

Jenna clung to Stefan with silent desperation as the fear and panic of the moments before washed over her. She leaned weakly against the strength of his lean, hard chest beneath her cheek.

"You are not harmed?"

Jenna shook her head firmly. Wide, dark eyes lifted to his, the amber depths suddenly awash with tears.

"Vasily . . ." Jenna pulled away from his embrace as she tried to go to the fallen Cossack. Stefan firmly refused to release her, his strong fingers closing over her shoulders.

"You will stay here. My men will see to Vasily."

"There may be others," Jenna warned, the fear still deep in her eyes.

"They were only deserters. Villandry is of little importance, except for the bounty they thought to find," Stefan whispered harshly, as he realized the cost might have been more than he could bear. The muscles in his jaw tautened visibly, hardening the line of his handsome face as he thought of the danger to Jenna. He reached out, his fingers brushing against the bloodstained muslin of her gown. Dmitri appeared in the doorway, the grim expression on his face softening when he was certain Jenna was not harmed.

"What of Vasily?" Stefan turned to his friend.

"He is badly wounded, but he lives. He managed to take two of them before he fell." Dmitri nodded grimly.

"I must go to him. I owe him my life." Jenna tried again to pull away from Stefan and found her way soundly blocked. He sighed heavily, recognizing the determined gleam in her wide eyes.

"I will have Vasily brought to the main house. I will not have you going to him in the stables."

Jenna quickly gave her orders to Marya for whatever

453

linens might still be found in the house, and hot water. Vasily was carried to the servants' quarters near the kitchen, and Jenna quickly set about her work. With Stefan beside her, Jenna cut away the blood-soaked tunic, exposing two blade wounds. Both were quite deep, but not as serious as the deep gash above his left eye where he had taken a blow from the butt of the pistol.

It was very near midnight when Jenna at last straightened and washed her hands in the basin of warm water that Marya had brought for her. Her back ached from leaning over all those long hours, cleaning and binding Vasily's wounds. Indeed, he would live. Wearily Jenna brushed back a stray wisk of dark hair as she again checked the bandage about his head. For now there was nothing more she could do. He slept peacefully, having drunk amply of Dmitri's freshly brewed tea laced with liberal doses of cognac. Stefan had been beside her during those long hours, refusing to leave her side, giving aid to Dmitri in holding Vasily when it was necessary for Jenna to remove the ball that had torn into his side. Now, as she arched against the stiffness in her back, Stefan drew her down on his knee and gently massaged her back. Jenna reached to pull aside the heavy mass of her long hair as his lean, strong fingers gently worked the ache from her tired muscles.

Stefan leaned forward, gently kissing the back of her neck, which smelled faintly of lavender. Jenna sighed, luxuriating in his kiss as much as in the comfort he brought with his soothing massage.

"Will he sleep the night?"

"I should think it would probably take one of Napoleon's cannons to waken him, for the amount of cognac you and Dmitri gave him with the tea. I fear his greatest discomfort will not be from his wounds, but from the size of his head in the morning from drinking so much." Jenna smiled at Stefan reproachfully.

"You might easily have been killed today," Stefan whispered solemnly. "You deliberately disobeyed my orders."

"And I would do so again," Jenna replied evenly as she turned to face him. "I could not run and hide, leaving Vasily to face the French alone. It would surely have meant his death."

"And you thought that your presence might make a difference?" Stefan stared into her wide amber gaze, already knowing he had lost the argument before it was begun, and yet somehow he had to make her understand the fear she had caused him that day.

"Did you think to take on the entire French army—a beautiful young woman, vulnerable and with child, with only an old woman for protection?" Golden lights glinted in the depths of his blue gaze as he held her firmly.

She was tired, and hungry, and she ached all over, and the last thing Jenna wanted was Stefan's criticism. When he had returned that afternoon, she had seen love in his eyes, and all the long hours of the evening that love had been there, in his touch, in his gently spoken words of encouragement. She had felt the tenderness in his hands only moments before when he had tried to take some of the pain from her. But now, he attacked her for something that was finished and gone, as if he sought somehow to punish her for some misdeed she could not understand. Jenna tried to twist from his grasp as tears of anger and frustration flooded her eyes. How could he be so cruel and hateful, when she loved him so desperately.

"Let me go!" Jenna whispered frantically, as she tried to move off his knee. "What would it have mattered if I had been killed? It is obvious these last weeks that you care little what might happen to me, and I hardly think you are concerned for the child." Jenna finally managed to gain her freedom as she sprang for the door of the small chamber, darting into the hallway beyond, concerned that their words might awaken Vasily. Stefan quickly followed, seizing her arm from behind and gently turning her about, closing her within the warmth of his embrace.

"How can I make you understand?" Stefan moaned harshly, staring down into the dark, stormy depths of her eyes, filled with the fire of her defiance. "How can I make you understand that you are more to me than life itself; more to me than I have ever allowed anyone to be?"

"You have never allowed me to understand. You have always loved me when you chose to love me, and then held me at a distance when I would have returned that love. From the very beginning, you told me that we were destined to love, but you have never asked for my love, as if you were commanding one of your men. I am not one of your men. I did not fall in love by royal decree; I loved you in spite of it. And now I carry your child because of that love. Will you now send me away to some far place to bear our child? Is that why you have brought me to Villandry?" Jenna sobbed softly as she held onto Stefan, all her fears of the last weeks spilling forth with her tears.

Her words tore at his heart. Stefan slowly pulled Jenna into his embrace, drawing her tightly against him in spite of her feeble protests. She struggled feebly, at last yielding to the fatigue and sadness that rose within her, drawing comfort from his nearness, no matter what his emotions for her might be. Stefan whispered softly against her ear, the words soothing her raw senses as he stroked the softness of her hair.

"I was angry because of my own doubts; doubts because I foolishly believed words spoken by a madman," Stefan whispered, hoarse with emotion.

Jenna pulled back, staring into the depths of his eyes, trying to gain some understanding of what he was saying.

"Was it something Charles said to you?"

"It is not important now. I know it was a lie. But once I had made the wall between us, I did not know how to remove it. Each day, it seemed that you were more distant from me, so that I began to fear you no longer cared. Today, when we returned to Villandry and I saw you covered with blood, my only thought was that I would be to blame if any harm had come to you. I know I could not continue in this life, if you were not there to share it." Stefan pulled Jenna gently against him, burying his face in the fragrant softness of her hair.

"You fear the child is not yours." Jenna spoke softly,

with sudden certainty.

"I no longer have those doubts." Stefan held her face in his hands, his fingers trembling as he gently stroked the silken softness of her cheek. "I know the child came from our last days together before I left for Vienna. I think I have known from the very moment the child was conceived."

Jenna sighed wistfully. "I can offer you nothing except my word, that the child is yours. Whatever Charles may have told you, you must believe the babe is yours. Only time will make you certain."

"I am certain now," Stefan whispered, bending to kiss her mouth tenderly, the touch of his lips filling her with longing.

"You must rest now. I could not bear for you to become ill from caring for Vasily. I will have Marya bring you something to eat, and then you will sleep."

"I do not want food, nor sleep. There is only one thing that I want at this very moment. I want to be with you." Jenna reached up, her arms entwining about Stefan's neck as she drew him down to her. Her lips sought his with growing hunger as the warmth of her touch fused with his.

Gently Stefan lifted Jenna in his arms, their kiss unbroken, as he bore her to his chamber, the emptiness and uncertainty of the last days slipping away.

Jenna stirred faintly, feeling a tickling against her cheek, and murmured softly in her sleep as she tried to brush the tickling away. When the tickling persisted, her eyes opened slowly, and she stared uncertainly at the lean form that filled her gaze.

"Stefan?" Jenna whispered as the room brightened with the first light of dawn.

"Merely a phantom, milady, come to bring you a summer flower," Stefan replied softly, stroking her cheek with a delicate pink daisy, his fingers then replacing the soft blossom as he caressed her skin and thought of the night they had shared. Faint circles of fatigue lingered beneath her eyes, after so little rest.

Jenna seized his hand, bringing it to her lips as she reached for him, feeling the exquisite warmth of his embrace closing around her. "I miss your warmth when you are not near," she murmured softly.

Stefan chuckled against the softness of her hair. "You were sleeping so soundly, you did not know I had gone," he teased playfully, his lips brushing against the soft skin across her forehead as his senses filled with the tantalizing pleasure of her nearness. It was a need that had very nearly driven him mad the last weeks. It was a need that surpassed his doubts of Charles Wingate's last words. She was his soul, his very life, each breath that he took. Once she had risked her life for him, and had been made to suffer because of him. She had risked her life for Vasily, because of some inner strength and courage he had only just begun to understand. She was soft and vulnerable beneath his hand, and yet as strong as the finest steel.

"I always know when you are not near. It is as if I am not whole without your strength beside me." Jenna curled within the safe haven of Stefan's embrace. He pulled her against him gently, stroking the silken softness of her hair.

"What will happen when Napoleon learns the conspiracy has failed? Is there any place that will be safe?"

"Napoleon has greater matters to concern him now than our presence at Villandry. He will need every available officer and soldier to hold back Wellington's advancing armies from Spain. We have learned that Wellington's army has defeated the French at Vittoria. With the English moving across Spain, it may now be safe for us to reach the coast of Spain. For Napoleon Bonaparte, it is the end," Stefan replied over the top of her head nestled in the curve of his neck. Beneath his arm that rested about Jenna's waist, he felt the faint stirrings of his child. Stefan's startled blue gaze met Jenna's. He smiled tenderly as he reached to spread his hand across the roundness of her stomach, feeling the strong movement beneath his fingers as the child moved again.

Jenna's hand moved over his, binding him to her, suddenly feeling an overwhelming happiness that Stefan wanted to feel the movement of his child within her.

Stefan lifted her chin to gaze into the depths of her eyes, where a myriad golden light glowed softly. Jenna reached up, her arm encircling his neck, pulling him closer, her lips demanding as his mouth closed over hers, hungering with growing need as Jenna responded with a passion to match his, drawing him down beside her with an urgency that left them both breathless. With fevered hands, Jenna stripped away his shirt, and then his breeches, her fingers igniting a multitude of flames upon his skin as they wandered across the browned surface with abandon.

Stefan reached to stroke his hands through the thick silken mass of her hair, holding her face tenderly as he bent to taste her lips. Her taste was the sweetest wine, which left him thirsting for more, until his senses could be filled with the sight, the touch, the taste of her. Slowly Stefan reached to draw the muslin gown over her head. Jenna's hands resisted him momentarily, suddenly uncertain what his reaction might be upon first seeing her rounded form. Stefan persisted, his lips tenderly persuading her of his love. Jenna's hands fell away, allowing him to pull the gown over her head. She sat before him, on bended legs, the cascading mass of her long hair forming a secretive veil about her slender body, momentarily shielding her from view. Stefan reached out slowly, smoothing back the rich, dark waves of her hair, exposing a silken shoulder. Jenna crossed her arms before her, feeling suddenly vulnerable and afraid. Her lips trembled as Stefan gently seized her wrists in his lean, strong fingers and drew her hands away. Her wide amber gaze searched his. He reached out, his fingers lightly tracing across the rounded curve of her belly. As if in response to his touch, the child moved sharply within her. Jenna's startled gaze met his. She reached for him, binding him to her with a longing and desire born of their time together, and their time apart.

Gently, Stefan pulled her beneath him, his knee moving between her thighs. "Our child seems to protest being awakened so early. Perhaps we should let him rest and not disturb him further." Stefan laughed good-humoredly against her neck as he nuzzled her playfully.

Jenna gave him her answer as she reached up, her arms entwining about his neck, drawing him to her with growing urgency. Her full breasts pressed against him wantonly, and her mouth hungered beneath his. She felt the longing within her burst forth like a ravaging flame, spreading through her entire being until it threatened to consume her. There was no measure of time, no world beyond the exquisite meeting of warmth against warmth, kindling into a flame of desire that surpassed all fears, all doubts. Stefan lingered over the silken smoothness of her skin, his hands exploring all the contours of his memory. It was as if a thousand days had separated them, and yet nothing was forgotten; indeed, each touch, each caress was heightened by the memory of other days and nights together. Stefan kissed her fingers, the back of her hand, and up the length of her arm. One kiss became another as he pressed a fevered path of kisses across the curve of her shoulder and up the column of her neck. His fingers entwined with hers, drawing her hands up beside her head as he leaned to taste the passion on her lips. He entered her slowly, savoring their joining. When he felt her impassioned response beneath him, he pressed deeper, feeling the tantalizing pleasure of her heat closing about him. Jenna marveled at the sight of Stefan's lean, bronzed body joining with hers. They moved together slowly, until their need of one another became a live creature that rose within them in a single passion that sought release. Jenna cried out, burying her face in Stefan's shoulder, feeling the warmth of his release flooding through her in recurrent waves of pleasure as he carried her with him. Slowly they drifted into slumber, his fingers entwined in the tangled mass of her hair, refusing to release her, even in sleep. Jenna curled into the curve of Stefan's body, murmuring softly, unintelligibly, her lips brushing against the smooth surface of his shoulder.

When Stefan rose again sometime later, Jenna stirred beside him, struggling out of the deep slumber that the child within her demanded. Stefan pressed her back into the softness of the bed, pulling the linen covers over her shoulders.

"I must attend Vasily," Jenna protested.

"You must rest. I will not have you or the child endangered again. I will attend Vasily. Rest, my princess," Stefan whispered gently as he pressed a kiss against her cheek, realizing she had hardly heard his last words as she drifted into sleep.

When Jenna rose, the day was well advanced, and she hastened from the chamber, drawing the muslin wrapper over her gown. No sounds came from the other chambers of the chateau. Her bare feet silent on the wood floors of the hall, Jenna went directly to the servants' chambers. Vasily slept soundly, an empty bowl beside the bed. Jenna checked the bandages, which had been replaced with fresh ones. His skin was cool, with no signs of fever. Jenna sighed, grateful that with rest and care, Vasily would live. She left the chamber, closing the door gently behind her as she heard voices coming from the kitchen. Dmitri and Stefan were seated at the long wood table at the far side of the kitchen. Marya had just served them a simple meal of bread and cheese, and fresh fruits from the gardens. Stefan reached for Jenna's hand, drawing her down on the long bench beside him. She leaned back into the curve of his body, drawing comfort from his nearness.

"Vasily rests well. It must have been the tea you brewed for him." Jenna's eyes sparkled with her good humor.

"Of course," Dmitri acknowledged. "But your care of the wounds might perhaps have had something to do with it."

Jenna laughed easily at his generosity. "I think the wounds might have fared well unattended, for the amount of cognac you and Stefan poured into the tea. It is a wonder he has awakened at all. I shall attend his care for the next days. If it were left to you, his head might pain him for a fortnight." Jenna was aware of a sudden silence that had fallen between Stefan and Dmitri. She glanced speculatively from the one to the other, wondering what had caused them to be so solemn. Stefan sighed heavily.

"We cannot remain here at Villandry. We must leave, and very soon. This very morning, my men returned with reports of a regiment of French soldiers marching from Orleans. There are rumors that Napoleon has retreated to Fontainebleu, to organize his defense of Paris against Wellington. In a matter of days the entire valley will be filled with French legions," Stefan said somberly.

"But what importance could Villandry possibly hold for the French? There is nothing here but farmlands." Jenna turned to Stefan.

"Villandry is very strategically located within the Loire Valley. We cannot risk being here, should Napoleon send his generals to establish a line of defense. There will be no safety for anyone here at Villandry," Dmitri answered.

"In a couple of days it might be possible for Vasily to ride in a cart, but it would surely mean his death to risk riding a horse. Could we possibly reach the coast, and from there England?"

Stefan shook his head. "Napoleon's army is amassed along the entire coast, in anticipation of an English offensive across the channel. We might possibly cross into Spain, and reach San Sebastian. It would mean a long journey, with no guarantee of passage from Spain."

Jenna sipped the cup of chocolate that Marya had placed before her, thoughtfully. "Could we go to your home at Varykein?"

Dmitri and Stefan both turned to stare at her, as if they thought she might have suffered some loss of common sense. Stefan laughed gently at the suggestion. "Varykein is very far away. It would take weeks to cross the eastern frontier, with no assurances of our arriving before the first snows of winter. Our fate would be no better than Napoleon's in Russia."

Dmitri propped his bearded chin on his hand thoughtfully. "It is impossible to reach England, and Napoleon prepares to meet Wellington's army pressing from Spain. We might easily be caught between the two. We cannot remain at Villandry, and it is well known that Napoleon's defenses against Austria are weakening. To the east lie the combined armies of the Austrian emperor, and your uncle, the Czar. Varykein would be a safe haven to spend the winter," Dmitri argued logically.

Stefan rose abruptly from the table, turning to face Jenna and Dmitri. "This is madness! Do you think me a complete fool to risk further injury to Vasily, or the life of my son? You know well the journey is long and difficult, under the best circumstances, let alone fleeing from the French."

Jenna went to him, reaching out to caress his cheek. "The entire summer lies before us; surely enough time for the journey. And I am strong, and the child is strong within me. In a very few days, Vasily will be able to ride. It seems any other choice would be most dangerous." She spoke softly, tearing away the resistance of logic. She gathered his hand in hers, pressing it against the firmness of his child. "I would like for my child to be born at Varykein. It is important to me." Jenna spoke convincingly.

Stefan sighed helplessly as he gazed into the liquid depths of her amber eyes, knowing he had lost the argument before it had begun.

"It is foolishness." He sighed unconvincingly.

"Surely no more foolish than riding into the middle of Napoleon's army, or waiting for them to come to us," Jenna countered.

Stefan nodded his resignation. "Very well. As soon as Vasily can ride, we shall leave for the eastern frontier."

Chapter Twenty-Four

By the second week in June, Vasily insisted he was strong enough to ride, and proved his fitness with a show of horsemanship in the yard of the chateau. Though Jenna was not fooled by his show of bravado and knew well that the effort greatly tired him, she could not argue against the growing danger of their remaining any longer at Villandry. Daily, Stefan's men rode the surrounding countryside, returning with reports of the advancing French legions that prepared for the defense of France against Wellington.

Preparations were made for their departure. The two wagons at the chateau were packed with provisions for the journey. They dare not take more. Each additional cart would only slow their pace, leaving them vulnerable to the French. There was very little for Jenna to pack; indeed her only garments had been the simple muslin gowns Marya had sewn to accommodate her increasing waistline. Though, even in this first month of summer, it was not obvious to the unsuspecting eye that she was with child. She remained slender, the only proof of the child evident when she undressed at night and crawled naked into Stefan's arms. Though Marya continually nagged at her to eat more, believing that ample roundness meant good health, Jenna was now silently grateful that she was not overly burdened with the child. It would make her condition less obvious, and the journey easier.

That last morning, Jenna stood in the middle of Stefan's chamber with her three high-waisted gowns spread before her, heartily wishing she were a man, with a few pairs of breeches for her wardrobe. She could hardly envision herself traveling for weeks, across the whole of Europe, in a flimsy gown, and yet there hardly seemed any choice in the matter. She turned suddenly, as Stefan entered the chamber.

"We are not planning to attend the opera or some grand ball, that you must delay us for the choice of an appropriate gown," Stefan teased playfully, his hands folded behind his back as he watched her with amusement.

"The latest French fashions hardly allow for traveling great distances on the back of a horse. I envy you the breeches and boots you wear." Jenna sighed uncertainly.

A smile pulled at the corners of Stefan's handsome mouth as he seemed to enjoy her dilemma. He was spotlessly dressed, in dark brown breeches that clung to his muscular body like a second skin, tucked into the tops of equally spotless gleaming black boots. A linen shirt was tucked inside the breeches, and over it he wore a loose vest of the same brown color. Under any other circumstances he might have seemed the gentleman, enjoying the splendor of a summer day at his palatial home in the Loire Valley.

Stefan reached out, encircling Jenna's rounded waist and drawing her against him intimately. He bent over, his lips seeking hers possessively, as he molded her still slender body against his.

"My men were concerned about the presence of a beautiful young lady on our journey from France. Through their combined efforts, they made you this gift, and asked that I give it to you. I will admit, my little princess, it was a most thoughtful gesture." Stefan presented her with a large bundle wrapped in plain cloth and tied all about with a cord.

Jenna took the bundle, a look of bewilderment crossing her lovely face as she untied the cord. Inside the cloth wrapping were an assortment of garments, the most notable being a pair of the loose-fitting Cossack pants Dmitri seemed to favor. And from their size it seemed that Dmitri had donated a pair of his own to the cause of her wardrobe. Jenna lifted the dark brown pants for a closer inspection.

"Have I grown so large that Dmitri thinks his pants of adequate size?" Jenna questioned. Stefan could no longer resist his humor at the expression on her face, and he burst out laughing.

"I think perhaps he thought more of the weeks to come, when the child grows larger. For now, I think you will find the others of more suitable fit, though I'll warrant you will hardly need a belt to make the fit more snug." Stefan chuckled as he reached out, measuring the width of her increased waistline with the span of his hands. He spread his long fingers wider apart to accommodate her increased measurement.

Jenna choked back a bloodcurdling oath. "You pompous ass, it is because of you that I grow fatter with each passing day. Very soon, I shall rival Marya in size, and you will seek your pleasure elsewhere."

Stefan's eyes filled with tears of laughter as he struggled to suppress his enjoyment of her high temper. He had not been wrong. Not only was she the most beautiful creature he had ever seen, she was certainly the most spirited. His brilliant blue eyes gleamed with his memory of other spirited moments they had shared. He reached out, brushing aside her protests as he pulled her into his embrace, smothering her objections beneath the warmth of his lips. For a moment she struggled against his hold, and then her arms locked about him possessively as she surrendered to a greater desire than vengeance. It was a full, long moment before Stefan regained his composure, pulling back suddenly as Jenna nipped at him. He felt his injured lip as he stared warily into the depths of her exquisite face, that which was a vision of feigned innocence.

"I think there are more dangers to be found here than in fighting duels with enemies," Stefan declared flatly.

Jenna's laughter filled the room as she whirled away from his embrace and seized a small broom, left at the hearth to sweep the ash and cinders. She turned on him with feigned bravado, assuming the position of an accomplished duelist. "Let that be a lesson to you." Jenna lunged playfully with the broom handle that had suddenly become an imaginary blade, shrieking with laughter, as Stefan seized her slender wrist and pulled her toward him, turning her in his embrace so that she was soundly caught.

"And let this be a lesson to you, milady." Stefan nibbled tenderly at the soft flesh across her bare shoulder and up the curve of her neck, sending shivers of delight down Jenna's back as his wanderings became bolder, his hand closing over the fullness of her breast as he pulled her into him.

"You take unfair advantage, your highness," Jenna murmured as she lay her head back against his shoulder, luxuriating in the warmth of his lips against her skin. Stefan leaned over her, his lips wandering across the fullness of her breast exposed above her muslin gown. She sighed heavily at the desire that flowed through her. She might easily have lingered with Stefan, to fulfill the passion that raged within her, had he not pulled away from her suddenly.

"You take unfair advantage," Stefan accused her. "All the preparations have been made. The horses are saddled and waiting in the yard. If we do not appear very soon, I fear my men will come looking for us. And though none of them are innocent in such matters, I do not think you wish them to find us abed. But I swear, milady, if you persist in such tactics, then we shall be forced to remain in France, and Napoleon will find us abed." Stefan fled for the door before his own desire betrayed him.

Jenna stared at him with wide-eyed innocence. "I am certain I have no idea what you are talking about." Jenna dissolved into fits of laughter as Stefan retreated from the chamber, slamming the door behind him.

A short while later, Jenna emerged from the chateau, dressed in much the same way as Stefan's men. The smaller pants had proven the better fit, for the time being, and Jenna was quite satisfied that there remained ample room in the waist for growth. Instead of belting the tunic snugly about her waist, as Marya had shown her, Jenna had chosen to wear the soft linen tunic loosely over the pants, discreetly hiding the roundness of the child. She had been surprised at the fit of the leather boots, unable to remember any of Stefan's men with such a small foot. Marya had informed her that the boots had once belonged to Stefan, when he was a young boy. She had pulled back the length of her hair, twisting it into a long braid that trailed down the length of her back. Indeed, it was impossible to determine that any woman rode among them, except for Marya's ample frame, atop the first cart. The old woman had steadfastly refused to consider the more functional costume of the men.

Jenna glanced about uncertainly, as it seemed no horse had been saddled for her. Stefan urged the black stallion forward, until he stood before her, the sun gleaming golden in the softness of his hair, his skin a deep bronze color.

"The black will easily carry us both," Stefan announced as he reached down to take Jenna's hand in his, easily drawing her into the saddle before him.

"I can handle a horse equal to any of your men," Jenna said flatly.

"That may be, but I will not take the risk of some harm coming to you or the child. The ride will be long, and hard. You will tire quickly. And there are comforts to be found in my saddle that cannot be found alone." Stefan grinned wickedly as he pulled her back against him.

Jenna could easily see that it was pointless to argue with him. She leaned back into the firmness of his chest, his strong arms closing about her protectively, as he gave a signal to his men. Slowly they traveled down the lane that led away from the chateau. Jenna turned about wistfully as she thought of the days they had shared there, and she silently wondered if they would ever return.

The sun had become a fiery red ball in the early evening sky, when they turned for one last glimpse of the magnificent chateau gleaming white in the last rays of light, on that distant hillside. In her heart, Jenna vowed they would return to Villandry.

The vastness of the eastern frontier was like a great tapestry of rivers, mountains, and forests as they traveled. They moved by day, staying away from more commonly traveled roads, making their encampments early, so there was less chance of their campfires' being seen in the full light of day. Only occasionally did Stefan's men return from riding ahead with some word of soldiers. Stefan continuously altered their course away from such encounters, easily realizing the vulnerability of their lesser numbers on the wartorn frontier.

Always riding northeast, Stefan led them across much the same route he had followed years before when his mother had sent her young son to the safety of France. Now, years later, he sought the safety of Varykein.

The first week in July, they left France behind them as they crossed the Rhine River, near Darmstadt. The mood of Stefan's men became less solemn and guarded as they traveled deeper into the countryside controlled by the combined armies of King Frederick William of Prussia and Czar Alexander.

Late in August, as they crossed Poland, Vasily returned after five days' absence to inform Stefan that a sizable army was encamped on the banks of a river that lay ahead of them. Jenna had awakened early, sleepily seeking Stefan's warmth from the early morning coolness, only to find the entire camp packed and prepared to ride, before first light. Stefan quickly sought her out, pulling her from the comforts of their crude bed on the ground, informing her they were riding immediately, and that there was no time for even the simplest meal. Indeed, Jenna could see that the carts had both been packed. Much too weary to be concerned with their course, Jenna snuggled into the warmth of Stefan's body atop the black stallion. When the sun warmed her in the seclusion of Stefan's embrace, Jenna awakened to the sight of a vast sea of soldiers encamped along the river. From among their midst emerged a man of stature to rival Dmitri. Jenna stared uncertainly as the mountainous man came forward, in the full dress uniform of his rank, a file of braided decorations draping the expanse of his chest. His well-trimmed beard and hair were gleaming black, and crisp, thick eyebrows of that same color arched above blue eyes that calmly regarded their slow approach. His personal guard stood warily, hands on their sabers against any unwarranted attack. Stefan reined the black stallion to a halt a few paces away, and slowly slid from the saddle. Jenna watched uncertainly, as Vasily and the others remained cautious. Only Dmitri seemed unconcerned. Jenna glanced about her frantically. Their fate would be certain, if the general gave the command to his men. Judging by their numbers alone, she knew there would be no hope for escape. Jenna's fingers tightened on the reins as she watched Stefan approach the general and his men. Words were exchanged. Most held no meaning for Jenna. The few that she heard were unknown to her. She watched with horror as the general's hand rested warily on the saber belted to his side. She felt a wave of fear wash over her as she imagined Stefan's death, after so many weeks of eluding Napoleon's army. Equal to Stefan in height, and far outweighing him, with his greater girth, the general leveled a blow to Stefan's shoulder. Jenna's breath caught in her throat as she forced back a cry of alarm. Beside her, Dmitri firmly restrained her hand as she reached for the pistol Stefan had left behind.

Jenna stared in stunned surprise as Stefan boldly returned the blow. The general staggered backwards, barking a sudden command as one of his soldiers leaped toward Stefan. The soldier held his position as the general straightened his uniform, his gaze never wavering as he watched Stefan warily. In the next moment the general roared with uncontrolled laughter, lunging toward Stefan and folding him in an embrace that would have broken any other man's back. Jenna's startled gaze flew to Dmitri. His dark eyes twinkling, he chuckled heartily as the moment of fear was suddenly broken. In mounting confusion, Jenna stared as Stefan was swung clear of the ground in the general's bearlike embrace. Instead of struggling to free himself, Stefan returned the embrace, his lean, handsome face breaking into a wide smile. Jenna's mouth dropped open as she realized it was no match to the death between adversaries, but a joyous reunion. Both men dissolved into roaring laughter, seeming oblivious of the stunned soldiers and men who watched their display. Words were exchanged between fits of laughter, the general clapping a massive arm about Stefan's shoulders as the two men approached.

"I see you still have this great bear Dmitri at your side." The general spoke in heavily accented English as he gazed up at the large Cossack.

Stefan laughed heartily. "Just when I think he is more trouble than he is worth, he redeems himself by saving my life." He gazed up at his lifelong friend teasingly. "He is like a weapon worn at one's side, a strong blade in the fiercest battle, even though a bit rusted from many storms."

Beside Jenna, Dmitri grumbled his pretended displeasure at such criticism. "If the cub would learn his lessons well and not venture into danger at every turn, perhaps I might find some peace and contentment in my life. But it is not so. Now he foolishly sets us on a path to Varykein."

The general roared his delight at the good-humored

camaraderie that rose easily among the three men, as if it was a habit enjoyed often before. His gaze immediately shifted to Jenna, who was sitting stiffly straight astride the black stallion.

"I see you still ride this great, black beast. I had always thought no other might ride him. Who is this lad? Are you now given to keeping company with young boys?" The general roared with renewed humor at the jest he had made, remembering well the first time he had caught Stefan with the young daughter of one of his captains.

Stefan's laughter quickly became hasty coughing as he noted well the warning fire that kindled in the depths of Jenna's amber eyes. He disengaged himself from the general's strong embrace, seizing Jenna's hand.

Jenna felt the warm rise of color across her cheeks as Stefan turned to make his introductions. She choked back her anger and frustration at her anticipation that he might be so crude as to introduce her as his mistress, when her condition would soon be obvious to every soldier in the encampment. She refused to meet Stefan's piercing blue gaze, which had suddenly turned the color of soft smoke as he gazed at her, and then said, "General Azimov, it is with honor that I present Princess Kalinsky."

Jenna's mouth flew open in stunned surprise as her dark amber gaze locked with Stefan's. The corners of his mouth twitched with his humor, and she realized that surely he made some jest, and at her expense. Never before had he ever chosen to discuss her status in his life, or the status of their unborn child. Though it plagued her constantly that she might well be no more than his mistress, Jenna had chosen not to think of the matter. Now, Stefan had deliberately forced her to confront her place in his life. She was convinced that he merely continued his jesting, though her surprise was no greater than that of General Azimov. Regaining his composure, the general came forward slowly, his clear blue eyes carefully scrutinizing the slender girl who sat astride the black stallion.

"So, the boy who would boldly defend you with the

473

pistol is no boy at all. The disguise is clever, but I see that it is not complete." The general nodded. Jenna was uncertain of the look in Stefan's eyes.

"I am honored, Princess Kalinsky. Of course, you will join our encampment. My men have traveled far in the last weeks, and though we have much further to go, we shall celebrate tonight," the general offered as he seized her hand, kissing the back with a certain eloquence and gentleness that Jenna had not expected. The general stepped back, quickly barking orders to his men as the festive mood descended on the entire encampment.

Stefan reached to help Jenna down from atop the black stallion. She handily avoided his arms, slipping easily from the saddle, carefully straightening the loose tunic over the increased roundness of her stomach. She threw him a murderous glare. Stefan only laughed at her sudden show of temper.

"You must take greater care, Jenna, not to draw the pistol so readily. Though we are friends of many years, I fear my life might have been forfeit had you moved more quickly."

Jenna regarded him coolly. "I think perhaps my target was ill-chosen. I will not play the fool before Dmitri and your men. Nor will I play that role to save your embarrassment."

Stefan smothered a smile behind a sober expression. "I merely thought to spare your embarrassment."

Jenna turned on him with a murderous glare. "You think to make something right with a lie?"

Stefan stiffened as he realized well that she hid some greater anger than the mere jesting of the moment before would suggest. "General Azimov has very generously offered us the use of his tent. You will find most of your comforts provided for." Stefan bowed stiffly as he turned to rejoin his men.

Indeed, all of Jenna's comforts were met by the general and his staff. She luxuriated in the warmth of the first bath in weeks not taken in a river or stream. While the boisterous sounds of the camp filled the air beyond the tent, Jenna attended to the comforts she had sorely missed the last weeks. When her bathing was completed, she wrung the water from her freshly washed hair and dried herself with a towel. Drawing the towel away, she noted that her slender figure had disappeared completely. She had little doubt that in the very near future she would be forced to don Dmitri's expansive pants. She sighed heavily as she pulled on a clean linen shirt. A short while later she emerged from the tent. Several heads turned admiringly toward her. She had left the long, flowing mane of her damp hair trailing loosely down the middle of her back to dry in the warm evening air. Her skin glowed brightly from a thorough scrubbing, and freshly polished black boots clung to her long legs. She was fascinatingly beautiful in the garments of a man, but undeniably a woman.

General Azimov came forward, his boisterous pleasure obvious in the flush that crossed his face. He bowed low before seizing Jenna's hand and drawing her to the table to sit beside him. A sumptuous feast of freshly roasted boar had been well prepared. Toasts were made round the table, and a goblet was quickly thrust into Jenna's hand. Across the table her gaze met Stefan's before she looked away, unable to remain aloof under the scrutiny of his mesmerizing blue eyes, which regarded her oddly. General Azimov introduced his aide, who came forward with a round, flat loaf of thickly crusted bread set upon a platter. Around the edge of the platter were several small dishes filled with salt. Jenna watched fascinated as the aide set the platter in the very center of the table. General Azimov turned to Jenna.

"The bread is the staple of life; the salt is the seasoning that makes life richer. It is an old custom among the Russian people that a guest is welcomed with a crust of bread to symbolize good life, and a bit of salt to symbolize the wish for richness in that life. Stefan has been gone from

475

us for a long time. Now he has returned. We welcome him. We welcome his princess." General Azimov toasted Jenna graciously.

Jenna turned uncertainly to Stefan. His eyes glowed warmly with his unspoken love for her. She reached and carefully tore off a piece of the thick-crusted bread. She ate the bread and then dipped her finger into a bowl of salt, tasting a pinch of it. A thunderous roar went up from the soldiers who had gathered about the table. Their boisterous celebrations quickly resumed, as everyone seated about the table, in turn, broke off a piece of the bread and tasted the salt. When it came Stefan's turn, he followed the ritual and then seized his goblet and rose to make a toast, in Russian, to the general's hospitality. General Azimov applauded his approval, and quickly gave his orders for the feasting to begin.

When she could eat no more, and felt fatigue stealing over her, Jenna sought the warmth of the campfire that glowed invitingly, chasing away the sudden chill of the summer evening. Stefan was deeply involved in exchanging stories with General Azimov, while Vasily and the others watched the sensuous movements of a dark-haired Gypsy girl who danced to the haunting melody of the balalaika, a triangular-shaped wooden instrument with three strings. Dmitri joined her at the edge of the fire, reaching his great, pawlike hands to catch the warmth.

"We will be leaving at first light. You should try to rest as much as possible," he advised her gently.

"I thought perhaps we would remain longer. It seems the general is an old friend," Jenna observed.

"General Azimov was a good friend of Stefan's father's. They trained together many years ago, as young men. It was General Azimov who forced Stefan's father to leave Russia, when the old Czar had ordered his death because of his affair with the princess, Stefan's mother."

"Stefan has never spoken of it," Jenna answered wistfully.

476

"It is a deep bond, stronger than that of blood brothers. Years later, Stefan returned to Russia, when I had taught him all that I could of being a Cossack. He trained with Azimov, as his father had trained with him years before. From Azimov, he learned the truth about his father." Dmitri glanced up as Stefan crossed the encampment, drawing the Gypsy girl with him. He sat down cross-legged beside Jenna, pulling the beautiful raven-haired girl with him.

Jenna regarded Stefan uncertainly, wondering at his mood, when he had remained distant the entire evening. She regarded the beautiful girl evenly, wondering if the dark-eyed temptress had been chosen as her replacement. The girl had refused several obvious invitations through the course of the evening, her dark eyes boldly seeking out Stefan. Whatever might have passed between them, the girl now regarded Jenna guardedly.

"Tonia is a Gypsy princess. I told her you were also descended from a Gypsy. I have persuaded her to read your fortune. It is an art perfected among her people." Stefan smiled secretively as he seized Jenna's hand and joined it with Tonia's. The dark-skinned woman smiled at him, her hopes high for the reward that would come later. She turned to Jenna, gently turning the slender hand and spreading Jenna's fingers open with her own fingers. She gazed into the depths of the amber gaze that met hers without faltering. Tonia pushed back a sudden uncertainty that possessed her. She immediately sensed a kindred spirit that she could not easily control, and she wondered if indeed the young beauty who sat unafraid before her did have the blood of a Gypsy princess. Tonia concentrated on the messages she saw etched in the lines of the slender hand. She glanced up in surprise at the sudden truth she saw there, and her mouth hardened in a sudden line.

"What do you see?" Stefan persisted.

Tonia met Jenna's gaze evenly, knowing her cause was lost. In the girl before her she had seen a power stronger than her own. "You will soon finish a long journey."

Dmitri scoffed at the Gypsy girl. "That is well known."

"At the end of the journey your child will be born. He will be strong and grow tall. You carry a son, descended from kings. And I see another journey, across a vast water. The land across the water will be your home," Tonia concluded as she rose. She made no attempt to conceal the disappointment in her eyes as she left to seek her pleasure in another part of the camp.

Dmitri laughed, in high humor. "So the child is a son. You must take care, little princess, that he does not grow obstinate and foolish like his father." Dmitri roared at his observation, and Jenna rose abruptly.

"You would both believe all this foolishness. It would serve you right if I have twin daughters. Then you will indeed have your hands full. Yes, I think daughters would be sufficient revenge. And surely you do not believe what she said about a great journey across water." Jenna huffed as she whirled about and sought the seclusion of the tent General Azimov had offered her for the night.

Dmitri chuckled at her fiery temper. "When will you tell her of the land in Virginia?"

"I will tell her later. At this moment, I don't think she would believe anything I would say," Stefan smiled wryly.

"It would ease her sadness for the loss of her grandfather to know that you owned the land in Virginia together."

"She will know of it soon enough. When the spring comes, and the child is strong, this war will be ended. Then it will be a good time to think of Virginia." Stefan sighed as he stood, contemplating the anger he would find in his bed. He smiled silently as he remembered other moments of anger that had quickly passed.

Jenna found no comfort in her anger, and she dozed into fitful slumber, rousing sometime later when she felt Stefan's warmth curving against her back. She tried to retreat from his nearness, but found her way blocked as his arms closed about her, drawing her against his naked warmth. His hands wandered possessively across the roundness of her stomach.

"It would serve you right if I did bear daughters," Jenna mumbled stubbornly, feeling her resistance draining away, as his hands wandered intimately over her.

Stefan kissed her shoulder. "I will accept what you give me, my princess. I intend to give you many babies. There will be at least one son among them," Stefan whispered softly into the mass of her hair.

Jenna could find no argument that might dampen his spirit, and soon surrendered to the passion he built within her. It was most enjoyable to take their pleasure in each other behind the seclusion of tent walls, when all the weeks before they had stolen their moments together beneath the meager shelter of blankets, to discreetly shield their lovemaking from Stefan's men. It would be a great many more days before they would again find such pleasure.

In the weeks that followed, they ventured into the stark forested beauty that was Russia. Their eyes constantly watching the flawless summer sky for early changes in the weather, they arrived at Varykein the last week in September, their journey slowed during the last weeks in deference to Jenna's condition. Indeed, Stefan feared his son might well be born on the back of his black stallion, but Jenna had solemnly promised her child would be born at Varykein. She never revealed her doubt of keeping that promise as the child grew heavy within her. She had long since resigned herself to the expanded size of Dmitri's loose-fitting woolen pants.

Varykein, Stefan's childhood home, hardly seemed the haven of a royal princess who had once awaited the birth

479

of her child. However, for Jenna, the rustic hunting lodge, which had been built from massive, hand-hewn timbers, was the perfect haven, tucked safely into the base of a mountain, surrounded by the trees of a nearby forest. Once the private hunting lodge of the royal family of Russia, it had stood closed and waiting since Stefan's last visit years before. The intervening years of war had allowed for little sporting pleasure. Though the outside had been built plainly and solidly to withstand the harsh winters, the inside of the massive lodge showed evidence of a fairer hand. Cloths were drawn back from elegant furnishings. Fine china and crystal was unpacked. Valuable portraits graced the walls, and linens were placed on the beds. The pantry was soon well stocked with provisions from a neighboring village as word spread quickly that Prince Kalinsky had returned to Varykein. Stefan and his men quickly bent to the task of replenishing the wood supply to fuel the fires for winter, and the larder was filled with freshly killed game, seasoned and hung. Jenna and Marya set about cleaning the lodge, driven by their instinct that their days for such tasks were limited. At night Jenna collapsed wearily into the shelter of Stefan's embrace, sharing the bed his mother and father had once shared, as lovers stealing the moments of their love when they might. Varykein had taken on new life.

By the first week of October the weather had grown unusually brisk, a heavy frost covering the landscape beyond the lodge. Dark clouds gathered across the crowning treetops, and a sudden gusting of wind warned there would be no hunting the next morning. Jenna was silently grateful that she would be able to sleep in later. Of late, she had begun to tire more easily with the burden of the child, and she silently longed to linger in bed on cold mornings.

Jenna roused slowly, prevented from curling into a tighter ball by her increased size, as Stefan slipped from the heavy blankets and threw more pieces of wood on the fire. He quickly returned, nuzzling her neck playfully as he tried to warm his hands in the soft curve of her body. Jenna moaned at his insistent intrusion into her sleep.

"Do you intend to sleep the entire day?" Stefan kissed her tenderly.

"It is too early. You and Dmitri are not hunting today," Jenna objected sleepily.

"That is true, but there is something you must see, and you can only see it this once." Stefan's hand wandered across the ample swell of his child within her. He gently caressed the taut hardness, which had lowered in the last few days, his hand deliberately seeking her full breast. Jenna moaned softly.

"You remind me of the pleasures I have missed these last days," Jenna whispered softly, reaching to entwine her arms about Stefan's neck, longing to feel his body pressed against hers. That was another pleasure she had missed, as her size had increased. "I think I should like to practice making another child, very soon." She sighed lustily as she buried her face in the hollow of his neck.

Stefan groaned at the desire that raged within him, thinking it indeed unfortunate that even with her increased size she should cause him such longing. "If you do not rise from this bed immediately, I swear I will forget your condition and take advantage of your slower pace."

Jenna grinned at him wickedly. "Then perhaps I shall linger. I think it a marvelous way to spend a cold morning."

Stefan rose abruptly, gently pulling her from the covers. "I think not, milady. I do not want my son telling me of it at a later time." When Jenna tried to sneak back under the covers, Stefan descended upon her, his arm slipping beneath her legs, lifting her and the bed covers clear of the bed as he swung her around, and carried her to the second-floor window of their bedroom.

"Behold, the first snow of the new winter at Varykein," Stefan announced. Jenna reached to draw back the heavy

481

velvet drapes. She gasped at the sight of a soft white mantle of fresh snow that blanketed the countryside beyond the lodge. She hugged him fiercely and squealed with childish delight at the gift Stefan had arranged for her. He gently released her.

"Will you take me for a ride in a troika, as you once promised?" Jenna gazed up at Stefan excitedly.

"I will have Dmitri harness the horse. You must dress quickly." Stefan leaned to kiss the tip of her nose before turning to quickly put on his pants. Before leaving the chamber he returned hastily, pressing an impassioned kiss against her lips.

Jenna quickly donned her warm woolen pants, boots, and heavy linen shirt. There was no time for more, as Stefan bounded up the wide stairs and burst into the room, quickly engulfing her in a rich, luxurious mantle of warm, soft sable.

"It will keep you warm for the ride," he announced as he scooped her into his arms and quickly descended to the waiting sleigh. He carefully placed Jenna in the single seat, pulling a fur lap robe about her before climbing in. Seizing the reins, Stefan called to the horse, and the sleigh moved slowly across the yard in front of the lodge, the runners making soft, squeaking sounds as they slid across the surface of the newly fallen snow.

Jenna snuggled into the warmth of her fur cocoon, dazzled by the dusting of snow that had sprinkled the tops of the trees with glistening powder. Stefan handled the reins with the ease of one born to such a task, his lean, strong fingers holding easy control of the strong beast that bore them across the countryside. He carefully turned the troika in the direction of a distant stand of aspen trees nestled among the towering junipers. When they reached the small grove of trees, stripped of their foliage and reaching starkly into the wintry sky, Stefan reined the horse to a stop. He turned to Jenna.

"It is beautiful here," she whispered as she gazed about her.

"This was a special place for my mother and father. They came to Varykein when my mother knew that she was with child, even though her father, the old Czar, was intent on her marriage to another man. They came in the winter, and found this place. They watched the first snow fall, and made their vows to each other here, even though they knew well that their time together would be brief. They remained at Varykein that winter, and I was born here. In the spring, when they knew the Czar would come for my mother, they came here again, and found wild daffodils blooming beneath the trees. My mother spoke of it often, and I saw them each new spring that I lived at Varykein, until I was older and had to leave. For them, the daffodils were the sign of love they vowed for each other, renewed each spring from beneath the mantle of snow. Jenna, I have brought you here to make those same vows of my love for you." Stefan leaned forward, his lips warm and tender against her own.

Jenna's eyes filled with tears of overwhelming tenderness as she reached to caress his brown cheek. She turned as a figure emerged from the stand of trees and approached the troika. An older man, dressed in long, flowing robes, with long, gray hair and beard, smiled at them. Stefan stepped down from the troika, reaching to lift her down gently. Jenna stared at Stefan in growing confusion as his arm encircled her waist and he drew her along with him. They stepped before the old man.

"I once vowed that you were mine. It has always been so. The priest from the village does not speak English. He will give the vows in Russian, but they will bind us beyond any language, if you will speak them with me." Stefan gazed down at her solemnly.

Jenna could only nod happily as tears again welled within her eyes. The priest smiled as Stefan spoke to him, and slowly began the ancient rites. Jenna repeated the words carefully, knowing every meaning within her heart. Stefan recited his vows clearly, holding her hand firmly in his. Together they knelt in the snow before the priest, as he intoned the ancient blessings that crossed all languages. The priest reached down, taking their joined hands and drawing them up together. Stefan seized a ring from his pocket inside his tunic, and reached for Jenna's hand.

"You left this behind once before. I trust you will not be so careless again." Stefan smiled as he placed the ring on her finger.

Jenna cried out joyously as she gazed down at the lovely ring Stefan had given her long ago in London. She had thought it surely lost, all these months since Charles had taken her to Mont St. Michel. Jenna threw her arms about Stefan's neck, melting into his embrace as the snow fell softly about them, the fine flakes catching and lingering in the waving mass of her hair. Her lips parted beneath Stefan's, tasting the exquisite pleasure of his kiss.

Jenna drew back suddenly, inhaling sharply as an unexpected pain twisted within her. Her gaze met Stefan's, and she realized her time was very near. Stefan smiled at her ruefully.

"Stefan?" Jenna breathed uncertainly.

Stefan's blue eyes twinkled softly as he gathered her in his arms and lifted her gently.

"I vowed I would have no bastard sons. You almost made a fool of me, little princess," Stefan smiled as he bore Jenna to the waiting troika for the return to Varykein.

Jenna smiled softly as he gently deposited her in the sleigh and carefully tucked the thick, warm sable about her. She reached up, pulling Stefan near as her lips sought his to reaffirm their promise of love.

"Stefan, please, I want to stay a while longer in our special place. I want our child to know it, to know the magic of the first snow of winter, as you promised me." They lingered a while longer, their fingers entwined, as the snow fell softly across the land, catching in the tops of the trees. Jenna's hand suddenly tightened about Stefan's as another pain moved through her. She knew no fear with Stefan's strength beside her. When the pain had receded, Jenna breathed deeply.

A tender smile formed on Stefan's lips. "If we do not hurry, Princess Kalinsky, my son will indeed see the first snow."

Jenna nodded, leaning against the firm strength of Stefan's shoulder, as he turned the sleigh about. Varykein awaited.

Epilogue

April 17, 1814

Jenna snuggled deeper into the warmth of the luxurious, dark sable cocoon that Stefan had wrapped about her as the chilling wind stung at her cheeks, bringing bright crimson patches of color to them. Stefan leaned forward, keeping a firm hand on the reins as he carefully guided the troika through the disappearing patches of snow. At long last spring had come to this frozen, white winterland where they had retreated from the war, from the world. Everywhere about Varykein the last two weeks the long-awaited season had poked tentatively through the frozen mantle that had sheltered their world in restful sleep.

Jenna blinked back the tears that welled in her eyes from the biting cold that belied the warmth of the sun, glistening in the myriad hues of the rainbow from the melting icicles that hung from the branches of the trees. Stefan called sharply to the large gray stallion that pulled the troika with ease through the rapidly disappearing drifts of snow and muddied patches that now appeared across the landscape. Jenna laughed gaily as the troika lunged uncertainly and then steadied with the firm pull of the powerful animal that pulled them with effortless ease. They reached the small clearing Jenna remembered well, and Stefan reined the horse to a halt. She had first seen it under the mantle of freshly fallen snow, that morning in

October. That day, he had given her another promise—to see it in spring. Now, Jenna stared in rapt silence at the magnificent scene that lay before her. The aspen trees were newly budded with yellow-green leaves. At the base of the trees, in shimmering waves of brilliant yellow, was a vast sea of wild daffodils in full bloom.

"It is beautiful," Jenna sighed softly, leaning forward in the troika to gain a better view.

Stefan reached down to take her gloved hand in his. "I wanted you to see this, as my mother and father saw it. In all the years that I have returned to Varykein, the daffodils always return in the spring. Marya has lived here all her life, and she cannot remember when the flowers were not here, and yet they are not found anywhere else in this region. Many in the village believe that long ago two lovers planted the flowers as a symbol that their love would be forever."

"Do you believe in the story?" Jenna gazed up at Stefan lovingly.

"The love my mother and father shared was forever. It endured beyond the power of kings to keep them apart. Yes, I believe it is true." Stefan leaned over, tenderly seeking her lips.

"There is another reason I wanted to bring you here today. Very soon warmer weather will be upon us, and we must think of leaving Varykein." Stefan secured the reins and swung down easily from the small sleigh. Gently he reached up, smiling softly as he took the well-wrapped bundle from Jenna's arms.

"I wanted my son to see this special place, so that he might also remember. It is a part of him." Stefan pushed back the hood of the fur-lined mantle that was wrapped warmly about the child. Startled by the cold air that invaded the warmth of his secluded haven, Prince Michael Alexander Kalinsky blinked uncertainly, his brilliant blue gaze meeting Stefan's evenly. Tiny fists poked through the dark fur lining, fingers locking around a gleaming button on Stefan's heavy coat. Jenna laughed softly as she watched father and son locked in a silent battle of wills over one brass button. At first, young Prince Michael seemed the victor as he tried to draw the button into his mouth.

"I think your son has other ideas of what is important," Jenna observed wryly.

Stefan smiled down at the robust infant in his arms, stroking his long fingers through the waves of dark hair, as rich as any sable. Gently he pried his son's fingers loose from the button, carrying him to the stand of aspen trees. Jenna waited a few moments longer before joining them, enraptured by this ageless communication between father and son.

Jenna slipped her arm through Stefan's as he knelt to give their son a better view of the brilliant yellow blooms. A small hand reached out tentatively, closing about a flower in curiosity.

"It is so beautiful here. Must we leave Varykein?" Jenna sighed wistfully, gazing toward the brilliant blue sky and the aspen trees that reached toward the beckoning warmth of the spring day. "These last months have been so happy, so simple, with just the few of us."

"Would you close out the world beyond, Jenna?" Stefan asked thoughtfully, as he played lovingly with his son's hand. "It is not possible. My mother and father thought to retreat from the world. But, in time, they found it was impossible. They were not so fortunate as we. They had to wait to find the happiness that would last forever. We have it now."

"Do you think to return to Villandry?"

"Perhaps someday, but that is far away." Possessed of a sudden passion, Stefan lifted his son high against the sky, like some ancient warrior king presenting his son to the gods. The babe gurgled gleefully at the sudden movement, unafraid, as he waved his small, round arms excitedly.

"I want a home that cannot be taken from me." Stefan spoke passionately. "I want a home for my son, which cannot be taken by Czar or emperor; a home that will stand for all the sons to follow," Stefan added, with such longing that Jenna felt an overwhelming ache deep inside

489

her for the pain in his voice. She reached up to stroke his cheek, turning his face toward hers, as her lips moved against his with a sudden longing and passion to take the pain away.

"My home is with you," she whispered huskily.

"Even if that home is not England?"

"I should like to return to England briefly, for a visit. Emma would never forgive me if she were not allowed to see our son. Just as it was important to you to bring our son here, it is important to me that he knows England. But our home will be where you will take us. I would have no other."

Stefan carefully handed his strong young son back to Jenna, as the child's interest turned in another direction. Prince Michael sucked hungrily on his tight fist, turning his head suddenly against the rounded warmth beneath the wool of Jenna's tunic against his cheek. Stefan eyed his son enviously, thinking that the baby had enjoyed more physical pleasure of late than he.

"Several years ago, I purchased several sections of land in Virginia. It was part of a business arrangement with a certain gentleman I thought very highly of." Stefan turned his thoughts to other matters.

"Virginia? The United States?" Jenna looked up with sudden curiosity. "My grandfather owned land there. I learned of it when his will was read."

"Yes, I know of his land. You see, it adjoins mine. It is a very rich area. There are fertile farmlands, and rich grazing lands, as well. Already my horses grow strong, and long-legged. They are the finest to be found anywhere. The prince regent has often said as much. The black stallion is one that was born and nurtured there. I think, perhaps, he would like to return to Virginia."

Jenna stared at Stefan speculatively. "And do you raise hunting dogs, as well?" she inquired, not quite seriously.

"The regent and I have an arrangement, whereby he acquires several pups from each litter, each spring," Stefan responded, a sly smile pulling at the corners of his lips.

"You are the one the stableboy spoke of at Foxmoor!" Jenna gasped incredulously.

"Too long, I have left the care of the Virginia farm to others. Would you like to see the land your grandfather intended for you?"

Young Prince Michael let out a disgruntled squall as Jenna snuggled into Stefan's embrace, ignoring her son's protests of hunger. A greater need hungered deep within her. Jenna closed her eyes rapturously as she kissed Stefan's neck, and then his lips as he bent over her.

"Yes, I think Virginia would make a fine home for our young prince," she murmured huskily, as Stefan's arms closed about her, his lips seeking her with breathless passion.

Jenna finally surrendered to her son's persistent wailings, turning back to the troika and there satisfying his appetite as she drew him to her breast. Stefan crawled into the sleigh beside her, drawing the heavy, warm sable about his wife and son, content to share the magic of Varykein with them this last time. Gently he reached to stroke his son's cheek. The child paid him little heed, seeking a greater satisfaction. Stefan's warm fingers grazed across the ample swell of Jenna's breast, igniting a heat where they touched, promising more rewarding moments later, when the baby was satisfied and sleeping.

"When will we leave?" Jenna asked shakily, vainly trying to draw his attention to other matters.

Stefan kissed her forehead tenderly. "I think the sooner the better, if you wish to see England first. If we delay much longer, in this remote wilderness, you will find yourself with child again, and the next child will be born at sea." Stefan's brilliant blue gaze burned into Jenna's with a sudden passion as his lips again sought hers. This time, Jenna did not think first of the child who rested contentedly in her arms, but of the man beside her, and the love he had promised. Their journey had only just begun.

CAPTIVATING ROMANCE FROM ZEBRA

MIDNIGHT DESIRE (1573, $3.50)
by Linda Benjamin

Looking into the handsome gunslinger's blazing blue eyes, innocent Kate felt dizzy. His husky voice, so warm and inviting, sent a river of fire cascading through her flesh. But she knew she'd never willingly give her heart to the arrogant rogue!

PASSION'S GAMBLE (1477, $3.50)
by Linda Benjamin

Jade-eyed Jessica was too shocked to protest when the riverboat cardsharp offered *her* as the stakes in a poker game. Then she met the smouldering glance of his opponent as he stared at her satiny cheeks and the tantalizing fullness of her bodice — and she found herself hoping he would hold the winning hand!

FORBIDDEN FIRES (1295, $3.50)
by Bobbi Smith

When Ellyn Douglas rescued the handsome Union officer from the raging river, she had no choice but to surrender to the sensuous stranger as he pulled her against his hard muscular body. Forgetting they were enemies in a senseless war, they were destined to share a life of unbridled ecstasy and glorious love!

WANTON SPLENDOR (1461, $3.50)
by Bobbi Smith

Kathleen had every intention of keeping her distance from Christopher Fletcher. But in the midst of a devastating hurricane, she crept into his arms. As she felt the heat of his lean body pressed against hers, she wondered breathlessly what it would be like to kiss those cynical lips — to turn that cool arrogance to fiery passion!

Available wherever paperbacks are sold, or order direct from the Publisher. Send cover price plus 50¢ per copy for mailing and handling to Zebra Books, Dept. 1741, 475 Park Avenue South, New York, N.Y. 10016. DO NOT SEND CASH.

CONTEMPORARY ROMANCE
FROM ZEBRA

ASK FOR NOTHING MORE   (1643, $3.95)

Mary Conroy lived her life as daughter and wife in the safest way possible—always playing by the rules. But this didn't guard her from cruelty and pain. Mary found a new way of experiencing the world as mistress to a very attractive, but married, man. A world where desires and betrayal were separated only by a plain band of gold.

WINTER JASMINE   (1658, $3.50)

The beautiful Beth wanted Danny and longed to be a part of his exciting life style, but Danny was tired of the fast lane and yearned for stability. Together they shared a searing passion and searched for a world in between.

SOMEBODY PLEASE LOVE ME   (1604, $3.95)

Cat Willingham was every woman's ideal of success. She was smart, wealthy, and strong. But it took Wall Street millionaire Clay Whitfield to bring out the sensuous woman trapped deep inside her, and to teach her the passions that love can bring.

WHITEWATER DYNASTY
by Helen Lee Poole

WHITEWATER DYNASTY: HUDSON! (1304, $2.95)
Amidst America's vast wilderness of forests and waterways, Indians and trappers, a beautiful New England girl and a handsome French adventurer meet. And the romance that follows is just the beginning, the foundation . . . of the great WHITEWATER DYNASTY.

WHITEWATER DYNASTY: OHIO! (1290, $2.95)
As Edward and Abby watched the beautiful Ohio River flow into the Spanish lands hundreds of miles away they felt their destiny flow with it. For Edward would be the first merchant of the river—and Abby, part of the legendary empire yet to be created!

WHITEWATER DYNASTY: WABASH! (1293, $3.50)
The American Revolution has begun, and Edward Forny's love for Abby must be tested—when he travels alone to the Wabash River to open up trade to the soldiers. By forging a new frontier, he will secure his family's future for generations to come, an unforgettable WHITEWATER DYNASTY!

WHITEWATER DYNASTY: MISSOURI! (1532, $3.50)
Lara, great-granddaughter of Edward, the founder of the river trade empire, is forbidden to join her brother and her husband on an expedition up the mighty Missouri. When the expedition fails to return, Lara joins Edward on a desperate rescue mission!

Available wherever paperbacks are sold, or order direct from the Publisher. Send cover price plus 50¢ per copy for mailing and handling to Zebra Books, Dept. 1741, 475 Park Avenue South, New York, N.Y. 10016. DO NOT SEND CASH.